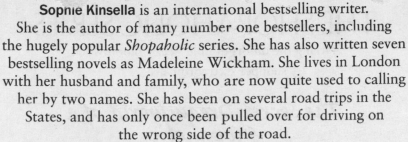

Sophie Kinsella is an international bestselling writer. She is the author of many number one bestsellers, including the hugely popular *Shopaholic* series. She has also written seven bestselling novels as Madeleine Wickham. She lives in London with her husband and family, who are now quite used to calling her by two names. She has been on several road trips in the States, and has only once been pulled over for driving on the wrong side of the road.

Visit her website at
www.sophiekinsella.co.uk
find her on Facebook at
www.facebook.com/SophieKinsellaOfficial
and follow her on Twitter **@KinsellaSophie**
and Instagram **@sophiekinsellawriter**

THE SHOPAHOLIC SERIES

Starring the unforgettable Becky Bloomwood,
shopper extraordinaire . . .

The Secret Dreamworld of a Shopaholic

(also published as *Confessions of a Shopaholic*)

Meet Becky – a journalist who spends all her time
telling people how to manage money, and all her leisure
time spending it. But the letters from her bank manager
are getting harder to ignore. Can she ever escape this
dream world, find true love . . . and regain the use of
her credit card?

Shopaholic Abroad

Becky's life is peachy. Her balance is in the black – well,
nearly – and now her boyfriend has asked her to move to
New York with him. Can Becky keep the man *and* the
clothes when there's so much temptation around
every corner?

Shopaholic Ties the Knot

Becky finally has the perfect job, the perfect man and, at
last, the perfect wedding. Or rather, *weddings* . . . How has
Becky ended up with not one, but two big days?

Shopaholic & Sister

Becky has received some incredible news. She has a
long-lost sister! But how will she cope when she realizes
her sister is not a shopper . . . but a skinflint?

Shopaholic & Baby

Becky is pregnant! But being Becky, she decides to shop around — for a new, more expensive obstetrician — and unwittingly ends up employing Luke's ex-girlfriend! How will Becky make it through the longest nine months of her life?

Mini Shopaholic

Times are hard, so Becky's Cutting Back. She has the perfect idea: throw a budget-busting birthday party. But her daughter Minnie can turn the simplest event into chaos. Whose turn will it be to sit on the naughty step?

Shopaholic to the Stars

Becky is in Hollywood and her heart is set on a new career — she's going to be a stylist to the stars! But in between choosing clutch bags and chasing celebrities, Becky gets caught up in the whirlwind of Tinseltown.
Has Becky gone too far this time?

Shopaholic to the Rescue

Becky is on a major rescue mission! Hollywood was full of surprises, and now she's on a road trip to Las Vegas to find out why her dad has mysteriously disappeared, help her best friend Suze and *maybe* even bond with Alicia Bitch Long-legs. She comes up with her biggest, boldest, most brilliant plan yet — can she save the day?

OTHER BOOKS
Sophie Kinsella's hilarious, heart-warming
standalone novels

Can You Keep a Secret?

Certain she's going to die in a plane crash, Emma blurts
out her deepest, darkest secrets to the sexy stranger next
to her. But it's OK, because she'll never have to see him
again . . . will she?

The Undomestic Goddess

Samantha works all hours, has no home life and thrives
on adrenalin. Then one day it all falls apart. She finds
herself a new life as housekeeper in a country house.
Will her old life ever catch up with her? And if it
does, will she want it back?

Remember Me?

What if you woke up and your life was perfect? Somehow
Lexi's life has fast-forwarded three years, and she has
everything she's ever wanted — the job, the house, the
man. Or does she? What went on in those missing
years, and can she cope when she finds out the truth?

Twenties Girl

Lara has always had an overactive imagination. But even she finds it hard to believe when the ghost of her great aunt Sadie shows up, asking for her help. Is Lara losing her mind? Or could two girls from different times end up helping each other?

I've Got Your Number

First Poppy loses her engagement ring – a priceless heirloom – and then she misplaces her phone. The only alternative seems to be to take a mobile she finds in a bin. Little knowing that she's picked up another man in the process . . .

Wedding Night

Lottie is determined to get married. And Ben seems perfect – they have history, he's gorgeous and he's willing to do it now. They'll iron out their little differences later. All that's left to do is seal the deal. But their families have different plans . . .

FOR YOUNGER READERS

Finding Audrey

Audrey can't leave the house. She can't even take off her dark glasses inside. But then Linus stumbles into her life. And with Linus at her side, Audrey can do things she'd thought were too scary. Suddenly, finding her way back to the real world seems achievable . . .

SOPHIE KINSELLA

Shopaholic to the Rescue

BLACK SWAN

TRANSWORLD PUBLISHERS
61–63 Uxbridge Road, London W5 5SA
www.transworldbooks.co.uk

Transworld is part of the Penguin Random House group of companies
whose addresses can be found at global.penguinrandomhouse.com

Penguin
Random House
UK

First published in Great Britain
in 2015 by Bantam Press
an imprint of Transworld Publishers
Black Swan edition published 2016

A CIP catalogue record for this book
is available from the British Library.

ISBN
9781784160364 (B format)
9781784161170 (A format)

Typeset in 11/14pt Giovanni Book by Falcon Oast Graphic Art Ltd.
Printed and bound by Clays Ltd, Bungay, Suffolk.

Penguin Random House is committed to a sustainable
future for our business, our readers and our planet. This book is made from
Forest Stewardship Council® certified paper.

MIX
Paper from
responsible sources
FSC® C018179

1 3 5 7 9 10 8 6 4 2

To Linda Evans
with love and thanks for everything

Dear Mrs Brandon

It has been a long time since I saw you last. I hope you and your family are flourishing.

As for myself, I am enjoying a life of retirement, but find my mind often casting back fondly to episodes from my professional life at Endwich Bank. I have therefore decided to embark upon an 'autobiography' or 'memoir', provisionally entitled: *Good and Bad Debts: The Ups and Downs of a Patient (and Not-so-Patient!) Fulham Bank Manager.*

I have written two chapters already, which were well received by members of my local horticultural club; several present even expressed the opinion: 'They should put it on TV!' Well, I don't know about that!!

I might say, Mrs Brandon, that you were always one of my more 'colourful' customers and had a 'unique' approach to your finances. (I heartily hope and believe that you have mended your ways with maturity.) We crossed swords many a time, but I trust we reached some sort of '*entente cordiale*' by the time of my retirement?

I therefore wonder if I might interview you for my book at a time convenient to yourself? I await your reply with pleasure.

Yours sincerely

Derek Smeath
Bank Manager (Retd)

From: dsmeath@locostinternet.com
To: Brandon, Rebecca
Subject: Re: Re: A 'request'

Dear Mrs Brandon

I write in disappointment. I approached you in good faith, as a fellow professional, or even, dare I say, friend. I hoped to be treated as 'such'.

If you do not wish to be interviewed for my 'memoir' then that is your choice. However, I am saddened that you felt the need to concoct an elaborate lie. Clearly this ridiculous, convoluted story about 'racing after your father towards Las Vegas', to 'uncover some mystery' and make sure 'poor Tarkie isn't being brainwashed', is entirely fictitious.

How many times, Mrs Brandon, have I held missives from you in which you have claimed to have 'broken your leg', 'suffered from glandular fever' or told me that your (imaginary) dog has died? I had hoped that as a mature, married mother, you might have grown up a little. However, I find myself sadly disappointed.

Yours sincerely

Derek Smeath

From: dsmeath@locostinternet.com
To: Brandon, Rebecca
Subject: Re: Re: Re: Re: A 'request'

Dear Mrs Brandon

To say I was astonished by your most recent email would be an understatement. Thank you very much for the series of photographs.

I can indeed see that you are standing on the edge of a desert. I see the RV that you are pointing at and the close-up of the map of California. I also observe your friend Lady Cleath-Stuart in one picture, although whether it is 'totally obvious from her tortured expression that her husband has gone missing' is not for me to say.

May I please ask you to clarify: your father has gone missing *and* so has your friend's husband? Both at once?

Yours sincerely

Derek Smeath

Dear Mrs Brandon

My goodness, what a story! Your email was a little garbled, if I may say – would these be the correct facts?

• Your father came to visit you in Los Angeles because he discovered some news regarding an old friend, Brent, whom he had not seen for many years.
• He then disappeared on a mission, leaving only a note in which he referred to 'putting something right'.
• He has enlisted the help of Lord Cleath-Stuart ('Tarkie'), who has been through a difficult time lately and is in a 'vulnerable state'.
• He has also coopted a chap named 'Bryce'. (Strange names they have, in California.)
• Now you are following the three to Las Vegas in the fear that Bryce is a nefarious character who may wish to extract money from Lord Cleath-Stuart.

In answer to your query, I'm afraid I do not have any 'blinding insights' with which to help you; nor did anything similar ever happen while I was at the bank. Although we did once have a rather 'shady' client who attempted to deposit a bin bag full of £20 notes, whereupon I phoned the financial authorities. I will be recounting that 'tale' in my book, believe me!!

I wish you every success in tracking down the missing three, and if I can be of any help whatsoever, please do not hesitate to contact me.

Yours sincerely
Derek Smeath

ONE

'OK,' says Luke calmly. 'Don't panic.'

Don't panic? *Luke* is saying 'Don't panic'? No. Noooo. This is all wrong. My husband never says 'Don't panic.' If he's saying 'Don't panic,' then what he really means is: 'There's every good reason to panic.'

God, now *I'm* panicking.

Lights are flashing and the police siren is still sounding. All I can think are wild random thoughts like, 'Do hand-cuffs hurt?' and 'Who shall I call from my jail cell?' and 'Are the jumpsuits *all* orange?'

A policeman is heading towards our hired Class C 26-foot motorhome. (Blue gingham drapes, flowery upholstery, 'six beds', although 'bed' is an exaggeration, try 'six skinny mattresses plonked on planks of wood'.) He's one of those cool-looking American policemen with mirror shades and a tan and he looks very scary. My heart starts to thump and I automatically start searching around for a hiding place.

OK, maybe this is a slight overreaction. But I've always

been nervy around policemen, ever since I smuggled six pairs of dollies' shoes out of Hamleys, aged five, and a policeman came up to me and boomed, 'What have you got there, young lady?' and I nearly jumped out of my skin. He was admiring my helium balloon, it turned out.

(We sent the dollies' shoes back in a padded envelope after Mum and Dad found them, with a letter of apology which I wrote myself. And then Hamleys wrote back and said 'Don't worry' very nicely. I think that's the first time I realized that writing a letter is actually a very good way to get yourself out of a tricky situation.)

'Luke!' I mutter urgently. 'Quick! Are we supposed to bribe them? How much cash have we got?'

'Becky,' says Luke patiently. 'I said, don't panic. There'll be a perfectly good reason why they've pulled us over.'

'Should we all get out?' says Suze.

'I say we stay in the vehicle,' says Janice, sounding edgy. 'I say we act perfectly normal as though we've got nothing to hide.'

'We *have* got nothing to hide,' says Alicia, sounding exasperated. 'Everyone needs to relax.'

'They've got guns!' says Mum wildly, peering out of the window. 'Guns, Janice!'

'Jane, please calm down!' says Luke. 'I'll go and talk to them.'

He gets out of the RV and the rest of us look around at one another anxiously. I'm travelling with my best friend Suze, my very much *un*-best friend Alicia, my daughter Minnie, my mum and *her* best friend Janice. We're on our way to Las Vegas from LA and already we've argued about

16

the air conditioning, the seating arrangements and whether Janice should be allowed to play Celtic pipe music to calm her nerves. (Answer: no. Five votes to one.) It's a tad fraught, this road trip, and we've only been going for two hours. And now this.

I watch as the cop approaches Luke and starts talking.

'Doggie!' says Minnie, pointing out of the window. 'Big, big, *big* doggie.'

A second cop has come up to Luke, with an intimidating-looking police dog. It's a German shepherd and is sniffing around Luke's feet. Suddenly it looks up at the RV and barks.

'Oh God!' Janice emits an anguished cry. 'I knew it! It's the narcotics squad! They're going to sniff me out!'

'*What?*' I turn to stare at her. Janice is a middle-aged lady who likes flower arranging and doing people's make-up in lurid shades of peach. What does she mean, 'sniff her out'?

'I'm sorry to have to tell you, everybody . . .' She gulps dramatically. 'But I have illicit drugs about my person.'

For a moment, nobody moves. My brain is refusing to compute these two elements. Illicit drugs? Janice?

'*Drugs?*' Mum exclaims. 'Janice, what are you talking about?'

'For jetlag,' Janice moans. 'My doctor was so unhelpful, I had to resort to the internet. Annabel at the bridge club gave me the website, but it had a disclaimer: "May be prohibited in certain countries." And now that dog will sniff them out and we'll get hauled in for questioning—'

She breaks off at the sound of frenzied barking. I have to admit, the police dog seems quite keen on coming over to the RV. It's pulling on its leash and yelping and the policeman keeps looking down at it in irritation.

'You bought *prohibited drugs*?' Suze explodes. 'Why would you do that?'

'Janice, you're going to jeopardize the whole trip!' Mum sounds apoplectic. 'How could you bring Class A drugs into America?'

'I'm sure they're not Class A,' I say, but Mum and Janice are too hysterical to listen.

'Get rid of them!' Mum is saying shrilly. 'Now!'

'Here they are.' Janice takes two white packets out of her bag, her hands fumbling. 'I never would have brought them if I'd known—'

'Well, what shall we do with them?' demands Mum.

'Everyone swallow one blister pack,' says Janice, pulling them out of the boxes in agitation. 'That's the only thing we can do.'

'Are you *nuts*?' retorts Suze furiously. 'I'm not swallowing unlicensed tablets from the internet!'

'Janice, you have to dispose of them,' says Mum. 'Get out and scatter them by the side of the road. I'll distract the police. No, we'll *all* distract the police. Everybody out of the RV. Now!'

'The police will notice!' wails Janice.

'No, the police won't notice,' says Mum firmly. 'Do you hear me, Janice? The police *won't* notice. Not if you're quick.'

She opens the door of the RV and we all pile out into the already blazing-hot day. We're parked by the side of the freeway, with scratchy, scrubby desert stretching away on either side, as far as you can see.

'Go *on*!' Mum hisses to Janice.

As Janice picks her way over the dry ground, Mum bustles up to the policemen, Suze and Alicia in tow.

'Jane!' says Luke, looking taken aback to see her by his side. 'It wasn't necessary for you to get out.' He shoots me a glance that says, *What-the-hell-are-you-doing?* and I shrug helplessly back.

'Good morning, Officer,' Mum says, addressing the first policeman. 'I'm sure my son-in-law has explained the situation. My husband has gone missing on a secret life-or-death mission.'

'It's not *necessarily* life or death.' I feel the need to clarify.

Every time Mum uses the phrase 'life or death', I'm certain her blood pressure goes up. I keep trying to soothe her, but I'm not sure she wants to be soothed.

'He's in the company of Lord Cleath-Stuart,' Mum continues, 'and this is Lady Cleath-Stuart. They live in Letherby Hall, one of the top stately homes in England,' she adds proudly.

'That's irrelevant!' says Suze.

One of the cops takes off his sunglasses to survey Suze.

'Like *Downton Abbey*? My wife is nuts for that show.'

'Oh, Letherby is *far* better than Downton,' says Mum. 'You should visit.'

Out of the corner of my eye I notice Janice, standing in the desert in her aqua floral two-piece, madly scattering pills behind a giant cactus. She could hardly be less discreet. But luckily the policemen are distracted by Mum, who is now telling them about Dad's note.

'He left it on his pillow!' she's saying indignantly. 'A "little trip", he's calling it. What kind of married man just ups and leaves on a "little trip"?'

'Officers.' Luke has been trying to get a word in. 'Thank you for informing me about the taillight. Perhaps we could carry on with our journey now?'

There's a short silence as the cops look consideringly at each other.

'Don't panic,' says Minnie, looking up from where she's been playing with her favourite dolly, Speaky. She beams up at one of the policemen. 'Don't panic.'

'Sure thing.' He beams back at her. 'Cute kid. What's your name, honey?'

'The police won't notice,' replies Minnie conversationally, and at once there's a prickly silence. My stomach clenches tight and I don't dare glance at Suze.

Meanwhile, the smile on the cop's face has frozen. 'I'm sorry, what did you say?' he asks Minnie. 'Notice what, sweetheart?'

'Nothing!' I say shrilly. 'We've been watching TV, you know what children are like . . .'

'There we are!' Janice arrives by my side, breathless. 'All done. Hello, Officers, what can we do to help you?'

The two cops look disconcerted to see yet another person joining the group.

'Ma'am, where've you been?' asks one.

'I was behind the cactus. Call of nature,' Janice adds, clearly proud of having a prepared answer.

'Don't you have facilities in the RV?' says the light-haired cop.

'Oh,' says Janice, looking thrown. 'Oh, goodness. I suppose we do.' Her confident air melts away and her eyes dart about wildly. 'Goodness. Um . . . well . . . in actual fact . . . I felt like a walk.'

The dark-haired cop folds his arms. 'A walk? A walk behind a cactus?'

'The police won't notice,' says Minnie to Janice confidingly, and Janice jumps like a scalded cat.

'Minnie! Goodness, dear! Notice what? Ha ha ha!'

'Can't you shut that child *up*?' says Alicia in a furious undertone.

'It was a nature walk,' Janice adds weakly. 'I was admiring the cacti. Beautiful . . . um . . . prickles.'

'Beautiful prickles'? Is that the best she could come up with? OK, I'm never going on a road trip with Janice again. She looks totally uncool and guilty. No wonder the cops seem suspicious. (I'll admit that Minnie hasn't exactly helped.)

The policemen are looking at each other meaningfully. Any minute now they're going to say they're bringing us in or calling the Feds. I have to do something, quick. But what? Think, *think* . . .

And then inspiration strikes.

'Officer!' I exclaim. 'I'm so glad we've met, because I have a favour to ask. I have a young cousin who'd love to become a police officer and he'd be so grateful for an internship. Could he contact you? You're Officer Kapinski . . .' I get out my phone and start typing in the name, copying it off his badge. 'Perhaps he could shadow you?'

'There are official channels, ma'am,' says Officer Kapinski discouragingly. 'Tell him to look on the website.'

'Oh, but it's all about personal connections, isn't it?' I blink innocently at him. 'Are you available tomorrow? We could meet after work. Yes! We'll be waiting for you outside the precinct.' I take a step forward and Officer Kapinski backs away. 'He's so talented and chatty. You'll love him. So we'll see you tomorrow, shall we? I'll bring croissants, shall I?'

Officer Kapinski looks utterly freaked out.

'You're good to go,' he mutters, and turns on his heel. Within about thirty seconds he, his colleague and the dog are back in the police car and zooming off.

'Bravo, Becky!' applauds Luke.

'Well done, love!' chimes in Mum.

'That was close.' Janice is trembling. 'Too close. We need to be more careful.'

'What *is* all this?' says Luke, looking baffled. 'Why did you get out of the RV?'

'Janice is on the run from the narcs,' I say, and almost want to giggle at his expression. 'Look, I'll explain on the road. Let's get going.'

TWO

They went missing two days ago. You might say, 'So what? They're probably just on a boys' trip. Why not relax and wait for them to roll on home?' Actually, that's what the police *did* say. But it's more complicated than that. Tarquin had a bit of a breakdown-type moment recently. He's also very rich and is apparently being targeted by Bryce with 'unhealthy practices', which Suze is worried means 'joining a cult'.

I mean, it's all just a theory. In fact, it's lots of different theories. To be honest – and I'd never say this to Suze – I secretly think we might find that Dad and Tarquin have been sitting in a 24-hour café in LA all this time. Suze, on the other hand, believes Bryce has already thrown Tarquin down a canyon after plundering his bank account. (She won't admit it, but I know it's what she thinks.)

What we need is some order. We need a *plan*. We need one of those incident boards like they have in cop shows, with lists and arrows, and pictures of Dad and Tarkie.

(Actually, no, let's not do that. Then they really would look like murder victims.) But we need *something*. So far, this road trip has been shambolic.

It was an utter kerfuffle this morning – what with packing and handing over Suze's three children to her nanny, Ellie (she's going to live in and have full charge while we're gone). Luke arrived with the hired RV at the crack of dawn. Then I woke Mum and Janice – they'd only had a few hours' sleep since they arrived from the UK – and we all jumped in and said, 'To Vegas!'

To be *absolutely* truthful, we probably didn't need to hire an RV. In fact, Luke was all for going in two saloon cars. But my argument was: we need to talk to each other, en route. Therefore we need an RV. Plus, how can you go on an American road trip and not get an RV? Exactly.

Since then, Suze has spent the whole time Googling cults, which I don't think she should do, because it's freaking her out. (Especially when she found one where they all paint their faces white and get married to animals.) Luke has mostly been on the phone to his second-in-command, Gary, who's at a conference in London, taking Luke's place. Luke owns a PR firm and has stacks of commitments right now, but he put them all aside to drive the RV. Which is really supportive and loving of him and I will do *exactly* the same for him when the situation arises.

Janice and Mum have been exchanging dire theories about Dad having a meltdown and going to live wild in the desert in a poncho. (Why a poncho?) Minnie has said, 'Cactus, Mummy! Cac-TUS!' about three thousand times. And I've sat there in silence, stroking her hair and just letting my thoughts swirl around. Which, to be honest, isn't a lot of fun. My thoughts aren't in a brilliant place right now.

I'm trying to stay as positive and buoyant as I can, I really am. I'm trying to keep everyone cheery and not dwell on the past. But every time I let my guard down, it all comes back, in a horrible rush of guilt. Because the truth is: this whole trip is down to me. It's all *my* fault.

Half an hour later we stop at a diner to have some breakfast and to regroup. I take Minnie to the Ladies, where we have a long conversation about different kinds of soap and Minnie decides she has to try each soap dispenser in turn and basically it takes for ever. When at last we make it back into the diner, Suze is standing alone, looking at a vintage-style poster, and I head towards her.

'Suze . . .' I say for about the billionth time. 'Listen. I'm sorry.'

'Sorry for what?' She barely looks up.

'You know. Everything—' I break off, feeling a bit despairing. I don't know how to continue. Suze is my oldest, dearest friend and being with her used to feel like the easiest thing in the world. But now it feels like I'm in a stage play and I've forgotten my lines and she's not about to help me out.

It was over the last few weeks, while we were both living in LA, that things went wrong. Not just between Suze and me, but altogether. I lost my head. I went careering off the track. I wanted to be a celebrity stylist so badly that I lost the plot for a bit. I can hardly believe it was only last night that I was standing on the red carpet outside a premiere, realizing quite how badly I *didn't* want to be inside the cinema with all the celebrities. I feel like I've been in a bubble, and now it's popped.

Luke gets it. We had a long talk last night and set a lot of things straight. What happened to me in Hollywood was freakish, he said. I became a celebrity overnight, without intending to at all, and it threw me. My friends and family won't hold it against me for ever, he said. They'll forgive me.

Well, maybe he's forgiven me. But Suze hasn't.

The worst thing is, last night I thought everything was healing. Suze stood there and begged me to come on this trip, and I promised her I'd drop everything. She cried, and said she'd missed me, and I felt this massive relief. But now that I'm here, everything's changed. She's behaving as though she doesn't want me here. She won't discuss it; she just exudes hostility.

I mean, I *know* she's worried about Tarkie, I *know* I need to cut her some slack. It's just . . . hard.

'Whatever,' says Suze brusquely. And without looking at me, she heads back to the table. As I follow her, Alicia Bitch Long-legs glances up and sweeps disdainful eyes over me. I still can't quite believe she's come on this trip. Alicia Bitch Long-legs, my least favourite person in the world.

I should say, Alicia Merrelle. That's her name now, ever since she married Wilton Merrelle, founder of the famous yoga and rehab centre, Golden Peace. It's a massive complex, with classes and a gift shop, and I used to be quite a fan. Well, we were all fans. Until Tarquin started going there all the time to hang out with Bryce, and told Suze she was 'toxic' and frankly became a bit weird. (I should say: a bit weirder. He's never exactly been the most normal knife in the drawer, old Tarkie.)

It was Alicia who discovered they were heading to Vegas. It was Alicia who brought a chiller full of coconut water for the RV. Alicia's the heroine of the hour. But I'm still wary of her. Alicia has been my bête noire ever since I first knew her, years ago, before I was married. She's tried to wreck my life, she's tried to wreck Luke's life, she's put me down at every opportunity and made me feel small and stupid. Now she says that's all in the past and we should forget it and she's moved on. But I'm sorry, I can't trust her, I just can't.

'I was thinking,' I say, trying to sound businesslike. 'We need to make a proper plan.' I get a pen and notebook from my bag, write *PLAN* in big letters and put it on the table for everyone to see. 'Let's go over the facts.'

'Your dad has dragged the other two off on some mission to do with his past,' says Suze. 'But you don't know what, because you didn't ask him.' With that, she shoots me a familiar, accusing look.

'I know,' I say humbly. 'I'm sorry.'

I should have talked to my dad more. If I could turn back time I'd do everything differently, of course I would, of *course* I would. But I can't. All I can do is try to make up for it now.

'So let's recap what we *do* know,' I say, trying to stay upbeat. 'Graham Bloomwood came to the US in 1972. He toured around with three American friends: Brent, Corey and Raymond. And they followed *this* route.' I open Dad's map and put it down with a flourish. 'Exhibit A.'

We all look at the map for the millionth time. It's a very basic road map, old and yellowing, with a red-biro route drawn in. It doesn't really help us, in truth, but we all keep staring at it, just in case. I searched my dad's room after he disappeared with Tarkie, and this is all I found, apart from an old magazine.

'So, they might be following this route.' Suze is still peering at the map. 'LA . . . Las Vegas . . . Look, they went to the Grand Canyon . . .'

'But they might *not* be following that route,' I say quickly, before she decides that Dad and Tarkie must be at the bottom of the Grand Canyon and we need to go there at once in a helicopter.

'Is your father the sort to retrace his steps?' says Alicia. 'I suppose what I mean is, is he redactive?'

Redactive? What's that?

'Well.' I cough. 'Sometimes. Maybe.'

Alicia keeps asking me really difficult questions like this. And then she blinks at me in silent triumph as though to say, *You don't understand, do you?*

Plus, she speaks in this soft, serene way which gives me the creeps. Alicia has totally changed style since she was a bossy PR girl in London. She wears yoga trousers and her hair in a low ponytail, and her speech is sprinkled with new-agey expressions. But she's still as patronizing as ever.

'Sometimes he retraces his steps, sometimes he doesn't,' I improvise. 'Depends.'

'Bex, you must have more information,' says Suze

tetchily. 'Tell me about the trailer park again. Maybe you missed something out.'

Obediently I begin: 'Dad wanted me to look up his old friend Brent. When I found the address, it was a trailer park and Brent had just been evicted.'

As I speak, a hotness comes over me and I take a sip of water. This is the point where I messed up most of all. Dad kept asking me to look up Brent, and I kept putting it off, because . . . Well, because life was so exciting, and it just seemed like a boring Dad-errand. But if I'd just done it, if I'd got there earlier, maybe Dad would have been able to talk to Brent *before* he got served with an eviction notice. Maybe Brent wouldn't have taken off. Maybe everything would be different.

'Dad couldn't believe it,' I resume, 'because he thought Brent would be rich.'

'Why?' demands Suze. 'Why did he think Brent would be rich? He hadn't seen him for what, thirty years? Forty years?'

'Dunno. But he was expecting Brent to be living in a mansion.'

'So your dad flew out to LA and went to see Brent?'

'Yes. It must have been at the trailer park. Apparently they "had it out" about something.'

'And it was Brent's daughter who told you that.' She pauses. 'Rebecca.'

We're both silent. This is the weirdest part of the story. Yet again, I replay the scene in my head. Meeting Brent's daughter on the steps of the trailer. Feeling the hostility burning off her like heat off a sun-baked tarmac road. Staring back at her in bewilderment; thinking, *What did*

I ever do to you? And then the killer line: 'We're all called Rebecca.' I still don't know what she meant by 'all'. She certainly wasn't about to explain.

'What else did she say?' Suze asks impatiently.

'Nothing! She said, "If you don't know, I'm not telling you."'

'Helpful.' Suze rolls her eyes.

'Yes, well. She didn't seem very keen on me. I don't know why.'

I don't add that she said I had a 'prinky-prinky voice' and that her last words to me were 'Fuck off, princess girl.'

'She didn't mention Corey at all?' Suze is tapping her pen on the table.

'No.'

'But Corey is the one who lives in Las Vegas. So your dad might be going to see him.'

'Yes. I think so.'

'You *think* so?' Suze suddenly lashes out. 'Bex, we need some solid facts!'

It's all very well, Suze expecting me to have all the answers. But Mum and I have no idea what Corey's or Raymond's surnames are, even, let alone anything else. Mum says Dad only ever mentioned them when he was reminiscing about the trip, which was once a year, at Christmas, and she never really listened. (She even said that if she'd heard about the searing heat of Death Valley once, she'd heard it a million times, and why hadn't they just stayed in a hotel with a nice swimming pool?)

I've Googled 'corey las vegas', 'corey graham bloom-wood', 'corey brent' and anything else I can think of.

The trouble is, there are a lot of Coreys in Las Vegas.

'OK.' Alicia comes off her mobile. 'Thanks anyway.'

Alicia's been phoning everyone she knows, to try to find out if Bryce mentioned where he's staying in Las Vegas. But so far, no one knows anything.

'No joy?'

'No.' She sighs deeply. 'Suze, I feel I'm letting you down.'

'You're not letting me down!' says Suze at once, and clutches Alicia's hand. 'You're an angel!'

They're both totally ignoring me. Maybe we should have a break, anyway. I force a friendly smile, and say, 'I'm going to stretch my legs. Apparently there's a barnyard at the back. Could you order me the maple waffles please? Plus some pancakes for Minnie, and a strawberry milkshake. Come on, sweetheart.' I take Minnie's little hand in mine and at once feel comforted. At least Minnie loves me unconditionally.

(Or at least, she will until she's thirteen and I tell her she can't wear a micro-mini to school and she'll hate me more than anyone in the world.)

(Oh God, that's only eleven years away. Why can't she just stay two and a half for ever?)

THREE

As I head to the back of the diner I see Mum and Janice exiting the Ladies. Janice is wearing a pair of white sunglasses on her head and Minnie draws breath at the sight.

'I like that!' she says carefully, pointing. 'Pleeeeeease?'

'Sweetheart!' says Janice. 'Would you like them?'

'Janice!' I exclaim in horror, as she hands Minnie the sunglasses. 'You mustn't!'

'Oh, it's quite all right.' Janice chuckles. 'I've hundreds of pairs.'

I have to say, Minnie looks adorable in oversized white sunglasses. But I can't let her get away with it.

'Minnie,' I say severely. 'You haven't said thank you. And you mustn't ask for things. What will poor Janice do now? She hasn't got any sunglasses!'

The sunglasses slither down off Minnie's nose and she holds them, thinking hard.

'Thank you,' she says at last. 'Thank you, Waniss.' (She can't quite manage 'Janice'.) She reaches up, tugs her pink gingham bow out of her hair and hands it to Janice. 'Wanniss bow.'

'Darling.' I can't help giggling. 'Janice doesn't wear hair bows.'

'Nonsense!' says Janice. 'That's lovely, Minnie, thank you.'

She clips the bow into her grey hair, where it perches incongruously, and I feel a sudden wave of affection for her. I've known Janice for ever, and she's a bit crazy – but look at this. She's flown out to LA at the drop of a hat, just to support Mum. She's kept us all amused with stories of her flower-arranging classes, and is a nice, cheery presence. (Except when she's dealing in illegal drugs, obviously.)

'Thanks for coming out, Janice,' I say impulsively and hug her as best I can, given that her money 'safety' belt is protruding like a pregnancy bump at the front of her top. She and Mum are wearing identical models, and if you ask me, they look exactly like an advert to a mugger: *Stacks of Cash Here*. But I haven't said that to Mum, because she's hassled enough already.

'Mum . . .' I turn to hug her too. 'Don't worry. I'm sure Dad's OK.'

But her shoulders are all tense and she doesn't hug me back properly. 'It's all very well, Becky,' she says, sounding agitated. 'But these secrets and mysteries. It's not what you want, at my age.'

'I know,' I say, soothingly.

'Dad didn't want to call you Rebecca, you know. It was *me* who liked the name.'

'I know,' I repeat.

33

We've had this conversation about twenty times. It was practically the first thing I demanded of Mum as soon as I saw her: 'Why was I named Rebecca?'

'After the book, you know,' Mum continues. 'The Daphne du Maurier book.'

'I know.' I nod patiently.

'And Dad didn't want it. He suggested Henrietta.' Mum's face starts to quiver.

'*Henrietta.*' I wrinkle my nose. I am so not a Henrietta.

'But *why* didn't he want to call you Rebecca?' Mum's voice rises shrilly.

There's silence, apart from a clicking sound as Mum fidgets with the pearls of her necklace. I feel a pang as I watch her trembling, anxious fingers. Dad gave her that pearl necklace. It's an antique, from 1895, and I went to help her choose it at the shop, and she was so excited and happy. Every year, Dad gets a BB – what we call his Big Bonus – and spends it on something nice for each of us.

The truth is, my dad's pretty amazing. He still gets his BB, even now he's retired, just for a bit of insurance consultancy. Luke says he must have some really impressive niche knowledge to command such high fees. But he's so modest, he never boasts about it. He always spends it on treats for us and we have a fun celebratory lunch in London. That's the kind of man Dad is. He's generous. He's loving. He cares about his family. This is all so out of character.

Gently I take Mum's hand and remove it from the pearls.

'You'll break them,' I say. 'Mum, *please* try to relax.'

'Come on, Jane.' Janice takes Mum's arm soothingly. 'Let's sit down and have something to eat. It's "bottom-less coffee" here, you know,' she adds as they head off. 'They come round with a pot and refill your cup when-ever you like! No limit! Such a good system. So much better than all those lattes and grandaccinos . . .'

As she and Mum disappear, I grab Minnie's hand, and carry on to the back of the diner. As soon as I step out-side I feel better, despite the scorching sun. I needed to get away. Everyone's so tense and ratty. What I'd really like to do is sit down with Suze and talk to her properly, but I can't with Alicia there—

Ooh, look!

I've stopped dead. Not at the 'barnyard', which consists of three mangy goats in a pen, but at a sign reading *Local Craft Sale*. Maybe I should go and buy something to cheer myself up. Give myself a little lift and support the local economy at the same time. Yes. I'll do that.

There are about six stalls, with crafts and clothes and artefacts. I can see a skinny girl in high-heeled suede boots filling a basket with necklaces, exclaiming to the stall holder, 'I love these! This is all my Christmas shopping done, right here!'

As I get near, a grizzled old lady appears from behind one stall, and I jump. She looks as if she's a hand-crafted artefact herself. Her skin is so brown and lined, it could be some ancient, grained wood, or hand-beaten hide. She's wearing a leather hat with a cord under her chin, and she has a tooth missing, and her plaid skirt looks about a hundred years old.

'You on vacation?' she enquires, as I start looking at leather bags.

'Kind of . . . Well, not really,' I say honestly. 'I'm on a trip. We're searching for someone, actually. Trying to track them down.'

'Manhunt.' She nods, matter-of-factly. 'My granddaddy used to be a bounty hunter.'

A *bounty hunter*? That's the coolest thing I've ever heard. Imagine being a bounty hunter! I can't help visualizing a business card, perhaps with a little cowboy hat printed in the corner:

Rebecca Brandon
Bounty Hunter

'I suppose I'm a kind of bounty hunter too,' I hear myself saying nonchalantly. 'You know. In a way.'

Which is sort of true. After all, I'm hunting for people, aren't I? And that makes me a bounty hunter, surely? 'So, can you give me any tips?' I add.

'I can give you plenty,' she says hoarsely. 'My granddaddy used to say, "Don't try to beat 'em, meet 'em."'

'"Don't try to beat 'em, meet 'em"?' I echo. 'What does that mean?'

'It means be smart. Don't go running after a moving target. Look for the friends. Look for the family.' She suddenly produces a bundle of deep-brown leather. 'Do you a fine holster, ma'am. Hand-stitched.'

A holster?

A holster, like . . . for a *gun*?

'Oh,' I say, discomfited. 'Right! A holster. Wow. That's
. . . um . . . gorgeous. The only tiny thing is . . .' I cough,
feeling embarrassed. 'I don't have a gun.'

'You don't got no weapon?' She seems staggered by
this news.

Now I feel totally wussy. I've never even *held* a gun, let
alone considered owning one. But maybe I should have
more of an open mind. I mean, it's the way out here in
the West, isn't it? You have your hat, you have your boots,
you have your gun. Probably girls in the West walk
around town and eye each other's guns up the way I eye
up Hermès bags.

'I don't have a weapon right *now*,' I amend. 'Not exactly
on me. But when I do, I'll come and get a holster.'

As I'm walking away, I'm wondering if I should quickly
have shooting lessons and get a firearms licence and buy
a Gluck. Or do I mean Glock? Or a Smith and Whatsit. I
don't even know which the coolest one is. They should
have *Vogue* for guns.

I head towards the next stall, where the skinny girl I
noticed before is filling up her second basket.

'Hey,' she says pleasantly, glancing up at me. 'These
shawls are all fifty per cent off.'

'Some are seventy-five per cent off,' chimes in the stall
owner. She has a greying braid with ribbons wound
around it, which looks stunning. 'I'm doing a big
clear-out.'

'Wow.' I pick up one of the shawls and shake it out. It's

37

really soft wool, with beautiful embroidered birds, and is amazing value.

'I'm getting two each for me and my mom,' the skinny girl says in chatty tones. 'And you should check out the belts.' She gestures at a neighbouring stall. 'I'm like, you can never have too many belts.'

'Totally,' I agree. 'Belts are a staple.'

'Right?' She nods enthusiastically. 'Can I have another basket?' she adds, to the stall owner. 'And do you take Amex?'

While the stall holder is getting out her credit-card machine, I pick up a couple of shawls. But it's strange. Maybe I'm not in a shawl mood or something, because even though I can *see* how gorgeous they are, I don't feel like buying them. It's as if I'm looking at some trolley full of delicious desserts, but I've lost my appetite.

So instead, I head over to the belt stall and have a look at those.

I mean, they're really well made. The buckles are nice and heavy, and they're in some good colours. I can't spot a single thing wrong with them. I just don't feel like *buying* them. In fact the thought makes me feel a bit ill. Which is weird.

The skinny girl has lined up five baskets of stuff and is scrabbling in her Michael Kors bag. 'I was sure that credit card was OK,' she says fretfully. 'Let me just try another one . . . oh shoot!' She drops her bag on the floor and bends down to pick up all her stuff. I'm about to help her, when I hear my name.

'Bex!' I turn to see Suze looking out of the back door

of the diner. 'The food's here—' She breaks off, and her eyes run along the row of five baskets. 'Oh, that's just typical! You've been shopping. What else would you be doing?'

She sounds so censorious, I feel the colour flood into my cheeks. But I just stare back silently. There's no point saying anything. Suze is determined to find fault, whatever I do. She disappears back into the diner, and I breathe out.

'Come on, Minnie,' I say, trying to sound light-hearted. 'We'd better get some breakfast. And you can even have a milkshake.'

'Milkshake!' exclaims Minnie joyfully. 'From a cow,' she tells me. 'A chocolate cow?'

'No, it's a strawberry cow today,' I tell her, tickling her under the chin.

OK. So I *know* we're going to have to put Minnie straight about cows one day, but I can't bear to just yet. It's so sweet. She honestly thinks there are chocolate cows and vanilla cows and strawberry cows.

'It's a very yummy strawberry cow,' comes Luke's voice, and I look up to see him coming out of the diner. 'Food's ready.' He winks at me.

'Thanks. We're just coming.'

'Swing time?' asks Minnie, screwing up her face in hope, and Luke laughs.

'Come on then, sausage.'

For a few minutes we walk around, swinging Minnie between our arms.

'How's tricks?' Luke asks me over Minnie's head. 'You've been pretty quiet in the RV.'

'Oh,' I say, disconcerted that he's even noticed. 'Well, I've just been, you know. Thinking.'

This isn't quite true. I'm quiet because I don't have anyone to talk to. Suze and Alicia are in their little twosome; Mum and Janice are in their little twosome. All I have is Minnie, and she's been glued to *Enchanted* on the iPad.

I mean, I've tried. As we left LA, I sat down with Suze and made to give her a hug but she went all stiff and cut me dead. I felt so stupid, I scuttled back to my seat and pretended to be interested in the landscape.

But I won't go into any of that right now. I'm not going to burden Luke with my problems. He's been such a star – the least I can do is refrain from dumping my stupid worries on him. I'll be dignified and discreet, as a wife should be. 'Thank you for coming,' I add. 'Thank you for doing this. I know you're really busy.'

'I wasn't about to let you drive off into the desert with Suze on your own.' He gives a short laugh.

It was Suze's idea to rush off to Vegas – she and Alicia were both convinced they'd soon track down Bryce. But they haven't yet, and here we are, halfway there, without a hotel reservation or a plan or anything . . .

I mean, believe me, I'm all for rushing off to places. But even I can see this is all a bit crazy. Except I don't want to be the one to say that, or I'll get my head bitten off by Suze. At the thought of Suze, I feel a fresh wave of distress, and suddenly I can't bottle it up any longer. I'll have to be dignified and discreet another time.

'Luke, I think I'm losing her,' I say in a rush. 'She never looks at me, she never talks to me . . .'

'Who, Suze?' Luke gives a little wince. 'I'd noticed.'

'I can't lose Suze.' My voice starts to wobble. 'I can't. She's my three a.m. friend!'

'Your what?' Luke looks puzzled.

'You know. The friend you could ring up at three a.m. if you were in trouble, and she'd come straight away, no problem? Like, Janice is Mum's three a.m. friend, Gary's your three a.m. friend . . .'

'Right. I see what you mean.' Luke nods.

Gary is the most loyal guy in the world. And he adores Luke. He'd be there at 3 a.m. like a shot, and Luke would be there for him, too. I always thought Suze and I would be like that, for ever.

'If I was in trouble at three a.m. right now, I'm not sure I could ring Suze.' I look miserably at Luke. 'I think she'd tell me to go away.'

'That's nonsense,' says Luke robustly. 'Suze loves you as much as she ever did.'

'She doesn't.' I shake my head. 'I mean, I don't *blame* her or anything, this whole thing's all my fault . . .'

'No it's not,' says Luke, with a surprised laugh. 'What are you talking about?'

I stare at him in bewilderment. How can he even ask that?

'Of course it is! If I'd gone to see Brent sooner, like I was meant to, we wouldn't be here.'

'Becky, this is *not* all your fault,' counters Luke firmly. 'You don't know what would have happened if you'd gone to see Brent sooner. And by the way, both Tarquin and your father are grown men. You mustn't blame yourself. OK?'

I can hear what he's saying, but he's wrong. He doesn't understand.

'Well, anyway.' I give a gusty sigh. 'Suze is only interested in Alicia.'

'You realize that Alicia's trying to psych you out?' says Luke, and he sounds so sure that I lift my head in astonishment.

'Really?'

'It's obvious. She talks a lot of shit, that girl. "Redactive" isn't a word.'

'*Really?*' I feel suddenly cheered. 'I thought I was just being stupid.'

'Stupid? You're never stupid.' Luke lets go of Minnie's hand, pulls me close and looks right into my eyes. 'Abysmal at parking, maybe. But never stupid. Becky, don't let that witch get to you.'

'You know what I think?' I lower my voice, even though no one's in earshot. 'She's up to something. Alicia, I mean.'

'Like what?'

'I don't know yet,' I admit. 'But I'm going to find out.'

Luke raises his eyebrows. 'All I'll say is, watch your step. Suze is pretty sensitive at the moment.'

'I know. You don't have to tell me.'

Luke hugs me tight for a minute, and I let myself relax. I'm pretty exhausted, actually.

'Come on, let's go in,' he says at last. 'By the way, I think Janice was done,' he adds as we head towards the building. 'Those tablets? I looked at the active ingredient and it's aspirin in fancy Latin.'

'*Really?*' I almost want to giggle as I picture Janice

frantically scattering the tablets over the desert. 'Well, let's not tell her.'

The table is covered with food when we arrive back in the diner, although no one seems to be eating except Janice, who's devouring scrambled eggs. Mum is stirring her coffee furiously, Suze is nibbling the side of her thumbnail (which she always does when she's stressed), and Alicia is pouring some kind of green powder into a cup. It'll be some revolting healthy thing.

'Hi everyone,' I say, and slide into my chair. 'How's the food?'

'We're trying to think,' growls Suze. 'No one's *thinking* hard enough.'

Alicia murmurs something in her ear and Suze nods and they both shoot sidelong looks at me. And just for one awful moment I feel as though I'm back at school and the mean girls are all pointing at my games kit. (Mum made me use the old games kit, long after everyone else had changed to the new version, because she thought it was a rip-off. I mean, I don't blame her, but I did get laughed at, *every single games lesson*.)

Anyway. I'm not going to get upset. I'm a grown-up with a job to do. I take a bite of my waffle, pull Dad's map towards me again, and stare at it until the lines blur. That wise old woman's words are ringing in my ears: *Look for the friends. Look for the family.*

Whatever this mystery is, it's all about those four friends. So let's go back to basics. Corey's the friend in Las Vegas. That's our biggest clue. We need to track him down. Be smarter. But how?

43

I must know more than I realize, I tell myself firmly. I *must* do. I just need to think harder. I close my eyes tight, and try to send myself back in time. It's Christmas. I'm sitting by the fire in our Oxshott house. I can smell the Chocolate Orange in my lap. Dad has spread his old map out on the coffee table and is reminiscing about his trip to America. I can hear his voice again, in random snippets of memory.

'. . . and then the fire got out of control; let me tell you, that was no picnic . . .'

'. . . they say "stubborn as a mule" and I know why – that wretched creature would *not* go down into the canyon . . .'

'. . . we used to sit late into the night, drinking the local beer . . .'

'. . . Brent and Corey were clever fellows, science grads they were . . .'

'. . . they'd discuss their theories and scribble down their ideas . . .'

'. . . Corey had the money, of course, wealthy family . . .'

'. . . there's nothing like camping out and seeing the sunrise . . .'

'. . . we nearly lost the car down a ravine because Raymond would not give in . . .'

'. . . Corey would be sketching away, he was quite an artist, as well as everything else . . .'

Wait a minute.

Corey was quite an artist. I'd forgotten that. And there was something else about Corey and his art. What was it? What *was* it . . . ?

The thing about me is: I'm quite good at bossing my brain about. It can forget about Visa bills if I want it to, and it can blur over arguments and it can see the plus side in almost any situation. And now I'm telling it to remember. To go into all those old dusty holes in my head that I never bother clearing out, and *remember*. Because I know there was something else . . . I simply know there was . . .

Yes!

'. . . he used to put an eagle in each picture, like a trademark . . .'

My eyes pop open. An eagle. I *knew* there was something. Well, it's not much, but it's a start, isn't it?

I whip out my phone, Google 'corey artist eagle las vegas' and wait for the results. There's something wrong with the signal, and I prod the keypad impatiently, trying to scour my brain for more information. Corey the artist. Corey the wealthy one. Corey the science grad. Were there any other clues?

'I've just heard from my last contact,' says Alicia, looking up from her phone. 'No luck. Suze . . .' She pauses, her face drawn. 'We might have to go back to LA and think again.'

'Give *up*?' Suze's face crumples, and I feel a pang of alarm. We've come rushing into the desert on a wave of adrenalin and drama. If we just give up and go home now, I think Suze will actually collapse.

'Let's not give up yet,' I say, trying to sound positive. 'I'm sure if we keep thinking we'll get somewhere—'

'Oh, really, Bex?' Suze spits. 'It's all very well saying that, but what are you doing to help? Nothing! What are you doing right now?' She waves a hand angrily at my phone. 'Probably shopping online.'

'I'm not!' I say defensively. 'I'm doing my own research.'

'Research into what?'

My stupid screen has frozen. I press Enter again, jabbing at it in my impatience.

'Luke, you must have influence!' Mum interjects. 'You know the prime minister. Can't he help?'

'The *prime minister*?' Luke sounds flabbergasted.

Suddenly my screen starts filling with Google results. And as I scan down the type, I feel an inner whoop. It's him! It's Corey from Dad's trip!

Local **artist Corey** Andrews . . . signature **eagle** . . . was exhibiting at the **Las Vegas** Gallery . . .

It *has* to be him, surely?

I quickly tap in 'Corey Andrews' and hold my breath. A few moments later, a page of entries appears. There's a Wikipedia page, business reports, property news, some company called Firelight Innovations, Inc . . . all the same guy. Corey Andrews of Las Vegas. I've found him!

'Or that chap you know from the Bank of England,' Mum is persisting.

'You mean the Governor of the Bank of England?' says Luke, after a pause.

'Yes, him! Ring him up!'

I almost want to laugh at Luke's expression. I honestly think Mum expects him to marshal the whole British Cabinet to come out here and hunt for Dad.

'I'm not sure that will be possible,' says Luke politely, and turns to Alicia. 'Do you really have no more leads?'

'No.' Alicia sighs. 'I think we've reached the end of the road.'

'I have a lead,' I begin nervously, and everyone turns to look at me.

'*You* do?' says Suze, suspiciously.

'I've tracked down Corey from the trip. Corey Andrews, he's called. Mum, does that sound right?'

'Corey Andrews.' Mum frowns. 'Yes, it might have been Andrews . . .' Her frown lifts. 'Becky, I think you've got it! Corey Andrews. He was the wealthy one, Dad always said. Wasn't he an artist, too?'

'Exactly! And he lives in Las Vegas. I've got his address.'

'Well done, Becky, love!' says Janice, and I can't help feeling a little glow.

'How did you work that out?' demands Alicia, looking almost affronted.

'Just . . . um . . . you know. Lateral thinking.' I hand my phone to Luke. 'Here's the zip code. Let's go.'

From: wunderwood@iafro.com
To: Brandon, Rebecca
Subject: Re: Applying to be a Bounty Hunter

Dear Ms Brandon

Thank you for your email. If you would like to join the
International Association of Fugitive Recovery Operatives,
please fill out the attached form, and return it, together with
the $95 membership fee. You will receive an ID card,
together with other benefits outlined on our website.

However, in answer to your query, we do not issue 'Bounty
Hunter' badges nor other 'bounty hunter accessories'.

We do provide an Apprentice Scheme; however, I regret we
do not offer specific workshops on 'How to Track Down a
Missing Dad'. Nor indeed 'How to Stay Friends With Your
Fellow Bounty Hunters'.

Good luck with your endeavors.

Yours kindly

Wyatt Underwood

Membership Manager
International Association of Fugitive Recovery Operatives

FOUR

As we travel towards Corey's Las Vegas address, the mood in the RV is subdued. Mum and Janice are silent. Suze and Alicia are sitting opposite me, still talking away in low voices. And I'm playing stickers with Minnie and thinking about Bryce.

His full name is Bryce Perry and he was – is – the Personal Growth Leader at Golden Peace. I came across him a lot when I was attending classes there, and what I'm pondering is: why has Tarquin fallen under his spell? Why has Dad asked him along on the mission? Why do the pair of them trust him? And I think I've hit on the answer: Bryce is really good-looking.

Which is not about being gay or anything. It's just, there's something compelling about very beautiful people. Especially strong-jawed men with stubble and intense eyes. You fall under their spell and believe anything they say. Like, if I met Will Smith tomorrow and he told me he was on the run from corrupt government officials and I must help him, no questions asked, I'd totally believe it.

Well, Bryce is the same. He has those captivating eyes that make you go weak-kneed. When he talks, it's mesmerizing. You start thinking, *Bryce, you're so right! About everything!* Even if he's only telling you the times of yoga classes.

Suze definitely felt the Bryce magic; I know she did. Everyone did. And the thing with Tarquin is that just before he met Bryce, he'd been in a fairly bad place. He'd fallen out with his family, and had an embarrassing business failure and he was generally feeling pretty down . . . when up pops Bryce with his beach volleyball sessions and his friendly chats and his charismatic personality. So it's no wonder that Tarkie fell under Bryce's spell.

It's also no wonder that Bryce is after his money. When you're as rich as Tarkie, everyone's after your money. Poor old Tarkie. He has all this cash and stately homes and stuff, but I don't think it makes him happy, really—

'OK, we're about twenty minutes away.' Luke interrupts my thoughts and I jump. In fact, we all jump.

'Twenty minutes?'

'Already?'

'But we're not in Las Vegas yet!'

'It's this side of Las Vegas,' says Luke, squinting at the sat nav. 'Looks like a residential area. Lots of golf clubs.'

'Golf!' exclaims Janice in excitement. 'Maybe Graham and his friend are playing golf! Could that be it, Jane?'

'Well, he does like his golf,' says Mum, sounding uncertain. 'Suzie, Tarquin plays golf, doesn't he?'

'A bit,' says Suze, sounding equally uncertain.

'That's it, then.' Janice claps her hands. 'It's golf!'

Golf?

We're all looking at each other, flummoxed. Is Dad on a golfing trip? Will we have rushed into the desert like mad things just to find him on the eighteenth green wearing Argyle socks and saying, 'Good shot, Tarquin'?

'Does Bryce play golf?' Suze turns to Alicia.

'I have no idea,' says Alicia. 'Seems unlikely. But I'd say there's no point speculating till we get there.'

This is such a sensible, dampening-down thing to say, it ruins the temporary excitement. So we sit in silence until Luke turns into a wide road lined with mansions and says, 'This is Eagles Landing Lane.'

We all stare out of the car, gobsmacked. I thought Las Vegas was all bright lights and hotels and casinos. I sort of imagined that everyone just lived in the hotels, all the time. But of course there are houses too. And these aren't just houses, they're *palaces*. The plots of land are huge, and they all have towering palm trees or vast gates or something, as if to announce, *I live here and I'm a pretty big deal*.

We arrive at No. 235 and gaze at it in silence. It's the hugest of the lot: grey with four castellated towers, like a proper princess's castle. It looks like it should have Rapunzel leaning out of an upper-storey window.

'What does Corey do, again?' says Luke.

'He owns a science company,' I say. 'He has all these patents registered. And he owns stacks of property too. He does lots of things.'

'What kind of patents?'

'I don't know!' I say. 'They're all in scientific gobbledegook.'

I scroll through my Google search and read out some of the entries. '*Corey Andrews, honored by the Institute of Electrical Engineers* . . . *Corey Andrews, stepped down as chairman of Firelight Innovations, Inc* . . . *Corey Andrews' growing property empire* . . . Oh. Wait. This is from the *Las Vegas Herald*, a few years ago. *Corey Andrews celebrates his fiftieth birthday at the Mandarin Oriental with friends and associates.*' I look up from my phone in consternation. 'His *fiftieth*? I thought he was the same age as Dad.'

'Shit.' Luke turns the engine off. 'Are we in the wrong place? Is this the wrong Corey?'

'Well, I don't know,' I say, confused. 'Because he's definitely a Corey Andrews who puts eagles in his pictures.'

'Could there be more than one who does the same thing?' suggests Suze.

There's silence as we all consider this.

'Only one way to find out,' says Luke at last. He jumps down and we watch him speaking into the intercom. A moment later he's back in the RV and the gates are swinging open.

'What did they say?' demands Janice eagerly.

'They thought we were here for a party,' says Luke. 'I didn't disabuse them.'

As we travel up the drive, a man in a grey linen outfit directs us to park the RV next to a building that looks like an aircraft hangar. This place is seriously huge, with massive trees and great potted plants everywhere. The netting of a tennis court is visible from where we've parked, and jazz from hidden speakers is filling the air. The other cars are all shiny convertibles, most with customized number plates. One says *DOLLAR 34*, another is *KRYSTLE* and a third is a stretch limo, spray-painted with a tiger print.

'Tiger car!' exclaims Minnie, looking transfixed with joy. 'Tiger car, Mummy!'

'It's beautiful, darling,' I say, trying not to giggle. 'So, where are we going to go now?' I turn to the others. 'You realize we're totally gatecrashing?'

'I've never been anywhere like this in my life,' says Suze, wide-eyed.

'Suze, you own a castle in Scotland,' I point out.

'Yes, but not like *this*,' she counters. 'This is like a Disney castle! Look, there's a helicopter pad on the roof!'

The man in the grey linen outfit approaches, eyeing us up and down dubiously.

'Are you here for Peyton's party?' he enquires. 'May I take your names?'

I must admit, we don't look like party guests. We don't even have a present for Peyton, whoever Peyton is.

'We won't be on the list,' says Luke smoothly. 'But we'd like to see Corey Andrews. It's a matter of some urgency.'

'It's a matter of life and death,' chimes in Mum wildly.

'We've come all the way from Oxshott,' Janice adds. 'Oxshott in England.'

'We want to find my dad,' I explain.

'And my husband,' says Suze, pushing her way to the front of the group. 'He's missing, and we think maybe Corey knows something about it.'

The linen-suit man is looking bewildered.

'I'm afraid Mr Andrews is tied up right now,' he says,

backing away from Suze. 'If you can give me your details, I'll pass them on—'

'But we need to see him now!' says Mum passionately.

'We'll be quick,' says Luke.

'Want to ride tiger car!' Minnie puts in emphatically.

'We won't be any trouble,' adds Mum eagerly. 'If you could just—'

'Please give Mr Andrews this.' A low voice comes from behind us and we all turn to see Alicia coming forward, holding out a Golden Peace card with its distinctive shiny insignia and some words scribbled on it.

The man takes it, reads it in silence and his expression changes.

'*Well*,' he says. 'I'll let Mr Andrews know you're here.'

He retreats and we all face Alicia, who's looking smug yet humble in that annoying way she has.

'What did you write?' I demand.

'Just a few words that I thought might help,' she says simply.

I can hear Mum and Janice agreeing in loud whispers that the name 'Alicia Merrelle' is like royalty in the States, and *think* how many celebrities she must have met at Golden Peace, not that she'd ever gossip, because she's such a nice discreet girl.

A *nice discreet girl*? I have explained to Mum about Alicia Bitch Long-legs, over and over—

Anyway. Whatever.

It's only a few moments later that our friend in the linen suit appears again, and ushers us silently towards the house – all except Luke, who stayed in the RV to talk to

Gary. (There's some big piece of gossip from the conference dinner involving a junior government minister.) The house has a massive studded front door, and just for a moment I think a drawbridge is going to come down. But instead we skirt round the house/castle/mansion altogether and file between some immaculate hedges like in the maze at Hampton Court, until we come out on to a great big lawn with a gigantic bouncy castle and a table covered in food and five zillion kids running about and a banner reading *Happy 5th Birthday, Peyton!*

Ah. So *that's* who Peyton is. Actually, you can't tell who she is, because every single little girl is wearing a shiny princess frock. But it's obvious who Corey is, from the way the guy in the linen suit approaches him deferentially and starts gesturing at us.

He's quite amazing-looking, Corey. He's very buff and tanned, with thick, black hair and what look like tweezered eyebrows. He looks way younger than Dad. Next to him is a woman who I guess is Mrs Corey, and when I look at her, the only word that comes to mind is 'frosted'. She has shiny blonde hair, a sparkly top, embossed jeans, diamanté sandals, zillions of rings and bracelets, and a jewelled clip in her hair. She basically looks like someone took the glitter pot and emptied it over her. She also has big, tanned breasts and a very low-cut top. I mean, *very* low cut. For a children's birthday party.

At last Corey heads towards us and we all glance at each other. We haven't decided who's going to speak or what we're going to say or anything. But as usual, Alicia gets in first.

'Mr Andrews,' she says. 'I am Alicia Merrelle.'

'Mrs Merrelle.' Corey takes her hand. 'Honoured to have you visit. How can I help?'

Close up, he doesn't look *quite* as young. In fact, he's got that over-tight, too-much-plastic-surgery look. And now I'm really confused. Is this Dad's Corey or not? I'm opening my mouth to ask him, when Mrs Corey appears by his side. If you put her in a cotton frock and wiped off all the shiny eyeshadow, she'd probably look about twenty-three. Maybe she *is* twenty-three.

'Honey?' she says questioningly to Corey. 'What's going on?'

'I don't know.' He gives a little laugh. 'What *is* going on? This is Alicia Merrelle,' he adds to his wife. 'Owns Golden Peace. My wife, Cyndi.'

Cyndi gasps and goggles at Alicia. 'You own Golden Peace? That place is inspirational! I have your DVD, my friend did the retreat . . . how can we help?'

'We're looking for my father,' I plunge in. 'He's called Graham Bloomwood, and we think you knew him years ago. Unless . . .' I add uncertainly to Corey, 'there's another Corey Andrews who's an artist who puts eagles in his paintings?'

Cyndi laughs. 'Only one Corey Andrews, isn't there, babe?'

'Great!' I say, encouraged. 'So, you went on a trip with my dad in 1972. A road trip. There were four of you.'

Something tells me I've said the wrong thing. Corey's face barely moves, but I can see it in his eyes. A flicker of hostility.

'In 1972?' Cyndi wrinkles her brow. 'Corey would

have been too young for a road trip back then! How old were you then, honey?'

'I can't help you, I'm afraid,' says Corey tightly. 'If you'll excuse us.'

As he turns away, I can see tiny scars behind his ears. Oh, for God's sake. This is about his personal vanity. That's why he's denying he knows Dad. Cyndi has hurried to help a fallen child, but before Corey can disappear too, Mum grabs his arm.

'My husband's missing!' she cries dramatically. 'You're our only hope!'

'Look, I'm sorry, but you *must* be the same Corey,' I say firmly. 'I know you are. Has my dad come here? Have you heard anything from him?'

'This conversation is over.' He glares at me.

'Are you in touch with Brent or Raymond?' I persist. 'Did you know that Brent's been living in a trailer? My dad says he's got to "put something right". Do you know what that is?'

'Please leave my property,' says Corey flatly. 'It's my daughter's birthday party. I'm sorry I can't help you.'

'Can you give us Raymond's surname, at least?'

'Raymond Earle?' says Cyndi brightly, rejoining the group. 'That's the only Raymond I ever heard Corey talk about.'

I glance at Corey, and he looks livid.

'Cyndi, don't talk to these people,' he snaps. 'They're just leaving. Go back to the party.'

'Cyndi, where does Raymond live?' I quickly ask. 'Isn't it Albuquerque? Or San Diego? Or is it . . . Milwaukee?'

I'm just plucking places from the air, hoping it'll prod her into answering, and it works.

'Well, no, he's down near Tucson, right?' She glances uncertainly at Corey. 'Only he's a bit nuts, isn't he, babe? Total recluse? I mean, I overheard you talking . . .' She quails at Corey's look and falls silent.

'So you are in touch with him!' I feel a surge of frustration. We're *so* on the right track. But if this stupid plastic-faced idiot won't help us, we'll be stuck again. 'Corey, what happened in 1972? Why's my dad gone on this mission? *What happened?*'

'Please get off my property,' says Corey, wheeling round. 'I'm calling my security team. This is a private birthday party.'

'My name is Rebecca!' I shout after him. 'Does that mean anything to you?'

'Oh!' exclaims Cyndi. 'Like your eldest, hon!'

Corey turns back and I can see him staring at me, the weirdest look on his face. No one else speaks. In fact, I think everyone's holding their breath. He has a daughter called Rebecca, too. What is going *on*?

Then he wheels round again and strides back towards the party.

'Well, great to meet you guys!' says Cyndi uncertainly. 'Pick up a party bag for your little one as you leave.'

'Oh, we couldn't do that!' I say at once. 'They're for your guests.'

'But we have way too many. Please, go ahead.' She hurries after Corey, stumbling a little on her heels. I can hear her saying in puzzled tones, 'Babe, what's up?'

A few moments later, the guy in the linen suit rounds

the corner of the house, accompanied by two guys who are *not* in linen suits. They're in jeans, and have crew cuts, and those expressionless faces which say *Only doing my job* as they beat you to a pulp.

You know. I'm assuming.

'Um, let's go,' I say nervously.

'Goodness,' gulps Janice. 'Those men do look rather *threatening*.'

'Big bullies!' says Mum indignantly, and I have a sudden dreadful image of her squaring up to them with her Oxshott Senior Ladies' Self-Defence Group moves.

'Mum, we need to go,' I say, before she can get any bright ideas.

'I think we should leave,' agrees Alicia. 'We've learned all we can for now.'

'Thanks!' I call to the crew-cut guys. 'We're just on our way out. Super party, we're just getting our party bag . . .'

As I steer Minnie to a table covered in massive loot bags, Cyndi reappears, holding a cocktail. She sees us approaching the table and hurries over.

'I'm so sorry about that,' Cyndi says breathlessly. 'My husband can be a grouch with people he doesn't know. I say to him, "Honey! Lighten up!"' She picks up a bag tied with purple ribbons and peeks inside. 'Oh now, this one has a ballerina doll in it.' She holds it out to Minnie. 'You like ballerinas, honey?'

'Party bag!' yells Minnie ecstatically. 'Tank-you-for-da-lovely-party,' she adds with care. 'Tank-you-for-da-lovely-parteee.'

'You're a darling.' Cyndi beams at her. 'That accent!'

'It's an amazing party,' I say, politely.

'I have a very generous husband,' says Cyndi earnestly. 'We're very lucky. But you know, we appreciate it. We don't take it for granted.' She nods at the table. 'Every one of these loot bags has a counterpart, going to an underprivileged kid.'

'Wow.' I blink at her. 'That's a great idea.'

'It's the way I like to do things. I wasn't born to this.' She sweeps an arm around, gesturing at the castle. 'We can always remember those less fortunate than ourselves. And that's what I want to teach Peyton, too.'

'Good for you.' I feel a tweak of admiration. I reckon there's more to Cyndi than meets the eye.

'Corey has his own charitable foundation, too,' she adds. 'He's the most generous, giving man. He constantly thinks of others.' She looks a little misty-eyed. 'But you must have picked that up from meeting him.'

'Er . . . absolutely!' I lie. 'Well, nice to meet you.'

'Great to meet you too! Bye-bye, pumpkin!' She pinches Minnie's cheek. 'Good luck with everything.'

'Oh, just one thing,' I add casually as we turn away. 'I was wondering . . . do you know why Corey called his first daughter Rebecca?'

'Oh my.' Cyndi looks awkward. 'I have no idea. You know, they don't really talk. I've never met her. It's kinda sad.'

'Oh.' I digest this.

'I shouldn't have mentioned her just now. Corey doesn't like to talk about the past at all. He says it brings him bad luck. I tried to invite her for Thanksgiving once, but . . .' She looks crestfallen for a moment, then brightens. 'Anyhow. Can I get you guys a snack for the road?'

FIVE

The party bag is *insanely* lavish.

It's half an hour later and we've stopped at another diner for lunch and a regroup. Minnie is unpacking the bag on to the table, and we're all staring, slack-jawed. The ballerina doll is just the start. There's also a DKNY watch, a Young Versace hoodie and a pair of tickets to Cirque du Soleil. Suze is especially horrified, because she's really not into party bags. She thinks they're common. (She never actually uses that word but she twists her fingers into knots and I know it's what she thinks. When she gives a children's party, the party bag consists of a balloon and a big piece of home-made toffee, wrapped in greaseproof paper.)

As Minnie pulls out a gorgeous pink Kate Spade clutch, Mum and Janice start Googling 'Las Vegas property prices' on their phones, to see how much Corey's house must be worth, while I quickly remove the Kate Spade for safekeeping. I'll look after it for Minnie till she's grown up enough to use it. (And in the meantime maybe borrow it just once or twice.)

'*How* does he make his money, exactly?' Janice asks. 'Goodness, this one is sixteen million dollars!'

'Property,' says Mum vaguely.

'No, he started out in patents,' I inform them. 'Science inventions or whatever. He invented a special spring, apparently.'

I got this from page 3 of my Google search, where there was a profile of Corey from the *Wall Street Journal*. According to that, the spring was the first thing he invented and it still makes him money today. Although, how can you invent a spring? It's just curly wire, isn't it?

'There, Becky, I *told* you to concentrate in your science lessons . . .' says Mum. 'Janice, look, this house has *two* swimming pools.'

'Now that's just vulgar,' says Janice disapprovingly as she leans over to see. 'But look at that view . . .'

'I just don't understand how he's managed to lie about his age,' I put in. Corey's *got* to be around the same age as my dad, but I've searched online and I can't find anything to disprove the so-called 'fiftieth birthday party'. 'I mean, you can't just invent an age these days. What about Google?'

'He probably started lying before Google was invented,' says Janice wisely. 'Like Marjorie Willis, remember, Jane? She shaved a year off, every other birthday.'

'Oh, that Marjorie!' exclaims Mum indignantly. 'She turned thirty-four at least twice, if not three times. That's the way to do it, love.' She turns to me. 'Gradually and early.'

'Yes!' Janice nods. 'Start now, Becky. You could lose a decade, easily.'

Should I do that? I hadn't even thought about shaving years off my age. Anyway, surely the most sensible thing is to pretend to be *older* than you are? And then everyone says, 'Wow, you look amazing for ninety-three!' when you're only seventy . . .

My thoughts are interrupted by Luke beckoning to me. He's standing by the window and has rather an odd expression.

'Hi,' I say as I join him. 'What's up?' Without answering, he hands me his phone.

'Now look, Becky,' says Dad into my ear with no preamble. 'What's all this nonsense about Mum flying out to LA?'

It's Dad's voice. It's my dad. He's alive. I think I might pass out, except I want to whoop as well.

'*Dad?*' I exclaim breathlessly. 'Oh my God. Is that *you?*'

Tears have already sprung to my eyes. I hadn't realized quite how worried I was. Or how guilty I felt. Or how many horrible images had been circling in my head.

'I've just received a very garbled message on my phone,' Dad says. 'As I've said to Luke, I want you to *put Mum off*, all right? Tell her to stay in the UK.'

Is he kidding? Does he have any idea what we've been going through?

'But she's already here! And so is Janice! Dad, we're worried about you!' My words tumble out. 'And we're worried about Tarkie, and we're worried about—'

'We're all fine,' says Dad testily. 'Please tell Mum not to fret. I'll only be a few days.'

'But where *are* you? What are you *doing*?'

'It doesn't matter,' responds Dad shortly. 'It's a small issue between friends, and it'll take no time at all to sort out, I'm sure. Try to amuse your mother in the meantime.'

'But we're following you!'

'Well, please *don't* follow me!' Dad sounds really quite angry. 'This is ridiculous! Can a man not deal with a small private matter without being trailed?'

'But you didn't even tell Mum what you were doing! You just disappeared!'

'I left you a note,' says Dad impatiently. 'You knew I was safe. Shouldn't that have been enough?'

'Dad, you need to speak to her, right now. I'll pass you over—'

'No.' Dad cuts me off. 'Becky, I'm trying to achieve an important task and I have to focus on that. I can't deal with your mother having hysterics at me for an hour.'

'She wouldn't—' I begin, then stop, mid-sentence. I hate to say it, but he's right. If Mum gets on the phone with him, the rant will last until the phone runs out of power.

'Take your mother back to LA,' Dad's saying. 'Go to a spa and . . . what do you call it? Chill out.'

'How can we chill out?' Now I'm starting to feel angry. 'You won't tell us anything, and we know Bryce is trying to brainwash Tarkie . . . I mean, is he OK?'

Dad gives a short laugh. 'Bryce isn't brainwashing anyone. He's a very helpful young man. He's been invaluable to me. Knows the area, you see. And he's quite taken Tarquin under his wing. They spend hours chatting with each other about this and that.'

Under his wing? Hours chatting about this and that? I don't like the sound of that one bit.

'Well, is Tarkie there?'

'He's here. D'you want to speak to him?'

What? I stare at the phone in disbelief. There's a scuffling noise down the line, then Tarquin's unmistakable, reedy voice says, 'Ahm, hello? Becky?'

'Tarkie!' I nearly explode with relief. 'Hi! I'll get Suze—'

'No, ahm . . . don't bother,' he says. 'Just tell her I'm all right.'

'But she's so worried! We're all worried. You know Bryce is trying to brainwash you? He's dangerous, Tarkie. He wants your money. You haven't given him any, have you? Because don't, OK?'

'Of course he wants my money.' Tarquin sounds so matter-of-fact, the wind is taken out of my sails. 'Asks me about it every five minutes. Not very subtle, either. I'm not giving it to him, though.'

'Thank God!' I exhale. 'Well, don't.'

'I'm not a *total* chump, you know, Becky.'

'Oh,' I say feebly.

'Chap like Bryce, you just have to keep your wits about you.'

'Right.'

I'm feeling totally confused right now. Tarkie sounds so together. I thought he'd been having a nervous breakdown.

But then, what was that whole act in LA about? I can still picture him, sitting at the table in our house, glowering at everyone, telling Suze she was toxic.

'Becky, I have to go,' Tarquin's saying. 'I'll put your father back on.'

'No, don't go!' I cry, but it's too late.

'Becky?' My dad's back on the line and I quickly draw breath.

'Dad, listen. Please. I don't know what you're up to, and if you don't want me to know, that's fine. But you *can't* leave Mum in the lurch like this. Are you anywhere near Las Vegas? Because, if you've ever loved us and you have any time at all, meet us there. Just so we can see you for a couple of minutes. Just so we know you're OK. And then go off on your mission. Please, Dad. Please.'

There's a long silence. I can *feel* Dad's unwillingness seeping down the phone.

'I'm a fair way away,' he says at last.

'Then we'll come to you! Give me an address!'

'No,' says Dad. 'No, let's not do that.'

There's another silence, and I hold my breath.

The thing about my dad is, he's actually a very reasonable man. I mean, he was in insurance.

'All right,' he says at last. 'I'll have a quick breakfast with you tomorrow in Las Vegas. Then you can all relax and go back to LA and leave me in peace. But no questions.'

'Absolutely,' I say hastily. 'No questions.'

I am *so* going to ask questions. I'll start a list straight away.

'Where shall we meet?'

'Er . . .'

My knowledge of Las Vegas is fairly limited. In fact, it basically consists of watching *Ocean's Eleven* about a thousand times.

'The Bellagio,' I say. 'Breakfast at the Bellagio, nine a.m.'

'Good. See you there.'

And I wasn't going to ask anything else, because clearly he doesn't want me to know, but I can't help myself, and I blurt out, 'Dad, why didn't you want to call me Rebecca?'

There's another prickly silence and I hold my breath. I know Dad's still on the line. He's on the line and he's not saying anything . . .

And then he's rung off.

I immediately press Call Return, but it goes straight to voicemail. I try Tarkie's phone, but the same thing happens. They must have switched them both off.

'Well done!' says Luke as I finally raise my head. 'You should be a hostage negotiator! Do I take it we have a breakfast appointment with the runaways?'

'Apparently so,' I say, blinking at him. I feel a bit dazed. After all the stressing and worrying, it turns out Dad and Tarkie are both fine. Not at the bottom of a ravine.

'Relax, Becky!' Luke puts his hands on my shoulders. 'This is good news! We've found them!'

'Yes!' And at last I feel a smile starting to spread across my face. 'We have! We've found them. Let's tell Mum and Suze!'

Well, honestly. I thought it was the bearers of *bad* news who were supposed to be given a hard time. There I was, imagining Mum and Suze would gasp and cheer and congratulate me on having pinned Dad down to breakfast in Las Vegas. There I was, hoping for a group hug. I must have been deluded.

Neither Mum nor Suze look any cheerier for the news that their beloved husbands are alive and well. There was a brief flicker of delight, and Suze breathed, 'Thank God.' But now both of them are back on their grievances.

Mum's line is: 'Why doesn't my own husband trust me?' At least, it's a kind of duet, with Janice taking the line: 'I know, Jane,' and 'You're so right, Jane,' and 'Jane, dear, have a Minstrel.' Mum's basic argument is that any husband who goes off with secrets is disrespectful, and he's a grown man, and who does he think he is, Kojak?

(I'm not sure how Kojak comes into it. In fact, I'm not sure who Kojak is. Someone off the telly, I think.)

Meanwhile, Suze's complaint is: 'Why didn't Tarkie want to talk to *me*?' She's tried Tarkie's number about ninety-five times, and each time it's busy and she darts me a resentful look, as though it's *my* fault. As we approach the looming skyline of Las Vegas, she's chewing her fingers and staring out of the window.

'Suze?' I say cautiously.

'Yes?' She turns her head impatiently as though I've distracted her from something really important.

'Isn't it great? Tarkie's fine!'

Suze looks blank, as though she doesn't even understand what I'm saying.

'I mean, you can stop worrying,' I persist. 'It must be such a relief.'

A pained expression comes over Suze's face, as though I'm too stupid to realize the truth.

'Not till I *see* him,' she insists. 'Not till I see for myself. I still think Bryce has got to him. He's messed with his head somehow.'

'He sounded OK to me,' I say encouragingly. 'He wouldn't want to have breakfast with us if he'd been brainwashed, would he? I mean, isn't it all good news?'

'Bex, you just don't get it,' says Suze aggressively and at once Alicia puts her hand on Suze's as though *she* gets it because she's a better friend than I am.

My heart sinks, and I pull Minnie on to my lap for comfort.

'Stop fretting?' Mum is muttering murderously to Janice. 'I'll give Graham something to fret about. Have I ever kept any secrets from him?'

'There was the sunbed in our garage,' points out Janice.

'That was *different*, Janice.' Mum nearly bites her head off. 'What Graham's doing, right now, it's shifty.'

'It's not like Graham,' agrees Janice sorrowfully, and she has a point. It's not that my mum and dad haven't had their ups and downs, discoveries and moments of drama. But I never remember him being secretive like this before, especially towards Mum.

'Where are we going to stay in Las Vegas?' I ask hastily, to change the subject. '*Not* in an RV park.'

'No, no,' says Luke from the driver's seat. 'We'll park the RV and check into a hotel.'

And despite everything, I feel a flicker of anticipation. I've never been to Las Vegas before in my life. Maybe, now we know that Dad and Tarkie are safe, we can unwind a little?

'You need to relax, Jane,' says Janice, as though reading my mind. 'Maybe we'll book some spa treatments.'

'Isn't there a hotel with a circus?' Mum seems a little mollified. 'I wouldn't mind seeing a circus.'

'Or the Venetian?' I suggest. 'We could go on the gondolas.'

'There's the Egyptian one . . .' Janice is scrolling on her phone. 'The MGM Grand . . . And we should pop into Caesars Palace. Fabulous shopping, Becky.'

'Elton John,' chimes in Mum suddenly. 'Is he still in Las Vegas?'

'Elton John?' interrupts Suze shrilly, and we all jump. '*Gondolas?* How can you all talk about Elton John and gondolas and Caesars Palace? This isn't some little vacation we're on! We're not here to *enjoy ourselves*!'

Her eyes glitter accusingly at us, and we all blink back in shock.

'OK,' I say cautiously. 'Well, let's just check into a hotel and take it from there.'

'Not one of the ghastly theme hotels,' says Alicia, wrinkling her lip in a sneer. 'I think we should find a non-theme hotel. Something conservative and businesslike.'

I stare at her in astonishment. Conservative? Businesslike? In *Las Vegas*? OK, first of all, my mum seriously needs to be distracted from her stress, not sit in some boring, businesslike room, looking at the PowerPoint facilities. And secondly, I want Minnie to have some fun. She deserves it.

'I expect we'll have to stay wherever we can get rooms,' I say quickly. 'Tell you what, I don't mind making the calls.'

'Sorry,' I say to Suze yet again. 'I know you wanted to stay somewhere businesslike.'

Suze darts me a suspicious look, and I arrange my features into an expression of regret, even though inside I'm saying, *Oh my Gooooood.*

We're standing in the lobby of the Venetian hotel, and it's the craziest place I've ever been. There's a gigantic, ornate dome above us, lined with what look like paintings by Venetian masters. (Maybe just a bit more lurid.) There's a fountain with a fantastic golden globe sculpture. A man in a red neckerchief is playing the accordion. I feel like we're already at a tourist attraction, and we haven't even left the lobby!

Luke returns from the desk, where he's been checking us all in. 'Here we are,' he says, waving a stack of room keys. 'I couldn't get all adjoining, but at least we're all in. And there's a promotion going on today, so we got a freebie,' he adds, brandishing the other hand. 'Complimentary chips for the casino.'

The chips come in a paper roll, like sweeties, and they look so *cute*. Except, they should put mottos on them, like Love Hearts. If I opened a casino, all my chips would say *Good luck!* and *Try again!*

'Complimentary chips? Typical.' Alicia makes a little *moue* of revulsion. 'Well, you can have mine.'

Honestly. We're in Las Vegas. You have to gamble in Las Vegas, surely. I've never gambled before, but I'm sure I can pick it up easily enough.

'So, let's make a plan,' says Luke, and shepherds us towards where Mum and Janice have plonked themselves on their suitcases, with Minnie.

'I like it,' Minnie stretches out her chubby little hands towards the casino chips. 'Dolly plate, pleeeeease?'

She thinks it's a dolly plate. That is so sweet.

'Here you are, darling,' I say, taking a chip from Luke and giving it to her. 'You can hold the dolly plate, but *don't* put it in your mouth.'

I look up, to see Suze regarding me, aghast. 'You're giving Minnie *gambling chips* to play with?'

What?

'Er . . . Minnie has no idea what it is,' I say carefully. 'She's using it as a dolly plate.'

'Still.' Suze shakes her head, as if I've broken some fundamental parenting rule. She glances at Alicia, who is looking equally disapproving.

'It's a piece of plastic!' I say, in disbelief. 'In a casino, yes, it's a gambling chip, but right now, in Minnie's hand, it's a dolly plate! What, you think I'm going to let her *gamble*?'

I don't understand Suze any more. To my horror, my eyes have filled with tears, and I turn away. How can she be like this? She barely meets my eye. She never jokes around with me.

It's Alicia, I think morosely. Alicia Bitch Long-legs has corrupted Suze. I mean, Alicia never had any sense of humour – but at least we *knew* that. We knew what Alicia was, and we hated her. Now she's all softly-softly, friendly-friendly on the outside, and Suze has been totally fooled. But the kernel of her is still the same as it ever was. Cold. Humourless. Judgy. And she's infecting my best friend.

I'm so lost in my miserable thoughts, it takes me a moment to realize that my phone has just beeped with a text.

On way!!! Will arrive las vegas later today!!! Kisses, danny

Danny! I feel a swell of relief. Danny will make me laugh again. Danny will make everything better.

Danny Kovitz is my famous fashion designer friend, and he's a total star. The minute he heard Suze was in trouble, he promised to fly out, commandeer his whole staff, whatever it took. He's really fond of Tarkie, too, so of course he wanted to help. (Well, actually, he fancies Tarkie rotten. But that's not something to mention to Suze.)

'Danny's nearly here!' I tell Suze. 'We can all meet up, have a nice dinner, relax . . .'

I'm desperately trying to inject a bit of positivity into Suze, but it's like trying to soften a brick wall.

'I can't *relax*, Bex,' she practically spits. 'I need to see Tarkie in the flesh. I need to know he's away from that . . . character.'

'Listen, Suze,' I say gently. 'I know you're still worried, but you should try to take your mind off things. I'm planning to take Minnie to the shark aquarium. D'you want to come too?'

'I don't think so.' Suze gives a dismissive shake of the head.

73

'But you need to do something—'

'I am going to do something. Alicia and I are going to try to find a yoga class. Do some emails, have an early night.'

I stare at her, trying to conceal my shock. *Emails? Early night?*

'But we're in Las Vegas! I thought we could go and watch the fountains at the Bellagio, and then have a drink . . .' I trail off at Suze's forbidding expression.

'I'm not into touristy gimmicks,' she says disdainfully, and Alicia nods in agreement.

I feel a dart of hurt. Since when? She was totally into touristy gimmicks when we went to Seville that time and bought flamenco dresses and wore them out to supper and kept saying 'Olé!' to each other. We couldn't stop laughing. It was one of the best nights of my life. In fact Suze was the one who had the idea to wear the dresses, now I come to think of it. *And* she bought a guitar with ribbons on it. How touristy is that?

'Suze, come and see the Bellagio fountains at least,' I say entreatingly. 'They're not gimmicky, they're iconic. Don't you remember when we went to see *Ocean's Eleven* for the first time and we made a pact to go to Las Vegas one day?'

Suze shrugs blankly, checking her phone as though she has no interest in anything I have to say, and I feel the tears threatening again.

'OK. Well. Enjoy your evening.'

'You do realize we have breakfast with Tarkie and your father at nine tomorrow morning?' Suze fixes me with an accusing gaze.

'Of course!'

'So you won't be up till all hours, drinking free cocktails and passing out over the roulette table?'

'No!' I say defiantly. 'I will not. I'll be sitting here, bright as a button at eight thirty a.m.'

'Well, see you then.'

Suze and Alicia head off down a corridor which looks just like the Sistine Chapel, and I stare after her miserably, then turn back to the others.

'*You'll* come and watch the fountains with me?' I appeal to Luke. 'And you, Mum? And Janice?'

'Of course we will!' says Mum, who procured a drink from somewhere while Luke was checking us in and is now swigging from it. 'You can't hold us back! My time has come, love. My time has come.'

'What do you mean?' I say, puzzled.

'If your father can go kicking his heels up, then so can I! If your father can run through the family fortune, then so can I!'

Mum has had a slightly mad look in her eye ever since we heard from Dad. Now, gulping her drink, she looks even madder.

'I don't think Dad's running through the family fortune,' I say warily.

'How do we know *what* he's doing?' counters Mum wildly. 'All these years, I've been that man's dutiful wife. I've cooked him supper, I've made his bed, I've hung on his every word . . .'

OK, that's rubbish. Mum has *never* hung on Dad's every word, and half the time she buys ready meals from M&S.

'And now I find that he has secrets and mysteries!' continues Mum. 'Lies and conspiracies!'

'Mum, he's just gone on a little trip, it's not the end of the world . . .'

'Lies and conspiracies!' repeats Mum, ignoring me. 'Janice, do you fancy a go on the slot machines? Because I know I do.'

'We'll be back in a jiffy,' says Janice breathlessly, as she follows Mum across the lobby.

Oooookay. I think I'll need to keep an eye on Mum.

'Minnie, shall we go and see the big fishies?' I turn and give her a hug. She's been such a poppet, sitting nicely all day in the RV. She deserves a bit of fun now.

'Fishies!' Minnie starts opening her mouth and gulping like a fish.

There's a little guide book in the welcome pack which Luke was given, and as I read through the 'Top Ten Attractions for Kids', I feel a bit gobsmacked. There's everything here! There's the Eiffel Tower and New York skyscrapers and Egyptian pyramids and dolphins *and* circus acts. It's like someone's crunched the entire world into one street and left out all the boring bits.

'Come on, sweetheart!' I say, and hold out my hand. I can give Minnie a good time, anyway.

SIX

Two hours later, my head is a whirl of lights and music and traffic noise. And above all, bleeps. Las Vegas is the bleepiest city I've ever known. It's like, everywhere you go there's a live band playing at full volume, and the only instruments are slot machines, and they only play one track: *bleep-bleep-bleepy-bleep*. And they never stop. Except when they occasionally disgorge money, which would be the percussion section.

I actually have a headache from all the clamour, but I don't care, because we're having a brilliant time. We've driven up and down the Strip in a limo which the Venetian concierge fixed up for us, and we've hopped out at this hotel and that hotel, and I feel as though I've been around the world. I even gave Minnie 'Parisian poulet' for supper. (It was chicken strips.)

Now we're back at the Venetian, which feels quite calm and normal compared to some of the places we've been. (Well, 'normal', bearing in mind that the sky, clouds, canals and St Mark's Square are all fake.) Luke has gone off to the conference centre to work through a backlog of emails. Mum and Janice have taken Minnie to investigate gondola rides, and I'm wandering around the shops. Or rather, 'Shoppes'. (Why do they call them 'Shoppes'? Isn't that olden-days English? And surely we're supposed to be in Italy?)

There are loads of 'Shoppes', from designer stores to galleries to souvenir outlets. It's pretty impressive, as malls go. As I walk along, the air is a perfect temperature and the fake sky is blue with wispy clouds. There's an opera singer wandering around in a velvet dress, trilling some lovely aria. I've just been into Armani and seen a grey cashmere jacket which would look *stunning* on Luke. (Except it's eight hundred dollars, so I hesitated. I mean, he should try it on first, at least.) The whole thing is amazing and I should be having the time of my life. But the truth is, I'm not.

I keep picturing Suze's face and feeling a great rolling sadness. It's as if she doesn't want to know me. But she's the one who begged me to come on this trip. She's the one who stood, holding my hands, saying, 'I need you.' It makes no sense.

I lost Suze once before, when I'd been away on honeymoon. But that was different. That was drifting apart. This is more like she's cutting me off.

By now I've wandered into The Big Souvenir Store, and as I start to fill my basket, my chest is heaving in distress. *Stop it, Becky*, I tell myself desperately. *Come on, focus on the souvenirs.* I have a snow globe of the Las Vegas skyline, and some dollar-sign fridge magnets, and a load of T-shirts saying *What Happens in Vegas.* I reach for an ashtray in the shape of a shoe, wondering if I know anyone who smokes . . .

But the thoughts keep piling in. Is this it? Is our friendship over? After all these years, after surviving all our ups and downs . . . are we really at the end of the line? I just can't work out what's gone wrong. I know I didn't behave brilliantly in LA. But did I really wreck things *this* badly?

There's a rack of jewellery made out of dice, and miserably I stuff a couple of necklaces into my basket. Maybe Mum and Janice will like them. In the old days, I would have bought matching ones for Suze and me and we would have thought it was hilarious, but I don't have the confidence to do that now.

What am I going to do? What *can* I do?

My feet are taking me round and round the shop and I keep passing the same items, over and over. I have to stop. *Come on, Becky,* focus. I can't just keep walking and brooding. I'll get these things and then see if Mum has had any joy with the gondolas.

The shop is pretty busy and has three checkout lines. As I finally reach the front of the queue, a pretty cashier in a sparkly jacket dimples at me.

'Hi! I hope your shopping experience today was enjoyable!'

'Oh,' I say. 'Well . . . yes. It was great, thank you.'

'If you could grade it for us, we'd really appreciate it,' she says, ringing up my items. She hands me a little card, which reads:

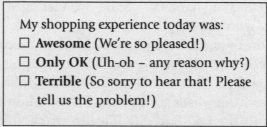

My shopping experience today was:
☐ **Awesome** (We're so pleased!)
☐ **Only OK** (Uh-oh – any reason why?)
☐ **Terrible** (So sorry to hear that! Please tell us the problem!)

I take the pen from her and stare at the card. I should tick *Awesome*. There was nothing wrong with the store and I got what I wanted. I have no complaints. Come on. *Awesome*.

But somehow ... my hand won't do it. I don't feel Awesome.

'That'll be sixty-three ninety-two,' says the girl, and peers at me curiously as I hand her the money. 'Are you OK?'

'Um ... I don't know.' To my horror, tears are suddenly trembling on my lashes. 'I don't know what to tick. I know I should choose *Awesome*, but I can't tick it, I just can't. I've fallen out with my best friend, and that's all I can think about, and so nothing's Awesome right now. Not even shopping.' I stare at her miserably. 'I'm sorry. I won't waste your time any more.'

I hold out my hand for my receipt. But the girl doesn't give it to me. She's gazing at me in concern. She's called Simone, I notice from her name tag.

'Well, are you happy with your purchases?' She opens the carrier bag for me to see them, and I stare at all the stuff, feeling a bit dazed.

'I don't know,' I say despairingly. 'I don't even know why I've bought all this stuff. It's meant to be presents for people. You know. Souvenirs.'

'OK . . .'

'But I don't know what I've bought for who, or anything, and I'm only supposed to buy meaningfully. I went on a whole programme at Golden Peace.'

'Golden Peace!' Her eyes light up. 'I did that programme.'

'No way.' I stare at her.

'Online.' She flushes faintly. 'I couldn't afford to visit. But, you know, they have an app, so . . . I was in big trouble, spending-wise. You can imagine, working here . . .' Simone gestures around at the shop. 'But I kicked my problem.'

'Wow.' I blink at her. 'Well then, you know what I'm talking about.'

'"Buy calmly and with meaning,"' she quotes.

'Exactly!' I nod in recognition. 'I have that in a frame!'

'"*Why* are you buying?"'

'Yes!'

'Do you need this?'

'Exactly! We had a whole session about that one issue—'

'No.' Simone looks at me directly. 'I'm asking you a question. Do you need this? Or are you just trying to soothe yourself?' Simone has taken the snow globe out of my carrier and is holding it up in front of me. '*Do* you need it?' she persists.

'Oh,' I say, disconcerted. 'I don't know. Well, I mean, obviously I don't *need* it. Nobody *needs* a snow globe. I thought I'd give it to . . . I don't know. Maybe my husband.'

'Great! Will it bring him consistent joy and pleasure?'

I try to picture Luke, shaking the snow globe and watching it whirl around. I mean, he might do it once.

'Dunno,' I admit, after a pause. 'It might do.'

'It *might* do?' She shakes her head. 'It only *might* do? What was your thought process when you put it in your basket?'

I stare at her, caught out. I didn't have a thought process. I just bunged it in.

'I don't think I need it.' I bite my lip. 'Or even want it, really.'

'So don't buy it. You want me to refund it?'

'Yes, please,' I whisper gratefully.

'These T-shirts.' Simone pulls them out of the bag. 'Who are they for, and will they really suit those people?'

I look at the T-shirts blankly. I hadn't worked out who was going to *wear* them. I bought them because I was in a souvenir shop and they were souvenirs.

Simone shakes her head at my expression. 'Refund?' she says, succinctly.

'Yes, please.' I pull out the dice necklaces. 'And these. I don't know what I was thinking. I'll give them to my mum and her friend and they'll wear them for five seconds and then they'll take them off, and they'll knock around the house and in about three years' time they'll go to the charity shop but no one there will want them either.'

'Oh my God, you're right,' comes a husky voice behind me and I turn to see a middle-aged woman pulling about six dice necklaces out of her basket. 'I got these for my girlfriends back home. They won't wear them, will they?'

'Never.' I shake my head.

'I want a refund.' A denim-clad woman at the next register has been listening in, and now she turns back to her cashier, who is a red-haired woman. 'I'm sorry. I just bought a heap of crap. I don't know what I was doing.' She pulls a diamanté Las Vegas baseball cap out of her carrier bag. 'My stepdaughter is *never* going to wear this.'

'Sorry, you want a refund?' The red-haired cashier looks affronted. '*Already?*'

'She's doing it.' The denim-clad woman points at me. 'She's returning everything.'

'Not everything,' I say hastily. 'I'm just trying to shop calmly and with meaning.'

The red-haired cashier gives me a nasty look. 'Well, please don't.'

'I *love* that,' the denim-clad woman says emphatically. '"Calmly and with meaning". OK, so what else in here don't I need?' She rootles in her carrier bag and brings out a Las Vegas hip flask. 'This. And this.' She produces a dollar-sign beach towel. 'This is going back.'

At the far register, I can see a third woman pausing. 'Wait a minute,' she says to her cashier. 'Maybe I don't need that flashing Las Vegas sign. Could I get a refund on that?'

'Stop it!' says the red-haired cashier, looking more and more flustered. 'No more refunds!'

'You can't refuse refunds!' objects the denim-clad

woman. 'I'm returning this, too.' She plonks a shiny pink photo album on to the counter. 'Who am I kidding? I'll never put an album together.'

'I don't want any of this!' The woman in the far line empties her entire carrier bag on to the counter. 'I'm only shopping because I'm bored out of my skull.'

'Me too!'

Down the lines, I can see other women listening in and looking in their baskets and taking things out. It's like some contagious wave of un-shopping has hit the crowd.

'What's going on?' A woman in a trouser suit is striding to the checkouts, and addresses the cashiers furiously. 'Why is everyone taking stuff out of their baskets?'

'All the customers are returning their goods!' says the red-haired cashier. 'They've gone crazy! *That* girl started it.' She points to me with a mean look.

'I didn't mean to start anything!' I say hastily. 'I just decided to – you know – think about my purchases. Buy only what I need.'

'Buy only what you *need*?' The woman in the trouser suit looks as though I've uttered something unspeakably profane. 'Ma'am, could you please finalize your purchases as quickly as possible and leave the store?'

Honestly. You'd think I'd been single-handedly trying to bring down capitalism or something. The manageress in the trouser suit actually hissed at me as she frogmarched me out, 'Did you see what happened in Japan? Do you want that happening here? *Do* you?'

I mean, I felt bad, because it did start getting a bit out

of hand. Everyone was taking stuff out of their baskets and dumping it back on the shelves, and asking total strangers, 'Why *are* we shopping?' and 'Do you *need* that?' – while all the sales staff were rushing around in a fluster, crying, 'Everyone loves a souvenir!' and 'This one is half price! Take three!'

Although it's not my fault, is it? I mean, all I did was point out that no one is ever going to wear a dice necklace.

In the end, the only thing I ended up buying was a little jigsaw puzzle for Minnie. I didn't feel any great buzz as I bought it, but it was a different sort of satisfaction. As I signed for my receipt ($7.32), I felt kind of calm. Empowered. I even took the feedback card and ticked *Awesome*.

But as I walk back along the parade of Shoppes, my mood starts sinking again. I pull out my phone and text Luke:

Where are you?

At once he texts back:

Conference centre still. Few more emails to deal with. Where are you?

I heave a sigh of relief at just being in contact with him, and type:

I'm at the Shoppes. Luke, do you think Suze is ever going to be my friend again? I mean I know things went bad between us in LA, but I'm doing my best now and she doesn't even seem to notice and the only person she cares about is Alicia and

Oh. I've run out of space. Well, he'll get the message. It's only after I've pressed Send that it strikes me:

maybe it was a mistake to launch into an outburst. Luke isn't brilliant at responding to endless angsty texts. In fact I have a sneaking feeling that whenever I send a really long text to him, he doesn't read it at all. Sure enough, a few moments later my phone beeps with a new text:

You need a distraction, my love. I'll be done in a while and then I'm taking you to the casino. I'll text when I'm on my way. Your mother will babysit Minnie, all fixed up. xxx

Wow. Gambling! I feel a thrill of excitement, mixed with trepidation. I've never gambled in my life, unless you count the Lottery. I mean, we always used to have a family flutter on the Grand National, but that was Dad's thing and he placed the bets. I've never been into a betting shop or even played poker.

On the other hand, I *have* watched loads of James Bond movies, and I think you can learn quite a lot from them. Like: stay impassive. Raise your eyebrows while you sip a cocktail. I'm sure I can do all that, it's just I'm not sure of the actual *rules*.

I pause at a coffee outlet and am getting myself a latte, when I see a woman nearby, sitting at a bistro table, with a bleached-blonde ponytail. She's in her fifties, I'd say. She's wearing a black denim jacket decorated with rhinestones and is playing some kind of card game on her phone. On the table in front of her is a massive great cup filled with change for the slot machines, and on her T-shirt is printed *Rockwell Casino Night 2008*.

She must know about gambling. And she'll want to

help a newcomer, surely? I wait till she pauses in her game, then approach her table.

'Excuse me,' I say politely. 'I was wondering, could you give me some gambling advice?'

'Huh?' The woman looks up from her phone and blinks at me. Oh my God, she has dollar signs on her eyelids. How on earth did she do that?

'Er . . .' I try not to stare too blatantly at her eyes. 'I'm a visitor and I've never gambled before, and I'm just not sure how to do it.'

The woman stares at me as though suspecting a scam.

'You're in Las Vegas and you've never gambled?' she says at last.

'I've just arrived,' I explain. 'I'm going to a casino later on, only I don't know which games to play, or where to start. I just wondered if you could give me any tips?'

'You want tips?' The woman's eyes are still fixed on me, unblinking. They're quite bloodshot, I notice. In fact, underneath all the rhinestones and make-up, she doesn't look in great shape.

'Or maybe you could recommend a book?' I suggest, as the thought strikes me.

The woman ignores the question as though it's too stupid to answer, and looks down at the card game again. I don't know what she's seen, but it makes her give a sudden, ugly scowl.

'You know what?' she says. 'My tip is, don't do it. Don't go near it. Save yourself.'

'Oh,' I say, discomfited. 'Well, I was only planning on having a quick go at a roulette table or something . . .'

'That's what we all said. Are you an addictive type?'

'Um . . .' I pause, trying to be scrupulously honest with myself. Am I an addictive type? I suppose you could say I am a *bit*. 'I do like shopping,' I confess. 'I mean, I've shopped too much in the past. I took out too many credit cards and it got a bit out of hand. But I'm much better now.'

The woman gives a short, humourless laugh.

'You think *shopping's* bad? Wait till you start gambling, hon. Just the feel of the chips in your hand. The rush. The buzz. It's like crystal meth. You only need one hit and that's it. You become a slave. And *that's* when your life starts to spiral. *That's* when the cops move in.'

I stare back at her, freaked out. She's actually quite ghoulish, close up. Her face muscles don't move properly and I can see where her hair extensions begin. She jabs at her phone and another card game appears on the screen.

'Right!' I say brightly, and start to back away. 'Well, thanks for your help, anyway . . .'

'Crystal meth,' the woman repeats in sinister tones, and locks her bloodshot eyes on mine. 'Remember that. Crystal meth.'

'Crystal meth.' I nod. 'Absolutely. Bye!'

Crystal *meth*?

Oh God. Should I be going to a casino at all? Is this all a bad, bad idea?

It's almost an hour later and I'm still feeling unnerved, even though I've been on a soothing gondola ride with Mum and Janice and Minnie. Now Mum and Janice have gone off for another 'sneaky cocktail', as Mum put it, while Minnie and I are upstairs in our hotel room. Minnie's playing 'shops' and I'm kind of playing too, only I'm also trying to put on my make-up whilst simultaneously worrying about my potential descent into gambling addiction.

Will I literally get hooked *straight away*? Like, on the first spin of the roulette wheel? I have a sudden, horrific vision of myself hunched over a casino table, hair askew, staring at Luke with dazed eyes, muttering, 'I'm going to win. I'm going to win,' while he tries to pull me away and Mum sobs quietly in the background. Maybe I shouldn't even go down there. Maybe it's too dangerous. Maybe I should just stay here in the room.

'More shops!' Minnie grabs the last remaining crisp packet out of the mini bar and puts it proprietorially in front of her. '*Shop*, Mummy, *shop!*'

'Right.' I come to, and hastily move the crisps away before she can squish them into bits and we have to buy them.

Parenthood is all about learning from experience. And the valuable rule I've learned today is: 'Don't say "mini bar" in front of Minnie.' She thought I meant 'Minnie bar' and that this was her own special cupboard, full of lovely things for Minnie. And it was impossible to explain. So in the end I let her get everything out and the carpet is strewn with little bottles and packets. We'll put them all back later. (If it's one of those electronic ones we may be in trouble, but Luke will call the front desk and sort it out. He's good at that kind of thing.)

I've already 'bought' a bottle of tonic and a Toblerone

from Minnie, and now I'm pointing at an orange juice.

'Please may I have an orange juice?' I say, brushing on mascara at the same time. I put out my hand for the bottle, but Minnie holds on to it firmly.

'You can't *have* one,' she says sternly. 'Must *wait*. We don't have any *money*.'

I blink at her in surprise. Who's she copying?

Oh.

Oh God. Actually, I think it's me.

Which makes me seem like a really mean, horrible mummy, but honestly, it's the only way I can deal with her when we're out shopping.

Minnie's speech has really come on recently. Which is wonderful, obviously. Every parent wants to hear their child articulate their innermost thoughts. The only *teeny* issue is, it turns out quite a lot of Minnie's innermost thoughts are about what she wants.

She doesn't yell 'Miiiiiiine' any more, which used to be her catchphrase. Instead, she says, 'I like it.' We'll walk around the supermarket and all she keeps saying is, 'I like it, I *like* it, Mummy,' more and more earnestly, as though she's trying to convert me to some new religion.

It's not even as though she likes sensible things. She grabs for mops and freezer bags and packets of staples. Last time we went out shopping, she kept telling me, 'I *like* it, pleeeeease,' and I kept nodding and putting the things back on the shelves, out of reach, until she suddenly flipped, and yelled, '*I want to buuuuuy something!*' in such desperate tones that all the nearby customers started laughing. Then she stopped and beamed around, and they all laughed even more.

(I do sometimes wonder if that's what I was like when I was her age. I must ask Mum.)

(Actually, on second thoughts, I'm not sure I want to know.)

So my new tactic when we go shopping is to tell Minnie that we don't have any money. Which she kind of understands. Except then she accosts total strangers and says, 'We don't have any *money*,' in a sorrowful voice, which can be embarrassing.

Now she's addressing Speaky, her dolly, in stentorian tones. 'Put. It. *Back.*' She confiscates a packet of peanuts from Speaky and eyes the doll fiercely. 'Is. Not. *Yours.*'

Oh God. Is that what I sound like?

'Talk kindly to Speaky,' I suggest. 'Like this.'

I take Speaky and cradle her in my arms, whereupon Minnie grabs her possessively from me. 'Speaky is crying,' she tells me. 'Speaky need . . . a sweetie?'

She has a sudden mischievous glint in her eye, and I can't help wanting to laugh.

'We haven't got any sweeties,' I tell her, totally straight-faced.

'This is a sweetie?' She picks up the Toblerone uncertainly.

'No, that's a grown-up, boring box,' I tell her. 'No sweetie.'

Minnie stares at the Toblerone, and I can see her little brain working hard. She's never actually eaten a Toblerone, so it was a pretty good guess on her part.

'It's not a sweetie,' I reiterate, matter-of-factly. 'We'll buy a sweetie *another* day. Now it's putting-away time.'

I can see Minnie's conviction wavering. She might think she knows everything, but at the end of the day, she's only two and a half.

'Thank you!' I take it neatly from her grasp. 'Now, can you count the bottles?'

This was a genius move, as Minnie adores counting, even if she always misses out 'four'. We've managed to get all the bottles back in the mini bar and are just moving on to light snacks and refreshments, when the door opens and Mum appears, with Janice in tow. Both are flushed in the face, Janice is wearing a plastic tiara and Mum is clutching a cup full of coins.

'Hello!' I say. 'Did you have a good cocktail?'

'I won over thirty dollars!' Mum says with a kind of grim triumph. '*That'll* show your father.'

Mum makes no sense. How will that show Dad anything? But there's no point questioning her when she's in this mood.

'Well done!' I say. 'Nice tiara, Janice.'

'Oh, it was free,' says Janice breathlessly. 'There's a dancing competition later, you know. They're promoting it.'

'We're going to take a breather while you go out with Luke and then we're going to hit the town,' says Mum, waving her cup for emphasis. 'Do you have any false eyelashes I can put on, love?'

'Well . . . yes,' I say, a bit surprised. 'But I've never known you to wear false eyelashes, Mum.'

'What happens in Vegas stays in Vegas,' she says, giving me a meaningful look.

What happens in Vegas? OK, does she just mean false

eyelashes or something else? I'm just wondering how I can ask her tactfully if she's OK or actually going off the rails, when my phone bleeps with a text.

'It's Danny!' I say, feeling a lift of delight. 'He's here! He's downstairs.'

'Well, if you're ready, why don't you go down and see him, love?' says Mum. 'We'll give Minnie her bath and put her to bed. Won't we, Janice?'

'Of course!' says Janice. 'Dear little Minnie is never any trouble.'

'Are you sure?' I wrinkle my brow. 'Because I can easily do it—'

'Don't be silly, Becky!' says Mum. 'I don't see enough of my grandchild these days. Now, Minnie, come and sit on Grana's knee.' She holds out her arms for Minnie to run into. 'We'll have a nice story and play some games and . . . I know!' She beams. 'Let's have a lovely yummy Toblerone!'

SEVEN

I find Danny at a corner table in Bouchon, which is a posh, linen-tablecloths kind of restaurant. He's deeply tanned (it's got to be fake), he's wearing a baby-blue biker jacket, and is sitting with a very blonde, very pale girl with no make-up except deep-purple lipstick.

'Danny!' I hurry over and throw my arms around his skinny frame. 'Oh my God! You're alive!'

I haven't seen Danny since he tried to cross the Greenland Ice Sheet for charity, and had to be airlifted out, because he grazed his toe or something, and go for a recuperative holiday in Miami.

'Only just,' says Danny. 'It was touch and go.'

It was so *not* touch and go. I've spoken to his business manager: I know the truth. Only he said not to contradict Danny because he thinks he nearly died.

'Poor you,' I say. 'It must have been terrifying! All that snow and . . . er . . . wolves?'

'It was a nightmare!' says Danny fervently. 'You know, Becky, I've left you a bunch of stuff in my will and you were *this* close to getting it.'

'Really?' I can't help feeling interested. 'You've left me stuff? Like what?'

'Some clothes,' says Danny vaguely. 'My Eames chair. A forest.'

'A *forest*?' I gape at him.

'I bought this forest in Montana. You know, for tax? And I figured Minnie could go play in it or whatever—' He breaks off. 'This is Ulla, by the way.'

'Hi, Ulla!' I wave a cheery hand, but Ulla just blinks nervously, mutters 'Hi' and returns to work. She's sketching something in a large artist's pad, and as I glance over, I see it's a close-up of the flower arrangement on the table.

'I just hired Ulla as my Inspiration Finder,' says Danny grandly. 'She's already filled that pad.' He gestures at it. 'My whole new collection will be Las Vegas inspired.'

'I thought it was going to be Inuit inspired?' I object.

Last time I was in contact with Danny, he was talking about raw bone and Inuit crafts and the infinite expanse of whiteness which he planned to represent in a pair of oversized men's culottes.

'Inuit meets Las Vegas,' says Danny, without missing a beat. 'So, did you gamble yet?'

'I don't dare.' I shudder. 'This woman has just told me gambling is like crystal meth and if I dip my toe in, I'll get sucked in for ever.'

I'm hoping he'll say, 'That's bullshit,' but Danny nods gravely.

'It could happen. My schoolfriend Tania never recovered from one night of online poker. It took hold of her and she was never the same person again. It was a pretty tragic story.'

'Where is she now?' I say fearfully. 'Is she . . . dead?'

'Pretty much.' He nods. 'Alaska.'

'Alaska's not *dead*!' I say indignantly.

'She went to work on an oil rig.' Danny takes a swig of wine. 'She's very successful, actually. I think she runs the whole thing. But before that, she was a gambling addict.'

'So it's not a tragic story at all,' I say crossly. 'She ended up being boss of an oil rig.'

'Do you have any idea what it's like, being boss of an oil rig?' counters Danny. 'Have you seen those places?'

I always forget how exasperating Danny is.

'Anyway,' I say, a little sternly. 'None of this is the point. The point is—'

'I know what the point is!' Danny cuts me off, sounding triumphant. 'I'm, like, ten steps ahead of you. I have flyers, I have leaflets, I have pens, I have T-shirts . . .'

'T-shirts?' I peer at him.

Danny takes off his biker jacket to reveal a T-shirt printed with an image of Tarquin. It's a black-and-white picture taken from a fashion shoot which Tarkie did a while ago, and it shows him naked from the waist up, with rope twined around his torso, his eyes staring soulfully into the camera. It's an amazing shot, but I recoil in dismay. Suze hates that picture. She thinks it makes Tarquin look like some gay supermodel. (Which, to be fair, it does.) She will *not* be happy to see it reproduced on a T-shirt.

At the bottom is printed FIND ME and Suze's mobile number.

'I have a whole bunch printed,' says Danny proudly, 'Kasey and Josh are handing out the flyers, all round Caesars Palace.'

'Kasey and Josh?'

'My assistants. See, what we do is, we get his face out there. First rule of finding a missing person. My PR people are trying the news channels, I have someone talking to the milk-carton guys . . .'

'Wait a sec.' The truth suddenly dawns on me. 'They're handing out pictures of Tarquin right now?'

'They're going to cover the whole city,' boasts Danny. 'We printed ten thousand.'

'But we've found him!'

'*What?*' Danny actually jolts in shock.

'Well, kind of,' I amend. 'I mean, we've spoken to him. We're having breakfast at the Bellagio in the morning.'

'The *Bellagio*?' Danny looks utterly affronted. 'Are you serious? I thought he'd been kidnapped. I thought he was being brainwashed.'

'Well, Suze still does. At least, she can't relax until she actually sees him . . . Anyway, show me the flyers,' I add hastily. 'You're amazing, Danny. Absolutely brilliant. Suze will be so grateful.'

'I produced three varieties,' says Danny, mollified. 'Ulla, the flyers?'

Ulla hastily reaches into her big leather bag and pulls out three leaflets, which she passes over the table. Each has a different, stunning, black-and-white picture of Tarkie looking like a moody gay-porn star – all from the same fashion shoot. One reads *FIND ME* like the T-shirt, one reads *WHERE AM I?* and the third reads *I AM LOST*, and they all have Suze's mobile number.

'Cool, huh?'

'Er . . .' I clear my throat. 'Yes! Wonderful!'

I *cannot* let Suze see these.

'I don't think Kasey and Josh need to hand out *all* the flyers,' I say carefully. 'Maybe not all ten thousand.'

'But what will I do with the rest?' Danny looks perturbed for a moment – then his brow clears. 'I know. An installation! Maybe my next collection will be based on this experience!' His face brightens. 'Yes! Entrapment. Kidnap. Bondage. Very dark, you know? Very *noir*. Models in shackles. Ulla!' he exclaims. 'Write down: "Bonds, chains, sacking, leather." "Hot pants",' he adds after a moment's thought.

'I thought your next collection was going to be Las Vegas meets Inuit?'

'OK then, the one after that,' he says easily. 'So where's Suze?'

'Oh.' My mood instantly falls. 'She's with Alicia. Remember Alicia Bitch Long-legs? Well, she married this guy called Wilton Merrelle, and—'

'Becky, I know who Alicia Merrelle is,' Danny cuts me off. 'She's a pretty big deal. Her house is, like, all over *Architectural Digest*.'

'You don't have to remind me,' I say, dolefully. 'Oh, Danny, it's awful. She's taken Suze away from me. The two of them spend the whole time together. Suze has totally lost her sense of humour and it's all because of Alicia—' I break off and rub my nose. 'I don't know what to do.'

'Well.' Danny thinks a moment, then shrugs philo-sophically. 'People move on. Friendships end. If you love Suze, maybe you need to let her go.'

'Let her *go*?' I gaze at him, stricken. He wasn't supposed to say that.

'People change, life changes . . . It's the way of the world. Maybe it's meant to be.'

I stare down at the tablecloth, my head a miserable whirl. It can't be meant that I lose Suze to Alicia Bitch Long-legs. It *can't* be.

'So how is she these days, Alicia?' says Danny. 'Still the sweet thing she always was? Still trying to wreck people's marriages?'

I feel a wash of relief. At least Danny knows what Alicia's really like.

'She pretends to be a reformed character,' I say darkly. 'But I don't trust her. She's up to something.'

'No way.' Danny perks up. 'Like what?'

'I don't know,' I admit. 'But she has to be. She always is. Keep your eye on her.'

'Got it.' He nods.

'Not that you'll see her tonight.' I hunch my shoulders gloomily. 'Here we are in Las Vegas. I've spoken to Tarquin and Dad and we know they're safe. We should be cele-brating. But Alicia and Suze are refusing to have any fun. They're going to have an early night. Can you believe it?'

'Well, *I'll* have fun.' Danny reaches over and clasps my hand with his warm, dry fingers. 'Don't look blue, Becky. What shall we do? Hit the casino?'

'I'm meeting Luke there in a little while,' I tell him. 'Although I'm a bit . . . you know. Freaked out.'

'Why?'

Honestly, wasn't he *listening*?

'Because!' I make agitated gestures with my hands. 'Crystal meth!'

'You're not taking that seriously?' Danny laughs. 'Becky, gambing is *fun*.'

'You don't understand! I'm the type of personality to get hooked! My whole life might spiral away in a toxic mix of addiction and dependence! You'll try to help me, but you won't be able to!'

I've seen true-life movies about drug addiction. I know how it goes. One minute you're saying, 'I'll just have one puff,' and the next minute you're in court with unwashed hair, fighting for custody of your children.

'Relax.' Danny gestures for the bill. 'Let's go and hit the tables. If you start to look anything like an addict, I'll drag you away. Promise.'

'Even if I swear and spit at you and say I don't care about my friends and family any more?' I say fearfully.

'Especially then. C'mon, let's go see if we can lose all Luke's money. Joke!' he adds at my expression. '*Joke*.'

It only takes a few minutes to reach the casino, and as we enter, I take a deep breath. So this is it. Las Vegas proper. The beating heart of the city. I look around, almost dazzled by the neon and patterned carpet and shiny outfits. Everyone seems to be gleaming in some way or other, even if it's just their diamond-encrusted watch glinting in the lights.

'Did you get any chips yet?' asks Danny, and I reach

for my complimentary chips. Luke gave me his too, so I've got loads.

'I've got fifty dollars' worth,' I say, totting them up.

'*Fifty?*' Danny stares at me. 'You can barely get a bet on a table for that. You need three hundred, at least.'

'I'm not spending three hundred!' I say in horror. God, gambling's expensive. I mean, you could get a really nice skirt for three hundred dollars.

'Well, I bought five hundred's worth earlier,' says Danny, his eyes gleaming. 'So I want to get going.'

'Five hundred?' I gape at him.

'I'll make ten times that much, you wait and see. I'm feeling lucky tonight.' He blows on his hands. 'Lucky fingers.' His glee is infectious, and as we turn to survey the room, chips in our hands, I can't help feeling thrilled. And terrified. Both.

I've never been anywhere like this. Even the *air* is infected with gambling. You can practically sense it in people's breath as you walk past the tables, a kind of heightened, tense feeling, like when you're in the queue outside a sample sale. All around I can hear roars and exclamations from tables as the customers win or lose, mixed with the clicking of chips and the clinking of cocktail glasses on trays held by skimpily dressed waitresses. And all the time, the continual background bleeping of the machines.

'What shall we play?' I demand. 'Roulette?'

'Blackjack,' says Danny firmly, and ushers me towards a big table.

It all looks so grown-up and serious and *real*. As we slide into a pair of empty seats at the table, no one even looks up to say hello. It's a bit like sitting at a bar, except the bar is covered in fabric and instead of handing out drinks, the croupier is dealing out cards. There are two elderly men at the table and a girl in a tuxedo and a sparkly trilby, who looks very bad-tempered.

'I don't know how to play!' I whisper in a panic to Danny.

At least . . . I *sort* of know how to play. It's the same as twist, isn't it? I play twist with Mum and Dad every year at Christmas. But are there special rules in Las Vegas?

'Easy,' Danny says. 'Put down some chips. Twenty dollars.' He takes the chips from my hand and places them firmly down in a circle on the table. The croupier is a Japanese-looking girl and she barely acknowledges my chips, just waits till everyone has bet, then deals out the cards.

I've got a six of hearts and a six of spades.

'Twist,' I say loudly, and everyone stares at me.

'You don't say "Twist",' says Danny, glancing at my cards. 'You want to split.'

I don't know what that is, but I'll trust Danny.

'OK,' I say boldly. 'Split.'

'Don't *say* "Split",' mutters Danny. 'Put your extra chips here' – he points at the table – 'and make a V with your fingers.'

'OK.' I follow his guidance, feeling suddenly very cool and professional. The dealer separates my two cards and deals again.

'Oh I *see*!' I exclaim as she gives me an eight of clubs and a ten of hearts. 'I have two piles now! I'm bound to win!'

I look around the table, watching as everyone plays. This is actually quite fun.

'Becky, you're up,' murmurs Danny. 'Everyone's waiting.'

'Oh right.' I peer at my cards. One pile totals fourteen and the other sixteen. What should I do? Twist or stick? Er . . . My mind flips backwards and forwards, undecided.

'Becky?'

'Yes, give me a second . . .'

God, this game is hard. I mean, it's *really* hard. How do I decide? I close my eyes and try to channel the Betting Gods. But they're clearly on a tea break.

'Becky?' prompts Danny again.

Everyone at the table is frowning at me. Honestly. Don't they realize how difficult this is?

'Ummm.' I massage my brow. 'I'm not sure. I just need to think . . .'

'Ma'am?' Now the croupier is looking impatient. 'Ma'am, you need to play.'

Argh. Gambling is so stressy! It's like trying to decide whether to buy a marked-down coat in the Selfridges sale, when there might be a better one at Liberty, but if you leave this one, it might get snapped up by someone else . . .

'What shall I do?' I appeal around the table. 'How do you all stay so calm?'

'Ma'am, it's *gambling*. You just make a choice.'

'OK, twist,' I say at last. 'Hit. Whatever. On both of them. Ooh, shall I double down?' I turn to Danny. I don't know what double down is, but I've heard it in films, so it must be a thing.

'*No*,' he says firmly.

The croupier deals a nine and a ten, finishes the round and scoops my chips towards her.

'What?' I say in bewilderment. 'What just happened?'

'You went bust,' says Danny.

'But . . . is that it? Doesn't she even *say* anything?'

'No. She just takes your money. And mine too. Bummer.'

I stare at the silent croupier, feeling a bit affronted. There should be more *ceremony* to gambling, I decide. Like when you buy something expensive and they hand it to you in a nice bag and say, 'Good choice!'

In fact, I reckon shops beat casinos, full stop. You spend the same amount of money, but in shops you *get* stuff. I mean, look, I've sat on a stool for about five seconds and I've spent forty dollars, and I've got nothing.

'I'll have a pause,' I say, sliding down off my stool. 'Let's get a drink.' I check my phone and see a new text. Luke's on his way.

'Sure,' agrees Danny. 'So, are you addicted to gambling yet, Becky?'

'I don't *think* so,' I say, prodding my feelings. 'Maybe I'm not a natural gambler after all.'

'You lost,' says Danny wisely. 'Wait till you start to win. *That's* when you can't stop. Oh, hey, Luke.'

I look up to see Luke striding towards us through the casino, his dark hair glossy under the lights and a confident set to his chin.

'Danny!' He claps Danny on the back. 'Have you thawed out yet?'

'Don't joke.' Danny shudders. 'It's still too raw to talk about.'

Luke meets my eye, and I shoot him a tiny grin. The thing about Danny is he takes himself *very* seriously. But he's so sweet, you just kind of go with it.

'So, Becky, have you made our fortune yet?' asks Luke.

'No, I've lost,' I say. 'I think gambling's rubbish.'

'You haven't got started yet!' says Danny. 'Let's hit another table.'

'Maybe,' I say, but don't move. I'm still not convinced by this whole gambling lark. If you lose, then that's crap, obviously. And if you win, then that's great, but you might get addicted.

'Don't you want to, Becky?' Luke looks at me curiously.

'Kind of. Except . . . what if I *do* start winning and get hooked?'

'You'll be fine,' says Luke reassuringly. 'Just decide on a strategy before you begin and stick to it.'

'What kind of strategy?'

'Like: I'll gamble for *this* long, then stop. I'll spend *this* much, then walk away. Or simply "quit while you're ahead". What you should never do is throw good money after bad. If you lose, you lose. Don't try to bet yourself back into winning.'

I'm silent for a moment, processing all this. 'Right. OK.' I look up at last. 'I have a strategy.'

'Great! So what do you want to play?'

'Not blackjack,' I say firmly. 'It's a stupid game. Let's play roulette.'

We head to an empty roulette table, and sit down on the high chairs. The croupier, a bald guy in his thirties, at once says, 'Good evening, and welcome to my table!' with a twinkly smile, and I beam back. I already like him better than that last croupier. She was a total misery. No wonder I lost.

'Hi!' I smile back, and put a single chip on red, while Luke and Danny opt for black. I watch, mesmerized, as the roulette wheel spins round. Come on red . . . come on red . . .

The ball clatters into a pocket, and I blink at it in astonishment. I won! I actually won!

'That's my first ever win in Las Vegas!' I tell the croupier, who laughs.

'Maybe you're on a lucky streak.'

'Maybe!' I put my chips on red again and focus on the table. It's quite a sight, the spinning wheel. It's almost hypnotic. We're all staring at it, unable to draw our eyes away, until it finally slows and the ball falls into a pocket . . .

Yes! I won again!

OK. Roulette is the most excellent game in the world, and I don't know why we ever wasted our time on that stupid blackjack. It's half an hour later and I've won so many times, I feel like the gambling goddess. Luke and Danny have both kept just about even, but I've accumulated a massive great pile of chips, and I'm still going strong.

'I'm brilliant at this game!' I can't help gloating as I win yet another stack of chips. I take a swig of margarita and survey the table, pondering my next move.

'You're *lucky*,' Luke corrects me.

'Luck . . . talent . . . same thing . . .'

I take all my chips, concentrate for a moment, then put them on black. Luke slides some chips on to odd and we all watch, rapt, as the wheel spins round.

'Black!' I whoop as the ball clatters on to ten. 'I won *again*!'

Next I put my chips on black and then red, then red again. And somehow I keep on winning! A group of guys on a stag night come over, and the croupier tells them I'm on a winning streak, and they all start chanting, 'Beck-ee! Beck-*ee*!' every time I win. I can't believe I'm doing so well. I'm charmed!

And you know what? Danny was right. Gambling is totally different when you're winning. I'm in the zone. The rest of life has disappeared. All I can see is the roulette wheel, blurring as it spins round and then settling down . . . and I've won *again*.

One of the stag guys, called Mike, taps me on the shoulder. 'What's your method?'

'I don't know,' I say modestly. 'I just concentrate, you know. I kind of *channel* the colour.'

'You a regular?' asks someone else.

'I've never gambled before in my life,' I say, heady with the attention. 'But maybe I should!'

'You should, like, move to Las Vegas.'

'I know!' I turn to Luke. 'We should totally move here!'

I pick up all my chips, hesitate a moment, then plonk them all on number seven.

'Really?' says Luke, raising his eyebrows.

'Really,' I say, and take another swig of margarita. 'Let's just say I feel a vibe about it. Number seven.' I address the whole group. 'That's my number. Seven.'

A couple of the stag guys begin to chant, 'Se-*ven*, se-*ven*!' Some of them quickly put their chips on seven too. As the wheel spins, we're all gazing at it like possessed people.

'Seven!' The table erupts as the ball clatters into the seven slot. I won! Even the croupier leans over to high-five me.

'The girl's on fire!' exclaims Mike.

'Which number next, Becky?' demands another of the stag guys.

'Tell us, Becky!'

'Becky!'

'What do we bet, Becky?'

Everyone's waiting for me to bet again. But I'm not looking at the wheel any more. I'm looking at my chips and doing a quick sum. Two hundred . . . four hundred . . . plus another . . . Yes! I can't resist a tiny fist pump.

'What?' demands one of the stag guys eagerly. 'What you got for us, Becky?'

I turn to the croupier with a triumphant smile. 'I'm cashing in, please.'

'Cashing *in*?' Mike's jaw drops. '*What*?'

'I've done enough gambling.'

'No, no, no!' Mike is practically gibbering in dismay. 'You're on a roll. You play! Play on!'

'But I've made eight hundred dollars,' I tell him.

'That's great! Keep going, girl! Put your chips down!'

'No, you don't understand,' I say patiently. 'Eight hundred dollars gets me this gorgeous jacket for Luke.'

'What jacket?' Luke looks puzzled.

'I saw it in Armani, when I was going round the Shoppes. It's grey cashmere. Let's go and look at it.' I squeeze his arm. 'It'll so suit you.'

'A *jacket*?' Mike looks uncomprehending. 'Honey, are you insane? You've got the magic touch! You can't leave the table now!'

'Yes, I can. That was my strategy.'

'Your *strategy*?'

'Luke said, have a strategy. So I decided my strategy was: win enough money to buy the Armani jacket. And I have.' I beam triumphantly. 'So I'm stopping.'

'But . . . but . . .' Mike seems almost speechless. 'You can't stop! You're on a *winning streak*.'

'But I might not win any more,' I point out. 'I might lose.'

'You won't lose! She's winning, right?' He looks around his friends for support.

'Becky for the win!' chimes in another.

'But I might start *losing*,' I explain carefully. 'And then I won't be able to afford the jacket.'

Don't they understand anything?

'Becky, don't go.' Mike drunkenly puts an arm around my shoulders. 'We're having a blast, aren't we?'

'Oh, it's been fab,' I say at once. 'You've been great company. And I do enjoy gambling, kind of . . . but I'll enjoy buying Luke this jacket *more*. Sorry,' I add politely to the croupier. 'I don't mean to be rude. You've got a lovely roulette table.' I hear Luke give a sudden snort of laughter. 'What?' I demand. 'What's funny?'

'Nothing, my love,' he says, picking up my hand and kissing it. 'Except, I wouldn't worry about your descent into gambling-addiction hell *just* yet.'

The jacket looks amazing on Luke. I knew it would. It's very close-cut and slimming, and brings out the chocolatey highlights in his hair. I can see all the assistants watching in admiration as he comes out of the changing room and looks at himself in the big mirror. I'm only sorry Danny isn't here to admire him too, but he's still gambling with the stag-night guys.

'Perfect!' I say. 'I knew it would suit you!'

'Well, thank you,' Luke says, beaming at his reflection. 'I'm very touched.'

I take out my winnings and carefully count out the cash, as an assistant packages up the jacket in a lovely square box.

'And now,' says Luke, as we head out of the shop, 'let me reciprocate, in the tiniest way. I meant to give you this earlier.' He hands me a printed-out email. 'One of the teams in the London office is advising MAC, so they've offered all the staff a ninety per cent discount voucher. For one glorious moment I thought she meant Apple Mac . . .' He gives a comical sigh. 'But of course it's make-up. So you can have mine.'

'Right. Thanks.' I skim the offer. 'Wow. Ninety per cent!'

'Where would they stock it?' He looks around. 'Barneys? Shall we head there?'

'Actually . . . don't worry,' I say after a pause. 'Let's not bother. It'll be really boring for you.'

'You don't want to go?' Luke seems surprised.

I'm studying the document, trying to work out my own reaction. The thought of choosing make-up for myself – even if it's reduced – is giving me this weird, twisting feeling in my stomach.

Oh God, I don't know *what's* going on with me right now. I loved buying that jacket for Luke. And I loved buying the little jigsaw for Minnie. But somehow, I can't go and buy make-up for myself. It's not . . . I feel so strange . . . I don't . . .

I don't deserve it. The miserable thought flashes through my head, making me wince.

'No, thanks.' I force a cheery smile. 'Let's go up and relieve Mum and Janice from babysitting duty.'

'You don't want to walk around any more? Look at the lights?'

'No, thanks.'

All my elation from earlier has melted away. The moment that Luke suggested treating me, it's as though a voice popped up inside my head to berate me. But it's not the nice, even-tempered, Golden Peace voice telling me to 'buy with meaning' and 'do everything in moderation'. It's a harsher voice, telling me I don't deserve anything at all.

We walk together away from the Shoppes, towards the elevators, letting the clamour of people and music wash over us. Luke keeps darting me thoughtful little glances, and at last he says, 'Becky, sweetheart, I think you need your mojo back.'

'What mojo?' I say defensively. 'I haven't lost any mojo.'

'I think you have. What's up, darling?' He swivels me round and puts his hands on my shoulders.

'Well . . . you know.' There's a lump in my throat. 'Everything. It's all my fault, this trip. I should have gone to see Brent sooner. I should have listened to Dad more. No wonder Suze—'

I break off, my eyes hot, and Luke sighs.

'Suze will come round.'

'But I was talking to Danny about it, and he said friendships end, and I should let Suze go.'

'No.' Luke shakes his head firmly. 'No, no. He's wrong. Some friendships end. You and Suze are *not* going to end.'

'I think we already have ended,' I say miserably.

'Don't give up! Becky, you've never been one to give up! OK, you've been in a bad place and Suze has been in a bad place . . . But I know the pair of you, and I know you're in it for the long haul. You'll be grandmothers together, exchanging tips on knitting baby bootees. I can see you now.'

'Really?' I say with a flicker of optimism. 'Do you think so?'

I can actually picture us as old ladies. Suze will have long white hair and an elegant walking stick and still be stunningly beautiful, just with a few lines. And I won't be beautiful but I'll wear great accessories. People will call me 'The Old Lady in the Fabulous Necklaces'.

'Don't give up on Suze,' Luke is saying. 'You need her. And she needs you, even if she doesn't realize it right now.'

'But all she can see is Alicia,' I say hopelessly.

'Yes, and one day she'll focus properly and see exactly who and what Alicia is,' says Luke dryly as he jabs the elevator button. 'Meanwhile, remember you *are* still her friend. She asked you to come on this trip. Don't let Alicia psych you out.'

'OK,' I say in a small voice.

'I mean it, Becky,' Luke insists, almost fiercely. 'Are you going to let Alicia walk all over you? Fight for your friendship. Because it's worth it.'

He sounds so forceful, I can feel a tiny smidgen of positivity returning.

'OK,' I say at last. 'OK. I'll do it.'

'Attagirl.'

By now we've reached our hotel room. Luke takes out the key, swipes it and pushes open the door – and I freeze in shock. Wh—

Whaaat?

'Good evening, Rebecca, Luke,' comes a familiar, icy voice.

OK, am I dreaming? Or did I have too many margaritas? This *can't* be true.

But I think it is. Elinor, my mother-in-law, is sitting bolt upright on a pouffe in a DVF wrap dress, gazing at me with that gimlet stare she has.

'Mother!' Luke sounds equally shocked. 'What are you *doing* here?'

I feel an inward wince as I glance up at his face. The relationship between Luke and his mother has never been straightforward, but recently it's plummeted to a new low. Two days ago, in LA, I staged the least successful mother–son reconciliation ever. Luke stalked out. Elinor stalked out. My dreams of being a Kofi-Annan-style conflict-resolver kind of disintegrated. I know Luke's been feeling raw, ever since. And now, with no warning, here she is.

'Elinor came to my rescue!' says Mum dramatically, from where she's sitting on the sofa with Janice. 'I had no one else to turn to, so I rang her up!'

No one else to turn to? What's she talking about? She's got a whole RV full of people.

'Mum,' I say, cautiously. 'That's not true. You've got me, Suze, Luke—'

'I needed someone influential!' Mum waves her wine glass at me. 'Since Luke *refused* to use his contacts . . .'

'Jane,' says Luke. 'I'm not sure what you expected me to do—'

'I expected you to pull out all the stops! Elinor couldn't have been more helpful. *She* understands. Don't you, Elinor?'

'But we've found Dad!' I expostulate. 'We've tracked him down!'

'Well, I didn't know that when I rang Elinor, did I?' says Mum, unabashed. 'She came rushing here to help. But then, she's a *true* friend.'

This is insane. Mum barely *knows* Elinor. It's not as though we're one of those big happy families that have blended together and have each other on speed-dial. As far as I know, our basic family arrangement, to date, is as follows:

Elinor looks down on Mum and Dad (too suburban).

Mum resents Elinor (too snooty).

Dad quite likes Elinor but thinks she's a stiff old stick (fair point).

Luke and Elinor are barely talking.

Minnie loves everyone, especially 'Grana' (Mum) and 'Lady' (Elinor). But she's asleep in bed, so she's not much help.

So. Nowhere in this scenario is 'Mum and Elinor are best friends.' In fact, I didn't even know Mum had Elinor's number. As I glance at Luke I see a darkening frown on his face.

'What are you expecting my mother to do?' he says flatly.

'We're going out now, to discuss the situation,' says Mum. 'She's never been to Las Vegas before and neither have we, so we're going to have a ladies' night out.'

'Girlpower!' chimes in Janice eagerly.

'You look nice, Elinor.' I can't help adding my bit. 'Lovely dress.'

It was me who suggested that Elinor wear a wrap dress instead of her endless stiff suits. And look, she's taken my advice again! She's in a black-and-white print dress which fits her perfectly – I think she must have had it altered – and makes her look so much more feminine. Next I'm going to suggest layering her hair. (One thing at a time, though.)

I can tell Luke is pissed off with Mum, although he's trying to hide it.

'Mother,' he says. 'Please don't feel you have to be dragged into this. It was inappropriate of Jane to call you.'

'*Inappropriate?*' retorts Mum. 'Elinor's family, aren't you, Elinor?'

'She's been in ill-health recently,' says Luke. 'The last thing she needs is to be drawn into some family drama. Mother . . .' He turns to Elinor. 'If you haven't already eaten, I suggest the two of us go out for dinner. Becky, you don't mind, do you?'

'No,' I say hurriedly. 'Not at all. You go.'

'Because the truth is . . .' Luke sounds awkward as he addresses Elinor. 'Well, the fact is, I didn't behave well the other night. And I'd like to make it up to you. I think we need an opportunity to build bridges . . .' Luke pauses, rubbing his neck, and I know he's finding this hard, especially in front of everyone. 'And I have some apologizing to do. Please let me start with dinner.'

'I appreciate your words, Luke,' says Elinor after a stiff little pause. 'Thank you. I think, if you are willing, that we could . . .' She seems just as awkward as Luke. 'We could . . . draw a line under the past and begin again?'

I catch my breath and glance at Luke. I can't quite believe I'm hearing the words *draw a line* and *begin again*. They're making up! Finally! Hopefully they'll have a lovely long bonding dinner, and talk it through and everything will be different from now on.

'Wonderful!' Luke's face breaks into a relieved smile. 'I can't think of anything I'd like better. Why don't I book us a table, we'll have dinner, maybe talk about that holiday in the Hamptons we were planning—'

'I haven't finished,' Elinor interrupts. 'I appreciate your words, Luke, and I would like to put our past difficulties behind us. But I have decided that tonight . . .' She pauses. 'I will go out with Jane and Janice.'

My jaw actually drops. Elinor and Mum? Out together? In Las Vegas?

'That's right.' Mum pats Elinor's shoulder. 'You come and have fun with us.'

'Girlpower!' exclaims Janice again. Her cheeks are pink and I wonder how many mini bottles of wine she's had.

'You want to go out with *them*? Not *me*?' asks Luke, as though he can't believe it.

To be fair, it is quite unbelievable. When Elinor first met my family, she was so snobby, she behaved as though all the Bloomwoods had some sort of plague.

'Jane has some photographs of Minnie she has promised to show me,' says Elinor. 'I should like to see her babyhood. I missed so much of it.'

Her eyes flicker as though with some distant emotion, and I feel an uncomfortable twinge. Poor Elinor has been on the outskirts of this family for too long.

'Quite right, Elinor! You have a look through my iPhone and I'll send you any piccies you like,' says Mum, pulling on her jacket and standing up. 'You could make a collage for your kitchen. Or . . . I know! You like jigsaws, don't you? Well then, have a jigsaw made of a picture of Minnie! They'll do it at Snappy Snaps.'

'A jigsaw?' Elinor frowns thoughtfully. 'A jigsaw of Minnie's likeness. What a good idea.'

'Oh, I'm full of good ideas.' Mum starts bustling her to

the door. 'Come on! Ready, Janice? Elinor, have you ever gambled before?'

'I play baccarat in Monte Carlo from time to time,' says Elinor stiffly. 'With the de Broisiers. An old Monaco family.'

'Good! Then you can show us how it's done. I need to let off some steam, Elinor, I don't mind telling you. Bye, Becky love. I'll see you at the Bellagio tomorrow morning, nine sharp. Your father had better be ready for some home truths. Now Elinor, do you enjoy a cocktail?'

As the door closes, Mum is still talking. And Luke and I just gape at each other.

Messages: Inbox (1,783)

From: Unknown Number
6.46 p.m.
Hey sexy!

From: Unknown Number
6.48 p.m.
I'll find you any day!

From: Unknown Number
6.57 p.m.
Meet me 10 pm flamingo ask for juan

From: Unknown Number
6.59 p.m.
How much by the hour?

From: Unknown Number
7.01 p.m.
Cool pecs!!!! Love the rope!!!!

From: Unknown Number
7.07 p.m.
I luv u lonelee guy

From: Unknown Number
7.09 p.m.
How much?

From Unknown Number
7.10 p.m.
Do me hot lips, any time ok

From: Unknown Number
7.12 p.m.
I want to book u

From: Unknown Number
7.14 p.m.
Men or women?

EIGHT

It's the morning after. Whoever invented mornings after should basically be *shot*.

It's quarter to nine and I'm sitting at a large circular table in the Bellagio restaurant, waiting for the others. My head is throbbing gently along with the background muzak, and I feel a bit green. Which goes to show that room service wine is just as potent as restaurant wine.

And so are room-service cocktails.

OK, *OK*. And room-service nightcaps.

It also didn't help that Minnie woke us up at about 3 a.m., shrieking that her bed was 'in the water'. It's all the fault of those stupid gondolas. They should have health warnings.

I look up to see Luke returning to the table from the buffet, along with Minnie, who is clutching a bowl of cornflakes.

'Mummy, flakes!' she says, as though she's discovered some rare delicacy. 'I got *flakes*!'

'Amazing, darling! Yummy!' I turn to Luke. 'She has

the whole of the Bellagio buffet to choose from and she goes for cornflakes?'

'I tried to get her interested in the fresh shrimp and lobster platter,' says Luke with a grin. 'Not so much.'

My stomach turns over at the sound of fresh shrimp and lobster. I mean, honestly, lobster for breakfast. What kind of madness is that?

'They have truffle omelettes,' says Luke, as Minnie starts to munch her cornflakes.

'Great,' I say without enthusiasm.

'And there's a chocolate fountain, and French toast, and . . .'

'Luke, stop,' I moan. 'Don't talk about food.'

'Are you suffering?' Luke grins.

'No,' I say with dignity. 'I'm simply not very hungry.'

Maybe I should start the 5:2 diet, it occurs to me. Yes. And today could be the eat-nothing day.

A waiter comes to refresh my coffee cup, and I sip from it gingerly. A moment later a familiar sound catches my eye and I look up. Is that Mum's voice? Oh my God, is that apparition *Mum*?

She's standing at the greeter's desk, her hair all messed up, her eyes smudged and with some kind of glittery flower behind her ear.

'My daughter,' she's saying. 'My daughter Becky. Can you find her, please? I really need a cup of coffee . . .' She clutches her dishevelled hair, 'Oh, my head . . .'

'Mum!' I wave frantically. 'Over here!'

As Mum looks up, I can see that she's wearing the same dress as last night. Has she *not been to bed*?

'Mum!' I exclaim again as I head across the restaurant to her. 'Are you OK? Where have you *been*?'

'Wait,' she says. 'Let me get the others. Girls! Here!'

She beckons to the restaurant entrance, and to my astonishment, I see the figures of Elinor and Janice approaching. They're walking arm in arm. No, they're staggering.

Both look dreadful. Both are in the same clothes as last night. Janice is wearing a shiny sash which reads *Karaoke Queen*, and Elinor has what look like burnt-out sparklers stuck into her hair.

Oh my God. I give a sudden snort of laughter and clap a hand over my mouth.

'So, it was a good night out?' I ask as they reach us. Janice looks up and murmurs weakly, 'Oh, Becky love. Never let me drink Tia Maria again.'

'I am not well,' announces Elinor, who is white as a sheet. 'My head . . . these symptoms . . . they are most alarming . . .' She closes her eyes, and I grab on to her to steady her.

'Did you get *any* sleep?' I look from face to face, feeling like I'm the parent. 'Did you drink any water? Did you eat anything?'

'We dozed,' says Mum, after a moment's thought. 'At the Wynn, was it?'

'I am not at all well,' says Elinor again, her head drooping like a swan's.

'You've got a hangover,' I say sympathetically. 'Come and sit down, I'll order some tea . . .'

As we move towards the table, Luke glances up from Minnie's cornflakes and starts in horror.

'Mother!' He leaps up. 'Oh my God! Are you all right?'

'Don't worry. She's just got a hangover,' I say. 'They all have. Elinor, have you ever had a hangover before?'

Elinor looks blank as I help her into a chair.

'Do you know what a hangover *is*?' I try again.

'I have heard the term,' she says, regaining some of her familiar snootiness.

'Well, welcome to your first ever hangover.' I pour her a large glass of water. 'Drink this. Luke, do you have any Nurofen?'

For the next few minutes, Luke and I are the Hangover Doctors, as we administer fluids, cups of tea and painkillers to Mum, Janice and Elinor. I keep catching Luke's eye and wanting to giggle, but Elinor looks so pained, I don't like to.

'But you had a good time?' I say at last, when a little colour has come back into her cheeks.

'I think so.' She looks baffled. 'I barely remember.'

'That means you did,' says Luke.

'You guys!' Danny's voice hails us and we all look round to see him approaching the table. He's wearing a full-length sequinned dress, and his face is made up with glittery purple eyeshadow. I'm guessing he hasn't been to bed either.

'Danny!' I exclaim. 'What are you *wearing*?' But he ignores me.

'You guys!' he says again, and I realize he's addressing Mum, Janice and Elinor. 'You rocked last night! They did karaoke at the Mandalay Bay.' He turns to me. 'Your mom can do a mean "Rolling in the Deep". And Elinor! What a class act!'

'Elinor did karaoke?' I stare at him.

'*No*,' says Luke, sounding absolutely poleaxed.

'Oh yes.' Danny grins. "Something Stupid". Duet with Janice.'

'*No*,' says Luke again, and we all turn to survey Elinor, whose head is drooping on the table again. Poor Elinor. The first time you get drunk is always horrendous, and this is obviously her first time.

'You'll be OK,' I say, and stroke her back. 'Hang in there, Elinor.' I'm just pouring her some more water, when I see Suze and Alicia out of the corner of my eye. Needless to say, they don't look one bit hungover. Alicia's got that burnished healthy glow which all the Golden Peace staffers have. (It comes from the Golden Peace bronzing serum, by the way, *not* healthy living.) Suze's blonde hair is freshly washed and she's wearing a white, long-sleeved top which gives her an angelic air. As they draw near, I get a waft of some fresh, breezy scent, as if they're both wearing the same perfume, which maybe they are, because they're such best, best friends.

'Hello, you two!' I say, compelling myself to sound polite. 'Did you have a good evening?'

'We had an early night,' says Alicia. 'And this morning, we found a t'ai chi class.'

'Great!' I force a smile. 'Lovely. Can I pour you some water? Have you seen Danny's here?'

As the two sit down, Danny approaches from the buffet. He's holding a plate piled high with lobster and grapes and nothing else.

'Suze! Darling.' He blows her a kiss. 'I'm here for you.

I mean, literally. I. Am here.' He points at himself. 'For you. Just tell me what I can do.'

'Danny!' says Suze with a ferocious glare. 'What the *hell* do you think you've been doing?'

'I flew here as soon as I could,' says Danny proudly. 'My assistants and I are at your disposal. Tell me what we can do.'

'I'll tell you what you can *not* do!' says Suze. She pulls out one of Danny's flyers and brandishes it at him. 'You can *not* plaster my husband's face all over Las Vegas so I get a million people wanting to "hook up" with him! Do you *know* the kind of calls I've been getting?'

'No!' says Danny in delight. 'What did they say?' Then he notices Suze's expression and draws himself up defensively. 'I was only trying to help, Suze. Excuse me for deploying my resources to aid you. Next time I won't bother.'

I can see Suze quivering, trying to get a grip on herself, and after a few moments she says, 'I'm sorry, Danny. I know you were trying to help. But *honestly*.'

'They're great pictures though, aren't they?' says Danny, looking lovingly at Tarkie's moody gaze.

'I hate them,' says Suze with fervour.

'I know, but they're still great. You have to admit it, Suze. You're an artist. You have an eye. Hey, I have a coat from my new collection that's perfect for you. It has, like, this mammoth ruff neckline? Like Elizabeth the First? You would totally pull it off. Peace offering?'

No one can stay cross with Danny for long. I can see Suze unbending and rolling her eyes at him, and eventually she leans back with a huffing sigh and turns to

Alicia. 'Alicia, you've met Danny Kovitz, haven't you?' she says. 'Danny, Alicia Merrelle.'

'I remember you from Becky's wedding,' says Danny blandly to Alicia. 'You made quite the entrance.'

I can see a flash of something pass across Alicia's face – anger? Remorse? – but she doesn't reply. Suze has poured out two glasses of water, and the two of them start sipping delicately.

'Where did you go last night?' says Danny to Suze, who shakes her head.

'We didn't. We stayed in all night. Shall we go to the buffet, Alicia?'

As the two of them get up, Danny leans across the table to me.

'Well, that's a lie,' he murmurs quietly.

'What's a lie?'

'Alicia wasn't in all evening. I saw her in the lobby of the Four Seasons, about midnight, talking to some guy.'

'You're kidding!' I say, agog.

'You're kidding!' mimics Minnie at once.

'What was she doing? And why would she lie about it?'

Danny shrugs and stuffs about six grapes into his mouth at once.

'I need ice water,' he says fretfully. 'This water isn't chill enough. Where's Kasey?'

He starts to text, and I lean back in my chair, watching Alicia as she selects pieces of grapefruit. I *knew* she was up to something. What was she doing in the Four Seasons lobby at midnight? It sounds totally suspicious, if you ask me. I'm about to ask Danny for more details when I suddenly notice that Elinor has fallen asleep on the table. Her face is squashed up and her hair is skew-whiff and I can hear a gentle snoring.

I am *so* tempted to take a selfie with her right now. But, no. That wouldn't be the act of a kind, mature daughter-in-law.

'Elinor.' I shake her gently. 'Elinor, wake up!'

'Huh?' She comes to with a start and rubs at her eyes while I watch in alarm, half-expecting flakes of skin to start falling off her face.

'Have some more water.' I hand her the glass and look at my watch. 'Tarkie and Dad should be here soon.'

'If they come,' says Luke, who is tucking into bacon and eggs and feeding every other forkful to Minnie.

'"If they come"?' I stare at him in dismay. 'What do you mean? Of course they'll come.'

'Kidding,' puts in Minnie emphatically. 'You're *kidding*.' She looks around proudly and pinches a strawberry off Mum's plate. But Mum doesn't even notice. She's also staring at Luke in consternation.

'What makes you say that, Luke? Has Graham been in touch with you?'

'Of course not,' says Luke patiently as Suze sits down again. 'But it's ten past nine now. If this appointment was going to happen, I think they'd be on time. I just have a hunch about it.'

'A *hunch*?' echoes Mum suspiciously.

'What do you know?' demands Suze. 'Luke, what aren't you telling us?'

'Luke doesn't know anything!' I say hurriedly. 'And his

127

instincts are usually wrong. I'm sure they'll turn up.'

But I'm lying, of course. Luke's instincts are usually spot on. Why else has he done so well in business? He can read people and situations and think ahead of everyone else. And then, as we're sitting there silently, sipping our drinks, my phone rings. I pull it out and see *Dad* on the screen and my heart plummets.

'Dad!' I exclaim determinedly. 'Great! Are you here? We're sitting on the big circular table, next to the huge display of fruit . . .'

'Becky . . .' He stops, and there's silence and I know, I just know.

'Dad, I'm passing you over to Mum,' I say in a kind of fierce, bright way. 'Right now! You're talking to Mum.'

I'm not being the messenger any more. I can't do it.

I hand the phone to Mum and furiously start cutting up a melon slice. My head is bowed over the plate but I can hear Mum's voice getting shriller and shriller:

'But we're all sitting here, waiting! Graham, don't you tell me not to worry . . . Well then, tell me the truth . . . I think *I'll* decide what's important or not . . . Go back to LA? . . . No, I haven't visited any vineyards . . . No, I don't want to visit any vineyards . . . *Stop talking about bloody vineyards!*'

'Let me talk to him!' Suze keeps chiming in. 'Is Tarkie there?' At last she wrests the phone off Mum and exclaims, 'I need to talk to my husband! Well, where is he? What do you mean, a "walk"?' She's practically snarling at the phone. 'I need to speak to him!'

At last she switches the phone off and slaps it back

down on the table. She's breathing hard and her cheeks are pink. 'If one more person tells me to relax . . .'

'I agree!' says Mum vociferously.

'How *can* I relax?'

'Vineyards! He wants me to go and visit the vineyards! I'll give that Graham what for when I see him. He kept spouting nonsense like, "This isn't a big deal . . . I've only been away for a couple of days . . . what's the problem . . . ?" The problem is, he's keeping secrets from me!' She bangs her cup down on the table. 'There's another woman. I know there is.'

'Mum!' I say, shocked. 'No!'

'There is!' Tears rise in her eyes and she dabs at them with a napkin. 'That's what he's "putting right". Something to do with another woman.'

'No he's not!'

'Well, what else can it be?'

And there's silence. The truth is, I have no idea what it can be.

We sit there for forty minutes longer, even though we know they're not coming. It's as though we've all been stunned into inaction.

Plus, you know, the buffet really *is* excellent. And my appetite has greatly recovered after a few cups of coffee. In fact, I've decided to switch from the 5:2 diet to the 'Get the most from your buffet because it's costing you a fortune' diet.

Meanwhile, Elinor has revived and is deep in conversation with Danny. It turns out they know all the same society ladies in Manhattan, because Elinor goes to events with them and Danny sells dresses to them. Danny has even opened up his sketchbook and is drawing outfits for Elinor, while she watches over his shoulder.

'This would do for the opera,' he's saying as he shades the skirt with cross-hatching. 'Or gallery events, tea parties . . .'

'Not too much of a peplum,' says Elinor, regarding his sketch with a critical eye. 'I do not wish to appear as a lampshade.'

'Elinor, I'll give you exactly the right amount of peplum,' Danny retorts. 'Trust me. I have the eye.'

'I have the money,' Elinor shoots back, and I stifle a snort. These two are a good match. Now Danny is drawing a sweeping coat with a massive funnel neck.

'This neckline is your friend,' he says to Elinor. 'Higher in back, lower in front. It's going to frame your face. It's going to look unbelievable. And we're going to edge it in faux fur.' He's drawing in the fur, and Elinor is watching avidly. To be honest, I'm quite fascinated myself. Elinor would look *amazing* in that coat.

'I need a muffin to help me think,' Danny says, suddenly leaping to his feet. 'I'll be back in a moment, Elinor.'

As I head to the muffin stand alongside him, Danny looks delighted with himself.

'I'm basing a whole new collection around Elinor,' he tells me. 'Danny Kovitz Classic. Like, a semi-couture line for the lady of silver years.'

'Silver dollars, more like,' I say, rolling my eyes.

'Both.' He winks at me. 'You know, Elinor has a very good sense of style.'

'Well, yes . . . Only, she's a bit rigid.'

'I don't find that,' says Danny complacently. 'I find her very receptive to new ideas.'

'Well, obviously she's hit it off with you,' I say, a bit jealously. I had been thinking of myself as Elinor's fashion guru. I mean, I'm the one who got her into wrap dresses. But now Danny will take over and claim all the credit. 'Anyway, enjoy. How much are you going to charge her for all this?'

'Oh, not more than the price of a small condo in Mexico,' murmurs Danny. 'I already Googled the one I want.'

'Danny!'

'I just need to sell her three more coats.'

'*Danny!*' I give him a push. 'Don't exploit my mother-in-law.'

'She's exploiting me!' retorts Danny. 'Do you know how much work this will all be? Hey, I might get myself a waffle.'

As he heads to the other side of the buffet, I wander over to the Italian-themed counter, and I'm just reaching for a cannolo when my phone rings. I pull it out and stare at the display in astonishment. It's Tarquin. Why's he phoning *me*? Did he get the wrong number?

'Hi!' I say breathlessly. 'Oh my God, Tarkie, hi! I'll just get Suze—'

'No!' says Tarquin. 'I don't want to talk to Suze.'

'But—'

'If you get her, Becky, I'll ring off.'

He sounds so adamant, I gape at the phone.

'But Tarkie . . .'

131

'I phoned to have a conversation with *you*, Becky. That's why I dialled your number.'

'But I'm not your wife,' I say, feeling stupid.

'You're my friend. Aren't you?'

'Of course. Tarkie . . .' I rub my head, trying to collect my thoughts. 'What's happened to you?'

'Nothing's *happened* to me.'

'But you've really changed. You sound fine. In LA, we all thought—' I stop before I can say, *We thought you were losing it.*

And I know that sounds extreme – but, honestly, Tarkie was in a mess. All he wanted to do was spend time with Bryce. All he could talk about was how Suze was sabotaging him. It was miserable.

'I was in a bad way in LA,' says Tarkie after a long pause. 'It was . . . claustrophobic. That can make any relationship go in a strange direction.'

He must be talking about himself and Bryce.

'But surely things are even more claustrophobic now?' I say, puzzled. 'I mean, now you're with Bryce all the time, things won't get any better—'

'I don't mean Bryce! Why would I mean Bryce? I mean Suze!'

'*Suze?*'

I blink at the phone. Does he mean— He doesn't mean—

'Tarkie?' I begin in slight dread. 'What do you—'

'You must have seen us, Becky,' says Tarkie, his voice gruff. 'You must have realized things weren't good between me and Suze. Well, they hit a real low in LA.'

'It was a stressy time for everyone,' I put in quickly.

132

'No, it was *really* bad for us.'

I feel a kind of knotting in my stomach. I've never had this kind of conversation with Tarkie before. Suze and Tarkie have never gone wrong before. They *can't* go wrong. I feel like the world isn't right if Suze and Tarkie aren't happy.

'You must have realized,' Tarkie repeats.

'I . . . well . . .' I stammer. 'I knew you were spending a lot of time with Bryce, but—'

'Yes, and why do you think that was?' Tarkie sounds so forceful, I jump. 'I'm sorry,' he backtracks immediately. 'I didn't mean to lose my cool like that.'

Tarkie is such a gentleman. I've barely ever heard him even snap before. My head is spinning with worry and distress, and all I can think is: *Suze*.

'Tarkie, you have to talk to Suze,' I say. 'Please. She's so worried about you, she's in a total state—'

'I can't talk to her,' Tarkie interrupts me. 'Not right now. Becky, I can't cope with her. She's so irrational. She makes accusations, she jumps down my throat . . . I needed to get away. Your father is wonderful. He's so balanced.'

'But Suze needs you!'

'I'll be back. We'll only be a few days.'

'She needs you now!'

'Well, maybe our marriage needs some time apart!' he practically shouts.

There's nothing I can say to that. I just stand there, quivering in shock, trying to think of how to turn this conversation round to a better place.

'So . . . why did you phone?' I say, finally.

'I think you should warn Alicia about Bryce. I've found out what he's up to.'

'Oh, wow.' My heart starts to beat faster. We've all known Bryce was up to no good – but what is it? A cult? A secret organization? Oh God, he's not a terrorist, is he?

'Bryce has been trying to get money out of me for a while. He talked of his "cause" but he was secretive as to what exactly this "cause" was.'

My heart lurches. A 'cause'. Oh my God, it's true. I stare at the phone in dread, imagining Bryce yelling instructions at a secret army of followers at a training camp in South America. Or hacking into Google, maybe.

'Now he's finally revealed the truth,' Tarkie continues. 'And his plan is . . .'

'Yes?' I prompt breathlessly.

'To set up a rival centre to Golden Peace.'

'Oh,' I say, after a short silence. 'Oh, right.'

I have to confess: I feel just a tad let down. I mean, obviously I'm *glad* Bryce isn't a terrorist or cult leader . . . but still. A new business venture. Bor-*ing*.

'He's been collecting a database of former clients of Golden Peace, many of whom were unhappy with their experience,' Tarquin is telling me. 'He's been working on it secretly. Alicia and her husband should watch out. Bryce is going to be extremely aggressive. I'm not the only person he's targeting for money, so I'm sure he'll succeed.'

'Oh,' I say again. 'Well, I'll tell Alicia.'

All my adrenalin has faded away. So Bryce is going

into competition with Alicia. So what? I'm far more concerned with Tarkie and what he's up to with my dad. And what's going on with Tarkie and Suze. And what on earth I do now.

I'm in an impossible situation, I suddenly realize. If I warn Alicia about Bryce's business venture, she'll say 'How did you find out?' and I'll have to admit I've spoken to Tarkie, and Suze will go mad.

'Tarkie, *can't* you tell me what you're up to with my dad?' The words tumble out. 'Please?'

'Becky . . .' Tarkie hesitates. 'Your father is a good man. And he's very protective. He doesn't want you to know what he's doing. Personally, I can't see why, but perhaps you should respect that.' I can hear a noise down the line which sounds like a car engine starting. 'I'm sorry, I have to go. But please don't worry.'

'Tarkie, wait!' I cry, but the phone goes dead, and I stand stock still, digesting what I've just heard.

'Becky?' I look up to see Luke in front of me. 'Who on earth was that? You look deathly.'

'It was Tarquin,' I say miserably. 'Oh, Luke, I don't think he's having a nervous breakdown at all. He's having a *marital* breakdown. He says he needs to spend some time away from Suze . . . things aren't going well between them . . .' I gulp. 'What do I say to Suze?'

'Nothing,' says Luke at once. 'Do *not* get involved in their relationship. She'll just transfer all her anger on to you.'

'He said she was . . .' I swallow. 'Irrational.'

'Well,' says Luke dryly, 'I think Suze is going through a

pretty odd phase. But if you tell her she's irrational, your friendship will *definitely* be at an end.'

We're silent for a moment. My stomach is churning, over and over. I hate this situation. I want someone to blame, but I'm not sure I can blame even Alicia for this.

'It's all so horrible,' I say miserably.

'This is big stuff. It's hard.' Luke wraps his arms around me tight and kisses my forehead. I sink into his embrace and breathe in his familiar scent: part aftershave, part laundered shirt, part Luke.

'Oh and by the way, Bryce isn't running a cult after all,' I tell him gloomily. 'He's trying to rip off Alicia. Tarkie wants me to warn her. But how can I? I can't say, "Guess what? Tarkie just rang me!"'

'It's awkward,' Luke agrees.

The idea suddenly hits me. 'Luke, *you* tell Alicia. Say you heard it on the grapevine. Keep me out of it.'

'Oh no, no.' Luke shakes his head with a short laugh. 'I'm not getting into this.'

'Please,' I wheedle. '*Please*, Luke.'

What's the point of having a husband if he won't cover your back, once in a while? I mean, it's practically in the vows.

There's silence as Luke pours himself a grapefruit juice. Then he looks up with a sigh.

'OK, I'll do it. But Becky, you're going to have to tell Suze *sometime* that you spoke to Tarquin. These things have a habit of coming out.'

'I know.' I nod fervently. 'I will. But I can't right now. She'll murder me.'

'What else did he say?'

'Not a lot. My father's a good man, apparently.'

'Well, we knew that.' Luke laughs at my expression. 'Becky, cheer up. It's good news, remember? A day ago we thought Tarquin had been kidnapped and left for dead.'

'Yes, but it's all so *complicated*.' Dolefully I select a pain au chocolat, an almond croissant and a Danish whirl. I'll put one in my bag for later, in case Minnie needs a snack. 'And what do we do now? You know what I think? If Tarkie's fine and Dad doesn't want us to find him, I think we should just go home.'

'Right.' Luke nods thoughtfully. 'Good point. Do you want to say that to your mother or shall I?'

OK, so that was a non-starter. I should have realized Mum was never going to agree to go home in a million years. By the end of what you could call an 'animated discussion' (the waiting staff had to ask us to keep it down), we've reached a compromise. We'll go to see Dad's other old friend, the one in Tucson. Raymond Earle. And if we can't find anything out from him, we'll go back to LA and wait for Dad to return.

Whereupon, no doubt, Dad will refuse to say what he was up to. And it will be one of the great unsolved puzzles of our time. And Mum will nearly expire in rage. But as Luke keeps telling me, that's not my problem.

We're all up at the buffet again now, having a last go round. I can't believe I'm putting yet more food on my plate, but there's just *so much*. Every time you think, 'I've had everything,' you turn a corner and see some huge pile of fresh waffles, or chicken skewers, or chocolate-covered strawberries, and a bit of your brain shouts, 'I've paid for this! I need to eat it!' even while the other bit is moaning, 'I'm full! Take it awaaaay!'

I pour a glass of milk for Minnie and glance over at Suze, who's getting some juice on the other side of the counter. My whole body is tense with guilt. I've never had secrets from Suze before.

Well, except the odd tiny one, like that time I borrowed her Monsoon top and it wasn't even hers and she only found out years later. But apart from *that*.

Alicia is taking some slivers of pineapple from a fruit display and as I watch, Luke approaches her, his phone in his hand.

'Oh, Alicia,' he says, sounding casual. 'Just heard a bit of gossip on the grapevine. Chap didn't want me to let on who he was, but he has it on good authority that Bryce Perry is intending to set up a rival establishment to Golden Peace.'

'*What?*' Alicia's cry of shock pierces the sound of buffet chatter.

'That's what I heard. You might want to check it out.'

He sounds totally laid-back and hasn't even glanced at me. God, I love Luke.

'So *that's* what he's up to?' Alicia's eyes glitter. 'That's why he's targeted Tarquin? For backing?'

'Could be.'

Alicia's new-agey, Zen-like manner seems to be fading away, fast. She looks absolutely livid.

'Anyway.' Luke shrugs. 'As I say, just a rumour, but you might want to investigate.'

'Yes. Yes.' She looks ferocious. 'Thank you for the tip,

Luke.' Already, she's heading over to Suze. 'You'll never *guess* what Luke just told me,' she begins, before lowering her voice discreetly.

'Really?' I can hear Suze saying in shock. 'Oh my God.'

'I know. I know!' Alicia's voice rises again in fury. 'All this time, he's been Wilton's trusted right-hand man, and now he's betraying us!'

'So *that's*—' Suze stops herself dead and there's a weird pause. Her eyes are distant, and I can't work out what she's thinking at all.

Alicia has pulled out her phone to start texting. 'I don't know what Wilton will say,' she mutters. 'It's taken years for him to build up such an amazing, blue-chip client list, and Bryce wants to *steal* it?'

I feel such a jolt of shock that I goggle at her. Hello? You want to talk about pinching clients?

Alicia, do you remember when you tried to steal all Luke's clients? I want to call out. *Do you remember when you tried to wreck everything he'd worked so hard for?*

But there's no point. I think she's airbrushed that whole incident out of her memory.

As she's texting away, Danny comes over to her and Suze, his plate piled high with bacon. I can see an evil gleam in his eye, and he shoots me a tiny wink before speaking.

'So I hear Bryce is going into competition with you!' he begins with great interest. 'That's a piece of news. Tell me, Alicia, is he going to charge any less than you? Because I have to tell you, Golden Peace is *waaaay* expensive.'

'I have no idea,' says Alicia stonily.

'I mean, I love a good mindfulness class as much as the next guy,' Danny continues airily. 'But if Bryce opens a more reasonable alternative then it'll be a no-brainer. I mean, who doesn't need to be price-conscious, right? Even movie stars. I'd think you would lose a lot of clients.'

'Danny!' says Suze sharply.

'Just being honest,' says Danny innocently. 'So, Alicia, if Bryce opens up a rival centre, will your empire collapse, do you think?' He blinks at her. 'Will you have to get a job?'

'Danny, shut up!' says Suze furiously.

'Wilton and I will not let some *employee* undermine us,' snaps Alicia. 'Who does this Bryce Perry think he is?'

He *is* very good-looking, I want to point out. And everyone does worship him. But I don't say this, because I think she'd probably attack me with a fork.

'Come on, Alicia.' Suze glares at Danny again. 'Let's sit down.'

As I'm wondering whether to follow them or just hide out by the muffins, I see Elinor approaching. She seems a *lot* better, which is either down to the fruit salad she's been nibbling or because of her impending custom-made Danny Kovitz Classic wardrobe (I still can't wait to see her in that coat).

'Would you like a muffin?' I venture politely, and she shoots a disdainful look at them.

'I hardly think so.' She glances over at Suze and Alicia. 'What was Luke saying about Wilton Merrelle?'

140

'One of his employees is planning to open a rival centre and steal all his customers. Why, do you know him?'

'He's an atrocious man,' says Elinor crisply, and I try not to beam in delight. A bit of bitching about Wilton Merrelle is just what I'm in the mood for.

'Why?' I repeat encouragingly. 'You can tell me. I'm really discreet.'

'He practically forced a friend of mine out of her Park Avenue condominium.'

'How did he do that?' I ask, agog.

'He bought the apartment next door and pestered and pestered. Poor Anne-Marie was quite beleaguered. She felt she had no choice but to sell to him.'

'Poor woman!' I say in sympathy. 'So, what happened to her?'

'She was forced to spend more time on her estate in the Hamptons,' says Elinor, without blinking.

OK, Elinor needs to work on her sob-stories a little. But even so, it feels cosy, sharing a common enemy with her.

'Well, Alicia's just as bad as Wilton,' I say. 'Worse.' I'm about to launch into a whole list of Alicia's dastardly deeds, when I see Elinor picking up a grape on a cocktail stick and looking at it curiously.

'This is a particularly minimalist canapé,' she observes.

'It's not a canapé, it's for the chocolate fountain.' I point. 'See?'

Elinor peers at the gushing chocolate as though she's none the wiser. I take the grape from her, dip it in the chocolate, let it cool slightly and hand it to her.

'*Ah*.' Her brow clears. 'I am reminded of the fondues one sees in Gstaad.'

'You've never dipped anything in a chocolate fountain before?'

'Naturally not,' she confirms with a supercilious air.

I love it. First ever hangover. First ever chocolate fountain. What else is there in the list of Elinor Sherman's Firsts?

'Elinor,' I say in sudden inspiration. 'Have you ever worn a pair of blue jeans before?'

'Never,' responds Elinor, looking slightly revolted.

That's it. I have her Christmas present. Dark-blue skinnies by J Brand.

Unless . . . do I dare give her *ripped* jeans?

The thought of Elinor unwrapping a pair of ripped jeans on Christmas Day cheers me up so much, I'm still smiling as I return to the table. But I hastily stop, as I see Suze's pained expression.

'I have to get Tarkie away from Bryce,' she's saying fervently. 'He'll be trying to fleece him for millions.'

'If not more,' says Alicia darkly, and jabs at her phone yet again.

'I mean, should we phone the police again?' Suze looks around the table for support. 'Now we have this new information?'

'Tarkie told me yesterday that he wasn't going to give Bryce any money,' I venture. 'I think he'll be strong. He'll just say no.'

'Bex, you don't know anything about it! Tarkie's extremely vulnerable. He hasn't called, he hasn't texted . . . he was snappy with me in LA . . . He's *not normal*.'

142

Her blue eyes are blazing and I lean away on my chair. Suze can be quite scary when she's on fire like this.

'Suze . . .' I begin cautiously. 'Look. I know Tarkie was a bit tense in LA. I know he said some weird stuff. But that doesn't necessarily mean he was being brainwashed. He might just . . . well . . .'

I trail off feebly. I can't exactly say, *He might just not want to talk to you right now.*

'What do you know about it?' Suze bites back.

'I was just giving you my point of view.'

'Well, don't! You're constantly trying to undermine me. Isn't she, Alicia?'

Suze's eyes are glittering, and she looks so hostile, it's as if something inside me snaps.

'You know what, Suze?' I cry out. 'Why did you even ask me to come on this trip? In LA you said you needed me, so I dropped everything. I was glad to! But you don't seem to want my companionship or my opinions or anything I have to offer. All you care about is Alicia. And by the way, guess what, she's been *lying* to you!'

I didn't mean to blurt that out. But now that I have, I feel an almighty satisfaction.

'Lying?' Suze's eyes darken in shock. 'What do you mean?'

'I mean, lying! You told me you both stayed in all evening last night?'

'We did.' Suze glances uncertainly at Alicia.

'Alicia didn't! Who were you meeting in the lobby of the Four Seasons at midnight, Alicia? And before you deny it, Danny saw you.' I throw this out with relish and sink back, folding my arms. At *last*. Alicia is totally exposed as a liar.

Except, she doesn't look exposed. She doesn't blush, or seem embarrassed, or drop her glass with a clatter, or do any of the things I would do.

'I was meeting a private detective,' she says coldly.

A *what*?

'Naturally, I've been using my own resources.' She shoots me a withering look. 'However, I didn't want to let Suze know I'd drawn a blank, in case it discouraged her. So thanks, Becky, for ruining all my efforts.'

There's a long and prickling silence around the table. My head's all hot and fuzzy. I can't believe Alicia's come out on top again. What is she, a *witch*?

'Do you have anything to say, Becky?' Suze asks, and she sounds exactly like my headmistress did when I started the whole Bring Your Teacher a Clothes Item craze (which I *still* think was a good idea).

'I'm sorry,' I mumble, staring down, exactly as I did back then in Mrs Brightling's study.

'Right. Well.' Suze finishes her coffee. 'I think we'd better move on.'

From: dsmeath@locostinternet.com
To: Brandon, Rebecca
Subject: Re: It's all going wrong!!!

Dear Mrs Brandon

Thank you for your email. I am most sorry to hear of all your difficulties.

We have indeed known each other a long time, and you are very welcome to 'pour your heart out' to me. I am flattered that you think of me as 'a wise old counsellor, like Father Christmas' and will do my best to advise you.

Mrs Brandon, for what it is worth: I suggest perhaps you try to bond a little more with Ms Bitch Long-legs. Lady Cleath-Stuart has clearly allied herself with this woman. If you set up in the opposite 'camp' you risk losing your friend. Find points of common interest and take it from there. I'm sure that with your ingenuity, you can do so with considerable effect.

I do hope your trip progresses with success and that you find happiness with your friend again.

Yours sincerely

Derek Smeath

NINE

Derek Smeath is so wise. He's always given me good advice over the years, which I really should have followed a bit more. (Or, you know. At all. Especially that time he told me not to take out any more store cards for the free presents. I never did use that set of heated rollers.)

So as we're heading out of Vegas, I decide this time I *will* follow his advice. If I have to bond with Alicia Bitch Long-legs to keep Suze's friendship, then I will. Somehow. I'll just have to channel Pollyanna and focus on all of Alicia's plus points. I've even Googled 'ways to bond with co-workers you don't like', and have got some useful tips like 'find a common hobby' and 'give them an affectionate nickname'. (Although how will I ever find a nickname to top 'Alicia Bitch Long-legs'?)

By now we're speeding along the freeway. I edge towards the table and benches where Alicia and Suze are sitting. Mum, Janice and Danny are perched on the little sofa along with Minnie, and they're playing bridge. (They work it so Minnie is 'dummy' every time, which is quite clever. The only thing is, Minnie has her own set of cards too, and keeps plonking them down and saying '*My* trick' and trying to scoop up all the other cards.) Meanwhile, Elinor has stayed in Las Vegas to 'rest' for a few days, and I really don't blame her. Your first ever hangover is always a shocker. I should think hers will last about a week.

Either side of us are wide desert plains, with mountains in the distance, and I feel a little thrill every time I glance out of the window. I mean, *this* is a view. *This* is scenery. Why can't England have anything like this? When I was a little girl, Mum and Dad used to say, 'Look at the lovely scenery, Becky!' and they were talking about three trees and a cow. No wonder I couldn't get excited and preferred reading *Debbie and Her Magic Sparkle Dress*.

As I approach the table, Suze looks up – and for an awful moment I think she's not going to shift up and make room for me. But after an awkward beat, she does, and I sit down, trying to appear normal. Like we three always hang out together. Like we're old mates.

'I really like your top, Alicia,' I say awkwardly. I've decided the quickest way to ingratiate myself is to compliment her. It's a totally boring top, but that's not the point.

'Oh.' Alicia gives me a wary look. 'Thanks.'

'And your hair,' I add randomly. 'I love your hair. It's so shiny.'

'Thanks,' she repeats shortly.

'And . . . er . . . your perfume.'

'Thanks,' she says yet again. 'It's the Golden Peace blend.'

'Well, it's really gorgeous on you, um . . . Ali,' I try, self-consciously.

As soon as I've said it I realize Alicia is definitely *not* an Ali. She turns, startled, and I can see Suze gawping at me, too.

'Ali?'

'I mean . . . Lissy,' I amend hastily. 'Does anyone ever call you Lissy? It suits you. Lissy. Liss.' I give her a friendly little squeeze of the arm, which really doesn't work.

'Ow!' She glares at me. 'No, they don't. And please leave my arm alone.'

'Sorry,' I say, and quickly cast around for more compliments. 'You've got a really pretty nose! It's so, um . . .' I swallow, playing for time. What can you say about a nose? 'I love the way your . . . nostrils go,' I hear myself saying feebly.

Argh. I love the way her *nostrils go*?

Suze is giving me a very strange look, which I pretend I can't see, while Alicia has turned to survey me with narrowed eyes.

'Oh, *I* get it,' she says. '*I* get what you're doing. You want the number of my plastic surgeon, don't you? Well, you're not getting it.'

What? I stare at her in bewilderment. Plastic surgeon? *What?*

Oh God, this is hopeless. Let's forget the compliments. And the nicknames.

'So, t'ai chi!' I say brightly. 'Is that good? Should I try it?'

'I wouldn't have thought it would suit you,' says Alicia. 'You need to be able to *control* your mind and body.' She

148

gives me a patronizing smile and flicks a glance at Suze.

'Oh.' I'm trying not to feel too snubbed. 'OK. Well—'

'So, *how* many bedrooms, did you say?' Alicia cuts across me, resuming the obviously much more fascinating conversation they were having before.

So much for bonding. Total fail. And what's so interesting about bedrooms, anyway? Why is it some people will *always* bring the conversation back to houses and house prices and how they can't decide whether 'feature' wallpaper is over, what do I think? (OK, that last one is just Mum. I keep telling her, I don't *know* anything about feature wallpaper.)

'Oh, I'm not sure,' says Suze. 'Twenty-eight? Half of them are crumbling away though. We never even go into them.'

'Twenty-eight,' echoes Alicia. 'Imagine that. Twenty-eight bedrooms.'

They must be talking about Letherby Hall. Poor Suze. She gets so bored when people start pestering her for details about Letherby Hall. Especially historical experts, who start saying things like, 'I believe you mean seventeen *fifteen*,' in a supercilious way. I was once in the local greengrocer's with Suze, when some old man accosted her. He started quizzing her on some important fireplace in the Great Hall, and putting her right on every detail. He was actually quite aggressive about which of Tarkie's ancestors had commissioned it (I mean, who cares?) and in the end I had to deliberately knock over a stack of tangerines and cause a distraction, so Suze could run away.

'And is it one of those houses that has a title attached?'

'I think so,' says Suze, sounding uninterested. 'Lord of the Manor.'

'Right.' Alicia delicately wrinkles her brow. 'So anyone who owns the house is entitled to call themselves "Lord".'

'I suppose.' Suze looks vague. 'I mean, in our case it doesn't arise, because Tarkie has this other title anyway.'

The truth is, Tarkie has about six other titles, although Suze is far too modest to bring that up. In fact, she hates talking about this stuff altogether. I, on the other hand, once looked it all up on a website, because I quite fancy being 'Lady Brandon of somewhere'. The titles don't even cost that much. They're, like, a few hundred pounds, for something that lasts your whole life. I mean, in a way, why *not* be Lady Brandon?

(Only then Luke caught me looking and teased me about it for a week.)

As Suze pops to the loo, I glance at Alicia. Her eyes are distant and thoughtful. And OK, I *know* I'm supposed to be channelling Pollyanna, but my brain won't do it. Instead of thinking, *Golly-gosh! I bet Alicia's a sweetheart really, maybe we could have milkshakes together*, I'm thinking, *Huh. What's she up to now?*

Maybe I'm just a naturally negative, suspicious person, I think morosely. Maybe I need therapy before I can get on with Alicia. I have a sudden image of us in couples' counselling, being forced to hold each other's hands, and I let out a strange little snort. Meanwhile, as soon as Suze returns, Alicia resumes quizzing her on Letherby Hall.

'My husband would love to see the place,' she says. 'He's such an Anglophile.'

'He's welcome to!' Suze rolls her eyes ruefully. 'It costs a fortune to run. We're always trying to think of new ways to make money out of it. You'll see when you come to stay.'

'Is Alicia coming to stay with you?' I ask, trying to sound as though this is a super-fab idea. 'When's that?'

'We don't *know* yet, obviously,' says Suze, her brow darkening as though I'm insensitive even to ask. 'We'll have to wait until everything with Tarkie is cleared up.'

'Great,' I manage. 'That sounds perfect.'

I sit for a bit, saying nothing, watching the landscape, thoughts bombing miserably around my brain. I'm getting so tired of my own suspicious mind. I'm supposed to be Pollyanna, I remind myself. *Pollyanna*. And there's no reason to be suspicious of Alicia. None.

But, oh *God*. Alicia has always been up to something, ever since I've known her, and I just can't help wondering what might be in this for her. Suze is so unsuspicious and her guard is down and Alicia knows it . . .

And then I sit up. *Wait* a minute. Wilton Merrelle is an Anglophile. A predatory, aggressive Anglophile who decides he wants something and gets it. And here's Alicia, interrogating Suze about Letherby Hall . . . What if Wilton Merrelle has decided the next thing he wants is a stately home and a title? What if he wants to be Lord Merrelle of Letherby Hall?

For about the next twenty miles, I'm silent, considering this theory. It's a ridiculous idea. Suze and Tarkie would never sell their ancestral home, even if they were put under pressure. Surely they wouldn't.

Surely?

I glance sidelong at Suze. Her hair is always scrunched in a knot these days, like she doesn't care about anything. Her lips are chapped and her face is strained. The truth is, I don't know what I think any more. Suze and Tarkie aren't in a good place, Tarkie finds Letherby Hall hard to run, Suze isn't thinking straight right now . . .

But they *can't* sell. That house has been in their family for a zillion years. Just the thought gives me a horrible pang. And to Alicia Bitch Long-legs of all people? I can just see Alicia wearing a tiara and making all the villagers curtsey while some little girl gives her a posy and whispers, 'You're so beautiful, Princess Alicia.' Ugh. It can't happen. It *can't*.

From: dsmeath@locostinternet.com
To: Brandon, Rebecca
Subject: Re: Disaster!!

Dear Mrs Brandon

Thank you for your email. I'm so sorry to hear that your efforts to bond with Ms Bitch Long-legs failed. I am also sorry to hear you feel so powerless and 'like everything's impossible'.

If I may be so bold, Mrs Brandon, I would say, 'Don't give up.' Positive action boosts the soul.

In all our years of knowing each other, I have observed with admiration your dynamic approach to life's problems and innate sense of justice. This has empowered you before and I feel certain it will again.

Things may seem difficult at the moment, but I feel sure that you will prevail.

With kindest best wishes

Derek Smeath

TEN

The only disadvantage to a road trip, I've decided, is the actual *road* bit. Everything else is brilliant – the RV, the diners, the views, the Country music. (I made Luke tune into a Country music radio station for a bit, and *God*, Country singers understand how you feel. One song, called 'Only Your Oldest Friend', almost made me cry.)

But the roads are a total pain. They're too long. I mean, it's ridiculous. Someone should rethink them. Plus the map is very deceptive and sneaky. It lures you in. It makes you think, *Oh I'll just zip along that bit of freeway, it's only one centimetre, it can't take long.* Ha! One centimetre? One whole day out of your life, more like.

It's quite a distance to Tucson, Arizona, it turns out. It's even more of a distance when you realize that the ranch you're after is *beyond* Tucson. By the time we roll up at the Red Ranch, Cactus Creek, Arizona, we've been on the road practically all day. I've taken turns driving and so has Suze and so has Alicia. We're all stiff, exhausted and out of conversation. Plus my head is ringing with the tunes of *Aladdin*, which Minnie has just forced me to watch along with her, with headphones on.

Before we got out, I brushed my hair, but it still feels all flat and weird from where I've been resting my head. My legs feel like they've seized up and my lungs are desperate for some fresh air.

As I glance around, no one else looks in great shape either. Mum and Janice are staggering around on the dusty ground, like cattle let out of a lorry into the light. Suze and Alicia are swigging Tylenol and water. Danny is doing a series of complicated yoga stretches. Minnie is the only one who's full of beans. She's trying to skip around a massive great boulder, only she can't skip yet, so she's basically just running and whirling her arms. As I watch, she stops dead, reaches down and picks the tiniest little white flower. Then she brings it to me, looking all pink and pleased with herself.

'Is a *rose*,' she says carefully. 'Is a rose for Mummy.'

Minnie thinks every flower is a rose, except daffodils, which she calls 'raffodils'.

'Lovely, darling, thank you!' I say. I put it in my hair, which is what I always do, and immediately she goes to pick another one, looking even more pink and pleased. (We play this game a lot. I'm getting used to my shower clogging up with wilted flowers.)

The sky is a deep blue and the air has that warm, expectant, twilight feel. In the distance are red rocky mountains which seem to go on for ever, and around us are scrubby trees which are giving off some herby scent.

And I think I just saw a lizard, running over the dust. I glance up at Luke, to see if he noticed it too, but he's squinting at the ranch.

The entrance is a few yards away. Huge great gates and CCTV and only a small wooden sign to tell you this is Red Ranch, home of Raymond Earle. It's all on its own, set way back from the road, with massive fences keeping out visitors. Apparently there are over a thousand acres attached to the property, but Raymond doesn't farm them himself, he rents them out, and lives in his compound, all alone.

We found this out at Bites 'n' Brunch, where we stopped twenty minutes ago for drinks. Megan the owner was very chatty, and my mum is the queen of getting information out of people, so basically we found out everything Megan knows about Raymond. Which is as follows:

1. He doesn't spend all his time at the ranch.
2. He doesn't socialize much.
3. He put in a new kitchen five years ago and the guys who worked on it said he was pleasant enough.
4. He's known for his pottery.

So, not a *huge* amount of information. But it doesn't matter. We're here now. Time for the big meeting. Time to find out what on earth has been going on.

'Shall we?' Danny comes out of his tree pose and gestures at the ranch.

'We can't all go in together,' I object. 'We'll look like a posse.' I'm about to add that I'll go on my own, when Mum gets in there first.

'I agree,' she says, reapplying her lipstick. 'If anyone sees this man, it should be me. Me and Janice'll go.'

'Janice and I,' corrects Alicia, and I shoot her daggers. Grammar? Really? At this moment in time?

'We'll go.' Janice nods enthusiastically.

'D'you want me to come too?' I suggest. 'For moral support?'

'No, love, I don't. Whatever I have to hear about Dad and his past . . .' Mum looks into the middle distance. 'The truth is, love, I'd rather you weren't there to hear about his other woman.'

'Mum, you don't know it's another woman!'

'I know, Becky,' she says, with a quivering voice like the heroine of a true-life mini series. 'I *know*.'

Oh God. Does she know? I'm torn between: a) Mum is just believing the worst because she's a drama queen . . . and b) After decades of marriage she has a wife's intuition and of *course* she knows.

'Well, OK,' I say at last. 'You go with Janice.'

'We're right here,' says Luke. 'Keep your phone with you.'

'Ask him about Tarkie,' puts in Suze. 'He might know something.'

'Ask him if his property is for sale,' adds Danny. 'I have a friend, works for Fred Segal, he's *longing* for a ranch and this looks perfect—'

'Danny!' I say crossly. 'This isn't about real estate! It's about . . .' I look at Mum, whose lips are tightly pursed. 'It's about finding out the truth.'

There's silence as Mum and Janice head over the arid scrubland to the huge wooden gates. There's an intercom system and I can see them talking into it. Mum speaks first. Then, to my surprise, Janice tries, then Mum again. But the gates remain stubbornly closed. What is going on?

At last, Mum and Janice head back, and as they near us, I can tell Mum's upset.

'He turned us away!' she exclaims. 'Can you believe it?'

At once a babble breaks out:

'Oh my God!'

'Turned you *away*?'

'Did you actually speak to him?' I demand above the noise. 'To Raymond himself?'

'Yes! At first it was some kind of housekeeper, but she went to fetch him and I said I was Graham's wife and explained what's happened—' She breaks off. 'Didn't I, Janice?'

'You did.' Janice nods. 'Wonderfully, love. Very clear, very to the point.'

'And . . . ?' I say.

'And he said he couldn't help!' Mum's voice rises in distress. 'We've driven over six hours, just to see him, and he can't help! Janice tried speaking to him, too . . .'

'We tried everything,' says Janice dolefully.

'But he wouldn't even let us in for five minutes. Even though he could see me! Through his video system! I know he could see how upset I was. But he still said no.'

'Could you see him?' I ask with sudden interest. 'What does he look like?'

'Oh no,' says Mum. 'We couldn't see him. He's hidden himself away, hasn't he?'

158

We all turn to look at the gates, resolutely closed against the world. There's a kind of burning in my chest. Who does this man think he is? How can he be so mean? To my *mum*?

'I'll go,' says Alicia firmly, and before anyone can protest, she's striding towards the gates, pulling out one of her Golden Peace business cards. We all watch dumbly as she presses the buzzer, speaks, holds up her card to the camera, speaks again, starts getting really angry, and eventually swings away.

'This is outrageous!' she's spitting as she rejoins the group. 'He claimed not to have heard of Golden Peace! Well, clearly he's a liar. I don't know why we're wasting our time with him.'

'He's the only lead we've got!' says Mum.

'Well, perhaps your husband should have chosen his friends more carefully,' says Alicia, her old snide manner reappearing.

'Well, perhaps you should keep your opinions to yourself!' responds Mum hotly, and for a moment I think she and Alicia might start some full-scale row, but Luke intervenes.

'Let me have a go,' he says, and heads off towards the ranch entrance. As he speaks into the microphone we're all watching agog, hoping maybe he knows the special magic words, like Ali Baba at the cave entrance. But soon he turns and shakes his head. As he rejoins the group, he's looking pensive.

'I don't think we'll crack him,' he says. 'He sent his housekeeper to talk to me. He doesn't want to engage.'

'So what do we do?' wails Mum. 'Here he is, he *must*

know the story . . .' She waves a hand angrily at the gates.

'Regroup,' says Luke. 'It's getting late. We need to eat and sleep. Maybe we'll come up with a bright idea over some food.'

I think we're all hoping that the food will trigger a moment of genius in one of us. As we tuck into steaks and fries and cornbread at the Tall Rock Inn, Cactus Creek, there's a feeling of optimism. Surely one of us will think of something brilliant?

Oh, come on. Someone has to think of *something*.

People keep starting sentences with 'Ooh! Maybe . . .' and then losing confidence and trailing off into silence. I've had about five ideas involving scaling the walls of Raymond's ranch, which I *haven't* shared.

The trouble is, I don't think any of us had thought much beyond finding Raymond, being welcomed into his ranch and offered beds for the night, and having a wonderful supper, while Raymond got Dad on the phone and sorted everything out. (Well, that's what I was expecting, anyway.)

As the steak plates are cleared away and the dessert menus handed round, conversation has died away to a minimum and I'm wondering who'll be first to say, 'Let's give up.'

It won't be me. No way. I'm here till the bitter end. But it might be Janice. She's looking a bit frayed around the edges. I bet she's longing to get back to Oxshott.

'So can I get you folks anything for dessert?' Our waitress, Mary-Jo, has approached the table.

'*You* don't know any way to get in touch with Raymond Earle, do you?' I say impulsively. 'We're here to see him but he's being a bit reclusive.'

'Raymond Earle?' She wrinkles her brow. 'Guy up at Red Ranch?'

'Exactly.' I feel a surge of hope. 'Do you know him?'

Maybe she works for him part-time, I think with sudden optimism. Maybe I can get into the ranch with her, pretending to be her assistant—

'Sorry, hon.' Mary-Jo's voice interrupts my thoughts. 'We don't see a lot of him. Hey, Patty?' She turns to the woman at the bar. 'These folks are after Raymond Earle.'

'We don't see a lot of him,' echoes Patty, shaking her head.

'That's right.' Mary-Jo turns back to us. 'We don't see a lot of him.'

'Oh well. Thanks anyway,' I say, deflated. 'Could I have apple pie please?'

'He'll be at the fair tomorrow.' A hoarse voice comes from the corner and we all turn to see an elderly guy with a beard and a proper cowboy shirt with those metal collar tips. 'He'll be showing his pots and such.'

Everyone at the table swivels round in excitement, even Minnie.

'Seriously?'

'Will he definitely be there?'

'Where's the fair?' Luke enquires. 'What time does it start?'

'It's up at Wilderness.' Mary-Jo looks surprised. 'Wilderness County Fair. I assumed that's why you folks were in town. It's on all week, you can't miss it.'

'And Raymond will be there?' persists Mum.

'He's usually there.' The bearded guy nods. 'Exhibits his pots in the Ceramics Tent. Charges silly dollars. No one buys 'em, far as I can make out.'

'Y'all should go, if you've never been,' says Mary-Jo with enthusiasm. 'It's the best fair in the state. You got the livestock show, the pageant, the line dancing . . .'

Line dancing? Oh my God, I've *always* wanted to do line dancing.

I mean, not that we're here to do line dancing. I shoot a guilty look at Suze, in case she read my thoughts.

'OK, this sounds like a plan.' Luke is addressing the table. 'We stay overnight, hit the fair first thing, find Raymond in the art tent and pin him down.'

There's a huge air of relief around the table. At last, Mum's anxious frown has melted away. Let's just hope this Raymond character comes up with the goods, I find myself thinking. Otherwise, we really will be at the end of the road, and I don't know *what* I'll do with Mum.

The next day I awake full of optimism. Wilderness County Fair, here we come! We slept at the Treeside Lodge, Wilderness, last night, which had a big cancellation and was very glad to have some last-minute visitors. Janice and Mum had to squash into one tiny room, which isn't ideal, but it was that or the RV.

Every other guest at the Lodge is here for the fair, which we discovered at breakfast. The other families were all wearing Wilderness County Fair T-shirts and baseball caps and talking about their plans for the day, and the excitement was contagious. I Googled the fair last night, and it's huge! It has a zillion tents and stalls, plus a rodeo, livestock shows and a huge Ferris wheel. According to the map the Ceramics Tent is situated in the north-west corner of the fair. It's near the Best-Decorated Sheaves Tent and the Clogging Festival, while nearby is the Rodeo Arena, which will hold the Wild-Cow Milking, the Pig Scramble and the Mutton Bustin'.

It's like a foreign language to me. A whole tent for decorated sheaves? How do you decorate a sheaf, anyway? And what's 'clogging'? And what on earth is a pig scramble? Let alone 'mutton bustin''?

'Luke, what do you think mutton bustin' is?' I say, looking up from the laptop.

'No idea,' he says, putting on his watch. 'A mutton-eating competition?'

'Mutton-eating?' I make a face.

'There's an Oreo-stacking contest, in case you're interested,' he adds. 'Saw it on the website last night.'

Now, *that* sounds good. I think I might be rather brilliant at stacking Oreos. I can already see myself, pre-siding over a ten-foot stack, beaming at the audience as I receive first prize, which is probably a packet of Oreos.

Not that we're going to enter the competitions, I hastily remind myself. We're here for business. We'll probably only stay for half an hour.

'Ready?' I say to Luke, as he reaches for his wallet. 'Ready, Minnie? Ready for the fair?'

'Fair!' shouts Minnie joyously. 'See Winnie-the-Pooh!'

Hmm. This is the trouble with taking your child to

Disneyland. They then think all other fairs are Disneyland too, and it's no use trying to explain to a two-year-old about branding and copyright, like Luke did last night.

'We *might* see Winnie-the-Pooh,' I say, just as Luke says, 'We *won't* see Winnie-the-Pooh.'

Minnie looks from Luke to me, confused.

'We *won't* see Winnie-the-Pooh,' I amend quickly, just as Luke says, 'We *might* see Winnie-the-Pooh.'

Argh. Every parenting book says the most important thing you can do is present a united front, otherwise your child gets confused and starts to exploit the differences between you. Which I do totally believe in, but it can be a challenge. There was one time when Luke said, 'Mummy's just going out now, Minnie,' when I'd changed my plans, and rather than contradict him, I went out of the front door shouting 'Byee!' then climbed back in through a window.

(Mum said I was totally mad and that parenting books cause more harm than good, and she and Dad never bothered with all that nonsense, and 'Look how *you* turned out, Becky.' Whereupon Luke made this stifled little noise and then said, 'No, nothing,' when we all turned to look at him.)

I've dressed Minnie up in her little blue jeans and a new fringed suede waistcoat, which Luke bought her yesterday, and she looks absolutely delicious: a proper Western girl. I'm wearing shorts and a sleeveless top and I've glanced at myself in the mirror and . . . I look fine. I'll do.

Somehow I can't get excited about what I look like any more. I'm waiting for some bit of my brain to click in – the bit that would normally go 'Woohoo! County fair! What's the perfect outfit for that?' But it doesn't. It's silent.

'Ready?' says Luke at the door.

'Yup.' I force a smile. 'Let's go.'

It's fine. Whatever. Maybe I'm just finally growing up.

As we arrive down in the lobby, everyone is assembled and there's an air of anticipation.

'OK, so we'll head straight for the Ceramics Tent,' Luke addresses the group. 'Jane will approach Raymond, along with Becky, with the rest of us on standby.'

There was a bit of a tussle last night about who should accompany Mum to accost Raymond. Janice reckoned she was Best Friend, but I countered with Daughter. Then Suze suggested, 'Couldn't we all go?' but got shouted down. Anyway, I won, on the grounds that whatever Raymond says about Dad, good or bad, Mum and I should hear it first.

The only person who wasn't remotely interested in meeting Raymond was Alicia. In fact, she's not even coming to the fair. She says she's arranged a meeting in Tucson. A *meeting in Tucson*? I mean, honestly. Who arranges meetings in Tucson?

Well, I suppose people who live in Tucson do. But, you know. Apart from them.

I don't believe this 'meeting in Tucson' story for a minute. Alicia's up to something, I'm convinced of it. And if I could, I'd keep tabs on her. But I can't, because: 1. I have to go to the fair, and 2. she's already left for the day in a limo.

Suze is sitting on a chair made out of a barrel, hunched

over her phone, frantically texting. Presumably she's texting Alicia, because they've been apart for, like, twenty minutes. She looks absolutely deathly, and I want to put an arm around her, or shake her out of her cloud of misery. But I don't even dare approach her. Not only is Suze not my 3 a.m. friend, I think dolefully, she's not even my 9 a.m.-sitting-five-feet-away friend.

'OK?' Luke interrupts my thoughts. 'Everyone ready? Ready, Jane?'

'Oh, I'm ready,' says Mum, with a meaningful, almost ominous look. 'I'm ready.'

We hear the fair before we see it. There's music blasting through the hot air as we snake along in the queue to the RV park. Once we're parked we have to buy passes, and then we have to find the right entrance, and we're all quite hot and bothered as, finally, we make it through Gate B.

(You'd think Gate B would be next to Gate A. You'd think.)

'Goodness!' says Janice, as we all look around. 'It's very . . . fulsome!'

I know what she means. Everywhere there's something bright or blaring or plain extraordinary. There are tents and stalls as far as the eye can see. Every loudspeaker seems to be playing a different tune. A blimp above us in the sky reads *Wilderness County Fair*, and beneath it are soaring a couple of helium balloons, silver dots against the blue, which must have been let go by mistake. A troupe of cheerleaderish girls in aquamarine costumes is hurrying into a nearby tent and I can see Minnie watching them in awe. A man leads a massive woolly sheep past us on a rope and I instinctively take a step back.

'Bex!' Suze rolls her eyes. 'It's only a sheep.'

Hmph. She may say, 'Only a sheep.' But that animal has huge curly horns and an evil eye. It's probably the prize-winning exhibit in the Killer Sheep Event.

The air is full of mingled smells – fuel, animal dung, roasting meat, and the sweet pungent aroma of freshly made doughnuts, which is particularly strong, as we're standing right by a doughnut stand.

'Cake!' says Minnie, suddenly spotting the stall. 'I *like* it, Mummy.' She tugs on my arm yearningly, almost pulling me over.

'No cake,' I say hurriedly, and start leading her away. 'Come on, let's find these ceramics.'

Even though it's early, there are already crowds of people everywhere: clustering to get into tents, queuing for food, wandering along the lanes between the attractions, and suddenly stopping to consult their fair maps. So it takes us a little time to make it all the way to the Creative Village, and then we can't work out which tent we want. Mum is totally focused, barging along, her chin set, but Janice keeps getting distracted by exhibits and I have to tug her away, saying, 'You can look at the embroidered pot-holders *later.*' Honestly, she's worse than Minnie.

At last we make it to the Ceramics Tent and consult the Exhibitors' Guide. Raymond is in the Adult Ceramics and China section, and has entered the Bowl class, the Container With Lid class and the Miscellaneous class. He's also got some pieces in the For Sale Gallery. It's easy to tell which are his, because they're about five times the size of anyone else's. It's also obvious that he's not here, because apart from us, only seven people are in the tent, and they're all women.

For a couple of minutes, Mum and I circle the exhibits in silence, pausing by each of Raymond's pieces as though it might give us a clue. He's put a piece of paper by each entry, which goes on about the influence of the French ceramicist Pauline Audette (who?) and how he takes inspiration from nature and some other waffle about glazes.

'Well, he's not here,' says Mum, finally, as we reach a wide bowl with green glaze on it, which takes up nearly a whole table.

'But he must have *been* here,' I point out. 'Maybe he'll come back. Um, excuse me?' I address a lady in a strappy vest-top, who's standing at the next table. 'We're looking for Raymond Earle. Do you know him? Do you think he'll come to the tent today?'

'Oh, Raymond,' says the woman, and rolls her eyes slightly. 'He was here earlier. He might be along later. But he doesn't hang around.'

'Thank you. Is that your vase?' I add. 'It's beautiful.'

This is a total lie, as it's the most ugly thing I've ever seen. But I'm thinking we should make a few friends and allies in case we have to tackle Raymond to the ground or anything.

'Why, thank you,' says the woman, and pats it protectively. 'I have pieces for sale, too, if you're interested.' She points to the gallery, which is at the far end.

'Great!' I say, trying to sound enthused. 'I'll look at

those later. So, are you influenced by Pauline Audette too?'

'Pauline Audette?' the woman says sharply. 'What is it with this Pauline Audette? I'd never even *heard* of her before I met Raymond. You know he wrote her in France? Asked her to come and judge the contest? Never heard back, *not* that he'll admit it.' Her eyes glitter at me. 'You ask me, it's pretentious.'

'Totally pretentious,' I hastily agree.

'Why do we need a French judge when we have Erica Fromm living right here in Tucson?'

'Erica Fromm.' I nod. 'Totally.'

'Do you throw yourself?' She focuses on me with renewed interest.

'Oh . . . Um . . .' I can't bring myself to say a flat no. 'Well . . . a bit. You know, when I have time.'

Which is sort of almost true. I mean, I did pottery at school, and maybe I'll take it up again. I have a sudden image of myself in a potter's smock, making some fabulous vase while Luke stands behind me nuzzling my neck. And everybody opening their presents on Christmas Day and saying, 'Wow, Becky, we didn't realize you were so artistic!' I don't know *why* I've never thought of doing pottery before.

'So . . . good luck,' I add. 'Lovely to meet you. I'm Becky, by the way.'

'Dee.' She shakes my hand and I beat a retreat to Mum, who is looking at a collection of tiny clay dolls.

'Well?' She looks up eagerly. 'Did you learn anything?'

'Apparently Raymond might be back later,' I tell her. 'We'll just have to stake out the tent.'

It's Luke who takes charge of the stakeout rota. Mum and Janice will do the first hour, because they both want to look at the pottery anyway. Danny will be on second, but first he's going to the refreshments tent for a traditional Wilderness Iced Tea, which is apparently 80 per cent bourbon.

'I'll take Minnie to Toddlerville, and buy her a balloon, and we'll be on third,' says Luke in that commanding way he has. 'And Becky, why don't you and Suze take the fourth hour? You could just hang out meanwhile. Enjoy the fair together. That OK by you, Suze?'

Oh God. I know exactly what Luke's doing. He's trying to push Suze and me together so we can make up. Which is really sweet of him. But I feel like a panda being told to mate with another panda that clearly doesn't fancy me. Suze looks totally unenthusiastic at the idea of hanging out with me. Her forehead is puckered in a frown, and she shoots me a dark, unfriendly look.

'I don't mind staking out the tent on my own,' she says. 'You and Becky and Minnie should stay together.'

I feel a little stabbing pain in my heart. Is she really that anti-me? She can't even bear to spend a couple of hours in my company?

'No, it's better to do it this way,' says Luke briskly. 'And as we're walking round the fair, we can all keep an eye out for Raymond.'

Last night, Luke found a photo of Raymond on a Tucson news website. And I don't want to boast, but my dad is *so* much handsomer than all his old friends. If Corey looks plasticky and weird, then Raymond looks ancient. He has these big, grey, tufty eyebrows, and in the picture he's frowning at the camera in a really moody way.

'There's a bit of phone signal,' Luke is saying, 'although it's patchy. So if anyone sees Raymond, immediately text the others. OK?'

As everyone disperses, Luke shoots me a little meaningful look, which I think is supposed to mean 'Chin up' – then he and Minnie disappear into the mêlée. And it's just Suze and me.

I haven't been alone with Suze for . . . I can't even remember. The sun suddenly seems hot on my head, and my skin feels prickly. I take a few deep breaths, trying to relax. As I glance at Suze, I see she's staring down at the ground, as though she doesn't even want to acknowledge my existence. I don't know what to say. I don't know where to begin.

She's sitting on a stack of upturned crates, wearing blue jeans and a white T-shirt and these ancient cowboy boots which she always used to wear in London. They look perfect here, and I want to tell her so, but something's blocking my throat. As I draw breath to say something – *anything* – her phone bleeps. She pulls it out, stares at it intently, and closes her eyes.

'Suze?' I say nervously.

'*What?*' she lashes out. I haven't even suggested anything yet and she's being aggressive.

'I just . . . What do you want to do first?' I pull out the Fair Guide with trembling fingers. 'Shall we go and look at the pigs?'

This is a supreme sacrifice on my part, because I'm

actually quite scared of pigs. I mean, I'm not wild about sheep either, but pigs are terrifying. Suze and Tarkie have some on the farm in Hampshire and honestly, they're like these malevolent, squealing monsters.

But Suze loves them and gives them all names. And maybe if we go and look at them here, we can bond over how pointy their ears are, or whatever.

'American pigs are probably really interesting,' I persist, as Suze hasn't replied. 'Or sheep? They have all these rare species . . . or look, there's a pygmy-goat event!'

As Suze looks up, her gaze is absent. I don't think she heard a word.

'Bex, I've got to do something,' she says. 'I'll catch up with you later, OK?' She swings her legs off the crates and is instantly gone, hurrying past the Ceramics Tent and into the crowd.

'Suze?' I stare after her in shock. *'Suze?'*

She can't just leave me like that. We're supposed to be a team. We're supposed to stick together. Before I stop to think whether this is a good idea or not, I'm following her.

Luckily Suze is so tall and her hair is so fair, it's easy to keep track of her, even though the crowds are getting heavier by the minute. She heads determinedly past the Rodeo Stadium, through the Food Village, past the kids' petting area and even stalks straight past an arena where a guy is getting his dog to jump through a hoop. She doesn't even *look* at all the stalls of cowboy hats and boots and saddles, even though I know she'd normally spend hours stroking them. She's tense and preoccupied. I can see it in the set of her shoulders. And I can see it in her expression as she finally comes to a stop, in a clearing behind the Hog Roast.

She leans against a tall wooden post, and gets out her phone. She looks worse than preoccupied, I realize with a lurch. She looks desperate. Who's she texting, Alicia?

As my own phone bleeps, I hastily back away, well out of sight. I'm fully expecting a text from Mum, or Luke, or even Danny – but it's from Tarquin.

Hi Becky. Just checking in. Is Suze OK?

I stare at the phone in sudden outrage. No, she is not OK. She is *not OK*! I jab at Tarkie's number and retreat yet further, into a tent full of home-made preserves.

'Becky?' Tarquin sounds surprised I've phoned. 'Everything all right?'

'Tarkie, do you have any idea what we're going through?' I practically scream. 'Suze is utterly miserable, we're staking out some guy at a county fair, my mum has no idea what my dad's been up to . . .'

'You're not still on that, are you?' Tarquin sounds shocked.

'Of course we are!'

'Can't you give your dad some privacy, for God's sake?' Tarquin sounds quite angry. 'Can't you *trust* him?'

I'm drawn up short. I hadn't thought of it like that. And just for a moment, I feel chastened – until my blood starts boiling again. It's all very well for these blokes to rush off on their mission, thinking they're all cool and hero-like. What about those of us left behind, who thought they were dead?

'Couldn't he trust my mum?' I counter furiously.

'Couldn't you trust Suze? You're married! You should share things!'

There's silence, and I know I've touched a nerve. I want to say more. I want to wail, 'Be happy with Suze! Be happy!'

But you can't interfere in another couple's relationship. It's like trying to step inside a cloud. The whole thing kind of dissipates, till you get back out again.

'Anyway, you can't follow us any more,' says Tarkie, after a painful pause. 'The three of us have split up. There's nothing to follow.'

'You've split *up*?' I stare at the phone. 'What do you mean?'

'We've all gone our separate ways. I'm helping your dad out with . . .' He hesitates. 'Something. He's doing his own thing. Bryce has disappeared off, God knows where.'

'Bryce has *disappeared*?' I say in shock.

'Left last night. No idea where.'

'Oh right.'

I feel totally wrong-footed. After all that. Bryce hasn't ensnared Tarquin in his evil plan at all. He hasn't brainwashed him or fleeced him or even made him start selling time-shares. He's just buggered off.

'Becky, go back to LA,' says Tarquin, as though reading my mind. 'Call off the search. Give it up.'

'But we might be able to help you,' I persist. 'What are you doing? What's going on?'

Let us in! I feel like shouting. *Please!*

'We don't need your help,' says Tarquin adamantly. 'Tell Suze I'm OK. I'm helping your dad. I'm feeling

174

useful for the first time in . . . for ever. I'm going to do this, OK? And I don't need any interference from you or Suze. Bye, Becky.'

And with that, he rings off. I've never felt so powerless in my life. I want to cry with frustration, or at least savagely kick a barrel.

OK, it turns out savagely kicking a barrel didn't make me feel any better. (I'm wearing flip-flops and barrels are really hard.) Nor did pounding a fist into my palm like they do in the movies. (I've never understood the appeal of boxing and now I understand it even less. My hand hurts just from *me* punching it. Imagine if it was someone else and you couldn't tell them to stop.)

The only thing that will make me feel better, I realize, is talking to Suze. I need to tell her about Tarkie's calls. I have to tell her that he's safe and away from Bryce. This is a matter of urgency and I must be brave and not shy away from the task.

But as I creep out of the Preserves Tent, I feel a swoop of nerves. Suze looks about as approachable as a lioness who's guarding her cubs, the family food and the Crown Jewels, all at once. She's prowling around the clearing, her phone grasped in her right hand, her brows lowered and her eyes flitting from side to side.

I've started to rehearse possible casual conversational openers in my mind – *Gosh, Suze, fancy bumping into you here* – when she stops dead. She's standing still, watching alertly. Waiting for something. What?

A moment later I can see what she can see, coming towards her and I gasp so strongly, I nearly black out. *No!* I must be hallucinating. I can't be seeing what

175

I'm seeing. But the tall, loping figure is unmistakable. It's Bryce.

Bryce. Himself. Here. At the Wilderness County Fair.

My jaw sags as I watch him approach Suze. He's as good-looking and burnished as ever, wearing cut-offs and flip-flops. He looks easy and relaxed whereas Suze looks absolutely desperate. But she doesn't look surprised to see him. Clearly this was all pre-arranged. But . . . what?

I mean, *what?*

How can Suze be meeting Bryce? How?

We've been chasing Bryce. We've been worrying about what Bryce was up to. We've been talking about Bryce, trying to get inside his mind, practically believing he was a serial killer. Was Suze *in touch with him all along?*

Inside, I'm whimpering with confusion. I want to cry out, *Whaaaaat? Explain!* I want to barge up and say, *You can't do this!*

But all I can do is watch mutely, as they have some kind of conversation I can't hear. Suze's arms are crossed protectively across her body and she's talking in short, jabbing sentences, whereas Bryce looks as calm and laid-back as he always did. I half-expect to see him produce a volleyball and start bouncing it around.

At last they seem to come to some conclusion. Bryce gives a single nod, then puts a hand on Suze's arm. She shakes it off with such ferocity that even I jump, and Bryce gives a shrug. He seems quite amused. Then he lopes away, through the crowd, and Suze is left alone.

She slumps down on a nearby decorative hay bale, her head bowed, looking so despairing that a couple of passers-by give her mildly concerned looks. She's in such a trance that I almost don't dare disturb her. Something tells me she's going to lash out at me even more viciously when she realizes I saw her with Bryce.

But I have to. This isn't just about our friendship any more. This is about everything.

I step forward resolutely, one foot in front of the other, and wait till she looks up. Her head jerks and for a moment she looks like a cornered animal. Every muscle in her body is tense. Her eyes dart about frantically, as though to check whether anyone else is with me – then, as she accepts I'm alone, they gradually settle back on me.

'Suze . . .' I begin, but my voice comes out all husky and I don't quite know where I'm going.

'Did you . . .' She swallows as though she can't bring herself to say it, and I nod.

'Suze—'

'Don't.' She cuts me off, her voice trembling. Her eyes are bloodshot. She looks ill, I think suddenly. Ill with worry. And it's not because she thinks Tarkie's unsafe. It's something else, something she's been keeping from all of us.

For what seems like an age, we just look at each other, and it's almost as if we're having a silent conversation.

I wish you'd talked to me.

I do too.

Things have got pretty bad, haven't they?

Yes.

So let's sort it out.

I can see Suze's defences lowering, little by little. Her

shoulders slowly drop. Her jaw relaxes. She meets my eye properly, for the first time in ages, and I feel a horrible pang at how desperate she looks.

But there's something else going on here. There's a kind of shift in the balance between us. For as long as I can remember, I've been the one to get in scrapes and Suze has been the one to help me out of them. It's just the way we are. Now, though, things feel reversed. I don't know exactly what's been going on – but I do know something. Suze is in a big old mess.

I have a zillion questions I want to fire at her, but I think she needs to calm down a bit first.

'C'mon,' I say. 'I don't care what time in the morning it is, we need a titchy.'

I lead her into the Tequila Tasting Tent, and she meekly follows, her face downcast. I order tequila shots and hand her one. Then I face her full-on, with a business-like look, and say, 'OK, Suze. You need to tell me everything. What's up with you and Bryce?'

And of course, as soon as I see her face, I know.

I mean, I pretty much knew as soon as I saw him appear. But it's seeing her face which drives a kind of dagger-blow into my heart. 'Suze, you *didn't*.'

'No!' she says, as though I've scalded her. 'Not *completely* . . .'

'What's not completely?'

'I . . . we . . .' She looks around the bar. 'Shall we find a better place to sit?'

'Suze. Just tell me.' There's a lump in my throat. 'Have you been unfaithful to Tarkie?'

I'm having a sudden flashback to their wedding. Suze

looked so radiant and beautiful. She and Tarkie were so hopeful and optimistic. We were all so hopeful and optimistic.

And OK, Tarkie may be a bit weird at times. He may have odd taste in clothes. And music. And everything. But there's no way he'd ever be unfaithful to Suze, no *way*. Just the thought of how hurt he'd be if he found out is bringing tears to my eyes.

'I . . .' Her hands flutter around her throat. 'What counts as unfaithful? Kissing?'

'You only kissed?'

'Not exactly.'

'Did you—'

'No!' She hesitates. 'Not *exactly*.'

There's a pause, while my imagination gallops around several assorted scenarios.

'Did you *feel* unfaithful?'

There's another long pause. And suddenly there are tears in Suze's eyes too.

'Yes,' she says, with a wretched defiance. 'Yes. I *wanted* to be. I'd just had enough. Tarkie was so miserable, and everything was so difficult in England, and Bryce was all fresh and positive and . . . you know . . .'

'Sex-god-like.'

I can remember Suze and Bryce meeting for the first time and thinking that there was a spark between them. But never in a million *years* did I think . . .

It just goes to show: I'm not suspicious enough. That's it. I'm never trusting anything again. I expect everyone's having affairs with everyone else and I just haven't noticed.

179

'Exactly,' Suze is saying. 'He was just so different. So confident about everything.'

'So when did you . . .' My mind is spooling back, trying to work it out. 'I mean, you didn't go to Golden Peace *that* much . . . Was it in the evenings?'

'Don't ask me when!' Suze cries out in anguish. 'Don't ask me for dates and times and places! It was a mistake, OK! I realize that now. But it's too late. He's got me.'

'What do you mean, he's got you?'

'He wants money,' says Suze flatly. 'Lots of it.'

'You're not *giving* it to him, are you?' I stare at her.

'What else can I do?'

'Suze! You mustn't!' I feel almost faint with horror. 'You mustn't give him anything!'

'But he'll tell Tarkie!' Tears start pouring down Suze's face. 'And my marriage will be over . . . the children . . .' She stares into her tequila glass. 'Bex, I've screwed up my whole life and I don't know what to do. I couldn't tell anyone. I've been so lonely.'

I feel a tweak of hurt. Well, possibly indignation. Well, possibly anger.

'You could have told me,' I say, trying to sound calm, as opposed to hurt and indignant and angry. 'You could always have confided in *me*, Suze.'

'No, I couldn't! You and Luke have this perfect relationship. You would never have understood.'

What? How can she *say* that?

'We nearly split up in LA!' I retort in disbelief. 'We had a terrible row and Luke went home to England and I didn't know if he'd even come back. So, I think I might have understood. If you'd given me a chance.'

180

'Oh.' Suze wipes her eyes. 'Well . . . Oh. I didn't know things were so bad.'

'I tried to tell you, but you weren't interested! You shut me out!'

'Well, you shut *me* out!'

We're gazing at each other, breathing hard, both with flushed cheeks and tequila glasses clutched in our hands. I feel as if finally I'm peeling away the layers and saying to Suze what I really want to say.

'OK, Suze, maybe I did shut you out.' My words erupt: 'Maybe I did get it wrong in LA. But you know what? I've said sorry a zillion times, I've come with you on this trip, I'm doing my best . . . and you haven't even *looked* at me. You won't talk to me, you won't meet my eye, all you do is criticize me. All you care about is Alicia. But I'm supposed to be your friend.' A mountain of old hurt is rising through me and my eyes are suddenly hot with tears. 'I'm supposed to be your *friend*, Suze.'

'I know,' she whispers, staring into her glass. 'I know you are.'

'So why are you treating me like this?' I wipe roughly at my face. 'And I'm not making it up. Luke's noticed it too.'

'Oh God.' Suze looks more anguished than ever. 'I know. I've been so horrible. But I couldn't even look at you.'

'Why not?' I feel so agitated, I'm practically shouting. 'Why not?'

'Because I knew you'd guess everything!' she bursts out. 'You *know* me, Bex. Alicia doesn't. I can get away with pretending when I'm with Alicia.' As she raises her

181

head, she's properly crying. I mean, her face is blotchy-red and her nose is running and everything. 'I can't keep anything from you.'

'You kept Bryce from me,' I point out.

'By avoiding you. Oh God, Bex.' Suze clutches her hair. 'I've been in such a state for so long . . . I wish I'd told you from the start . . .'

I've never seen Suze look so piteous. She seems kind of smaller and all her Suze-ebullience has gone. Her face is drawn and her hair is all greasy underneath the extensions.

'What if my marriage ends, Bex?' she gulps, and I feel an answering thud of dread in my chest.

'It won't. Suze, it'll be OK.' I fling my arms around her. 'Don't cry. We'll work it out.'

'I've been so stupid,' Suze sobs. 'Soooooo stupid. Haven't I?'

But I don't say anything in return. I just hug her tighter.

I've been stupid before. I've had things catch up with me before. And Suze has never been mean or told me off. She's always been supportive. So that's what I'll be, too.

As we sit there, letting the Mexican music wash over us, I'm thinking back to when things first started going wrong between me and Suze. I thought it was all my fault. I thought it was because of me and my preoccupations. It never occurred to me that she might have a preoccupation of her own.

'Oh my God.' I look up as it hits me. '*That's* why you've been so desperate to get Tarkie away from Bryce. In case Bryce tells him.'

182

'That was part of it,' Suze admits.

'Wait.' I give a tiny gasp. 'Did you *invent* the whole brainwashing thing?'

'No! I was genuinely worried about Tarkie!' says Suze defensively. 'He's really vulnerable. And Bryce is an evil, manipulative—' She stops herself and takes a deep breath. 'He's after money wherever he can get it. At first he thought Tarkie had all the money, so he went after him. Then he worked out I have my own money too, so he . . . Well.' She swallows. 'He moved on to me.'

'You can't give him any. You do know that.' Suze doesn't react and I eye her sternly. 'You do know that, don't you, Suze? What have you said to him?'

'I've said I'll meet him at seven p.m. and give him some money,' mumbles Suze.

'*Suze!*'

'Well, what else can I do?'

'If you pay him once, he'll have you in his power for ever. Never give in to a blackmailer. Everyone knows that.'

'But what if he tells Tarkie?' Suze puts down her empty shot glass and thrusts her hands through her hair again. 'Bex, what if I've really fucked up? What if Tarkie and I split up? What about the children?' Her voice is trembling. 'I've jeopardized my whole life, everything . . .'

A guy from the Mexican band comes up and shakes his maracas at Suze with a beam on his face. He offers her one to shake too, but he's picked the wrong girl.

'Leave me *alone!*' yells Suze, and the maracas man backs away, startled.

For a while we both sit there in silence. My head is spinning a bit, and it's not just from the tequila. I still have a zillion questions for Suze, like, *Who made the first move?* and *What do you mean, 'not exactly'?* But I can't start quizzing her now. The important thing is to get rid of Bryce.

'Suze, Tarkie won't leave you,' I say abruptly.

'Why wouldn't he? *I'd* leave me.' She looks up with miserable eyes. 'I can be a real nightmare. I lose my temper with him and I say all kinds of frightful things . . .'

'I know,' I say awkwardly. 'He told me. Look, Suze, you should know something. I've been in contact with Tarkie without telling you.'

Her eyes spark in shock and she draws a long breath. For an awful moment I think she's going to shout at me. But then she exhales and the rage sort of subsides.

'Right,' she says at last. 'I might have known. And he said, "My wife's a bitch."'

'No! Of course he didn't!' I try to think of how to put it tactfully. 'He said . . . um . . . you'd had difficulties.'

'Difficulties!' She gives a short bitter laugh.

'No, but listen, Suze,' I continue eagerly. 'It's all *good*. Tarquin's far stronger than you think. He's separated from my dad now, he's doing his own thing to help and he sounds really positive. I don't reckon Bryce brainwashed him at all. I think the reason he was so ratty in LA was . . . other things.'

'Me.'

'Not just you. The whole situation. But now he's got away . . . he feels useful . . . I think he's in a better place.'

Suze is silent for a moment, mulling this over.

'Tarkie adores your dad,' she says at last. 'Your dad is the father he would have loved to have had.'

'I know.'

'Did he say what they're doing?'

'Of course not.' I roll my eyes. 'He told me to give my dad some privacy and go back to LA.'

'Maybe he's got a point.' Suze draws her feet up on to her bar stool and wraps her arms around her knees. 'I mean, what are we doing? What are we all *doing*?'

I think this is one of those questions that you don't actually reply to. So instead of saying, *We're tracking Tarkie because you told us to, Suze*, I just sip my tequila.

'I feel like I've been in this horrible crazy place,' Suze says suddenly. 'And I took it out on you, Bex.'

'No you didn't.' I shrug, feeling embarrassed.

'I did.' She gazes at me with huge, miserable eyes. 'I've been hateful. I can't believe you're still talking to me.'

'Well . . .' I hesitate, trying to find the words. 'You're my friend. And I was pretty hateful in LA. We've both been hateful.'

'I was *more* hateful,' says Suze emphatically. 'Because I tried to make you feel guilty all the time. But what was I doing? *What was I doing?*' Her voice rises in distress and fresh tears start flooding down her face. 'It's been a kind of madness. Ever since I came out to LA, I felt like I wanted to escape my boring old British life. But now I'd give anything to . . .' She trails off and scrubs at her eyes. 'I'd give anything for . . .'

'You *can* have your life back. But first, you have to *not* give any money to Bryce.'

185

Suze is silent for a while, twisting her hands round and round.

'But what if he tells Tarkie?' she whispers at last.

'You can't wait for that.' I steel myself to say what I know is right. 'Suze, you have to tell Tarkie yourself. As soon as possible.'

As she gazes back at me, she looks utterly ill. But after what feels like about half an hour, she nods.

I think I feel nearly as sick as Suze does. I've had to admit plenty of awkward things to Luke over the years, like when I sold his six Tiffany clocks on eBay without telling him. But selling Tiffany clocks and kissing another man aren't even in the same *category*.

And when I say 'kissing' I'm being kind to Suze, because it was obviously far more than kissing. (Although exactly what? She still won't tell me and I'm obviously too mature to ask her to draw a stick diagram. I'll just have to use my imagination.)

(Actually, no, don't do that. Urgh. *Bad* imagination.)

We've agreed that I'll make the call and then pass the phone over to her, and as I press the speed-dial button, my heart is pumping.

'Tarkie!' I say fiercely as soon as he answers. 'Listen. You have to talk to Suze, right now, and if you don't, I'm never speaking to you again, and when I tell my dad, he won't either. This is *stupid*. You can't keep phoning me and avoiding Suze. She's your *wife*. And she has some very important things to say.'

There's silence at the other end, then Tarkie says, 'OK, put her on.' He sounds a bit chastened, actually.

186

I pass the phone to Suze, then retreat. I was half-hoping Suze would ask me to stay with her, so I could press my ear to the back of the phone and hear Tarkie's side of the conversation. But she said she had to talk to him in private.

Which . . . you know. It's her marriage and everything. Although I *would* have been very helpful and given her Dutch courage and prompted her when she ran out of words. I'm just saying.

Anyway, it's fine. She's gone outside the tent and I'm sitting by the Mexican band, drinking a Diet Coke to dilute the tequila. A guy in a poncho handed me a tambourine a few moments ago and he looked so eager I didn't have the heart to say no. So I'm banging it and singing in what I *think* is pretty good Spanish ('Aheya-aheya-aheya-aheya') and trying not to picture Suze and Tarquin standing on the steps of a divorce court, when suddenly there she is, back again.

My heart gives this almighty swoop and my tambourine falls limply to my side. She's standing by the flap of the tent, her face flushed, breathing hard, looking totally freaked out.

'What happened?' I venture as she approaches. 'Suze, are you OK?'

'Bex, the trees on our estate,' she mutters feverishly. 'The trees. Do you remember anything about them? Anything at all?'

Trees? What *is* she going on about?

'Um, no,' I say cautiously. 'I don't know anything about trees. Suze, focus. What happened? How were things left?'

'I don't know.' She's looking bleak.

'You don't *know*?' I stare at her. 'How can you not know? What did he say?'

'We talked. I told him. I mean, he didn't quite understand to begin with . . .' She rubs her nose.

OK, I can just imagine the conversation. Suze saying, 'I've had this dreadful thing happen, Tarkie,' and Tarkie thinking she's lost her mascara.

'Did you actually *tell* him?' I demand severely. 'Does he actually know what's happened?'

'Yes.' She swallows. 'Yes, he . . . he got it in the end. I mean, the signal was patchy . . .'

'And?'

'He was really shocked. I think I'd kidded myself he might have guessed . . . but he hadn't.'

Honestly. Of course he hadn't guessed. This is Tarkie. Only I don't say this to Suze, because she's in full flight.

'I kept saying I was sorry and it wasn't as bad as he probably imagined' – Suze gulps – 'and that I couldn't, you know, bring myself to go the whole way with Bryce, and he said, was he supposed to be *grateful* for that?'

Good point, Tarkie, I think silently. Although also: good point, Suze. I mean, she wasn't *actually unfaithful*, was she? In the legal sense.

(Is there a legal sense? I must ask Luke, he'll know.)

(Actually, no, I won't ask Luke or he'll wonder why I want to know, and that could lead to all sorts of misunderstandings which I *really* don't need right now.)

'Anyway, in the end I said we need to meet up and talk, as soon as possible,' Suze continues, her voice quivering. 'And he said no.'

'*No?*' I gape at her.

'He said he was doing something very important for your dad and he wasn't going to interrupt it. And then the signal finally went. So.' Suze shrugs, as though she's not bothered, but I can see her hands clenching and unclenching nervously.

'So that was the end of the conversation?' I say disbelievingly.

'Yes.'

'So you don't know how things stand?'

'Not really.' She sinks on to a bar stool next to me and I gaze at her, feeling slightly dumbstruck. This is all wrong. The whole point of ringing your husband for a full and frank confession is that you talk everything through, and by the end you're either going to split up or you've made up.

I mean, *isn't* it?

The trouble with Tarkie is, he doesn't watch TV, so he has no idea how these things go.

'Suze, you need to buy some box sets,' I say fervently. 'Tarkie has no point of reference.'

'I know. He didn't say anything like I thought he would.'

'Did he say he needed some space?'

'No.'

'Did he say, "How can I trust anything you say now?"'

'No.'

'Well, what *did* he say?'

'He said he could understand me being tempted by Bryce and he'd fallen under Bryce's spell too . . .'

189

'Very true.' I nod.

'. . . but we were Cleath-Stuarts, and Cleath-Stuarts don't compromise, it's all or nothing.'

'All or nothing?' I pull a face. 'What did he mean by that?'

'I don't know!' wails Suze. 'He wasn't clear. And then he started talking about this famous tree we have on the Letherby estate, Owl's Tower.' The freaked-out look returns to her eyes. 'You know how all our biggest trees have names?'

I do know. In Suze's spare room, there's a booklet about the trees, and I *have* tried to read it, except I fall asleep every time I reach Lord Henry Cleath-Stuart bringing back seeds from India in 1873.

'Talking about a tree is good!' I exclaim encouragingly. 'It's a very good sign. It says, "I want our marriage to last." Suze, if he's talking about trees, I think you're OK.'

'You don't understand!' wails Suze again. 'I don't know which tree Owl's Tower is! We've got millions of trees called Owl's Something. And there was one really famous one which was struck by lightning and died. He might be talking about that one.'

'Oh God.' I stare at her, my confidence slightly dented. 'Really?'

'Maybe Tarkie's saying that Bryce is the lightning bolt and now our marriage is a charred stump with smoke rising from it.' Suze's voice quivers.

'But maybe he's not,' I counter. 'Maybe Owl's Tower is some really healthy oak which is still standing after lots of trials and tribulations. Didn't you *ask* him which tree it was?'

Suze looks more agonized than ever.

'I couldn't admit I didn't know,' she says in a small voice. 'Tarkie always says I should take more interest in the trees on the estate. So last year I told him I'd been round with the head groundsman and it was all really interesting.'

'Had you?'

'No,' she whispers, and buries her head in her hands. 'I went riding instead.'

'Let me get this straight.' I put my tambourine down on the bar, because you can't think properly with a tambourine in your hand. 'Tarkie thought he was giving you a coded message that you would understand due to your shared love of the family trees.'

'Yes.'

'But you haven't the foggiest what he meant.'

'No.'

Honestly. This is the trouble with living in a stately home with great poetic symbols everywhere. If they lived in a normal house with one apple tree and a privet hedge, there'd be none of this hoo-ha.

'OK,' I say firmly. 'Suze, you need to find out which tree Owl's Tower is. Phone your parents, phone his parents, phone your head groundsman . . . anyone!'

'I already have,' admits Suze. 'I've left them all messages.'

'So what do we do now?'

'I don't know. Wait.'

I can't quite believe this. Basically Suze's marriage is either over or not, depending on a tree. This is *so bloody Tarquin.*

Although, I suppose it could have been worse. He could have expected her to know the whole plot of a Wagner opera.

Suze gets down from her bar stool and starts pacing around on the spot, nibbling her fingers and checking her phone about every two seconds. Her eyes are wild and she's muttering to herself, 'Is it the chestnut? Maybe it's that big ash.' She's going to drive herself insane like this.

'Look, Suze.' I try to grab her arm, but miss. 'Calm down. There's nothing you can do now. You need to think of something else. Let's go and look at the fair. Suze, *please*,' I beg, making another swipe at her arm. 'You've had a really stressful time. It's not good for you. It's all cortisol and stuff in your veins. It's poison!'

I learned this at Golden Peace. In fact, I went to a whole series of classes called Limit Your Stress Levels, which would have been really useful if I hadn't always arrived late after yoga, and spent the whole class feeling totally hassled. (I actually think I'd have felt less stressed if I *hadn't* gone to the class.)

'OK,' says Suze at last, still pacing. 'OK. Maybe I should try to get my mind off things.'

'Exactly! Look, we've got ages till we're on duty in the Ceramics Tent. Let's go and find a distraction.'

'Right.' Suze stops pacing, but her eyes are still wild. 'You're right. What shall we do? I wonder if I can borrow a horse. I could enter some events. I've never done a rodeo before.'

A rodeo? Is she *nuts*?

'Er . . . maybe!' I say warily. 'I was actually thinking

more like, wander round? Look at the displays? They've got chickens, you know.'

Suze has always had a soft spot for chickens (which I understand even less than the pig thing). I unfold my guide and I'm about to tell her some of the breeds, when her eyes light up.

'*I* know.' She clasps hold of my arm and marches me off. 'I've got it.'

'Where are we going?' I protest.

'You'll see.'

Suze seems so determined, there's no point arguing. And at least she's stopped nibbling her fingers like a mad-woman. We skirt round all the food tents, wind our way through the livestock arenas and pass the Creative Village. (We pass it twice, in fact. I think Suze gets a bit lost, not that she'll admit it.)

'Here we are.' Suze draws up at last in front of a tent with a sign reading *Heel to Toe*. I can hear 'Sweet Home Alabama' being played on the sound system inside.

'What's this?' I say blankly.

'We're buying boots,' says Suze. 'We're at a proper county fair, so we need proper cowboy boots.' She sweeps me inside the tent and I inhale a solid smell of leather. In fact, I'm so overcome by the smell, it takes me a moment to register the spectacular sight before me.

'Oh my *God*,' I stutter at last.

'Isn't it just . . .' Suze seems as overwhelmed as I am.

We're standing, arm in arm, staring upwards in total awe like a pair of pilgrims at the holy shrine.

I mean, I've seen cowboy boots for sale, plenty of

times. You know. A shelf here and there. But I've never seen anything like this. The racks reach the top of the tent. Each rack has about fifteen shelves, and each one is covered in boots. There are brown boots and black boots; pink ones and aquamarine ones. Some have rhinestones. Some have embroidery. Some have rhinestones *and* embroidery. Under a sign reading *Luxury Boots*, there's a white pair with inlaid python print which cost $500, and a pair made from pale-blue ostrich leather which cost $700. There's even a black pair which are thigh-high and marked *Latest Fashion* but they look a bit weird, to be honest.

It's all so dazzling, neither of us can quite speak. Suze takes off her old brown cowboy boots which she got in Covent Garden and slips on a pair of pink-and-white boots from the rack. With her blue jeans and blonde hair they look *amazing*.

'Or look at these.' I grab her a pale-tan pair, with delicate rhinestones tracing a pattern up the sides.

'They're beautiful.' Suze practically swoons in lust.

'Or these!' I've found a dramatic pair of black and dark-brown leather boots which smell all rich and dark and saddley. 'For winter?'

It's like gorging on chocolates. Every pair is more alluring and delicious. For about twenty minutes I do nothing but chuck boots at Suze and watch as she models them. Her legs look endless and she keeps swishing her hair around and saying, 'I wish I had Caramel here.'

(Caramel is her latest horse. And I have to say, I'm very glad she *doesn't* have him here, if she's thinking of riding in a rodeo.)

At last she's narrowed it down to the tan boots with rhinestones and a black pair with amazing white embroidery. I bet she buys both.

'Hang on.' Her chin suddenly jerks up. 'Bex, what about you? Why aren't you trying any on?'

'Oh,' I say, caught out. 'Actually, I don't really feel like it.'

'Don't feel like it?' Suze stares at me, puzzled. 'What, trying on boots?'

'Yes. I suppose.'

'Not at *all*?'

'Well . . . no.' I gesture at the boots. 'But you carry on.'

'I don't want to carry on.' Suze seems a bit crestfallen. 'I wanted to buy us *both* a pair of boots. You know, to make up. To be friends again. But if you don't want to . . .'

'No, I do! That would be lovely,' I say hastily.

I can't hurt Suze. But I'm feeling that same weird, twisting-in-my-stomach feeling as before. Trying to ignore it, I take a pair of boots off the nearest rack and Suze hands me some socks.

'These are nice.' I slip them on. They're brown with a black laser-cut design and fit me perfectly. 'Good size, too. There we are. Done.' I try to smile.

Suze stands in her socks, holding two pairs of boots in her hands, her eyes narrowed.

'That's *it*?'

'Er . . . yes.'

'Aren't you going to try any more on?'

'Well . . .' I run my eyes over the boots, trying to feel

like I used to. *Boots!* I tell myself. *Suze wants to buy me some cool boots! Yay!*

But it all feels false to my own ears. When it's Suze trying them on I get all excited for her – but when it's me, somehow it's different. To show willing, I quickly pull down a turquoise pair and slide my feet inside. 'These are nice, too.'

'Nice?'

'I mean . . .' I cast around for the right word. 'Gorgeous. They're gorgeous.' I nod, trying to look enthusiastic.

'Bex, stop it!' says Suze in sudden distress. 'Be normal! Be excited!'

'I *am* excited!' I retort – but even I can tell I'm not convincing.

'What's happened to you?' Suze gazes at me, her face pink with agitation.

'Nothing!'

'It has! You've gone strange! You've gone all—' She stops herself suddenly. 'Wait. Are you in debt, Bex? Because I'm paying for this—'

'No, I'm not in debt, for once. Look . . .' I rub my face. 'I've slightly gone off shopping. That's all.'

'You've *gone off shopping*?' Suze drops both pairs of boots with a thud.

'Just a bit. You know. For myself. I mean, I love buying Minnie things, and Luke . . . Look, you buy yourself a pair of boots.' I smile at her. 'I'll get some another time.' I pick up the boots she dropped and proffer them. 'They look fabulous.'

But Suze doesn't move a muscle. She's staring at me warily.

'Bex, what's up?' she asks at last.

'Nothing,' I answer at once. 'I just ... you know. Everything's been a bit stressy, I suppose ...'

'You seem flat,' she says slowly. 'I didn't notice it before. I've been too wrapped up in—' She halts. 'I wasn't taking notice of you.'

'There's nothing to take notice of. Look, Suze, I'm *fine.*'

There's silence. Suze is still regarding me with that wary look. Then she comes over, grabs my arms and stares into my face.

'OK, Bex, what do you want most of all in life, right now? Not only things, but, like, *experiences.* A holiday. A job. An ambition ... anything!'

'I ... well ...'

I try to summon up some kind of desire. But it's weird. It's like, that place inside me is hollow.

'I just want ... everyone to be healthy,' I say lamely. 'World peace. You know. Usual stuff.'

'You're not right.' Suze releases my arms. 'I don't know *what's* up with you.'

'What, because I don't want a pair of cowboy boots?'

'No! Because nothing's *driving* you.' She peers at me in distress. 'You've always had this ... this energy. This engine. Where's it gone? What are you enthusiastic about, right now?'

I don't say anything, but inside, something's quailing. Last time I was enthusiastic about something, it nearly cost me all my relationships.

'Dunno.' I shrug, avoiding her eye.

'Think. What do you *want*? Bex, we're being honest with each other.'

197

'Well,' I say, after a gigantic pause. 'I suppose . . .'

'What? Bex, *talk* to me.'

'Well,' I say again and give an awkward shrug. 'I suppose most of all I'd like another baby one day. But it hasn't happened. So. I mean maybe it'll never happen. But whatever.' I clear my throat. 'You know. It's no big deal.'

I raise my eyes to see Suze gazing at me, stricken.

'Bex, I didn't realize. You've never said anything.'

'Well, I don't go *on* about it.' I roll my eyes and take a few steps away. I don't want any sympathy. In fact, I should never have mentioned it.

'Bex—'

'No.' I shake my head. 'Stop it. Honestly. It's all good.'

We walk on a little, neither speaking, into an adjoining tent which is full of leather accessories laid out on tables.

'So . . . what are you guys going to do after this?' says Suze at last, as though she's thinking this all through for the first time. 'Is Luke going back to the UK?'

'Yes.' I nod. 'When we've finished this trip we'll pack up and go back. I suppose I'll try to get a job in England. Although I don't know if I'll find one. It's pretty tough out there, you know.' I pick up a plaited-leather belt, look at it blankly and put it down again.

'I wish you'd made it as a Hollywood stylist,' says Suze wistfully, and I feel so shocked I actually lurch against the table.

'No you don't! You gave me a hard time about it!'

'I did at the time.' Suze chews her lip. 'But I'd love to

have seen your name on a cinema screen. I'd have been so proud.'

'Well. All that's over.' I look away, my face set. It's still quite painful to think about. 'And I don't have a job to go back to.'

'You can pick up your career in England. Easy!'

'Maybe.'

I walk over to another stall, away from her penetrating eyes. I don't want Suze getting under my protective shell. I feel too sore inside. And I think she senses this, because when she comes over, all she says is, 'D'you want one of these?'

She holds up the most hideous leather necklace, decorated with wine corks.

'No,' I say firmly.

'Thank God. Because that *would* worry me.'

Her eyes are dancing comically, and I can't help giving a little smile. I've missed Suze. The old Suze. I miss the old us.

I mean, it's wonderful being a grown-up wife and mother and all of it. It's fulfilling. It's joyful. But sometimes I'd love to be pissed on a Saturday night, watching *Dirty Dancing* and deciding to dye our hair blue.

'Suze, d'you remember when we were single, in our flat?' I say abruptly. 'D'you remember when I tried to cook you curry? And neither of us was anywhere near getting married. Let alone having children.'

'Let alone committing adultery,' Suze puts in heavily.

'Don't think about that! I was just wondering . . . is this what you thought married life would be like?'

'Dunno,' she says, after mulling it over for a while. 'No, not really. What about you?'

'I thought it would be simpler,' I admit. 'My mum and dad always made it look so easy. You know, Sunday lunch, rounds of golf, glasses of sherry . . . Everything seemed so calm and ordered and sensible. But now look at them. Look at us. It's all so *stressy*.'

'You're OK,' says Suze at once. 'You and Luke are fine.'

'Well, you and Tarkie will be fine, too,' I reply as robustly as I can. 'I'm sure of it.'

'And what about us?' Suze's face is uneasy. 'Bex, I've been so mean to you.'

'No you haven't!' I say at once. 'I mean . . . we're . . . it's . . .'

I break off, my face hot. I don't know what to say. I know Suze is being all warm and lovely now – but what about when Alicia comes back? Will I be all left out again?

'Friendships move on.' I try to sound bright. 'Whatever.'

'Move *on*?' Suze sounds shocked.

'Well, you know,' I say awkwardly. 'You're better friends with Alicia now . . .'

'I'm not! Oh God . . .' Suze shuts her eyes, looking agonized. 'I've been obnoxious. I just felt so *guilty* . . . but it came out wrong. It came out as being horrible.' Her blue eyes pop open. 'Bex, Alicia's not my best friend. She could never be my best friend. You are. At least . . . I hope you still are.' She comes to face me, head on, her eyes all anxious. 'Aren't you?'

My throat is tight as I stare back at her familiar face. I feel like a cord is being untied from my chest. Something that had been hurting for so long that I'd even kind of got used to it is being released.

'Bex?' Suze tries again.

'If I phoned you up at three a.m ...' My voice is suddenly small. 'Would you answer?'

'I'd come straight round,' Suze replies forthrightly. 'I'd be there. Whatever you needed, I'd do it.' Suddenly tears are glistening in her eyes. 'And I don't have to ask you the same, because when I was in trouble you came. You're here.'

'It wasn't three a.m. though,' I say, to be fair. 'More like eight p.m.'

'Same thing.' Suze gives me a push, and I laugh, although I almost feel like crying. I'd felt unmoored, losing Suze. And now I have her back. I think I have her back.

I take a step away, trying to gather myself. Then, on impulse, I pick up an ugly leather bracelet decorated with beer-bottle tops – it's even worse than the wine-cork necklace – and hold it out to Suze, deadpan. 'You know what? You'd *really* suit this.'

'Is that right?' counters Suze, her eyes sparkling. 'Well, you'd look *divine* in this.' She picks up a hairband covered in lurid fake grapes and we both snuffle with laughter. I'm just searching for the worst possible thing I can find on the table, when my eye is distracted by a familiar figure coming through the tent.

'Hey, Luke!' I wave an arm. 'Over here! Any news from Mum?'

'Mummy!' yells Minnie, who is dragging on Luke's arm. 'Sheep!'

'No news that I know of,' says Luke over the noise. 'How's it going?' He greets me with a kiss, then his gaze travels from me to Suze and back again. I can see the question in his eye: *Have you two made up?*

'All good,' I say emphatically. 'I mean, not *all* good, but . . . you know.'

Good apart from Suze being blackmailed by her secret lover and possibly facing the end of her marriage, I try to convey with my eyes but I'm not sure he gets it.

'Luke, have you ever been round the trees at Letherby Hall?' Suze asks, the tense tone suddenly back in her voice. 'Or has Tarkie told you about them? Do you remember one called Owl's Tower?'

'Um, no. Sorry.' Luke seems a bit puzzled at the non sequitur, as well he might be.

'Right.' Suze slumps.

'I'll explain later,' I say. 'Er . . . Suze, you don't mind me telling Luke, do you? About . . . everything?'

A pink flush whips over Suze's face, and she stares at the ground.

'I suppose not,' she says morosely. 'But not in front of me. I'd *die*.'

What? Luke mouths at me.

Later, I mouth back.

'Sheep!' Minnie is still yelling passionately. 'Sheeeeeep!' She's dragging on Luke's arm so hard, he winces.

'Wait, Minnie! We need to talk to Mummy first.'

'What does she want? Does she want to buy a sheep?'

'She wants to *ride* a sheep,' says Luke with a grin. 'That's what "mutton bustin'" is. Small children riding on sheep. It's in the arena.'

'No *way*.' I goggle at him. 'They ride on sheep? Is that a thing?'

'Well, cling on for dear life, more than ride.' He laughs. 'It's quite comical.'

'Oh my God.' I stare at him in horror. 'Minnie, darling, you're not doing that. We'll buy you a lovely toy sheep instead.' I put a hand on Minnie's arm but she bats it away.

'Ride sheeeeep!'

'Oh, let her!' says Suze, coming out of her trance. 'I used to ride sheep in Scotland.'

Is she serious?

'But it's dangerous!' I point out.

'No it's not!' says Suze scoffingly. 'They wear helmets. I've seen them.'

'But she's too young!'

'Actually, they start at two and a half.' Luke raises his eyebrows. 'I was coming along to suggest we let her do it.'

'Let her do it?' I'm almost speechless. 'Are you *nuts*?'

'Where's your spirit of adventure, Bex? I'm Minnie's godmother and I say we let her ride a sheep.' Suddenly Suze's eyes are shining in the old Suze way. 'Come on, Minnie, we're in the Wild West now. Let's bust some mutton.'

Am I the only responsible adult around here? *Am* I?

As we arrive at the mutton bustin' arena, I'm silent with shock. I don't even know where to start. These are wild animals. And people are putting their *children* on them. And *cheering*. Right now, a boy in a bandana, who looks about five years old, is grasping on to the back of a big white woolly sheep, which is cavorting around the arena. The audience is yelling encouragement and filming on their phones, and the man on the mic is giving a running commentary:

'And young Leonard's still holding on . . . You go there, Leonard . . . He's got some grit . . . Aaaaaah.'

Leonard has fallen off the sheep, which is no surprise, because, honestly, it looks like a savage beast. Three men rush forward to catch the sheep, while Leonard leaps to his feet, beaming proudly, and the crowd goes even wilder.

'Let's hear it for Leonard!'

'Leo-nard! Leo-nard!' A whole group of people, who must be Leonard's adoring family, are chanting. Leonard gives a cocky little bow, then rips his bandana from around his neck and throws it into the crowd.

He *what*? He's a child who just fell off a sheep, not a Wimbledon champion! I look at Suze, to share my disapproval with her, but her whole face is lit up.

'This reminds me of my childhood,' she says enthusiastically. Which makes no sense. Suze was brought up in an aristocratic family in Britain, not on a ranch in Arizona.

'Did your mum and dad wear cowboy hats?' I say, rolling my eyes.

'Sometimes,' says Suze without batting an eyelid. 'You know what Mummy's like. She used to come to gymkhanas in the most frightful outfits.'

Actually, that I *can* believe. Suze's mum has such an eclectic collection of clothes, it should be in *Vogue*. She's also very attractive, in that bony, horsey way. If she had a good stylist on hand all the time – e.g. me – she'd look brilliantly, wonderfully weird. (As it is, most of the time she just looks weird.)

Another child has entered the arena, on the same sheep. Or maybe a different one. How am I meant to tell? It looks equally lively, and the little girl is almost falling off already.

'And here's Kaylee Baxter!' proclaims the announcer. 'Kaylee is six years old today!'

'Come on!' says Suze. 'Let's get Minnie entered!'

She grabs Minnie's hand and heads towards the Entry Tent. There's a form to fill in, and places to sign, and Luke does all that, while I try to think of more reasons why this is a bad idea.

'I think Minnie's feeling a bit unwell,' I tell him.

'Sheep!' chimes in Minnie, jumping up and down. 'Ride-da-sheep. Ride-da-sheep.' Her eyes are bright and her cheeks are flushed with excitement.

'Look, she's feverish.' I clamp a hand on her forehead.

'No she's not.' Luke rolls his eyes.

'I mean . . . I think she twisted her ankle earlier.'

'Does your ankle hurt?' Luke enquires of Minnie.

'No!' Minnie replies emphatically. 'Does not hurt. Ride *sheep*.'

'Becky, you can't wrap her up in cotton wool.' Luke addresses me directly. 'She needs to experience the world. She needs to take some risks.'

'But she's *two*! Excuse me.' Crisply, I address the woman who's collecting the forms. She's skinny and tanned, and her bomber jacket reads *Wilderness Junior High Twirlers: Head Coach.*

'Yes, hon?' She glances up from the table. 'Got your form?'

'My daughter's only two,' I explain. 'I think she's probably too young to enter. Aren't I right?'

'She two and a half yet?'

'Well, yes, but—'

'Then she's fine.'

'She's not fine! She can't ride a sheep! No one can ride a sheep!' I throw my hands in the air. 'This is all crazy!'

The woman gives a throaty laugh. 'Ma'am, don't panic. The dads hold on to the littl'uns.' She gives me a hearty wink. 'They don't really get to ride. They just think they do.'

She pronounces it 'rahd'. *They don't get to rahd.*

'I don't want my littl'un to rahd at all,' I say firmly. 'But if she does rahd, I really, *really* don't want her to fall off.'

'She won't, ma'am. Her daddy'll hold her firm. Won't you, sir?'

'I will,' says Luke, nodding.

'So, if she's gonna rahd, I need her form.'

There's nothing I can do. My precious daughter is going to rahd a sheep. A *sheep.* Luke hands over the form, and we head to the competitors' entrance. A guy in an Arizona State Fair T-shirt fits Minnie with a helmet and a body protector, then leads her to a little pen with about six sheep of different sizes in separate chutes.

'Now, you rahd that sheep good,' he instructs Minnie,

who's listening avidly. 'You don't let go that naughty sheep. Don't let go, you hear me?'

Minnie nods with eager eyes, and the guy laughs.

'The littl'uns crack me up,' he says. 'She'll be off before you know it. Sir, you keep a tight grip on her.' He looks at Luke.

'OK.' Luke nods. 'Let's do this. Ready, Minnie?'

Oh God. I feel sick. I mean, basically it's a rodeo. They're putting her on to a sheep. And they'll open the gate and she'll be in the arena . . . It's like *Gladiator*.

OK, it's not exactly like *Gladiator*. But it's almost as bad. My stomach is churning as I watch through my fingers, while Suze takes pictures on her phone and whoops, 'Go, Minnie!'

'Now we both run alongside,' the guy's saying to Luke. 'Don't take your hands off her and whip her off soon's you can.'

'OK.' Luke nods.

'This sheep's an old, docile one. We keep her for the littl'uns. But still and all.'

I glance at Minnie. Her eyebrows are lowered with intent. I've never seen her look so focused, except for that time she wanted to wear her fairy dress and it was in the wash, and she refused to put anything else on, the whole day.

Suddenly a buzzer is sounding. It's happening. The gate is opening.

'Go, Minnie!' Suze yells again. 'You can do it! Stay on!'

My whole body is braced, waiting for the sheep to start bucking crazily and throwing Minnie ten feet in the air. But it doesn't, partly because the guy in the Arizona State Fair T-shirt has a firm hold of it. It's squirming, but basically it can't go anywhere.

Oh. Oh, I see.

OK, it's not *quite* as bad as I thought.

'Good job, honey!' says the guy to Minnie after about ten seconds. 'You rode the sheep good! Off you come now . . .'

'Is that *it*?' says Suze as Luke steps away and takes a picture. 'For God's sake, that was nothing!'

'Ride sheep!' shouts Minnie with determination. 'Want to ride sheep!'

'Off you come . . .'

'Ride *sheep*!'

And I don't know what happens – if Minnie kicks the sheep or what – but suddenly the sheep gives a leap, dodges the grasp of the guy in the T-shirt, and starts off round the arena at a brisk trot, with Minnie clutching on for dear life.

'Oh my God!' I scream. 'Help!'

'Stay on, Minnie!' Suze is screaming beside me.

'Save my daughter!' I'm almost hysterical. 'Luke, get her!'

'Well, look at this!' the announcer is booming through the loudspeaker. 'Minnie Brandon, aged two, ladies and gentlemen, only two years old and she's *still on*!'

The sheep is trotting and wriggling all over the place with Luke and the guy in the T-shirt trying to catch it, but Minnie is grimly fastened to its back. The thing about Minnie is, if she wants something badly, her fingers get a kind of super-strength.

'She's amazing!' Suze is gasping. 'Look at her!'

'Minn-eeeee!' I cry in desperation. 'Heeeelp!' I can't watch any more. I have to do something. I clamber over the fence, and run into the arena as best I can in my flip-flops, my breath coming fast and hard. 'I'll save you, Minnie!' I yell. 'You put my daughter down, you sheep!'

I charge at the sheep, and grab it by the wool, intending to wrestle it to the ground in one simple move.

Bloody hell. Ow. Sheep are *strong*. And it trod on my *foot*.

'Becky!' Luke yells. 'What the hell are you doing?'

'Stopping the sheep!' I yell back. 'Get it, Luke!'

As I start chasing the sheep, I can hear laughter from the audience.

'And Minnie's mom has joined the fray!' booms the announcer. 'Go, Minnie's mom!'

'Go, Minnie's mom!' a crowd of teenage boys at once echoes. 'Minnie's-*mom*! Minnie's-*mom*!'

'Shut up!' I say, flustered. 'Give me my *daughter*!' I launch myself at the sheep as it trots by, but it's too quick, and I end up crashing down into a patch of mud, or even worse. Ow. My *head*.

'Becky!' cries Luke from the other end of the arena. 'Are you OK?'

'I'm fine! Get Minnie!' I flail my arms. 'Get that bloody sheep!'

'Get that bloody sheep!' the teenage boys immediately echo, in fake-British accents. 'Get that bloody sheep!'

'Shut up!' I glower at them.

'Shut up!' they joyfully return. 'Oh, guv'nor. Shut up!'

I hate teenage boys. And I hate sheep.

By now Luke, the guy in the Arizona State Fair T-shirt and a couple of others have cornered the sheep. They pin it down and try to remove Minnie, who is totally ungrateful for their help.

'Ride sheeeeep!' I can hear her yelling crossly as she clutches on to its wool. She looks around the audience, realizes she's the star of the moment, and beams, lifting one hand to wave at everyone. She is *such* a show-off.

'Well, look at this, ladies and gentlemen!' The announcer is chortling. 'Our youngest competitor stayed on the longest! Let's give her a huge hand . . .'

The audience erupts in a cheer as finally Luke gets Minnie off the sheep and holds her aloft, still in her little helmet and body protector, her legs kicking in protest.

'Minnie!' I run towards her, dodging the sheep, which is now being manhandled back into its pen. 'Minnie, are you OK?'

'Again!' Her face is pink with triumph. 'Ride sheep again!'

'No, sweetheart. *Not* again.'

My legs are all wobbly with relief as I lead Minnie out of the arena.

'You see?' I say to Luke. 'It *was* dangerous.'

'You see?' replies Luke calmly. 'She *did* manage it.'

OK. I can tell this is one of those marital 'we'll agree to disagree' moments, like when I gave Luke a yellow tie for Christmas. (I *still* say he can carry off yellow.)

'Anyway.' I take off Minnie's helmet and body protector. 'Let's go and have a cup of tea or a double vodka or something. I'm a total wreck.'

'Minnie was amazing!' Suze hurries up to us, her face shining. 'I've never seen anything like it!'

'Well, she's still in one piece, that's the main thing. I need a titchy.'

'Wait.' Suze grabs Minnie's hand from mine. 'I want to talk to you. Both of you.' She seems quite stirred up. 'I think Minnie has a real talent. Don't you think?'

'At what?' I say, puzzled.

'At riding! Did you see how she stayed on? Imagine putting her on a horse!'

'Er . . . yes,' I say without enthusiasm. 'Well, maybe she'll go riding one day.'

'You don't understand,' says Suze fervently. 'I want to train her. I think she could make it as a top eventer. Or a show-jumper.'

'*What?*' My jaw sags slightly.

'She's got amazing natural balance. I know these things, Bex. You have to spot the promise early on. Well, Minnie has astounding promise!'

'But Suze . . .' I trail off helplessly. Where do I start? I can't say, *You're mad, all she did was hold on to a sheep.*

'It's a bit early days, I'd say.' Luke smiles kindly at Suze.

'Luke, let me do this!' she persists, with sudden passion. 'Let me turn Minnie into a champion. My marriage might be over, my life might be ruined . . . but I can do this.'

'Your marriage is *over*?' exclaims Luke in shock. 'What are you talking about?'

OK, *this* is why Suze is fixating on Minnie.

211

'Suze, stop it!' I grab her shoulders. 'You don't know your marriage is over.'

'I do! The tree's a withered stump of charcoal,' says Suze with a sudden sob. 'I'm sure it is.'

'The tree?' Luke looks baffled. 'Why are you still going on about trees?'

'No, it isn't!' I say to Suze, as confidently as I can. 'It's leafy and green. With fruit. And . . . and birds tweeting on the branches.'

Suze is silent, and I grip her shoulders harder, trying to inject some positivity into her.

'Maybe,' she whispers at last.

'Come on,' says Luke. 'I'm getting everyone a drink. Including myself.' Taking Minnie by the hand, he strides off, and I hurry to catch him up. 'What the hell is going on?' he adds in a murmur.

'Bryce,' I whisper back, trying to be discreet.

'*Bryce?*'

'Ssh!' I mutter. 'Blackmail. Tarkie. Tree. Owl's Tower.'

I jerk my head significantly, hoping he'll read between the lines, but he just gives me a blank look.

'No. Idea,' he says. 'What. Fuck. Going. On. About.'

Sometimes I despair of Luke. I really do.

From: dsmeath@locostinternet.com
To: Brandon, Rebecca
Subject: Re: Would you like a hat from a county fair?

Dear Mrs Brandon

Thank you very much for your offer of a personalized
Stetson reading 'Smeathie' on one side and 'Is a Star' on
the other. Although this is very kind of you, I must decline.
I'm sure you are right, that it would look 'fabulous' while I
am gardening, but I am not sure it is a 'look' I can quite carry
off in East Horsley.

On another note, I am truly glad to hear that you and Lady
Cleath-Stuart have gone some way to mending your
differences, and hope you have success with your other
endeavours.

Yours sincerely

Derek Smeath

ELEVEN

OK, here's my verdict on county fairs. They're really fun and interesting and have millions of different types of pig. Which, you know, is good if you're into pigs. The only *tiny* downside is, it's absolutely exhausting spending all day at one.

It's five thirty in the afternoon, and we're all totally fried. We've done two turns each at staking out the Ceramics Tent, but no one has seen even a shadow of Raymond. Nor has Suze heard anything more from Tarkie, but she's being very brave and not talking about it. She spent ages on the phone to her children this afternoon, and I could hear her trying to sound merry – but she wasn't doing the most brilliant job of it. This is our third day away now and Suze isn't great at leaving the children at the best of times. (And this is hardly the best of times.)

Now Danny is doing another stint in the Ceramics Tent, Mum and Janice have gone shopping, and I'm feeding Minnie French fries in the *That Western Feelin'*

Tent, which has bales of hay and a dance floor. At the same time, I'm giving Suze a pep talk about her meeting later on with Bryce.

'Don't get into conversation,' I instruct her firmly. 'Tell Bryce you're not playing ball. And if he wants to get confrontational then you'll play hardball.'

'I thought I wasn't playing ball.' Suze looks confused.

'Er . . . you're not,' I say, a bit confused myself. 'You're playing *hardball*. It's different.'

'Right.' Suze still looks perplexed. 'Bex, will you come along too?'

'Really? Are you sure you want me there?'

'Please,' she begs. 'I need moral support. I'm afraid I might go to pieces when I see him again.'

'OK, then. I'll be there.' I squeeze her hand, and she squeezes it back gratefully.

It's been restorative, just wandering around the fair with Suze. Just drifting and chatting and pointing things out to each other. I've missed her *so* much.

As if she can read my mind, Suze gives me a sudden hug. 'Today's been lovely,' she says. 'Even despite everything.'

The band is playing some jaunty Country tune, and a woman in a leather waistcoat has climbed on to the stage. She's giving instructions on how to line-dance, and about twenty people are out on the floor. 'Come on, Minnie,' Suze says. 'Dance with me!'

I can't help smiling as Suze leads Minnie away. This afternoon she bought Minnie a teeny pair of cowboy boots, and the pair of them look like proper Western girls, doing heel-toe-kick-swivel.

Well, Suze is swivelling and kicking. Minnie's just kind of hopping from foot to foot.

'May I have this dance?' Luke's voice takes me by surprise, and I look up with a laugh. He's been doing some massive great work email all afternoon, so I've barely seen him. But here he is, smiling down, his face tanned from spending so much time in the sun.

'Do you know how to line-dance?' I parry.

'We'll learn! Come on.' He takes my hand, pulls me up, and leads me on to the dance floor. It's filled with people now, and everyone's moving backwards and forwards together in sync. I start trying to follow the instructions, but it's a bit difficult in flip-flops. Your heel doesn't hit the ground properly. And you can't swivel. And one of my flip-flops keeps falling off altogether.

At last I give up and gesture over the music to Luke that I'm sitting down again. As he follows me off the floor, he looks puzzled.

'What's up?'

'My flip-flops.' I shrug. 'I don't think they're designed for line dancing.'

A moment later, Suze and Minnie join us at the table.

'Come and have a go, Bex!' Suze holds out a hand, her eyes bright.

'I can't dance in my flip-flops. It doesn't matter.' I'm expecting Suze to shrug and return to the dance floor, but instead she glares at me, almost angrily.

'Suze?' I say in surprise.

'It *does* matter!' she bursts out. 'I tried to buy you

216

cowboy boots.' She turns to Luke. 'But she wouldn't let me. And now she can't dance!'

'Look, it's no big deal,' I say, feeling rattled. 'Leave me alone.'

'Bex has gone all weird.' Suze appeals to Luke. 'She won't even let me give her a present. Bex . . . *why*?'

She and Luke are both surveying me now, and I can see the concern in their faces.

'I don't know, OK?' With no warning, tears spring to my eyes. 'I just don't feel like it. Look, I want to do something useful. I'm going back to the Ceramics Tent. Luke, why not go and catch up with some more work. I know you need to. I'll see you later, Suze. Seven p.m. at the Hog Roast Tent, right?' And before either of them can reply, I hurry away.

As I stride towards the Ceramics Tent, my mind is miserably whirling. I don't know why I wouldn't let Suze get me the cowboy boots. I know she could easily afford to. Am I punishing her? Or am I punishing myself? Or am I punishing . . . Er . . .

Actually, I don't know who else I could be punishing. All I know is that Suze is right: I'm a bit messed up inside. I got it all wrong with my job, with Dad, with everything . . . I feel like I've made mistake after mistake without even realizing it. And then, as I reach the Ceramics Tent it suddenly hits me: I'm scared. Deep down, I'm scared I'm going to screw up even more. Some people lose their nerve for riding or skiing or driving . . . well, I've lost my nerve for life.

The Ceramics Tent is far more crowded than before,

and it takes me a little time to find Danny, sitting in the corner. He has his sketchbook open and is drawing an outfit, totally absorbed. I can see more sketches piled up by his feet and it looks like he's been at it a while. Isn't he keeping a lookout for Raymond at *all*?

'Danny!' I say, and he jumps. 'Any sign of Raymond? Are you watching?'

'Sure.' He nods alertly. 'I'm on it.' He focuses on the crowd in the tent for a few seconds – then his gaze drifts down and his pencil starts moving again.

Honestly. He is so *not* on it.

'Danny!' I plant a hand on his sketch. 'What happened to staking out the tent? If Raymond walked past right now, would you notice?'

'Jeez, Becky!' Danny raises his eyes to heaven. 'Face it, Raymond's not coming. If he wanted to be here, he'd be here. All the other artists are here.' He gestures around the tent. 'I chatted to them. They said Raymond hardly ever shows up.'

'Well, still. We should at least try.'

But Danny isn't listening. He's drawing a belted dress with a cape, which actually looks amazing.

'You carry on with your sketches,' I say with a sigh. 'Don't worry about Raymond. I'll stake out the tent.'

'I'm off duty?' Danny's eyes light up. 'OK, I'm getting a drink. Catch you later.' He gathers up his sketches, stuffs them into his leather portfolio and heads off.

As he disappears, I turn my attention to the people in the tent. My eyes are narrowed and I feel on red alert. It's all very well Danny saying Raymond won't turn up – but

218

what if he does? What if it's all down to me to discover the secret? If I could do that, if I could actually *achieve* something . . . maybe I wouldn't feel so pointless.

I check the photo of Raymond on my phone, and scan the faces around me, but I can't see him anywhere. I circle the tent a few times, weaving through the crowd, looking at all the pots and plates and vases. I quite like a cream-coloured bowl with red splatters, but as I get near I see it's called *Carnage*, and my stomach turns. Are those red splatters supposed to be . . .

Argh. Yuck. Why would you do that? Why would you call a bowl *Carnage*? God, potters are *weird*.

'You like it?' A slight, blonde woman in a smock comes up. 'It's my favourite piece.' I can see a tag reading *Artist* on a cord around her neck, so I guess she made it. Which means she's Mona Dorsey.

'Lovely!' I say politely. 'And that one's lovely too.' I point to a vase with big black random stripes, which I think Luke would like.

'That's *Desecration*,' she smiles. 'It comes in a set with *Holocaust*.'

Desecration and *Holocaust*?

'Excellent!' I nod, trying to look unfazed. 'Absolutely. Although I was just wondering, do you have anything with a slightly jollier title?'

'Jollier?'

'Happier. You know. Cheery.'

Mona looks blank. 'I try to give my pieces meaning,' she says. 'It's all in here.' She hands me a pamphlet entitled *Wilderness Creative Festival: Guide to Artists*. 'All the artists in the exhibition explain their life and working process. Mine is to depict the blackest, most morbid and nihilistic urges of human nature.'

'Right.' I gulp. 'Er . . . great!'

'Were you interested in a piece?'

'I don't know,' I say honestly. 'I mean, I love the way they look. Only I'd prefer one that's just a *tad* less depressing and nihilistic.'

'Let me think,' says Mona, considering. She gestures to a tall, narrow-necked bottle. 'This one is entitled *Hunger in a Plentiful World.*'

'Hmm.' I pull a thoughtful face. 'Still *quite* depressing.'

'Or *Ruined*?' She picks up a green-and-black lidded pot.

'It's really beautiful,' I hasten to assure her. 'But it's still a *teeny* bit of a gloomy title.'

'You think *Ruined* is a gloomy title?' She seems surprised, and I blink back in confusion. How could *Ruined* not be a gloomy title?

'A little bit,' I say at last. 'Just . . . you know. To my ear.'

'Strange.' She shrugs. 'Ah now, *this* one is different.' She seizes a dark-blue vase with white brushstrokes. 'I like to think this has a layer of hope beneath the despair. It was inspired by my grandmother's death,' she adds.

'Oh, how touching,' I say sympathetically. 'What's it called?'

'*Violence of Suicide,*' she announces proudly.

For a moment I can't quite speak. I try to imagine having Suze for supper and saying, 'You must look at my new vase, *Violence of Suicide.*'

220

'Or there's *Beaten*,' Mona is saying, 'that's quite lovely . . .'

'Actually, I'll leave it for now.' I hastily back away. 'But, you know . . . fab pots. Thanks so much for showing them to me. And good luck with the black and morbid human urges!' I add brightly, as I swivel on my heel.

Crikey. I had no *idea* pottery was so deep and depressing. I thought it was, you know, just clay and stuff. But on the plus side, a bright idea came to me while we were talking. I'll read Raymond's entry in the booklet about the artists, and see if any clues come up.

I retreat to the side of the tent, perch myself on a handy stool, and flick through until I find him: *Raymond Earle, Local Artist.*

Born in Flagstaff, Raymond Earle . . . blah blah . . . career in industrial design . . . blah blah . . . local philanthropist and supporter of the arts . . . blah . . . love of nature . . . blah. . . greatly inspired by Pauline Audette . . . has for many years corresponded with Pauline Audette . . . would like to dedicate this exhibition to Pauline Audette . . .

I turn the page and nearly fall off my stool in shock.

No way. No *way*.

That can't be—

I mean . . . *Seriously?*

As I stare at the page, I suddenly find myself laughing out loud. It's too extraordinary. It's too weird! But can we use this?

Of course we can, I tell myself firmly. It's too good a chance. We *have* to use it.

A couple nearby is eyeing me oddly, and I beam back at them.

'Sorry. I just saw something quite interesting. It's a great read!' I wave the booklet at them. 'You should get one!'

As they move away, I stay perched on my stool, glancing down at the booklet every so often, my mind spinning with ideas. I'm making plans upon plans. I'm getting little adrenalin rushes. And for the first time in ages, I'm feeling a kind of excitement. A determination. A positive spirit.

I stay in the tent for a while longer, till Mum and Janice come back. As I see them making their way through the mêlée, I can't help blinking in astonishment. Mum is wearing a pink Stetson and matching belt with silver studs all over it. Janice is lugging a banjo and wearing a fringed leather waistcoat. Both are flushed in the face, although I can't tell if that's from sunburn or rushing about or too much bourbon-laced iced tea.

'Any sign?' demands Mum as soon as she sees me.

'No.'

'It's nearly seven!' Mum looks fretfully at her watch. 'The day's almost gone!'

'He might come along at the end of the exhibition,' I say. 'You never know.'

'I suppose so.' Mum sighs. 'Well, we'll take over till it closes. Where are you going to go now?'

'I've got to shoot off and—' I stop myself mid-sentence. I can't say, *I've got to support Suze while she confronts her*

222

blackmailing former lover. I mean, Suze and my mum are close, but not *that* close.

'I'm going to see Suze,' I say at length. 'I'll catch up with you later, OK?' I smile at Mum, but she doesn't see. She's looking around the tent bleakly.

'What if we don't find this Raymond?' As she turns back, her face has sagged into little creases of dejection. 'Are we going to give up? Go home?'

'Actually, Mum, I've got a bit of a plan,' I say encouragingly. 'I'll tell you later. But now you should have a nice sit-down and relax.' I drag a couple of spare chairs from the side of the tent. 'There we are. Why don't I buy you each a lovely cool drink? Janice, is that a banjo?'

'I'm going to teach myself, love,' answers Janice enthusiastically as she sits down. 'I've always wanted to play the banjo. We can have a nice sing-along in the RV!'

If I had to picture the one thing *most* likely to get on Luke's nerves as he's driving, it's a sing-along with a banjo.

'Er . . . great!' I say. 'Sounds perfect. I'll just get you both an iced tea.'

I quickly buy a pair of peach iced teas from the refreshment stand, give them to Mum and Janice, and then dash away. It's very nearly seven, and I'm starting to feel horrible jitters in my stomach, so God only *knows* what Suze is feeling.

We've agreed to meet at the Hog Roast Tent and then head together to the meeting spot. But as I round the corner of the tent, I receive a shock. Alicia is standing with Suze. Why is Alicia standing with Suze?

'Oh, hi, Alicia,' I say, trying to sound friendly. 'I thought you had a meeting in Tucson.'

Meeting in Tucson. Honestly. It sounds less and less likely, the more I say it.

'I thought I'd come on afterwards and meet you,' says Alicia, in sober tones. 'And a good thing I did. This is unbelievable.'

'I've told Alicia,' says Suze tremulously.

'You mustn't feel guilty, Suze.' Alicia puts a hand on Suze's elbow. 'Bryce is poison.'

I shoot Alicia a look of dislike. I hate people who say, *You mustn't feel guilty.* What they really mean is: *I'm just reminding you that you should feel guilty.*

'Everyone makes mistakes,' I say briskly. 'The important thing is to get rid of Bryce, once and for all. So we'd better go.'

'Alicia's going to come for moral support, too,' says Suze – and is it my imagination, or is there an apologetic tone to her voice?

'Oh, right.' I force myself to smile. 'Great! So you're all set?' I look at Suze. 'You know what you're going to say?'

'I think so.' Suze nods.

'Hey, you guys! Here you are!' Danny's voice hails us. We all swivel round to see him carrying a stick of cotton candy in one hand and an iced tea in the other, his portfolio wedged awkwardly under one arm. He comes to a halt and surveys us more closely. 'Hey, what's going on?'

If Suze can tell Alicia, then I can tell Danny, I decide. And he'll find out, anyway.

'Bryce is here,' I say succinctly. 'Suze is going to confront him. He's been trying to blackmail her. Long story.'

'I *knew* it!' exclaims Danny. 'I said that all along.'

'No you didn't!' I protest.

'I suspected it.' He turns to Suze. 'You slept with him, right?'

'Wrong,' snaps Suze.

'But you fooled around. Does Tarkie know?'

'Yes. I've told him everything.'

'Oh, wow.' Danny raises his eyebrows, nibbling his cotton candy. 'Kudos to you, Suze.'

'Thank you,' says Suze in dignified tones.

'But . . . wait.' I can see Danny's mind is working hard. 'I thought Bryce was trying to rip off Tarkie for his new yoga centre. You mean he's trying to rip you off too? Husband *and* wife?'

'Apparently,' confirms Suze frostily.

'He's *good*,' says Danny with feeling. 'Hey Alicia, what do you make of all this? Looks like Bryce might just build that centre. Ready for the competition?'

Danny's so wicked. I know he's just trying to wind Alicia up.

'He will not,' says Alicia coolly. 'There is absolutely no way that *character* is going to threaten Golden Peace with some second-rate rival outfit. Believe me, Wilton will not let it happen.' She looks at her watch. 'We should go.'

'Yes, we should,' Suze agrees.

'Let's do it.' Danny nods.

'*You're* not coming,' insists Suze.

'Sure I am,' says Danny, unfazed. 'You can't have too much moral support. You want an iced tea?' He hands her his plastic glass. 'It's practically a hundred per cent bourbon.'

'Thanks,' says Suze reluctantly, and takes a sip. 'Bloody hell!' she splutters.

'Told you.' Danny grins. 'Want some more?'

'No thanks.' Suze lifts her chin in determination. 'I'm ready.'

As we march towards the meeting place, no one says anything. We're a posse, flanking Suze, ready to defend her. And we're not going to take any shit from Bryce. We're going to stand firm, and resolute, and *not* get distracted by his looks—

Oh God, there he is. He's leaning casually against a closed-up coffee stand, his skin all burnished and golden, with denim-blue eyes focused on something in the distance. He looks like a Calvin Klein model. *Mmmm* shoots through my brain before I can stop it. Argh. Bad, bad brain . . .

And then his eyes snap to, and his personality rushes into his face, and my *Mmmm* instantly withers. I can't believe I ever saw him as anything but odious.

'Suze.' He seems taken aback to see all of us. 'You brought reinforcements, huh?'

'Bryce, I have something to say to you,' Suze begins, her voice trembling and her eyes fixed on a point past his shoulder, just like I told her. 'You can't blackmail me. I'm not giving you any money and I request that you leave my husband and me alone. There is nothing you can tell him that will damage me. I have been utterly frank and open with him. You have no power over me and I request that you desist from contacting me.'

Desist was my word. I think it sounds nice and legal.

I squeeze Suze's hand encouragingly, and whisper, 'Brilliant!' She's still staring fixedly into the middle distance, so I take the opportunity to sneak a quick look at Bryce. His face is calm, but I can tell from his eyes that he's thinking.

'Blackmail?' he says at last, and breaks into a hearty laugh. 'Now, that's an extreme word. I ask you for a donation to a worthy cause and you call it blackmail?'

'A worthy cause?' echoes Suze in disbelief.

'A *worthy cause*?' exclaims Alicia, who seems more outraged than anybody. 'How *dare* you! I've heard what you're up to, Bryce, and believe me, you will never succeed.' She takes a step forward, her chin thrust out aggressively. 'You will never have our resources. You will never have our power. My husband will *crush* your paltry efforts to rival us. I've already informed him of your plan, and it won't even see the light of day. And by the time Wilton has finished with you, Bryce . . .' She pauses. 'You'll wish you'd never even thought of it.'

Wow. Alicia sounds like a Mafia boss. If I were Bryce, I'd be terrified. But I must say, he doesn't look remotely scared. He's gazing back at Alicia as though he can't figure her out. Then he gives a small, incredulous laugh.

'Jeez, Alicia, are we really doing this?'

A strange little flicker passes across Alicia's face.

'I don't know what you mean,' she says, in the most

icy, Queen Alicia tones I've ever heard. 'And I would remind you that you are still in the employ of my husband.'

'Sure. Whatever,' says Bryce.

There's an odd pause, during which no one speaks. I'm trying to work out the vibe. Suze is breathing hard beside me, her fists clenched; Alicia is glaring at Bryce; Danny is watching, agog. But it's Bryce who isn't behaving as I expected. He's not even looking at Suze. He's still looking appraisingly at Alicia.

'Or maybe . . . I quit,' he says slowly, and there's a kind of defiant glint to his eye. 'Maybe I've had enough of this bullshit.'

'In which case, you will be bound by our confidentiality agreement, as per your contract,' Alicia replies before anyone can speak. 'May I remind you that we have a very, *very* strong legal team?'

Alicia's tone has got sharper and the rest of us are exchanging puzzled glances. What's this got to do with Suze?

'So sue me,' says Bryce, and snaps his gum. 'It's never gonna happen. You'd let all this out into the media?' He spreads his arms wide.

'Bryce!' Alicia exclaims. 'Consider your position.'

'I've had enough of my "position"! You know what, I'm *sorry* for you poor saps.'

'Sorry for what?' Suze seems to wake up. 'Alicia, what's he talking about?'

'I have *no* idea,' she returns furiously.

'Oh, *please*!' Bryce shakes his head. 'You are one manipulative woman, Alicia Merrelle.'

'I will not be insulted in this way!' Alicia seems incandescent. 'And I suggest that this meeting ends right now. I will be on the phone to my husband, and he will be taking steps—'

'For Christ's sake!' Bryce sounds at the end of his tether. 'Enough already!' He turns and addresses Suze directly. 'I'm not in competition with Wilton Merrelle. I'm working *for* him. Of course I was trying to get money out of you, but it wasn't for me, it was for the Merrelles.'

There's a stunned silence. Did I hear that right?

'What?' falters Suze at last, and Bryce gives an impatient sigh.

'Wilton is setting up a rival establishment. He figures if he can fill one Golden Peace centre, he can fill two. Only this one will be branded differently. Lower price points. Scoop up all the customers who fell out with Golden Peace and want an alternative. It's a win-win.' He looks at Alicia. 'As you well know.'

I look at Suze, utterly speechless, then turn to Alicia. She's gone a kind of mauve colour.

'You mean . . .' My mind can't process all this. 'You mean . . .'

'You mean Wilton Merrelle is behind all of this?' says Danny, his eyes dancing with relish. 'So when you targeted Tarquin . . .'

'Sure.' Bryce nods. 'That was Wilton's idea. He thought he could get a few million out of him.' He shrugs. 'Wasn't so easy. You Brits are tight.'

'You've been *using* us?' Suze lashes out suddenly at Alicia, whose face has gone from mauve to a kind of deathly white. 'All this time you've been pretending to be my friend . . . and all you wanted was our *money*?'

OK, you have to admire Alicia. I can practically *see* the muscles of her face forcing themselves back into their old, haughty expression. She's like the Olympic champion of 'regaining control of yourself'.

'I have no idea what Bryce is talking about,' she says. 'I deny everything.'

'You want to deny these emails?' says Bryce, who seems to be enjoying himself now. He holds out his phone to Suze, who looks helplessly at Alicia. 'Wilton wanted me to target the pair of you,' he tells Suze, 'and Alicia knew that.' He swivels to Alicia. 'Didn't you just meet up with him in Tucson to talk about it?'

Tucson?

OK. So I take it back about Tucson. People do have meetings there. Who knew?

The muscles in Alicia's face are working hard again, in fact there's a spasm in her cheek. Her eyes are like two livid stones. She draws breath, then rounds on Bryce.

'We are suing your *ass*,' she spits at him, so vituperatively, I shrink back.

'So it's true.' Suze looks totally dazed. 'I can't believe it. I've been such a *fool*.'

Bryce looks around the whole group and shakes his head. 'This is fucked up. I'm out. It was fun playing with you, babe,' he adds to Suze, and she shudders. 'Becky, come back to one of my classes sometime.' His eyes crinkle in that sexy smile of his. 'You were making some good progress.'

'I'd rather rot in hell,' I say fiercely.

'Your choice.' He seems amused. 'See you around, Alicia.'

With a couple of strides of his long legs, he's gone. And the rest of us are left in silence again. It's like an earthquake has happened between us. I can practically see the dust in the air.

'Becky knew,' says Danny at last, breaking the quiet.

'*What?*' Suze's head whips round in astonishment.

'I didn't *know* . . .' I amend hurriedly.

'She guessed Alicia was up to something,' Danny maintains. 'She's been watching your back, Suze'

'Really?' Suze raises her huge blue eyes to mine, and I can see fresh pain in them. 'Oh God. Oh Bex. I don't know how I could have thought Alicia was *anything* but a wicked, two-faced—' She turns on Alicia with sudden passion. 'Why did you even come on this road trip? To make sure Bryce got the cash out of me? And who were you meeting in the Four Seasons? *Not* a private detective.'

'Suze, there's something else,' I whisper with urgency. 'You need to beware. I think Alicia is after Letherby Hall.'

'What do you mean?' Suze takes a step towards us and away from Alicia. She's eyeing Alicia warily, as though she's a bomb that might go off.

'Letherby Hall?' scoffs Alicia. 'Are you *nuts?*'

But I ignore her. 'Look at the facts, Suze. Why does Alicia keep asking questions about your house? Why is she interested in the title that goes with the property? *Because* . . .' I count off on my fingers: 'Her husband's an Anglophile. They'd love to be Lord and Lady of the Manor.

She wants your house. She wants your title . . . and probably all your family jewellery too.'

This last has only just occurred to me, but I'm sure I'm right. Alicia would love all those ancient tiaras and stuff. (Suze thinks most of them are gross and I kind of agree.)

'Becky, you're even more deluded than I thought.' Alicia bursts into mocking laughter. 'Why would I want Letherby Hall, for Christ's sake?'

'You don't fool me, Alicia.' I give her a glacial look. 'It's a top stately home and you're a snob. Don't think we don't know you're a social climber.'

Alicia glances from me to Suze and back again – but this time she doesn't turn mauve. She seems genuinely incredulous.

'Social climber? In *England*? You really think Wilton and I want to spend our days in some freezing-cold monstrosity with no underfloor heating and yokels for neighbours?'

Monstrosity? I feel such a surge of indignation on Suze's behalf, I can't help crying out, 'Letherby Hall isn't a monstrosity! It's a highly regarded Georgian house, with an original panelled library and particularly fine parkland, landscaped in 1752!'

I had no idea I knew any of that. I must have been concentrating harder than I thought when Tarkie's dad was telling me about it.

'Whatever. Believe me.' Alicia looks pityingly at Suze. 'There are things I'd rather spend my money on than a pile of crumbling old bricks.'

'How dare you!' I'm totally fired up now. 'Don't you

insult Suze's house! And why were you asking about it so much if you're not interested?'

There. Ha! I've got her.

'I had to make small talk *somehow*.' Alicia flicks her eyes disparagingly at Suze. 'There's only *so* much one can say about that ridiculous husband of yours. I mean, really, Suze. Yawn.'

I think I could hit Alicia right now.

But I won't do that. Instead, I glance over at Suze, who says in a shaky voice, 'I think you should go, Alicia.'

And we all stand like statues as she stalks away.

Some things are almost too big to talk about straight away. It's Danny who comes to life first, says, 'Drink,' and leads us into a nearby bar tent. As we sip some apple punch, he tells us all about his new collection for Elinor and shows us his drawings – and actually, it's the perfect thing to do right now. That's exactly what Suze needs to focus on: something that isn't her own messed-up life.

At last he closes his sketchbook, and we all meet eyes, as though picking up where we were. But still I can't bear to bring up the topic of Alicia. I don't even want to give her air space.

'Bex.' Suze takes a deep shuddery breath. 'I don't know how— I can't *believe* I fell for her—'

'Stop.' I cut her off gently. 'Let's not do this. If we talk about Alicia, she's still winning, because she's messing up our lives. OK?'

Suze thinks for a moment, then bows her head. 'OK.'

'Good call,' applauds Danny. 'I say we airbrush her out of existence. Alicia *who*?'

233

'Exactly.' I nod. 'Alicia *who*?'

I mean, obviously we *will* talk about Alicia. We'll probably spend a solid week bitching about her and maybe throwing darts at her picture. (In fact I'm quite looking forward to it.) But not yet. This isn't the time.

'So,' I say, trying to move the conversation on. 'Quite a day.'

'I guess your mum hasn't had any luck with Raymond,' says Suze.

'She would have texted if she had.'

'I can't believe we staked out that tent for a whole day. And nothing.'

'Not nothing,' I say. 'Janice got a banjo.'

Suze gives a feeble snort of laughter, and I can't help smiling, too.

'So . . . what are we going to do? Where do we go next?' Suze bites her lip. 'Let's face it, there's not much point me trying to chase Tarkie any more.' She speaks calmly, but there's a wobble in her voice.

'Maybe not.' I meet her eye, then quickly look away again.

'But what about your mum and dad?'

'Oh God.' I slump in my chair. 'I have no idea.'

'Should we try Raymond's house again? Or just go back to LA like your dad said all along? I mean, maybe he was right.' Suze lifts her gaze to mine, and I can see it's taking her a lot to say this. 'Maybe this *was* a stupid idea.'

'No!' I say automatically.

'We can't go back already,' protests Danny. 'We're on a mission. We need to see it through.'

'That's all very well.' Suze turns to him. 'But we have absolutely no idea what to do next. We've failed at getting through to Raymond, we don't have a single other lead, a single idea—'

'Actually . . .' I break in. 'I did have one idea.'

'Really?' Suze stares at me. 'What?'

'Well, a kind of idea,' I amend. 'It's a bit far out. In fact, it's a bit mad. But it's one last possibility. And if it doesn't work, maybe we give up and go back to LA.'

Both Danny and Suze are regarding me with interest.

'Well, go on then,' says Suze. 'What's this crazy, last-ditch idea?'

'OK.' I hesitate, then reach into my bag for the *Wilderness Creative Festival: Guide to Artists* booklet. 'Before I say anything, have a look at this.'

I watch as they survey the page; I watch as their faces jolt in surprise, just like mine did.

'Oh my *God*,' says Suze, and looks up at me incredulously. 'So what . . . I mean, how do we . . .'

'Like I said, I have this idea.'

'Of course you do,' says Danny. 'You always have great ideas. Spill, Beckeroo.'

He gives me an encouraging smile and sits back to listen, and once again I feel that flicker of adrenalin inside. That positive spirit. Like old friends coming to give me a little inner hug.

TWELVE

Having said that, everyone thinks it's a mad idea.

Even Suze, who thinks it's a good idea, thinks it's also mad. Luke thinks it's a terrible idea. Mum doesn't know if it's good or bad but is desperate for it to work. Janice keeps flitting between wild optimism and utter pessimism. Danny's really into it – but that's only because he's created my costume.

'There.' I give a final adjustment to my scarf. 'Perfect.' I turn to survey my audience. 'What do you think? Identical twins, no?'

'You don't look anything like her,' says Luke flatly.

'I look exactly like her!'

'Sweetheart, I think you need your eyes tested.'

'No, I can see it,' says Danny. 'You look quite like her.'

'Only *quite*?' I feel a bit crestfallen.

'Everyone looks different from their photos,' says Danny firmly. 'It's fine. It's good.' He takes the *Guide to Artists* booklet and holds it up next to me, open at the page with the photo of Pauline Audette. And I don't care what Luke says, I *do* look like her. It's uncanny – even more so now I've dressed up like her.

I'm wearing a smock-type shirt which Danny bought at the fair yesterday evening, over some loose trousers belonging to Janice. My hair is held back by a piece of tie-dye cloth, because Pauline Audette always has some boho scarf in her hair. All morning, Danny has been tugging and pinning and adding artistic streaks of paint and clay, which we bought in the Craft Tent. To my eye, I look *exactly* like a French potter.

'OK, I'll practise,' I announce. 'My name, eet ees Pauline Audette.'

Luckily there are lots of clips of Pauline Audette on YouTube, because she does this thing called 'Mini-sculpt' where she takes a handful of clay and models it into something in about five seconds flat. Like, a tree or a bird. (I must say, she is pretty amazing.) So I've watched her over and over, and I *think* I've got the accent. 'I am ceramic *artiste*,' I continue. 'My inspiration, eet come from ze nah-toor.'

'What's that?' says Janice, looking baffled.

'Nature, love,' explains Mum. 'Nature, in French.'

'I 'ave come to Arizona for 'oliday. I 'ave remember Monsieur Raymond who write me ze kind lettairs. I seenk, "*Zut!* I will *visite* Monsieur Raymond."' I pause and look around. 'What do you think?'

'*Don't* say "*Zut*",' says Luke.

'You sound like Hercule Poirot,' says Suze. 'He's never going to fall for it if you talk like that.'

'Well, it's our only shot,' I retort. I feel a bit offended, actually. I thought my accent was pretty good. 'And all right, I won't say *"Zut"*. Come on, assistant, let's go.'

Suze is playing my assistant in an all-black outfit with fake spectacles. Her hair is in a sleek ponytail and she's got just a slash of red lipstick, which Danny says is definitely the 'French art assistant' look.

I head to the door of the RV and look around the eager, hopeful faces. 'Wish us luck!'

Alicia isn't with us any more, obviously. I have no idea what she did yesterday evening. Called another limo service, I expect, and went back to LA. (She left some things in the RV, and Danny was all for making a bonfire of them, but we've decided to send them back with a dignified note.) Over supper last night, I explained to Mum and Janice about how Alicia and her husband had been trying to rip off both Tarkie and Suze and how evil she was. Whereupon they both instantly said that they'd *suspected* she was up to something all along, and they'd felt it in their bones, and what a good job they'd warned me about her!

I mean, honestly.

'Becky, what if you're arrested?' says Janice in a sudden panic. 'We've already had one run-in with the police.'

'I won't be arrested!' I scoff. 'It's not against the law to impersonate people.'

'Yes it is!' says Luke, smacking a hand against his forehead. 'Jesus, Becky. It's fraud.'

Luke's always so *literal*.

'Well, OK, maybe in some cases. But this isn't fraud,' I say firmly. 'It's a quest for the truth. Anyone would understand that, even a policeman. And I've dressed up now, I can't bottle out. See you later.'

'Wait!' calls Luke. 'Remember, if there isn't any house-keeper or household staff; if your phone loses signal; if anything feels wrong, you *leave*.'

'Luke, it'll be perfectly safe!' I say. 'This is a friend of my dad's, remember?'

'Hmm.' Luke doesn't look impressed. 'Well, you be careful.'

'We will. Come on, Suze.'

We hurry down the steps of the RV and towards Raymond's ranch. Luke drives off to hide the RV out of view just round the next bend. As we approach the massive gates, I start to feel quite severe jitters, but I'm not going to mention them to Suze. She'll only say, *Let's not do it, then*. And I really, really want to do this. It's our last chance.

Plus . . . there's more to it than that. Putting this plan into action, even if it is a bit ridiculous, I feel like I've come alive. I feel dynamic. And I think it's the same for Suze. She's still in a real state – she hasn't heard anything from Tarkie, nor about Owl's Tower, nor *anything*. But it's, like, channelling her energies into this is making her feel better.

'Come on!' I clasp Suze's hand briefly as we approach. 'We can do this! You went to drama school, remember? If I get into trouble, you take over.'

The gates to the ranch are vast and wooden and I count three cameras trained on us. It's all a bit intimidating but I remind myself that I'm Pauline Audette and head confidently to the intercom panel. I press the entry button and wait for someone to reply.

'Wait, Suze!' I say in a sudden undertone. 'What's our code word?'

239

'Shit.' She stares at me, wide-eyed. 'Dunno.'

We've been talking about having a code word all morning, but we haven't actually thought of one.

'Potato,' I say hurriedly.

'Potato?' She stares at me. 'Are you *nuts*? How am I supposed to bring "potato" into conversation?'

'Well, you think of a better one. Go on!' I add, as she looks blank.

'I can't,' she says, sounding cross. 'You've put me on the spot now. All I can think of is *potato*.'

'Hello?' A woman's tinny voice comes over the intercom and my stomach turns over.

'Hello!' says Suze, stepping forward. 'My name is Jeanne de Bloor. I have Pauline Audette here for Mr Raymond Earle. Pauline Audette,' she repeats, enunciating clearly.

Suze came up with the name Jeanne de Bloor. She's decided that Jeanne was born in The Hague, has settled in Paris but has a long-term lover in Antwerp, speaks five languages and is learning Sanskrit. (Suze is very thorough, when it comes to creating a character. She's made notes, and everything.)

There's silence from the intercom, and Suze and I exchange questioning glances. Then, just as I'm about to suggest Suze tries again, a man's voice comes from the speaker.

'Hello? It's Raymond Earle here.'

Oh my God. Now my stomach is churning furiously, but I step forward to speak.

"Allo,' I say into the intercom. 'My name, eet ees Pauline Audette. We 'ave corresponded.'

240

'You're Pauline Audette?' He sounds gobsmacked, as well he might.

'I 'ave see your exhibition at ze fair. I weesh to talk to you about your work, but I cannot find you. So I come to your 'ouse.'

'You saw my work? You want to talk about my work?'

He sounds so excited, I feel an almighty stab of guilt. I shouldn't be doing this to a poor, innocent potter. I shouldn't be raising his hopes. I'm a bad person.

But then, he shouldn't have sent Mum and Janice away. Tit for tat.

'May I come into your 'ouse?' I say, but already the gates are swinging open.

We're in!

'Jeanne,' I say briskly, for the cameras' benefit. 'You weel accompany me and take ze notes.'

'Vairy gut,' says Suze, in what I think is supposed to be a Dutch accent and nearly makes me double over.

The house is about half a mile away, up a badly kept track, and I realize he was expecting us to be in a car. But I can hardly go and get the RV. As we trudge along the track, I keep seeing weird sculptures everywhere. There's a bull made out of what looks like car parts, and a man's yelling face made out of iron, and lots of strange abstract pieces made out of what look like old tyres. It's all a bit freaky, and I'm glad to reach the house, until I hear the frenzied barking of dogs.

'This place is *spooky*,' I mutter to Suze as we ring the bell pull.

The house was probably really impressive once, but it's a bit dilapidated. It's made of stone and wood, with gables

241

and a verandah and a massive carved front door, but some of the wooden railings look rotten and I can see two patched-up broken windows. The dogs' barking gets even louder, and we both shrink back.

'Have you still got a signal?' I murmur to Suze, and she checks her phone.

'Yes. You?'

'Yup. All good,' I say more loudly, for Luke's benefit. Suze's phone is recording in her pocket and mine is connected to Luke's, so everyone in the RV should be able to hear what's going on.

'Down!' comes Raymond's voice from inside the house. 'You get in there.'

Inside, a door bangs shut. The next moment, we hear what seem like about twenty-five locks being undone, then the front door swings open and Raymond Earle greets us.

The first word that hits my mind is *grizzled*. Raymond's beard is like a grey furry blanket, and reaches all the way down to his chest. He's wearing a blue and white bandana around his head and his ancient jeans are covered in mud or clay or something. The house smells of dogs and tobacco and dust and old food, with a faint reek of rotting vegetation.

He could *really* do with a scented candle or two. I'm tempted to give him the link to Jo Malone.

'Miss Audette.' He bows low and his beard flops down. 'I'm honoured.'

Oh God. I feel even more guilty about tricking him, now we're here. We need to get into his studio as quickly as possible and action my plan.

'I am *enchantée* to meet you after all zis time,' I say gravely. 'When I come to Wilderness, I remember Monsieur Raymond who has written me ze kind lettairs.'

'Well, I'm delighted to meet you!' He grabs my hand and shakes it heartily. 'This is such an unexpected pleasure!'

'Let us go straight to ze studio and observe ze work,' I say.

'Of course.' Raymond seems totally overcome. 'I'll just . . . come in. Come in.'

He ushers us into a wide hall with a fireplace and a wooden vaulted ceiling, which would be stunning if it weren't such a mess. There are dusty boots, coats, dog baskets, a bucket of old bricks and a rolled-up carpet all just lying around.

'Can I get you a beer? Some iced water?' Raymond leads us into a messy kitchen, which smells of some meaty dish. The back wall is covered in shelves, on which are propped-up paintings and drawings and a few weird-looking sculptures. A housekeeper is trying to dust them, but I can see she's not finding it easy.

'Careful!' Raymond suddenly snaps at her. 'Don't move anything!' He turns back to me. 'Miss Audette?'

'*Non, merci*. I would like to see your work. Ze piece most dear to you in ze world.' I'm trying to hurry him along, but Raymond doesn't seem the hurrying type.

'I have so much to ask you,' he says.

'And I 'ave much to ask you,' I counter. Which, at least, is the truth.

'You'll have noticed my Darin.' He nods towards the shelves.

Darin? What's a Darin? Is Darin an artist?

'*Absolument*.' I nod briskly. 'Shall we go?'

'What's your take on his use of form?' His eyes blink at me earnestly.

OK, this is *exactly* the kind of question I didn't want him to ask me. I need to come up with some convincing artisty answer, quick. Something about form. Except I never listened in art lessons.

'Form is dead,' I pronounce at last, in my most Gallic accent. '*C'est morte*.'

Perfect. If form's dead, I don't have to talk about it.

'Let us go to ze studio,' I add, trying to usher Raymond out of the kitchen. But he doesn't move. He seems slightly staggered.

'Form is *dead*?' he echoes, finally.

'*Oui, c'est fini*.' I nod.

'But—'

'Form, eet ees no more.' I spread my hands, trying to look convincing.

'But Miss Audette, h-how can this be?' stammers Raymond. 'Your own design . . . your writings . . . your books . . . are you really giving up on a life's work? It can't be!'

He's staring at me in consternation. Clearly that was the wrong thing to say. But I can't backtrack now.

'*Oui*,' I say after a pause. '*C'est ça*.'

'But *why*?'

'I am *artiste*,' I say, playing for time. 'Not woman, not human, *artiste*.'

'I don't understand,' says Raymond, looking unhappy.

'I must seek ze truth,' I add, with sudden inspiration. 'I must be brave. *Ze artiste* must always be brave, above all,

244

you understand? I must destroy ze old ideas. Zen will I a true *artiste* be.'

I hear a tiny snort from Suze, but ignore her.

'But—'

'I do not weesh to speak of it further,' I cut him off firmly.

'But—'

'To ze studio!' I wave my hands. '*Allons-y!*'

My heart is thumping hard as I follow Raymond through the house to the far end. I can't cope with any more conversations about art, I just want to know about my dad.

'Are you supposed to be Pauline Audette or Yoda?' Suze's murmur comes in my ear.

'Shut up!' I mutter back.

'We need to cut to the chase!'

'I know!'

We arrive at a big room, with white walls and a glass roof. It's bright and messy, with a heavy wooden table in the centre and two potter's wheels, all covered with splotches of clay. But that's not what I'm seeing. I'm eyeing up the big set of display shelves at the far end of the room. They're covered with clay statues and sculptures and weird-looking vases. Bingo. *This* is what we wanted.

I glance at Suze, and she gives a tiny nod back.

'You must tell me, Raymond,' I order. 'Which, to you, are ze most precious pieces in ze room?'

'Well.' Raymond hesitates. 'Let me see. Of course, there's *Twice*.' He gestures at a sculpture which seems to be of a man with two heads. 'That was nominated for the Stephens Institute Prize, few years ago. It was mentioned on a couple websites, I don't suppose you . . .' He shoots me a hopeful look.

'A fine piece,' I say, with a brisk nod. 'And which ees precious to your *heart*?'

'Oh I don't know.' Raymond gives an awkward, heavy laugh. 'I have a fond spot for this one.' He points at a much larger, abstract piece, glazed in lots of different colours.

'Aha.' I nod. 'We will examine zem . . .' I pick up *Twice* and Suze picks up the multicoloured one. 'Let us study zem in ze light . . .' I move away from Raymond and Suze follows. 'Aha. Zis one, it remind me of . . . a *potato*.'

Suze was right. *Potato* is a really, *really* bad code word. But it works. In one seamless movement, Suze and I hold the sculptures above our heads.

(Suze's looks much heavier than mine. I feel a bit bad. But then, she's got strong arms.)

'All right,' I say, in my most menacing voice. 'Here's the truth. I'm not Pauline Audette. My name is Rebecca. Graham Bloomwood is my father. And I want to know the truth about what happened on your road trip. If you won't tell us, we'll smash the pieces. If you fetch help, we'll smash the pieces. So you'd better start talking.' I break off, breathing hard, wondering whether to add, 'Buster,' then think better of it.

Raymond is clearly one of those very slow, think-everything-through types. It feels like about half an hour that we're standing there, our arms aching, our pulses racing, waiting for him to respond. He looks from me to Suze. He blinks. He screws up his face. He opens his mouth to speak, then stops.

'We need to know,' I say, trying to prod him into action. 'We need to know the truth, right here, right *now*.'

Again, Raymond frowns, as though pondering the great mysteries of life. God, he's frustrating.

'You're not Pauline Audette?' he says at last.

'No.'

'Well, thank God for that.' He shakes his head in wonder. 'I thought you'd gone crazy.' He peers more closely at me. 'You look like her, though. Just like her.'

'I know.'

'I mean, that is *incredible*. You're not related?'

'Not as far as I know. It is incredible, isn't it?' I can't help unbending to him a little. I *knew* I looked like Pauline Audette.

'Well, you should look that up.' His eyes brighten with interest. 'Maybe you have some ancestor in common. You could go on one of those TV shows . . .'

'Enough of zis chit-chat!' barks Suze, sounding like a Nazi Kommandant. 'We need the truth!' She frowns disapprovingly at me, and I see I've let myself get side-tracked.

'That's right!' I say hastily, and hold *Twice* up even higher. 'We're here for a reason, Raymond, so you'd better give us what we need.'

'And don't try any funny business,' adds Suze menacingly. 'The minute you call the cops, your two pieces of pottery will be in smithereens.' She sounds like she can't wait to get smashing. I didn't realize Suze had quite such a violent side.

There's another minute or so of silence – which feels like half an hour – as Raymond digests this.

'You're Graham's daughter,' he says at last, staring at me. 'Don't look like him.'

'Well, I am. And he's gone missing. We've been trying to track him down and help him out, but all we know is, he's trying to put something right. Do you know what that is?'

'Has he been here?' puts in Suze.

'Has he made contact?'

'Can you tell us what this is all about?'

Raymond's face has closed up as we've been talking. He meets my eye briefly, then glances away, and I feel a twinge in my stomach. He knows.

'What is it?' I demand. 'What happened?'

'What's he *doing*?' chimes in Suze.

There's another flicker in Raymond's eye, and he stares at the far corner of the room.

'You know, don't you?' I try to catch his eye. 'Why won't you speak? Why did you turn my mum away?'

'Tell us!' exclaims Suze.

'Whatever he's doing, that's his business,' says Raymond, without moving his gaze.

He knows. We've come all this way and he knows and he's not telling us. I feel such a surge of fury, I start quivering.

'I'll throw this to the ground!' I yell, brandishing *Twice*. 'I'll throw everything to the ground! I can do a lot of damage in thirty seconds! And I don't care if you call the police, because this is my dad and I *need* to know!'

'Jesus!' Raymond seems shocked at my outburst. 'Chill out. You really Graham's daughter?' He turns to Suze. 'Graham was always Mr Calm.'

'He still is,' says Suze.

'I take a bit more after my mum,' I admit.

'So . . . you're Graham's daughter,' he says for a third time. God, is he always this slow on the uptake?

'Yes, I'm Rebecca,' I say pointedly. 'But my dad didn't want to give me that name. For some reason. Which no one will tell me.'

'And Brent's and Corey's daughters are Rebecca too,' puts in Suze.

'Brent's daughter said, "We're all called Rebecca," but I don't know why, and basically, I'm tired of not knowing about my own life.' My voice is shaking as I finish, and a weird little silence falls over the room.

Raymond seems to be processing everything. He looks at me and at Suze. He looks at the pots, still above our heads. (Suze must have such bad pins and needles by now.)

Then, at last, he seems to give in. 'OK,' he says.

'OK, what?' I say warily.

'I'll tell you what your dad's doing.'

'So you *do* know?'

'He was here.' He gestures to a paint-stained sofa. 'Sit. I'll tell you what I know. You want some iced tea?'

Even though Raymond seems to have decided to play along, we don't relinquish the pottery, just in case. We sit on the sofa, clutching the two sculptures on our laps while Raymond pours out iced tea from a jug, then arranges himself on a chair opposite.

'Well, it comes down to the money,' he says, as though this is perfectly obvious, and takes a thoughtful sip from his glass.

'What money?'

'Brent signing away his rights. I mean, that's years ago, now. But your dad only just found out, thought it was wrong. Wanted to do something about it. I said, "That's their business." But your dad got the bit between his teeth. He and Corey always did have that . . . I don't know what you'd call it. A spark. Corey wound your dad up. Anyway, so that's what he's up to.'

Raymond leans back as though all is now perfectly clear and takes another sip of iced tea. I stare at him, nonplussed.

'What?' I say at last. 'What are you talking about?'

'Well, you know,' says Raymond with a shrug. 'The spring. The money.' He eyes me closely. 'I'm talking about *the money*.'

'What money?' I retort with a flash of irritation. 'You keep talking about money, but I don't know what you're going on about.'

'You don't know?' Raymond gives a little whoop. 'He never told you?'

'No!'

'Oh Graham. Not so holier-than-thou now.' He gives a sudden guffaw.

'What are you *talking* about?' I'm exploding with frustration.

'OK.' Raymond flashes me a sudden grin. 'Now, you pay attention. This is a good story. We all first met in New York, the four of us, waiting tables. Corey and Brent were science grads. I was a design postgrad. Your dad was . . . I don't remember what your dad was. We were young men, waiting to see where life would

250

take us and we decided to go west. Have an adventure.'

'Right.' I nod politely, though my heart is sinking. People say, 'This is a good story,' and what they mean is, 'I'm going to share a random slice of my life with you now, and you have to look fascinated.' The truth is, I've heard this story a million times from Dad. Next we'll be on to the sunsets and the shimmering heat and that time they spent the night in the desert. 'So, where does money come into it?'

'I'll get to that.' Raymond lifts a hand. 'Off we went, travelling around the West. And we talked. A lot. No phones back then, remember. No wifi. Just music and conversation. In bars, sitting around the campfire, on the road . . . wherever. Corey and Brent used to spitball ideas. They used to talk about setting up a research company together. Bright boys, both of them. Corey had money, too. And looks. He was what you might call "the alpha male"'.

'Right,' I say, dubiously, remembering the tanned, weird-looking guy we met in Las Vegas.

'Then one night . . .' Raymond pauses for effect. 'They came up with the spring.' A little smile dances around his mouth. 'Ever heard of a balloon spring?'

Something is ringing in my mind and I sit up straighter. 'Hang on. Corey invented a spring, didn't he?'

'Corey *and* Brent invented a spring,' corrects Raymond.

'But . . .' I stare at him. 'I saw articles about that spring online. There's no mention of Brent anywhere.'

'Guess Corey had him airbrushed out of the story.' Raymond gives a wry chuckle. 'But Brent helped invent it, all right. They came up with the first notion together one

251

night, by the fire. Sketched out the concept, right then and there. It was four years before it was actually developed, but that's where it all began. Corey, Brent, your dad and me. We all had a stake in it.'

'Wait, *what*?' I stare at him. 'My dad had a stake in it?'

'Well, I say, "stake".' Raymond begins to chuckle again. 'He didn't put any money in. It was more like a "contribution".'

'Contribution? What contribution?'

I'm half-hoping to hear that my dad was the one who had the blinding insight that kickstarted the whole invention.

'Your dad gave them the pad of paper they wrote it on.'

'*Paper*,' I say, deflated. 'Is that all?'

'It was enough! They joked about it. Corey and Brent were desperate for something to write on. Your dad had a big sketchbook. He said, "Well, if I give you my sketchbook I want in on this," and Corey said, "You got it, Graham. You're on one per cent." I mean, we were all joking. I helped them sketch out their ideas. It passed a few evenings.' Raymond takes another glug of iced tea. 'But then they made the spring. The money started pouring in. And as far as I know, Corey stuck to his word. Sent your dad a dividend every year.'

I'm dumbstruck. My dad has a stake in a spring? OK, I take it back. This is a pretty good story.

'I had an inheritance around that time,' Raymond adds, 'so I put some real money in. Set me up for life.'

'But how can a spring make so much money?' says Suze sceptically. 'It's just a piece of curly wire.'

That's *exactly* what I was thinking, only I didn't want to say it.

'It's a kind of folding spring?' Raymond shrugs. 'Useful thing. You'll find it in firearms, computer keyboards . . . you name it. Corey and Brent were smart. Corey had a gun; he did some hunting. They'd take it apart in the evenings, play around with the spring-loading mechanism. It gave them ideas. You know how it is.'

No, I don't know how it is. I've sat around loads of times with Suze, and we've taken plenty of things apart, like make-up kits. But I've never invented a new spring.

I suddenly understand why Dad was always so interested in my physics report. And why he used to say, 'Becky, love, why not go into engineering?' and 'Science is *not* boring, young lady!'

Hmm. Maybe he had a point. Now I half-wish I'd listened.

Ooh, maybe we can train up Minnie in science and she'll invent an even more advanced spring and we'll all be squillionaires. (When she's not winning the Olympics at show-jumping, of course.)

'When they got back from the trip,' Raymond is saying, 'they hired a lab and developed it properly. Four years later they launched it. Leastways, Corey launched it.'

'Only Corey? Why not Brent?'

Raymond's face kind of closes up. 'Brent bowed out after three years,' he says shortly.

'*Three years?* What do you mean, before it launched? So he didn't make any money?'

'Not to speak of. He pretty much just signed away his rights.'

'But why on earth would he do that?' I demand in horror. 'He must have known it had huge potential.'

'I guess Corey told him—' Raymond breaks off, then says, with sudden heat, 'It's in the past. It's between the two of them.'

'Corey told him what?' I narrow my eyes. '*What*, Raymond?'

'*What?*' echoes Suze, and Raymond makes an angry, huffing sound.

'Corey had taken over the business side. Maybe he gave Brent the wrong impression. Told him the investors weren't coming forward, told him it wasn't developing commercially, told him it was going to be expensive to take it to the next level. So Brent sold out for . . . well. Pretty much nothing.'

I stare at Raymond in utter dismay. 'Corey *conned* Brent? He should go to prison!'

Into my head flashes an image of Corey's Las Vegas palace, followed by Brent's trailer. It's so unfair. I can't bear it.

'Corey didn't break any law as far as I know,' Raymond replies stolidly. 'He was right in some of what he said – it *wasn't* a sure thing. It *did* need investment. Brent shoulda looked into it. Shoulda been smarter.'

'You know Brent's been living in a trailer?' I say accusingly. 'You know he's been *evicted* from a trailer?'

'If Brent was fool enough to fall for Corey's patter, that's his problem,' returns Raymond aggressively. 'I believe he attempted legal action, but the facts didn't stack up strongly enough. Corey's word against Brent's, see.'

'But that's so *wrong*! Brent helped invent it! It's made millions!'

'Whatever.' Raymond's face closes up even further, and I feel a surge of contempt for him.

'You just don't want to know, do you?' I say scathingly. 'No wonder you hide yourself away from the world.'

'If Brent's so talented,' puts in Suze, 'why didn't he make something of himself anyway?'

'Brent was never the strongest character,' says Raymond. 'I think it ate him up, seeing Corey succeed. He drank, married too many times . . . that'll burn through your money.'

'No wonder it ate him up!' I almost yell. 'It would eat anyone up! So, you think this is OK, do you? One of your friends conned the other and you don't want to do anything about it?'

'I don't get involved,' says Raymond, his face expressionless. 'We lost touch.'

'But you still take the money,' I say pointedly.

'So does your dad,' returns Raymond, equally pointedly. 'He still gets his dividend, as far as I know.'

My racing thoughts are brought up short. My dad. The money. The dividend. Why did he never tell us about this? He told us everything else about that holiday, over and over. Why did he leave out the best bit?

I'm sure Mum doesn't know any of this. She would have said. Which means . . . He's been keeping it secret, *all these years*?

I feel a bit hot. My dad is the most open, straightforward person in the world. Why would he keep a massive great secret like this?

255

'Bex, didn't you know anything about it?' says Suze in a low voice.

'Nothing.'

'Why would your dad hide something like that?'

'I have no idea. It's weird.'

'Is your dad secretly a billionaire?' Her eyes widen.

'No! No. He can't be!'

'I don't think Corey sends your dad much,' says Raymond, who's blatantly listening in. 'It's more of a token between friends. A few thousand dollars, maybe.'

A few thousand dollars . . . every year . . . And like a flash, it hits me. The BB. Dad's Big Bonus.

He's had these bonuses my whole life. He's always told us they come from consultancy work, and has taken us out for treats, and we've all raised a glass to him. Do the big bonuses come . . . from Corey?

I look at Suze, and I can see she's had the same idea.

'The BB,' she says.

One year Suze was staying with us when Dad got it, and he bought her a Lulu Guinness bag, even though she kept saying, 'Mr Bloomwood, you mustn't!'

'The BB.' I nod. 'I think that's it. It's not consultancy. It's this spring.'

My head is spinning. I need to talk this out. My dad has a whole secret thing going on. Why didn't he *tell* us?

'Does Corey *know* Brent was evicted?' Suze is asking Raymond.

There's a pause. Raymond shifts around a little in his chair, and stares out of the window.

'I believe your dad told him. I believe your dad was appealing to Corey for a financial settlement for Brent.'

'So that's what he's been trying to "put right"'. I glance at Suze. *Now* it's all starting to make sense. 'And what did Corey say?'

'I believe Corey refused.'

'But you didn't get involved?'

Raymond gazes steadily back at me. 'Not my life.'

I can't believe how much I loathe this man. He's just bowed out. Looked the other way. It's all right for him, living off his lucky investment, with his pottery and his ranch and his messy house. What about Brent? Brent who probably doesn't even *have a* house?

Tears have started to my eyes. I feel so proud of my dad, standing up for his old friend, trying to right this wrong.

'Doesn't Corey feel *guilty*?' persists Suze. 'Weren't you all supposed to be friends?'

'Well. It's more complicated than that with Brent and Corey.' Raymond steeples his fingers. 'It all goes back, you see.'

'To what?'

'Well, I guess you could say it goes back to Rebecca.'

Both Suze and I inhale sharply. I feel my skin prickling all over. *Rebecca.*

'Who . . . what . . .' My voice isn't working properly.

'We need to know who Rebecca is,' chimes in Suze firmly. 'We need to know what this is all about. Start from the beginning and don't leave out a single detail.'

She sounds just a *teensy* bit bossy, and I see irritation sweep over Raymond's face.

'I'm not starting anywhere,' he lashes back. 'I'm tired of re-hashing the past. If you want to know about Rebecca, ask your dad.'

'But you have to tell us!' protests Suze.

'I don't have to do anything. I've told you enough. Interview over.' He gets up, and before I know what's happening, he's grabbed *Twice* out of my hands. 'Now, put down my piece,' he says, glowering at Suze. 'And leave my property before I call the police.'

He looks quite menacing, and I gulp. Actually, it might be time to go. But as I get up from the sofa, I can't help shooting him my most scornful look.

'Well, thanks for filling us in on the story. I'm glad you can sleep at night.'

'You're welcome. Goodbye.' He jerks a thumb at the door. 'Hey, Maria!' he adds in a yell.

'Wait! One more thing. Do you have *any* idea where my dad might be?'

There's silence, and I can see in Raymond's eyes the thoughts passing through his mind.

'You tried Rebecca?' he says at last – and again I feel a weird little zing at hearing my own name.

'No! Don't you understand? We don't know anything about Rebecca. Not her surname, or where she lives—'

'Rebecca Miades,' he cuts me off short. 'Lives in Sedona, about two-fifty miles north of here. Your dad was talking about contacting her. She was there that night, see? She saw how the idea was born.'

She was *there*? Why didn't he mention that before? I'm about to ask more – but before I can draw breath, the housekeeper arrives.

'Maria, show these girls out,' says Raymond. 'Don't let them take anything.'

Honestly. We're not *thieves.*

And then, without another word, he opens the far door and stalks out of the studio into the yard. I can see him taking out a pipe and lighting it. I meet Suze's eyes and I can tell we're both thinking the same thing: *what an awful, awful man.*

My phone's been on the whole time in my pocket. Which means, assuming that the signal was OK, Mum must have heard at least some of the conversation. I can't quite face seeing her yet, so as soon as we've got through Raymond's gates, I find a bare patch of ground and flop down. I text Luke **All fine, on way**, and then sink back on the scrubby earth and look up at the huge blue sky.

I feel a bit overwhelmed, to be honest. I'm proud of my dad, trying to help out his old friend – but I'm kind of perplexed, too. Why wouldn't he tell us the truth? Why would he invent some 'bonus'? Why the *mystery*, for God's sake?

'It's weird, isn't it?' says Suze, echoing my thoughts. 'We *have* to go to Sedona now.'

'I suppose so,' I say after a pause. Although the truth is, I'm just a teeny bit over chasing my dad around the country.

I have a sudden pang of longing for simple, family life at home in Oxshott. Watching the telly and praising Mum for some M&S ready meal, and arguing over whether Princess Anne should cut her hair.

'I get that Dad wanted to make things right for Brent,' I say, still gazing at the blueness. 'But why didn't he *tell* us?'

259

'No idea,' admits Suze, after a pause. 'The whole thing is just weird.' She sounds fairly wiped out, too, and for a while we're quiet, breathing in the arid air; feeling the American sun on our faces. There's something about that great big sky. I feel a million miles from anyone. I feel like things are clearing in my head.

'This has been splitting us up too much,' I say suddenly. 'This whole affair, everyone's been split up. My mum and dad . . . you and Tarkie . . . me and my dad . . . we're all splintering away into separate bits, with secrets and mis-understandings and confusion . . . it's horrible. I don't want to be separate any more, I want to be *solid*. I want to be *together.*' I raise myself on to one elbow. 'I'm going to Sedona, Suze. I'm going to find my dad. Whatever he's doing, whatever his plan is, he can do it with us along-side. Because we're a *family.*'

'He can do it with me, too,' says Suze at once. 'I'm your best friend. I'm practically family. So count me in.'

'Count me in, too,' comes a voice, and Luke appears round the bend in the road, holding Minnie by the hand. 'We wondered where you'd got to,' he says mildly. 'Darling, you can't just go AWOL.'

'We haven't gone AWOL, we're making plans.'

'So I hear.' Luke meets my gaze with warm eyes. 'And like I say, count me in.'

'Count us both in,' says Janice eagerly, hurrying behind him. 'I'm practically family, love. You're right, it sounds like your dad needs a bit of moral support.'

'You can count me in, too,' says Danny, appearing from behind Janice. 'We heard the whole story over the phone. Jeez, that Corey! What a scumbag! And Raymond's not much better. But your dad rocks. We should totally help him.'

He's so animated, I feel a sudden tug at my heart. Danny's an important person with a big career. He doesn't have to be here. No one has to be here, in some remote corner of Arizona, focusing on an injustice that happened to my dad's friend, a long time ago. I mean, really. People must have better things to do, surely? But as I look around, I see a bank of such eager, loving faces, it makes me blink a little.

'Well . . . thanks,' I manage. 'My dad would really appreciate this.'

'Becky?' We all look round and I see Janice wincing. Mum is trudging along the side of the road, and I can tell she's in a bit of a state. Poor Mum. Her face is pink and her hair is askew.

'Why would he lie?' she says simply, and I can hear the hurt crackling through her voice.

'I don't know, Mum,' I say hopelessly. 'I'm sure he'll explain . . .'

Mum's hands are twisting at her pearls. Her Big Bonus pearls. Or do we still call them that?

'So, we're going to Sedona now?' She seems a bit defeated, as though she wants me to take the lead.

'Yes,' I nod. 'It's our best way of finding Dad.'

Plus – I don't say this – it's my best way of getting to meet my anti-namesake, Rebecca. And honestly, I cannot *wait*.

THIRTEEN

Oh my God. Why didn't I know about Sedona before? Why did no one tell me? It's breathtaking. It's . . . indescribable.

Well, all right, not literally indescribable. You *can* describe it. You can say, 'There are these huge red sandstone rocks everywhere, jutting up from the desert, making you feel all tiny and insignificant.' You can say, 'There's a kind of rawness to the landscape which gives you goosebumps.' You can say, 'There's a solitary bird of prey hanging above us, high in the sky, which seems to put all of humankind into perspective.'

You can say all that. But it's not the same as being there.

'Look at—' I keep pointing, and Danny will chime in, '*I know!*'

'Oh my God! The—'

'I know. It's awesome!'

For once, the anxiety has lessened in Suze's face. Mum and Janice are staring out of the opposite window, and exclaiming to each other too. In fact, everyone seems uplifted by the landscape.

We stayed another night in Wilderness in the end, because Luke said there was no point dashing off to Sedona that day and we all needed a decent night's sleep. Suze spent about two hours Skyping her children back in LA, and then Minnie and I joined in, and we played 'Skype charades', which is actually a very good game. I know Suze is longing for home life. She's desperately miserable and I don't think she's sleeping. She *still* hasn't heard from Tarkie, nor about this stupid tree, which seems really crap on the part of her parents and the head groundsman. I've actually been quite angry on her behalf. I mean, can't *one* of them call her back?

Except, when I pressed her on it, she admitted that she'd only left super-casual messages because she was paranoid that otherwise they'd guess it was all about her marriage. So they probably think they can leave it till she returns to the UK. *Honestly.*

And meanwhile, she's in a total state. I can practically *see* the worry cranking round her veins. She needs to know the answer, now. Surely *somebody* could help—

Ooh. Wait a minute. I've had a sudden idea.

Surreptitiously I fire off a quick email, hiding my phone under a magazine so Suze doesn't ask what I'm doing. It's a total long shot . . . but you never know. I press Send, then put my phone away and focus again on the spectacular views.

Today we've been driving since the crack of dawn, which makes about five hours on the road, including a stop for early lunch. The sky has that very blue, middle-of-the-day intensity, and I'm dying for a cup of tea.

Our destination is the High View Resort. According to the website, it has 'floor-to-ceiling red-rock views', plus it's 'only moments away from the chic shops and galleries of uptown Sedona'. But that's not why we're heading there. We're heading there because the in-house Meditation Leader and New Age Guide is guess who? Rebecca Miades.

There's even a headshot of her on their website, which I *haven't* shown to Mum. Because it turns out that this Rebecca is very pretty, especially for a woman of her age. She has all this fantastic long hair, dyed pinky-red. And quite an intense, sexy stare.

Not that it's relevant, whether she's pretty or not. I mean, I'm sure Dad . . . I'm *sure* . . .

I don't know quite where I'm going with this. Let's just say, I don't think Mum needs to see that photo.

Every time I look at Rebecca's staring face, I feel a little internal 'Eek!' I'd almost started to think this 'Rebecca' didn't exist – but here she is. Finally I'm going to find out what this is all about. And it's about bloody time, too. Honestly, not knowing stuff is totally exhausting. How do detectives do it? How do they stay sane? I keep wondering *What if* . . . and *Could it be* . . . and *But surely* . . . until my brain feels like it might explode.

'We're here!' Luke interrupts my thoughts, and I look eagerly out of the RV. The hotel is set way back from the road, with palm trees lining the driveway. It's only a few storeys high and is constructed out of some sort of red stone, so it blends perfectly into the landscape.

'I'll park the RV,' says Luke. 'You go and check in. Find your anti-namesake.' He raises his eyebrows at me, and I grin back. I think he's quite interested to meet this Rebecca, too.

It takes a bit of time at the front desk to organize all the rooms, and in the end Suze takes over. Danny spies a poster for the Restorative Spa Package and instantly decides he's going to do that, because apparently his muscles and nerves have been 'shot' by all this travelling. (Obviously it's the travelling, not the staying-up-all-night-in-Las-Vegas and drinking-bourbon-laced-iced-teas-at-the-fair, which is to blame.) Meanwhile, I've found a whole leaflet about Rebecca Miades. I withdraw to the corner of the lobby, curl up in a big wooden chair and start reading it avidly.

We at the High View Resort are proud to have Rebecca Miades as our resident spiritual counselor and psychic reader. Rebecca began her psychic studies while a student in India, and has trained at the Alara Institute of Mysticism. She is delighted now to be practicing in the spiritual power center of Sedona, where beneath the famed red rocks swirl age-old vortexes, energies and mystic forces that strengthen and empower the soul.

Wow. I didn't realize Sedona had age-old vortexes. Let alone mystic forces. I glance around the hotel lobby, half-hoping to see evidence of a mystic force, but all I can see is an old lady tapping at her iPad. Maybe you have to go outside.

Rebecca can offer Sacred Vortex Tours, Intuitive Counseling, Healing, Aura Reading, Celestial Art, Angel Communication . . .

Angel Communication? I blink at the leaflet. As in . . . *Angels*? I've never even heard of that. Or Celestial Art, which I suppose might be drawings of stars. A wind-chimey-type sound draws my attention, and I see a young man with longish hair coming through a beaded curtain. A badge on his shirt reads *Seth Connolly, Customer Welfare*. He smiles at me in an open friendly way, and notices the leaflet I'm holding.

'Are you interested in our New Age Center?' he asks pleasantly. 'Would you like me to direct you there?'

'Um, maybe,' I say. 'I'm just reading about Rebecca Miades.'

'Oh Rebecca.' His face creases into a smile. 'She's, like, my favourite person in the world.'

'Really?' I wasn't expecting that. 'Er . . . why? What's she like?'

'She's so sweet and *good*, you know what I mean? And her work is amazing,' he adds earnestly. 'She really helps the guests find spiritual enlightenment. She's a qualified Angel Therapy Practitioner, if you were interested in that? Or, she can do card readings, aura readings . . .'

'Perhaps. She looks really attractive,' I add, trying to prod him into further revelations. 'That hair!'

'Oh, her hair is her glory.' He nods. 'She colours it every year. Blue . . . red . . . green . . . We told her she should change her name to Rainbow!' He gives a boyish laugh.

'So, could I see her, do you think?' I try to sound casual. 'Make an appointment or something?'

'Sure!' he says. 'She's based at the New Age Center. She's been away, but she might be back by now. If you go along, one of the Spirit Mentors will be able to help you. Through there' – he points at the bead curtain – 'all the way through the seating area, and you'll find the New Age Center in back.'

'OK. Well, maybe I'll stroll along. Thanks.'

As Seth walks off, I glance furtively around the lobby. Mum, Minnie and Janice are looking at a display of dream catchers. Suze is still talking to the woman at the front desk. Danny is following a lady in a white spa uniform towards the Spa Center.

I think I might pop along and see this Rebecca for myself. Just quietly. Just me. As I stand up, I feel a spasm of nerves, and firmly tell myself off. There's no need to be nervous. This is only some woman from Dad's past. No big deal.

With a musical clatter of beads, I push my way through the curtain. I'm standing in a large, airy area furnished with sofas and chairs, in which a few people are sitting, reading newspapers and magazines. There are palms in pots, a huge skylight, and a sign reading *New Age Center*, and I'm about to head in that direction, when a pair of shoes suddenly catches my attention. They're sticking out from a large wicker armchair – a pair of scuffed, suede men's loafers. I know those shoes, I *know* them. There's an elbow on the arm of the chair, too. A very, very familiar elbow, just a little more tanned than usual.

'Dad?' My voice rockets out of me before I can stop it. *'Dad?'*

The tanned elbow instantly jerks off the arm of the chair. The shoes move. The chair is pushed back with a scrape on the terracotta-tiled floor. And the next moment, I'm staring at Dad. Right here. In the flesh. My missing dad.

'Dad?' I almost yell again.

'Becky! Darling!' He seems as shell-shocked as I am. 'What— How on earth— Who told you I was here?'

'No one! We've been looking for you! We've been tracking you! We've been— Do you realize—' My whirling thoughts won't quite make it into words. 'Dad, do you realize—'

Dad closes his eyes as though in disbelief. 'Becky, I *told* you not to, I *told* you to go home—'

'We were worried about you, don't you understand?' I yell. 'We were *worried*!'

All sorts of emotions are pushing their way through me, like hot lava through a volcano. I'm not sure if I feel relieved, or happy, or furious, or just want to scream. Tears are on my face, I suddenly realize, but I have no idea how they got here. 'You just went off,' I say, breathing fast. 'You *left* us.'

'Oh Becky.' He holds out his arms. 'Love. Come here.'

'No.' I shake my head furiously. 'You can't just . . . Do you know what a state Mum's been in? Mum!' I scream. 'Muuuuuum!'

A moment later there's an almighty clatter of beads as Mum, Janice and Minnie all pile through the curtain.

'GRAHAM?'

I have literally never heard anything so shrill as Mum's voice. It's like a train whistle. We all flinch and I can hear more chairs scraping as people turn to watch.

As she approaches Dad, her eyes are sparking with fury and her nostrils are flared.

'Where have you BEEN?'

'Jane,' says Dad, looking alarmed. 'Now, Jane, I told you I had a little errand . . .'

'Little errand? I thought you were DEAD!' She collapses into racking sobs, and Dad throws his arms around her.

'Jane,' he croons. 'Jane, my love. Jane, don't worry.'

'How can I not worry?' Mum's head jerks back like a cobra's. 'How can I not worry? I'm your WIFE!' She swings her arm and slaps Dad across the cheek.

Oh my God. I've never seen Mum hit Dad before. I feel quite shocked. Thankfully, Minnie is playing with the beaded curtain, so I don't think she saw anything.

'Um, Minnie,' I say hastily. 'Grandpa and Grana need to . . . er . . . talk.'

'Don't you ever, ever disappear again.' Now Mum is clinging to Dad, tears running down her face. 'I thought I was a widow!'

'She did,' confirms Janice. 'She was looking up her insurance policies.'

'A *widow*?' Dad gives a shout of incredulous laughter.

'Don't you laugh at me, Graham Bloomwood!' Mum looks like she might wallop Dad again. 'DON'T YOU DARE!'

'Come on, sweetheart.' I grab Minnie's hand and push through the beaded curtain, my heart still thumping. A moment later, Janice joins me and we look at each other in disbelief.

'What's up?' says Suze, turning from the front desk. 'What's your mum yelling about? She's not on about the correct pronunciation of "scone" again, is she?'

Mum once took Suze and me out to tea at a posh hotel and had an altercation with a member of staff about how to say 'scone' and Suze has never forgotten it.

'No,' I say, feeling almost hysterical. 'She's not. Suze, you will not *believe* this . . .'

It takes two large Arizona Breezes to calm me down. (Gin, cranberry juice, grapefruit juice – *delicious*.) So God knows how many drinks Mum will need. Dad's here. We've found him. After all our searching, all our angst . . . He was just calmly sitting in an armchair, reading the paper. I mean . . . *what*?

I can barely sit still. All I want to do is go back into that seating area and quiz Dad relentlessly, till I understand everything: every single tiny little thing. But Suze won't let me.

'Your mum and dad need space,' she keeps saying. 'Let them alone. Give them time. Be patient.'

She won't even let me creep past them to go and check out the famous Rebecca. Nor has she run in to demand news of Tarkie. So we've all come outside on to the front verandah of the hotel, and are sitting on wicker chairs, swivelling round sharply whenever we hear a sound. I say 'all' – actually, Luke has gone off to the business centre to catch up on his emails. But the rest of us are sitting here, feeling like life has been put on hold while we wait. It's been half an hour, at least—

And then suddenly, there they are, swooshing back through the beaded curtain. Mum looks like she's run a marathon, while Dad seems startled to see the assembled group, and flinches as everyone starts exclaiming, 'Graham! We've found you!' and 'Where've you been?' and 'Are you all right?'

'Yes,' he keeps saying. 'Ah, yes. I'm fine, we're all fine . . . Goodness, I had no idea . . . Well, here we are, anyway. Would anyone like a snack? Drink? Ah . . . shall we order something?' He seems pretty flustered. Which is also unlike Dad.

When we're all seated with drinks and snacks and 'light bites' menus, the chatter dies down. One by one, we turn again towards Dad.

'So, come on,' I say. 'Why did you dash off? Why the big secret?'

'Why couldn't you just *tell* us what was going on?' says Suze tremulously. 'I got so worried . . .'

'Oh, my dear Suze.' Dad's face creases in distress. 'I know. I'm so sorry. I had no idea . . .' He hesitates. 'I simply came across a huge injustice. And I had to right it.'

'But Graham, why was it all so cloak and dagger?' says Janice, who is sitting beside Mum. 'Poor Jane's been beside herself, thinking all sorts!'

'I know.' Dad rubs his face. 'I know that now. I suppose I was foolish enough to think that if I told you not to worry then you wouldn't. And the reason I didn't tell you the whole story at first . . .' He gives another sigh. 'Oh, I feel so ridiculous.'

'The Big Bonus,' I say, and Dad nods, without looking up.

'It's a fine thing,' he says heavily, 'to be caught out in a lie like that at my time of life.'

He looks really unhappy. I don't know whether to feel sorry for him, or angry.

'But Dad, *why*?' I can't help my exasperation slipping out. '*Why* did you tell us you were earning consultancy money? You didn't need to invent a Big Bonus. You could have told us it was money from Corey. It wouldn't have mattered!'

'Darling, you don't understand. Not long after you were born, I lost my job. No reason in particular: it was a time of general cut-backs. But your mother . . .' He hesitates. 'She didn't react very well.'

He says this with typical Dad understatement, but he probably means, *She threw the crockery at me*.

'I was anxious!' says Mum defensively. 'Anyone would be anxious! I had a little one, our income had plummeted . . .'

'I know,' says Dad soothingly. 'It was a worrying time.'

'You coped very well, love,' says Janice, putting a supportive hand on Mum's. 'I remember that time. You did wonders with mince.'

'I was out of work for a few months. Things were tricky.' Dad takes up the story. 'And then, out of the blue, I received a letter from Corey. Not just a letter, a cheque too. He'd been making an income for a while, but suddenly he was into serious money. He remembered our joky deal and he'd actually honoured it. He sent me five hundred pounds. I couldn't believe my eyes.'

'You have no idea what five hundred pounds was in those days,' chimes in Mum eagerly. 'You could buy . . . a house!'

'Not a house,' corrects Dad. 'Maybe a second-hand car.'

'That money saved our lives,' says Mum with typical drama. 'It saved your life, Becky love! Who knows if you wouldn't have starved to death?'

I can see Suze opening her mouth to protest something like *Surely there was a welfare system?* and I shake my head. Mum's in the moment. She won't want to hear about welfare systems.

'But that's when I made my huge mistake.' Dad is silent for a long moment, and we all wait, hardly even breathing. 'It was vanity,' he says at last, 'sheer vanity. I wanted your mother to be proud of me. Here we were, not long married, new parents, and I'd gone and lost my job. So . . . I lied. I invented a piece of work and told her I'd earned the money.' His face kind of crumples. 'Stupid. So stupid.'

'I remember you running round to see me, Jane!' Janice's face brightens. 'I was hanging out my washing, remember? You came sprinting in, saying, "Guess what my clever husband's done!" I mean, we were all so relieved.' She looks around the group. 'You don't know what the strain had been like, what with Becky's arrival and bills going up every day . . .' She leans across and pats Dad's arm. 'Graham, don't blame yourself. Who wouldn't tell a little fib in those circumstances?'

'It was pathetic,' says Dad, with a sigh. 'I wanted to be the saviour.'

'You *were* the saviour,' confirms Janice firmly. 'That money came into your family because of you, Graham. It doesn't matter how.'

'I wrote back and said, "Corey, you've just saved my marriage, old friend." He replied, "Well, let's see if I can do the same next year!" And so it began.' Dad takes a slug of his drink, then looks up at me and Mum. 'I meant to tell you the truth. Every year. But you were both so proud. It became such a tradition for us to spend the Big Bonus together.'

I can see Mum fingering her pearls, and my mind ranges back over the years. All the lovely lunches we've had, celebrating Dad's Big Bonus. All the treats he's bought us. Hours of happiness and pride in him. No wonder he never let on. I totally understand it.

And I also understand how shocked he was when he heard Brent had been evicted from his trailer. I mean, look at them. Dad all comfortable and prosperous, and Brent penniless. But *how* could he have thought he could disappear for days at a time with no explanation and still keep his secret intact?

'So let me get this straight, Dad.' I lean towards him. 'You were hoping that you'd just go off to Vegas, see Corey, somehow put things right for Brent, come home . . . and we'd never ask about the details.'

Dad thinks for a moment, then says, 'Yes, that's about the sum of it.'

'You thought we'd just sit at home and wait patiently.'
'Yes.'

'When we thought you'd been kidnapped by Bryce and he was going to brainwash you and Tarkie.'

274

'Ah . . .'

'You thought you'd come back and Mum would say, "Good trip, dear?" and you'd say, "Yes," and that would be the end of the conversation.'

'Um . . .' Dad looks a little foolish. 'I hadn't really thought that far.'

Honestly. *Men.*

'So, what has happened about Brent?' A deep voice comes from behind my seat and I look round to see Luke standing there. 'Good to see you, Graham,' he adds with a little smile, and holds his hand out and shakes Dad's. 'Glad you're safe and sound.'

'Ah, Brent.' Dad's face twists in anguish again. 'It's a bad situation. I'm doing my best. I've appealed to Corey. I've appealed to Raymond. But . . .' He sighs. 'There were personality clashes, you see.'

'But it makes no sense!' I say impatiently. 'Why would Corey send you money every year but totally con Brent out of everything? What's he got against Brent?'

'Well. It goes back to the trip. It was all to do with . . .' He glances awkwardly at Mum.

'*Cherchez la femme,*' says Mum, rolling her eyes. 'I knew it. Didn't I know it? Didn't I say, "This is all about a woman"?'

'You did!' exclaims Janice, wide-eyed. 'You did, love! So, who was the woman?'

'Rebecca,' answers Dad, and some last bit of tension seems to sink out of him. There's a dead silence. I can sense eyes flickering avidly about the group, but no one dares even breathe.

'Graham,' says Luke at last, in such calm, even tones

275

that I want to applaud. 'Why not explain about Rebecca?'

I've learned a lot of useful lessons on this road trip. I've learned you can't line-dance properly in flip-flops. I've learned that grits are definitely not my favourite food. (I ordered them in Wilderness; Minnie hated them too.) And now I'm learning that when your dad spills the beans on some ancient, complicated three-way love affair, you should take notes. Or ask him to do a PowerPoint presentation with a handout.

I am *so* confused. In fact, I'm going to run over the facts again, privately to myself, leaving out the talk of sunsets and young men's blood, and the heat of the day and all the other poetical stuff which Dad throws in.

Come on. If I can follow DVD box sets about serial killers, surely I can follow this story? Maybe I'll *think* of it like a box set. With episodes. Yes. Good idea.

Episode 1: Dad, Corey, Brent and Raymond were on a road trip, and met a beautiful girl called Rebecca Miades in a bar. Corey fell for Rebecca in a big way, but she went off with Brent instead.

(So far so good.)

Episode 2: Corey never got over Rebecca. (Fast-forward: He even called his first daughter Rebecca. And his first wife found out and called him obsessed and left him.) When Brent and Rebecca broke up, Corey made a renewed pitch for Rebecca, but she played him around and then went back to Brent.

(I *think* I'm still following . . .)

Episode 3: Brent and Rebecca had an on-off relationship for some years and had a baby, also called Rebecca.

(I've met her! The girl on the steps of the trailer who called me 'Princess Girl'. I kind of understand why she was so hostile now, although she did *not* have to say I have a 'prinky-prinky voice'.)

Episode 4: Dad knew Rebecca had played Corey around and decided she was bad news. So when Mum insisted they call me Rebecca, he didn't want to.

Episode 5: Meanwhile, they'd all lost touch, because they didn't have Facebook and phones were expensive or whatever.

(You do have to feel sorry for the older generation. I mean, all this 'pay phones' and 'telegrams' and 'air mail'. How did they *cope*?)

Episode 6: Then Corey started making big money. Dad got his first cheque and he just assumed Brent was loaded, too. Little did he realize that Corey had deliberately cheated Brent out of everything, because of his raging jealousy over Rebecca.

(Again, if they'd only had Facebook. Or, you know, ever called each other, ever.)

Episode 7: Years later, Dad found out that Brent was penniless. He was so shocked, he flew to the States and saw Brent, but it didn't go well and then Brent disappeared. So he co-opted Tarquin and Bryce as fellow Musketeers and headed off to see Corey. But Corey wouldn't even take his call, let alone have a meeting.

(Which makes me hate Corey even more. How could anyone refuse to see my dad?)

Episode 8, Season Finale: So Brent's probably homeless but Corey doesn't care. Raymond just hides away on his ranch. And no one knows where Brent is, and—

'Wait!' I cry suddenly. 'Rebecca!'

How could I have got so distracted that I forgot about Rebecca?

'Dad, did you know she works here?' My words tumble out in excitement. 'Rebecca, who I'm *not* named after, works in this very hotel! She's here!' I flail my hands. 'Rebecca! Here!'

'Love, I know.' Dad looks perplexed. 'That's why I'm here. That's why I came to Sedona.'

'Oh,' I say, feeling stupid. 'Of course.'

'She's been away but she's due back today.' Dad gestures around the seating area. 'That's why I've been waiting here.'

'Right. I see.'

Honestly, I *so* need the printed handout.

'So, is there *any* hope for Brent?' Luke says to Dad, as a waiter brings another round of drinks. 'What's your strategy?'

'At first I thought Corey might have mellowed with age.' Dad pulls a rueful face. 'I was wrong about that. Now I've got a lawyer involved and we're examining the case again. But it's difficult without Brent himself. It was a long time ago . . . there are no records . . . I thought perhaps Rebecca could help.' He breaks off and sighs. 'But I don't know if we'll get anywhere.'

'And what's Tarkie doing?'

Poor Suze has been waiting all this time to ask. She's sitting on the edge of her seat, her hands squishing together. 'Is he OK? Only, I haven't heard from him for . . . a while.'

'Suze, my dear!' Dad quickly turns to her. 'Don't worry. Tarquin is just preoccupied. He's gone off to Las Vegas to find out more about Corey. Without giving away the connection to me, you see. He's a very resourceful man, your husband.'

The crease in Suze's brow doesn't lessen.

'Right,' she says, her voice trembling. 'OK. Um, Graham, has he mentioned any . . . *trees* at all?'

'Trees?' Dad sounds surprised.

'Never mind.' Suze looks a bit desperate. 'It doesn't matter.' She picks up a piece of bread and starts ripping it to bits without eating it.

'I just hope this Brent appreciates what you're doing!' says Mum, her face a bit pink. 'After all we've been through.'

'Oh, he probably won't,' says Dad, with an easy laugh. 'I'd like you to meet him, though. He's a pig-headed old soul, and he can be his own worst enemy, but he's wise. "You can CB or you can MMM," he used to say. I've always remembered that.' Dad sees Janice's confused look. 'Cut Back or Make More Money,' he explains.

'That's very good!' says Janice in delight. 'CB or MMM. Oh, I like that. I'm going to write it down.'

I'm staring at Dad in stupefaction. 'CB or MMM'? That came from *Brent*?

'But that's Becky's motto!' says Suze, in equal disbelief. That's like, her *Bible*.'

'I thought that was your saying!' I say almost accusingly to Dad. 'That's what I always tell people. "My dad says you have to CB or MMM."'

'Well, I do say that.' He smiles. 'But I learned it first from Brent. I learned a lot from him, in fact.'

'Like what?'

'Oh, I don't know.' Dad leans back in his chair, his glass in his hand, his eyes distant. 'Brent was always philosophical. He was a listener. I was going through some anxieties about my career path at the time, and he'd put everything in perspective. His other saying was, "The other person always has a point." He'd bring that one out when Raymond and Corey were arguing, which they often did after a few beers.' Dad laughs at the recollection. 'They'd be going at it, hammer and tongs, and Brent would be lying there, feet up on a rock, smoking, saying, "The other person always has a point. Listen to each other, and you'll hear it." It drove the others *mad*.' He pauses and I can tell he's lost in his memories.

OK, next Christmas, when Dad starts telling us about his trip again, I am *so* going to lap up every word.

'But why couldn't Brent sort out his own life a bit better?' I venture. 'I mean, if he was so wise and everything?'

A strange, melancholy expression passes over Dad's face.

'Not so easy when it's your own life. He knew he drank too much, even then, although he hid it. I tried to talk to him about it, but . . .' His hands fall to his lap. 'We were young. What did I know about alcoholism?' He looks so downcast. 'What a waste.'

There's a kind of sober little silence. This is such a sad story. And I'm feeling like Dad now. I'm burning with righteous indignation. I want to sort everything out for Brent and *crush* that vile Corey.

'But I'm not sure where to go from here.' Dad rubs his eyes wearily. 'If I can't get access to Corey . . .'

'I can't believe he wouldn't meet up with you,' I say hotly. 'His old friend.'

'He's built a fortress around himself,' says Dad with a shrug. 'Gates, guards, dogs . . .'

'We only got in because they were holding a children's birthday party and thought we were guests,' I tell him.

'You did well, love,' says Dad, wryly. 'I didn't even manage to get through on the phone.'

'We met his new wife and everything. She actually seems lovely.'

'From what I hear, she's very sweet-natured.' Dad nods.

'I thought perhaps I could get at Corey through her. But Corey controls her. He wants to know where she is at all times, reads her correspondence . . .' He sips his drink. 'I tried to get a meeting with her, after I'd failed with Corey. She emailed back and said it wasn't possible and not to contact her again. I wouldn't be surprised if Corey sent the email.'

'Oh, Dad,' I say with sympathy.

'Oh, that wasn't the worst! I even stood outside the house and called out as they drove out in their Bugatti. Waved my arms, shouted . . . But no joy.'

I feel a surge of fresh fury at Corey. How *dare* he demean my dad like that?

'If Brent only knew how much you were doing on his behalf,' I say. 'Do you think he has any idea?'

'I doubt it,' says Dad with a rueful chuckle. 'I mean, he knew I wanted to help. But I don't expect he imagined I'd end up in such an escapade—'

He stops at the sound of clicking beads. Something weird passes over his face and he blinks several times. At once I turn to see what it is – and freeze dead.

No way. No *way*.

It's all happening! The box-set plot is unfolding before my eyes. It's like a whole new season is kicking off.

Season 2
Episode 1: Forty-something years later, in a hotel in Sedona, Arizona, Graham Bloomwood and Rebecca Miades finally come face to face again.

She's standing at the beaded curtain, curling a strand

282

of long, dyed-red hair around one finger. She has lots of amber eyeshadow around her green eyes, too much kohl and a long floaty skirt in burgundy. Her matching top is low-cut, displaying lots of cleavage. Her nails are painted black, and she has a henna tattoo snaking up her arm. She looks at Dad and says nothing, but smiles slowly in recognition, her eyes crinkling up like a cat's.

'Oh my God,' says Dad at last, and his voice sounds a little faint. 'Rebecca.'

'Oh my God,' comes an abrasive-sounding voice from behind Rebecca. 'Princess Girl.'

From: dsmeath@locostinternet.com
To: Brandon, Rebecca
Subject: Re: Massive, MASSIVE favour

Dear Mrs Brandon

I received your email an hour ago, and was taken by its 'urgent' tone. I do not quite understand how 'lives can be hanging in the balance' over such a matter, but I do perceive your anxiety and as you reminded me, I did indeed 'offer to help'.

I therefore set out immediately, with a small packed supper and my Thermos. I am writing now from a service station on the A27.

I hope to reach my destination before too long and will keep you abreast of 'developments'.

Yours sincerely

Derek Smeath

FOURTEEN

OK, there are officially way too many Rebeccas at this gathering.

There's me, Becky.

There's Rebecca.

And there's 'Becca', who is Brent and Rebecca's daughter. She's the one I met at the trailer park, the one who calls me Princess Girl, even though it's getting quite annoying.

It's about half an hour later. Dad's ordered more food and drinks (we don't really want them, but it gives us something to do), and we're all trying to get to know the two new additions. But it's not the most relaxed group, I must say. Mum keeps eyeing Rebecca with deep suspicion, especially her outfit. Mum has views on how ladies of a certain age should dress, and they involve not having lots of cleavage showing, nor henna tattoos, nor a nose-ring. (I only just noticed it. It's teeny.)

Becca is sitting next to me, and I can smell some really strong fabric conditioner on her T-shirt. She's wearing cut-off jeans and is sitting with her legs sprawled, unlike her mother, who looks like an elegant witch perched on her broomstick.

It turns out that Becca is on her way to a new job at a hotel in Santa Fe, but has stopped off here for a night. I asked about her little dog Scooter – I met him at the trailer park – and she told me she can't have a pet at her new job, and she's had to give him away. And then glared at me like it's all my fault.

She's so unfriendly, and I can't understand it at all. What you'd *think* is that the two of them would marvel at Dad's plan to help Brent, and offer assistance. Instead, Becca answers every question with a defensive monosyllable. She doesn't know where her dad is right now. He'll be in touch when he's ready. She doesn't see how Dad can right the wrong that was done to Brent. No, she doesn't have any ideas. No, she doesn't want to brainstorm.

Meanwhile, Rebecca just wants to tell us about the amazing, 'spirit-cleansing' hikes we can do in the area. When Dad brings her back to the subject of Brent, she starts reminiscing about the time they all met a shaman at a reservation.

'Look, help me here, Rebecca!' Dad erupts at last. 'I'm trying to get justice for Brent!'

'Oh, Graham.' Rebecca gives her mysterious smile. 'You're such a good man. You always were. You have a wonderful flow.'

'Justice,' mutters Becca, with an eye-roll, and I feel a spike of irritation.

'What's your problem?' I demand. 'Why are you being so negative? We're here to help your dad!'

286

'Maybe you are.' She glowers back at me. 'But maybe it's too late. Where were you in 2002?'

'What?' I look at her blankly.

'Dad asked Corey for help back in 2002, when he was at a real low. Put on a suit, went to see him in Vegas. He could have used your dad by his side then.'

'But my dad was in England,' I say, puzzled. 'He didn't know.'

'Of course he knew,' says Becca scathingly. 'Dad wrote him.'

OK, I'm not having this.

'Dad!' I interrupt the conversation he's having with Rebecca. 'Did you know about Brent asking Corey for help in 2002?'

'No.' Dad looks blank. 'I heard nothing about that.'

'You never got a letter?' I gesture at Becca. 'She thinks you got a letter from Brent.'

'Of course I didn't!' says Dad hotly. 'Do you think if I'd got a letter from Brent about this horrendous situation, I would have *ignored* it?'

Becca seems taken aback by this response.

'Well, Corey told Dad you knew. Corey told Dad you'd been in touch about it, and your view was . . . He said—' She stops herself, and I find myself wondering what exactly Corey said.

'Becca, I think Corey must have lied,' says Dad more gently.

OK. Now this all makes sense. Corey stitched up my dad, and that's why Becca hates us.

'Do you understand now?' I turn to Becca. 'My dad *didn't* say whatever heinous thing Corey said he did.'

So you didn't need to be so hostile, I add silently. *Or say, 'Fuck off, Princess Girl.'*

I'm hoping Becca will respond with something like *Oh my God. Now I see it all. I've wronged you; please accept my apologies.*

But she just shrugs and looks at her phone and mutters, 'Anyway, you'll never get anything out of Corey. No chance.'

God, real people are so disappointing. I'm sure she would have done it better in the box-set version. A minute or two later, she says she has to leave, and I'm really not sorry.

'Bye, Princess Girl,' she says as she shrugs her bag on to her shoulder.

I want to say, *Bye, Horribly Rude and Negative Girl,* but instead, I just smile and say, 'Keep in touch!'

Not, I add in my head.

When she and Rebecca have gone, the atmosphere eases a little. Suze heads off to her room, to check in with her kids. Mum is wondering whether we should order more snacks or whether that will spoil our dinners, and Janice is reading out loud from a leaflet about 'spirit guides', when Rebecca appears again.

'I thought you'd like to see this.' Her eyes glimmer at Dad as she holds out an old, faded black-and-white photograph.

'Goodness me!' says Dad, and gets out his reading spectacles. 'Let me look at that.' After he's had a good long peruse, he puts it on the table and I lean over to see. There they all are, sitting on rocks in the desert.

Dad is recognizably Dad. Corey looks like a

completely different person from the tight-faced weirdo we met in Las Vegas. Raymond probably looks the same, except his greying beard is so big now, it's hard to tell. But the person I'm focusing on is Brent. I peer more closely, trying to get a sense of this man we're all trying to win justice for.

He has broad features. A square forehead. There's a stubborn look to him, even in the photo. But he looks like he could be kind and wise, too, just like Dad said. Then my gaze transfers to the young Rebecca, and I blink in amazement. God, she was beautiful! In the photo, she's sitting apart from the others, her head thrown back, her hair cascading down and her breasts almost popping out of her low-cut prairie-style dress. I can see exactly why Corey might have fallen for her. And Brent. I mean, to be honest, who *wouldn't* fall for her?

Did Raymond? Did *Dad*?

I feel an uncomfortable little flip in my stomach.

'Let me see!' says Mum, pulling the photo towards her, and I can see her studying Rebecca, her mouth pursed. As she lifts her gaze to the current Rebecca, her expression doesn't change.

'So, I took the liberty of booking massages for all of you tomorrow,' says Rebecca, in her soft, mesmerizing voice. 'Then maybe the hotel could organize a picnic lunch? And you *must* see the juniper trees while you're here.'

'We're not here for pleasure,' says Dad. 'So we'll have to cancel the massages.'

'You can take a few days off.' She gives him her catlike smile. 'You don't want to burn out, all of you.'

'I'm afraid we can't.' Dad shakes his head. 'We need to press on with the task.'

'You're in Sedona, Graham. Centre of relaxation. You need to kick back. Enjoy it!'

'Not really,' points out Dad. 'Helping Brent is our priority. He's the victim.'

'*Victim*,' mutters Rebecca, her eyes raised to heaven. She speaks so quietly I'm not sure if I actually heard it – but Dad did.

'Rebecca?' He turns to her. 'What does that mean?'

'Well, really.' Her voice bursts out. 'I can't keep quiet any more. What do you all think you're doing? Because it's *crazy*.'

'We're trying to put things right for Dad's old friend!' I say hotly. 'That's not crazy!'

'Put things right?' Her eyes flash at me. 'You know nothing about it. If Brent was swindled, it was his own fault. Everyone knew Corey was a liar. If Brent hadn't *drunk* so much, maybe he would have kept his wits about him.'

'That's very harsh,' says Dad, sounding shocked.

'It's the truth. He's just a loser. Always was. And now you all want to prop his life back up for him.' She sounds almost savage. 'Why should Brent get his life propped up?'

We're all exchanging shocked looks. Now I'm guessing that Rebecca and Brent's relationship didn't end too brilliantly.

'But he's almost certainly homeless!' I point out. 'And he's your daughter's father!'

'What does that mean to me?' Rebecca snaps. 'If he's homeless, it's his own damn idiot fault.'

I've never seen someone change so fast. All the syrupy charm has slid away, and with it has gone her veneer of attractiveness. She looks older and bitterer, and kind of pinched around the mouth. All in ten seconds. I almost want to whisper in her ear, *You know, being mean is really bad for your looks.*

Dad is watching her appraisingly, and I wonder if she was like this all those years ago. Maybe she was worse.

At any rate, something tells me: Mum doesn't need to worry.

'Well,' he says at last, in pleasant tones. 'We'll do our thing. And you do your thing. It was nice to see you again, Rebecca.'

He gets to his feet and waits meaningfully. After a moment, Rebecca stands up too, and picks up her tasselled leather bag.

'You'll never succeed anyway,' she says scathingly. 'Becca's right. Not a chance.'

My blood is starting to boil. This woman is a total *witch*.

'Hey, wait a moment, Rebecca,' I say as she reaches the door. 'You think I'm named after you, don't you? Just like Becca is, and Corey's daughter.'

Rebecca says nothing, but turns to face us again and shakes back her long hair, all the time looking at Dad with this self-satisfied smile. She clearly believes every man gets so besotted by her that he names his child after her. Ugh. Ugh!

'I knew it!' I glare at her. 'That's what your daughter thought, when I met her at the trailer park. You must have looked Dad up online and found out about me,

291

and you simply assumed that he'd called me Rebecca after you.' I lift my chin firmly. 'Well, guess what? He *didn't*. I'm named after the *book*.'

'Hear! Hear!' chimes in Mum wildly. 'The *book*!'

'And you want to know something even more interesting?' I add, in my most lacerating tones. 'Dad didn't *want* to name me Rebecca. He wanted to name me anything *but* Rebecca. I wonder why?'

Rebecca says nothing, but I can see two little pink dots appear on her cheeks. Ha. That tells *her*. A moment later, the beads have fallen in a noisy clatter behind her, and we all look at each other.

'Well!' says Mum, breathing hard. '*Well!* Of all the . . .'

'Dear oh dear,' says Dad, shaking his head, in that understated way he has.

'She reminds me of that Angela who used to run the church tombola,' muses Janice. 'Do you remember her, Jane? With the bracelets? Drove a blue Honda?'

Only Janice could bring up the church tombola at this moment in time. I feel a giggle rising, and then it's a snuffle, and then it's a full-blown burst of laughter. I feel like I haven't laughed in *so long*.

Dad's smiling too, and even Mum seems to see the funny side. As I glance at Luke, he's also grinning, and then Minnie decides that she finds it all hilarious, too.

'Funny!' she announces, clutching her stomach with laughter. 'Funny lady!'

'She *was* a funny lady,' agrees Janice, and that sets us all off again. As Suze rejoins us, we're still giving the occasional giggle, and she stares at us all in astonishment.

'Sorry.' I wipe my nose. 'I'll explain later. What's up at home?'

'Oh, everything's fine,' says Suze. 'I was just thinking, it's still a nice afternoon. D'you want to go for a little walk?'

FIFTEEN

Sedona's an amazing place to walk. The panorama of towering red rocks is like some kind of film backdrop, and all of us keep glancing up as though to check it's still there. As we stroll past the 'chic shops and galleries', Mum and Dad are walking arm in arm which is very sweet. Suze and Janice are holding Minnie's hands and showing her things in windows. Luke is typing an email. And I'm walking along in a bit of a trance. I'm still seething with indignation at Rebecca. (And her daughter.) The more people tell me I can't succeed at something, the more I want to prove them wrong. We will right this injustice. We *will*. She'll see.

Ideas are seeding in my brain, thoughts, half-plans . . . I keep taking a pen out of my bag and scribbling odd words on a scrap of paper. *Surely* we can do it, somehow?

'What are you up to, love?' says Mum, noticing me, and I pause, mid-word.

'Thinking of a plan to squash Corey. But I'm not sure

yet . . .' I glance down again at my page. 'I've got a *bit* of an idea . . .'

We're going to have a meeting later to discuss everything, and I might raise my plan as a possibility. Maybe.

'Well done, love!' says Mum, and I shrug.

'I don't know. It's only a few thoughts so far. I need to work on it.'

'Look at that!' says Suze, and we all pause at a shop called Someday My Prints Will Come. The window is full of gorgeous books, folders, boxes and cushions – all covered in hand-blocked prints of trees, birds and other nature-y stuff.

'Beautiful!' Mum agrees. 'Becky, look at those dinky little suitcases! Let's go in!'

We leave Luke outside, finishing his email, because he says it's super-urgent and otherwise he would *absolutely* have loved to go and browse photo-frames covered in cactuses. (He's such a fibber.) As we enter, a woman behind the till wearing a feather-print dress rises with a smile.

'Welcome,' she says in a soft voice.

'Did you create these prints?' asks Suze, and as the woman nods her head, she adds, 'I love them!'

As I stroll around, I can hear Suze asking lots of questions about print-making. The thing about Suze is, she's very artistic. She could totally open a shop like this. In fact, maybe that's what she should do at Letherby Hall. *The Letherby Print Collection*. It would be fantastic! I'm just squirrelling this idea away to tell her later, when I come across a display of pencils and stop dead. Wow. I've never *seen* such amazing pencils.

They're a little thicker than normal pencils, and each is covered in a different print. But not just that: the wood's coloured, too. There are orange-print pencils with lavender-coloured wood . . . turquoise-print pencils with crimson wood . . . They're just stunning. As I raise one to my nose, I can smell this gorgeous, wafty, sandal-woody scent.

'Are you buying one, Becky?' says Mum, and I swivel round to see her, Dad and Janice approaching. Mum's carrying three box files decorated with a tree print, and Janice has about a dozen tea towels covered in pumpkins.

'Oh no,' I say automatically, and put the pencil back. 'They're lovely, though, aren't they?'

'They're only $2.49,' says Mum, picking up a green leaf-print pencil with amber wood. 'You should get one.'

'It's fine,' I say hastily. 'What are you getting?'

'I'm organizing my life,' says Mum with a flourish. 'It's all changing.' She taps each box file in turn. 'Letters, warranties and printed-out emails. They'll be the *death* of me. All over the kitchen.'

'Why do you print out your emails?' I say, puzzled.

'Oh, I can't read emails on the *screen*.' Mum wrinkles her nose as though this is a mad idea. 'I don't know how you do that, love. And Luke! Doing all his business on a tiny little phone! How on earth does he manage it?'

'You could increase the font size?' I suggest, where-upon Mum looks as though I've said, *You could travel to Mars.*

'I'll buy myself a set of box files.' She pats them fondly. 'Much simpler.'

OK. I already know Mum's next birthday present. A day with an IT tutor.

'So, what *are* you getting?' Mum looks over the display. 'What about a pencil? They're lovely.'

'Nothing.' I smile. 'Let's go and pay for your box files.'

'Bex doesn't shop any more,' says Suze, joining us. 'Even if she can afford it.' She's holding Minnie's hand and they're both clutching what look like aprons decorated with rabbits.

'What do you mean, she doesn't shop any more?' says Mum, looking baffled.

'I tried to buy her a pair of cowboy boots. She wouldn't let me.'

'I didn't *need* cowboy boots.'

'Well, you *need* a pencil!' says Mum brightly. 'You can use it to write out your plan, love.'

'I don't.' I abruptly turn away. 'Let's go.'

'They're only $2.49,' points out Suze, picking one up. 'Wow, they smell amazing.'

I let my gaze run over the pencils again, feeling all twisty and miserable again. They *are* gorgeous. And of course I can afford one. But something's blocking me. I can hear that horrible voice inside my head again.

'Let's go and explore the rest of the town,' I say, trying to move everyone on, trying to get away. But Mum is gazing at me, her brow all wrinkled up.

'Becky, love . . .' she says gently. 'This isn't you. What's happened to you, love? What's going on inside?'

There's something about hearing Mum's kind voice;

the voice I've been listening to since before I was born. It seems to wriggle past all my defences, all the other voices, and get to the kernel of me. I can't not listen to her. And I can't not reply. This is my *mum*.

'It's just . . . you know,' I say at last. 'I messed up. All this trouble was all my fault. So . . .' I swallow hard, avoiding everyone's eye. 'You know. So I don't deserve to—' I break off and rub my nose. 'Anyway. It's fine. It's all good. I'm supposed to be stopping shopping. So.'

'Not like this!' says Mum in horror. 'Not like this, *punishing* yourself! I never heard of such a thing! Is this what they told you at that centre? "You don't deserve to buy a pencil"?'

'Well, not exactly,' I admit after a pause.

The truth is, at Golden Peace they said it was all about 'getting shopping in proportion' and 'spending meaningfully' and that the aim was to 'find a balance'. Maybe 'finding a balance' isn't really my strong point.

Now Mum is glancing at Suze and Dad, as though for support. 'I don't care what happened in LA!' she says hotly. 'What I can see in front of me is a young lady who's dropped everything to help her friend . . .' She starts counting off. 'Who found the address of Corey, thought of a way to get through to Raymond . . . What else?'

'Saw through Alicia,' adds Suze.

'Exactly!' says Mum. 'Exactly! You've been a little star, Becky! You don't need to feel guilty!'

'Becky, why do you think this trip is all your fault?' puts in Dad.

'Well, you know!' I say, desperately. 'Because I should

have gone to see Brent sooner, then he wouldn't have been evicted and he wouldn't have disappeared . . .'

'Becky.' Dad puts his hands on my shoulders and looks at me with his wise-Dad gaze. 'Not for one moment have I blamed you for this. Brent disappeared for many reasons. The truth is, he didn't need to leave. I'd paid off the arrears, and the rent on his trailer for the next year.'

He . . . *what?*

I stare at Dad, staggered – then almost at once realize: well, of course Dad would have done something lovely like that.

'But his daughter never said . . .'

'His daughter may not have known.' Dad sighs. 'These matters are complex, Becky, and that's no one's fault. And the idea that you would *blame* yourself for everything . . . it's appalling.'

'Oh,' I say, feebly. I don't know what else to say. It's like a great rock is rolling off me.

'And in light of this . . .' Dad steps forward. 'Please, my darling, let *me* buy you a pencil. You certainly deserve it.'

'No!' Mum steps in front of Dad before he can choose a pencil, and we all stare at her in surprise. 'That's not what this is about. This is about Becky. And what's going on *inside* Becky.' She pauses, as though marshalling her thoughts and everyone exchanges uncertain looks. 'I refuse to have brought up a daughter who can't buy herself a pencil because she feels too bad about herself,' she says at last. 'Becky, there's not-shopping for good reasons. And there's not-shopping for bad reasons. And they're *not* the same.' She's breathing hard and her eyes are glittering. 'No one wants you to go back to the way you were. No one wants you to be hiding Visa bills under the bed . . . Sorry, love,' she adds, a little pink in the face. 'I didn't mean to bring that up.'

'It's OK,' I reply, feeling my cheeks flush, too. 'Everyone here knows, we're all friends.' I catch the eye of a woman in blue lurking nearby, *totally* eavesdropping, and she hastily moves away.

'But this isn't the way to do it. This isn't my Becky.' She gazes at me in concern. 'Are you overdrawn?'

'Actually . . . no, I'm not,' I admit. 'In fact, I just got paid for my styling work in LA. I'm doing pretty well for money.'

'Would you like a pencil?'

'Um . . .' I swallow hard. 'Yes. I suppose I would. Maybe.'

'Well. It's up to you, love. You have to make your own choices. Maybe you don't want to buy anything.' Mum steps back, and blows her nose. 'But no more of this talk about "not deserving" it. The idea!'

There's a short silence as everyone moves away a little and pretends not to be watching. I feel so, *so* weird. Everything's reshuffling in my mind. Bits that have felt stuck for so long are coming free. It wasn't my fault. At least . . . it wasn't *all* my fault. Maybe . . .

Maybe I could get myself a pencil. Just as a souvenir. Maybe that beautiful purple one with the grey bird print and the pale-orange wood. I mean, it's only $2.49. And pencils are always useful, aren't they?

Yes, I, Becky Brandon, née Bloomwood, am going to buy myself a pencil.

I reach for it, and as my fingers close over it, I feel a happy beam spreading slowly over my face. A kind of warmth in my stomach. *I have so missed this feeling* . . .

Ooh. Wait a minute. So, am I shopping 'calmly and with meaning'? The thought passes through my mind and I pause, trying to examine myself. Oh, for God's sake, *I* don't know. I feel calm-ish, I suppose. As for 'meaning' . . . Well. The fact is, this one little pencil seems to have taken on a ridiculous amount of meaning.

The thing is, it *is* a gorgeous pencil. I'm not just saying that. Suze said so, too.

'Nice pencil, Bex,' says Suze with a grin as though she can read my mind. Dad nods his head and Janice says encouragingly, 'You'll enjoy using that, love!' And basically I feel like I'm five years old again. Especially when Mum and Dad meet eyes and Mum says, 'Do you remember the going-back-to-school shopping trip every September?' and I suddenly feel like I've whooshed back in time, and we're looking at pencil cases and I'm begging for a pink furry one and next they'll be asking if I *really* need a new set-triangle thing, or whatever it's called.

(The truth is, I bought a shiny new triangle thing every year and I never used it for any maths sum, ever. Not that I will mention this fact to Mum or Dad.)

'And when we've bought our things, we'll go and take some nice photos of the nature,' says Mum, firmly. *'That'll* clear your head, Becky, love. Doing something artistic. You can take a piccie of Minnie and me on a big red rock and we'll send it to Elinor.'

Minnie? On one of those huge great rocks? Is she joking?

'Great!' I say. 'Or, you know. Beside a rock.'

We all head to the till to buy our items, and the lady in the feather-print dress looks delighted. And then, just as it's my turn and I'm about to hand over my five-dollar bill, I see a big box of the same hand-printed pencils, marked *Special Offer: ten for the price of five.* And I pause.

Ten for the price of five. That's actually a pretty good offer. Let's see . . . I do a quick calculation in my head. That's ten hand-printed pencils for . . . $12.45. Wow. That's not bad, is it? It'll be plus tax, but still. And I've got an old twenty-dollar bill that's been sitting in my jacket pocket for ever . . . so I could give everyone a pencil as a present! Like a mascot.

'Bex?' says Suze, watching me hesitate. 'Are you going to get the pencil?'

'Yes,' I say, absently. 'I am. Although actually, I was just thinking. That's quite a good deal, isn't it?' I gesture at the box. 'Don't you think? Ten for the price of five? Because I was *thinking* I'd love to get you all a little souvenir, and I mean, everyone needs pencils . . .'

There's a kind of explosion next to me. I think it's Suze. How did she even *make* that sound?

'What?' I turn and stare at her. '*What?*'

But she doesn't reply at first. She's gazing at me with an expression I can't read. Then suddenly she grabs me for a hug, so tight I can hardly breathe.

'Nothing, Bex,' she says into my ear. 'Nothing.'

* * *

As we head out of the shop, I feel content in a way I haven't for so long. It *wasn't* all my fault. I hadn't realized quite how much I'd been blaming myself. And now I feel free.

We bought the ten pencils in the end, but everyone chipped in a dollar or two. Mum and Janice have already chosen one each, and Suze is hesitating between the turquoise and the pale pink.

'Turquoise goes with your eyes,' I advise, as she holds them up to compare. 'But pink goes with everything. Actually, have you seen the pale-blue one? Because it's really gorgeous—' I break off. 'Suze?' She isn't even listening. Her fingers have slackened around the pencils and her gaze is locked over my left shoulder. As I turn to see what's going on, I hear a kind of whimper come from her.

'Tarkie?'

Tarkie? Oh my God. *Tarkie?*

He's standing there, almost silhouetted in the late-afternoon sunlight, so I can't see his face properly. But even so – and this is really weird – he looks different. Like he's grown a couple of inches. Is he standing in a new way? Does he have a new suit?

'Tarkie,' Suze whispers again – and as I turn back to her, I see two tears spilling on to her cheeks. The next moment she's running so fast to Tarquin, I think she might knock him over.

The light is so bright she's in silhouette too, so all I see is their two figures melding together in this endless, tight hug. I have no idea what's happening within the hug, whether they're saying things, or not saying things, or what . . . It's like the black box in an aeroplane. I'll find out afterwards.

If Suze tells me. Which she may not. Some things are private. I mean, we're grown-ups now. You don't share everything. (Except, I really, really hope she tells me.)

I'm watching, transfixed, a hand to my mouth, and I can see that the other grown-ups are equally riveted. Even a few passers-by have stopped to watch, and I hear one say 'Aah' in fond tones.

'Look, Becky.' Luke has joined me. 'Tarquin's here. Have you seen?' He gestures with his head.

'Of course I've seen!' I hiss. 'But has he forgiven her? Is it all OK? What's he *saying*?'

'Their business, I would have thought,' says Luke in mild tones, and I stare at him crossly. I know all that. But this is *Suze*.

At that moment, my phone bleeps, and as I glance down at it, my heart skips a beat. Oh my God, Suze needs to see this. Right now. Surreptitiously, I edge a little closer to the couple, trying to hear Tarkie's voice, trying to glean what's going on.

'We both went a bit mad in our different ways,' Tarkie is saying, his eyes fixed firmly on Suze's. 'But that wasn't the real me. And it wasn't the real you, either.'

'No,' gulps Suze. 'No, Tarkie, it wasn't. I don't know what happened to me.'

'The real you isn't that girl in LA with hair extensions. The real you loves . . . nature.' He makes a sudden sweeping gesture with his hand. 'The real you loves . . . trees.'

There's a long pause, and I can see Suze's eyes skittering about with nerves.

'Um, yes,' she says at last. 'Trees. Absolutely. Um . . . speaking of trees . . .' Her voice has gone all squeaky and she keeps rubbing her face. 'I was thinking . . . *wondering* really . . .' I can see her screwing up her courage. 'How's . . . how's Owl's Tower?'

'It's just as it ever was,' says Tarkie. 'Just as it ever was, Suze.' His eyes are grave and his voice unreadable. Poor Suze is peering at him desperately, and I can see her mouth quivering.

'So, it's . . . no better?' she hazards. 'No worse?'

'Suze, you know Owl's Tower,' says Tarkie, his eyes flickering as though he's picturing it. 'You don't need me to describe it to you.'

God, this is *torture*.

'Suze!' I call as discreetly as I can. 'You need to see something!' Suze swivels her head in shock, and makes a furious batting-away gesture.

'Bex, this isn't the moment! Can't you *see* that?'

'Yes it is! Suze, honestly . . . Sorry, Tarkie, I'll be two secs . . .' I hurry up to Suze before she can refuse again, and show her my phone.

Derek Smeath's wrinkled face is beaming out from the screen. He's standing in a dark wood, shining a torch up at a tree which has a nail hammered into it. As I zoom in, you can see a metal tag reading *Owl's Tower*.

'That's not . . .' falters Suze, her eyes widening in shock. '*No*.'

'He's there right now. It's super-healthy, Suze,' I whisper, scrolling through the photos of thick, leafy, flourishing branches. 'It's here for the duration. Like you and Tarkie. It's strong and thriving and majestic. It's not going anywhere.'

Tears spring to Suze's eyes and she gives a tiny sob, then clamps her mouth shut. I put an arm around her shoulders and squeeze. This has all been so hellish.

'But—' At last she manages to speak, and gestures at the screen in bewilderment. 'How on earth—'

'Tell you later. Er . . . hi, Tarkie!' I add awkwardly, with a little wave. 'How are you? So . . . I'll leave you guys to it . . .' I back away. 'Sorry for interrupting . . .'

'Tarkie.' Suze suddenly dissolves into full-blown sobs, as though she can't keep up a front any more. 'Tarkie, I am so, *so* sorry . . .'

And then Tarquin's arm is around her, strong and firm, and he leads her away to a quiet spot, in the garden of a nearby café. Luke and I look at each other, and I feel a shiver pass over me. I hope everything turns out OK between them. I mean, I *think* it will. Tarkie's here. They'll talk it out.

But it just shows. Things can disintegrate so easily. Only one mistake . . .

'Luke, let's not have affairs,' I say abruptly, grabbing his arm for comfort, and Luke's face twitches as though in amusement.

'OK,' he agrees solemnly. 'Let's not have affairs.'

'You're teasing me!' I pinch his arm. 'Stop it! I mean it!'

'I'm not teasing you. Really.' He looks at me again and I can see something deeper in his gaze. Like an acknowledgement; like he gets it. 'Let's not have affairs. And let's not use some bloody stupid tree code, either,' he adds, with a glint in his eyes. (Luke thought the whole 'Owl's Tower' thing was *nuts*. It's really not his style.)

'Agreed.' I nod, and Luke bends to kiss me. And I find myself squeezing him back so tightly, I probably wind him or something. But I don't care. It needed doing.

It's a bit like waiting for a baby. We go into the café garden, staying well away from Suze and Tarkie, and we order drinks and make small talk. The garden's quite big, with rocks and trees and shrubs, so I take a photo of Mum next to a boulder, and Minnie sitting on the boulder, and a lizard which we spy in the shade. And Mum says brightly, 'You see, Becky, darling? There are *lots* of things you could do, if you wanted to. You could be a wildlife photographer!'

A *wildlife* photographer?

At once I know she's talked to Suze, or maybe Luke, or maybe even both of them, about me having no job and feeling worried about it. And even though I'd make the worst wildlife photographer ever, I feel incredibly touched. Mum will never give up on me. Her basic world view is that I can do anything. So I smile and say, 'Yes! Good idea, Mum! Maybe!' and take about ninety-five shots of a shrub that we'll delete later.

Then the drinks arrive and we sit down again. But all the while, we keep glancing over to where Suze and Tarkie are *still* talking. On the plus side, Tarkie's holding her hand, and she's speaking very fast and volubly at him, and tears are running down her face and he keeps wiping them away with his handkerchief. Which I reckon is a positive sign?

The thing about Suze and Tarkie is, I think they both *do want* to be married to each other. And that's quite a good start, for a marriage.

Then suddenly they've stood up and they're walking towards us, and we all get in a bit of a fluster trying to look like we've been having a normal conversation, not beadily watching their every move and speculating about what it means.

'So, these red-rock canyons,' begins Mum loudly, just as Janice chimes in, 'Super lemonade, don't you think?'

'Hi, everyone,' says Suze, tremulously, as she gets near, and we adopt expressions of 'surprise'.

'Oh Suzie, *there* you are!' exclaims Mum as though she's been wondering where Suze could have got to. 'And Tarquin, too. Don't you look well, Tarquin!'

This is actually a very perceptive comment. Tarquin looks totally together. His hair has grown back a little from the dreadful style he got in LA, and he's wearing a sleek navy linen suit, and his jaw seems firmer than it ever did.

'Great to see you, Jane,' he says, bending to kiss her. 'And Janice. I gather you've had quite a journey.'

Is his voice deeper, too? And he hasn't stammered, once. I mean, he's only uttered a few words, but still. Where's the shy, stuttering, bony-headed aristocrat who used to jump if you said 'Boo'?

I glance again at Suze, and she's hanging back, as though she doesn't want to be noticed.

'Suze.' I pat the empty chair next to me. 'Come on. Have some lemonade.' Then, 'Are you OK?' I murmur as she takes her seat.

'I think so.' Suze seems emotionally shattered, but raises a smile. 'We need to talk a lot. Tarkie's so generous . . .' She squeezes her eyes shut a moment. 'He's trying not to be hurt, because he wants to mend everything. He wants to focus on your dad and that whole affair. But he *should* be hurt. He *should* be furious with me. Shouldn't he?'

I survey Tarkie, who's shaking Dad's hand vigorously, his face shining.

'Excellent to see you again, Graham,' he says, and I can hear the pleasure in his voice.

'He'll work it out in his own time,' I say. 'Let him do it his way, Suze. You're together again, that's the main thing.' I glance at her in sudden terror. 'I mean, *aren't* you?'

'Yes!' Suze gives a sudden half-laugh, half-sob. 'Oh God. Yes. We are. Yes.'

'Did you tell him about Owl's Tower?'

'I will,' says Suze, and bites her lip, looking ashamed. 'When we get home, I'll tell him everything. *Everything*. But not now. He's . . . he almost doesn't want to know. He's like a tennis player in the zone.'

'You're right.' I watch him curiously. 'He's transformed!'

'Now, Graham,' Tarkie is saying as he takes a seat. 'Did you get my texts?'

'Absolutely,' Dad says. 'Absolutely. But I'm a little confused. You say you've made "contact" with Corey. Do you mean you've written to him? Sent him an email?'

'Not at all,' says Tarquin. 'I've had a meeting with him.'

'A meeting?' Dad's jaw drops. 'A face-to-face meeting?'

'Over lunch.'

There's a flabbergasted silence. Tarkie has had lunch with Corey?

'Tarkie, you're . . . amazing!' stutters Suze.

'Not at all,' says Tarkie modestly. 'The title helped, of course.'

'But what was your meeting *about*?' says Dad incredulously.

'About my new venture capital company, seeking partnership with his.' Tarkie pauses. 'My fictitious venture capital company.'

Dad throws back his head and guffaws. 'Tarquin, you're a wonder.'

'Tarkie, you're brilliant,' I say sincerely.

'Oh, please,' says Tarkie, looking embarrassed. 'Absolutely not. But the good news is that I have access to Corey. The question is how we can best use this access. It's a place to start, anyway.'

I blink at Tarkie, feeling impressed. He looks so grown up and determined, in a way he never really has before.

'Well.' Dad seems a bit shell-shocked. 'Tarquin, this is far, far better progress than I ever could have hoped for.'

My mind is digesting this new fact. This changes everything. This could mean . . . I grab for my little notebook, start crossing out ideas and adding others.

'We were planning a meeting to discuss the matter,' says Dad. 'Later on perhaps, when everyone's feeling' – he glances kindly at Suze – 'a little more composed.'

'Great,' says Tarkie. 'I'll tell you everything I know. And now, how about a titchy, to celebrate?'

We sit there for a while longer, quietly drinking and chatting and looking at the red rocks. And maybe there *is* something mystical in the Sedona air which empowers the soul, because I feel like finally, *finally* we're all calming down.

As we wander back to the hotel, Suze and Tarkie keep touching hands as though for reassurance, and every time they do, I feel a swell of gladness. Because I do *not* want to be a friend-of-divorce. It scars you for life.

'Your father's wonderful,' says Tarkie, as we wait to cross the street.

'I know,' I say proudly.

'He's Tarkie's hero,' says Suze, and she squeezes his hand fondly.

'What did you talk about, all that time on the road?' I ask with genuine curiosity. I mean, I know Tarkie and my dad like each other, but I wouldn't have thought they had that much in common. Apart from maybe golf.

'He gave me a talking-to, as it happens,' says Tarquin. 'Quite a stiff one.'

'Oh,' I say in surprise. 'Yikes. Sorry.'

'No, I needed it.' Tarkie frowns. 'He said we all have roles in life and that I was running away from mine. It's true. Being who I am – well, it's a big job. I didn't choose it . . . but I can't dodge it. I have to take it on.' He pauses. 'And I will. I'm going to carry on with my plans for Letherby Hall, no matter what my parents think.'

'They're brilliant plans,' says Suze loyally. 'It's going to be another Chatsworth.'

'Well, not quite,' says Tarkie. 'But the plans *do* make sense. They *will* work.' He sounds like he's fighting with someone in his head. 'They *will*.'

I shoot him a sidelong glance. I don't know what Dad's done to him, but he's grown. He sounds older. More assured. Like a guy who *could* take charge of a great big empire and not let it weigh him down.

When we've crossed the road, Suze walks alongside me, and we splinter off into a little twosome, just for a bit. (Two-and-a-half-some, actually. I'm holding Minnie's hand.)

'So, Bex . . .' she says softly. 'Guess what?'

'What?'

'I'm . . .' She waves her hands in a vague, Suze-ish way.

'What?' I gawp at her. 'Not . . .'

'Yes.' Her cheeks pinken.

'*Not* . . . You're *not* . . .'

'Yes!'

OK, I have to make sure we're on the same page here. Because I might mean one thing, and she might mean 'intending to start a Cordon Bleu course when I get back to England.'

'*Pregnant?*' I whisper, and she nods frantically. 'How long have you known?'

'Since the day after Tarkie left. I did the test that day. I totally freaked out.' Her face tightens with remembered stress. 'Oh God, it's been awful, Bex. So awful. I thought . . . I didn't know what to do . . . I was so afraid that . . .'

312

She trails off. 'It's been a nightmare,' she whispers.

OK, this explains a lot. A *lot*. For a start, is this why she's been so ratty? She always gets ratty in early pregnancy. And no wonder she was so freaked out about Bryce. She thought her marriage was going to fall apart and Tarkie didn't even know he was going to be a father again . . . I wince at the thought. And she's been dealing with it all on her own; saying nothing to anybody.

Or . . . has she?

'Does Alicia know?' I ask, more abruptly than I meant to.

'No!' Suze sounds shocked. 'Of course not. I would never have told her before you.' She puts an arm around me and squeezes. 'I wouldn't, Bex.'

I turn to face her and, of course, now I see all the tell-tale signs that only a best friend can pick up. Her skin is flaring up around her nose. That always happens when she's pregnant. And . . .

Well actually, that's the only tell-tale sign. That, and—

'Hey!' I take a step back. 'You've been drinking! All that tequila, the bourbon iced tea . . .'

'Faked it,' says Suze succinctly. 'Chucked it away when no one was looking. I knew if I was obvious about it, you'd guess.'

'Fair enough.' I nod. 'Oh my God, Suze, four children.' I stare at her wonderingly. '*Four*.'

'I know.' She gulps.

'Or five, if you have twins. Or six, if you have triplets . . .'

'Shut up!' says Suze, looking freaked out. 'I won't!

313

Bex . . .' Her expression becomes agonized. 'I wish . . . I wish you . . . I just wish—'

'I know,' I cut her off gently. 'I know you do.'

'It doesn't seem fair.' She swallows. 'We didn't even plan this. Total surprise.'

She gestures at her stomach, and deep inside I feel a little wrench of jealousy. I'd love a total surprise. To my horror, tears prick at my eyes, and I quickly turn away.

Anyway. It's fine. We have Minnie and she's perfect. She's more than perfect. We don't need anything else. I bend down to kiss the smooth, two-year-old cheek that I love so much it hurts inside. And as I straighten up, I see Suze watching me with a shimmer in her own eyes.

'Stop it,' I say, swallowing hard. '*Stop* it. Look. OK. You can't have everything. Can you?'

'No,' says Suze after a pause. 'No, I suppose not.'

'You can't have everything,' I repeat, as we resume walking. This is my favourite ever saying, in fact I've got it on a fridge magnet. 'You can't have *everything*,' I emphasize. 'Because where on earth would you put it?'

Suze gives a snort of laughter and I can't help grinning. She nudges me with her shoulder and I bash her back with my hand, and then she takes Minnie's other hand and we start swinging her along the road, and Minnie exclaims, 'Again! Again!' And just for a few minutes, all the angst and urgency dissipates into the sky. And we're just two friends, walking along down a sunny street, swinging a little girl.

SIXTEEN

Tarkie has taken a conference room for our meeting, and he even negotiated a deal on it. He is *so* the man of the moment. We've all got pads of paper and our lucky-mascot pencils and glasses of water and I've already written *Get Justice For Brent* at the top of my pad and underlined it three times, which I think gives it purpose.

Suze and I are sitting next to each other, and we keep nudging each other and admiring our new cowboy boots. It was Suze who bought them. She practically manhandled me into the shop, and said to the store owner, 'We're buying boots,' so firmly she almost sounded aggressive. And then we tried on nearly every pair, and *God*, it was fun.

I don't know quite what happened to me, before. How could I not want to buy cowboy boots? How could *anyone* not want to buy cowboy boots? I feel like a weird fog has lifted from my brain and I'm back to who I was.

My pair are anthracite grey with silver studs, and

Minnie absolutely adores them. She grabbed them and put them on as soon as I got them out of the box, and tottered around in them all evening. Then she wanted to go to bed in them. When I said, 'No, darling, you can't wear boots in bed,' she wanted to hug them in bed, like a teddy. And then, when I finally exclaimed, 'No! Mummy is wearing them tonight!' she said, 'But da boots love *Minnie*,' and gave me this sad, reproachful look that actually made me feel really bad, even though they're *my boots*. I mean, honestly.

Anyway, she's asleep now. We've found a really nice, highly recommended babysitter called Judy, and she's staying in our bedroom till we've finished our meeting. I mean, yes, I could have brought Minnie along and sat her on my knee. But first: it's past her bedtime. And second: this is business. As I look around, I can see that all our faces are taut with intent. (Except Danny's, which is taut with the 'firming serum' he got at his facial. Apparently his afternoon at the spa was so blissful, he doesn't care if he missed all the action, and he can always get it on 'catch-up', i.e. me telling him all about it.)

'Corey is like a fortress, we all know that.' Dad's voice brings me back to the room. 'Nevertheless, Tarquin has managed to get into the inner sanctum.'

'Corey's asked me to meet his board members.' Tarquin gives an affirming nod. 'I have his cell number. He's told me to call any time.'

'That's amazing!' I say. 'Well done!' I break into applause and everyone joins in, while Tarquin looks modest.

'It's still tricky, though,' Tarkie continues. 'First, because Corey has stepped back from the day-to-day running of his business. His new wife and daughter are the apple of his eye, and that's all he's interested in. Second, because he doesn't like talking about the past.'

'Because his wife thinks he's fifty-something,' I put in, and Dad gives a wry chuckle.

'It's not just that,' says Tarkie. 'He's almost phobic. He ducks any question about the past. I asked him directly if he'd ever travelled around the States as a young man, whereupon he flinched and started talking about his last holiday in Hawaii.'

'So we can't appeal to the goodness of his heart,' says Dad. 'Or any sense of nostalgia.'

'Not at all,' agrees Tarkie. 'We'll somehow have to force him into doing the right thing. Now as I said, I'm having lawyers look at the deal that Brent did. But unfortunately, there's no hard evidence that Corey ever lied to or misled Brent. This all happened a long time ago, and it's one man's word against the other's.'

'But Raymond told us!' puts in Suze.

'Maybe. But do you think Raymond will ever agree to appear in court to support Brent?' Tarkie shakes his head. 'Corey's story will be that Brent is simply bitter after having made a poor business decision.'

'Like EMI turning down The Beatles,' puts in Janice helpfully. 'Brent would be EMI.'

'No, he'd be the drummer,' says Mum. 'The other drummer.'

'Ringo Starr?' says Janice, looking baffled.

'No, love, the *other* drummer. Pete Whatsit—'

317

'Fascinating stuff, Jane,' Tarkie interrupts briskly. 'But if we *could* return to the business in hand . . . ?' He fixes Mum with a look which, for Tarkie, is almost stern, and to my astonishment, she shuts up.

'There's one arcane point of law that the lawyers are still looking into,' Tarkie continues. 'But meanwhile, our dilemma is this: do we contact Corey *before* we have any legal backing, or do we wait?'

'What will we say if we contact him?' says Mum.

'We'll pressure him,' says Tarkie. 'Bring influences to bear, introduce the element of threat, perhaps.'

'*Threat?*' echoes Janice in alarm.

'I have a client who'd help,' volunteers Danny. 'She's Russian. Spends a ton every year. Believe me, if you want any threatening done, her husband's the one.'

'Are you talking about the Russian Mafia?' Dad stares at him in horror.

'Of course I'm not talking about it.' Danny mimes a zip pull across his mouth. 'First rule of the Mafia: you don't talk about the Mafia.'

'That's *Fight Club*,' objects Suze.

'*Fight Club* and the Mafia.' Danny shrugs. 'And my haute couture show in Qatar.'

'I never knew you had a haute couture show in Qatar!' I say, avidly.

'I know.' Danny gives me an enigmatic eyebrow raise. 'That's because I can't talk about it.'

Since when did he have secret haute couture shows in Qatar he didn't tell me about? I want to ask him more, only it's not exactly the time.

'We can't get involved with the Mafia!' Janice looks

like she might hyperventilate. 'Graham, you never mentioned the Mafia!'

'*Obviously* we're not going to involve the Mafia,' says Dad, impatiently.

'I don't think threatening Corey is the way forward, anyway,' I put in. 'People like that – the more you try to threaten them, the more aggressive they get. We need to coax him. *Persuade* him. Like that story about the man in his cloak – the wind can't blow it off him, but the sun makes him take it off of his own accord? Remember that story you used to read me, Mum?' I turn to her. 'With the lovely illustrations?'

I'm trying to get Mum on-side, but she looks a bit perturbed. 'Becky, love, I'm not sure picture books are the best reference right now.'

'Why not? Persuading is definitely the way to go.' I look around the table. 'Forget the lawyers, forget the Mafia, he won't take any notice of them, anyway.'

'But darling, how on earth can we persuade him?' says Dad gently.

'Well actually, I have an idea,' I confess.

'What idea?' demands Suze at once.

'It's a bit complicated,' I admit. 'We'll need to use all our forces for it. We'll need to go back to Las Vegas and hire some rooms. And we'll need to plan it really carefully. We'll need to trap him. Con him. We want Elinor for this, too,' I add. 'We'll have to talk her into it.'

'My mother?' Luke sounds incredulous. 'Becky, what have you got up your sleeve?'

'You want to *con* Corey?' Dad looks anxious.

'You said *persuade*!' says Mum. 'Conning a man like that is dangerous!'

'Darling, is this wise?' reiterates Dad.

'We'll only con him a bit,' I say robustly. 'If we all work together, we can do it. I know we can.' I look around the table, trying to whip up some enthusiasm. 'We can work together, can't we? We've got this far, haven't we? Everyone will have their own job to do; it'll be all about timing and planning.'

'How many are we?' says Suze, and starts counting off on her fingers. 'You, me, Luke, Tarkie, Jane, Graham, Janice, Danny, Elinor . . .'

'Can we use Ulla, too?' I turn to Danny. 'She might be useful.'

'Sure.' Danny nods. 'Anything you want.'

'So that makes ten of us.' Suze finishes counting. 'Ten of us, conning a businessman in Las Vegas. You realize what this is?' She shoots me a wicked grin. 'It's Becky's Ten.'

'Ooh, Becky, love!' exclaims Janice. 'Well done you!'

'Becky's Ten?' echoes Dad, looking puzzled.

'The film,' explains Suze. '*Ocean's Eleven*. With Brad Pitt in it? And George Clooney?'

'Ah, *yes*.' Recognition comes to Dad's face. 'Now, I enjoyed that film.'

'This is very cool,' Danny is saying with approval. 'I'll be the billionaire. I can *so* play that role. "Greetings, hotel underling."' He puts on a mittel-European accent. "I weesh to place a nuclear weapon in your high-security wault."'

'We aren't placing anything in any high-security "waults".' I roll my eyes. 'And actually, it'll be Becky's Eleven,' I tell Suze. 'There's someone else we need on the team. Someone crucial.'

'Who?'

But I don't answer. My mind is buzzing with the plan. I need to write it all down in full, look at it properly and see if it'll work.

Except: no I don't. I already know it'll work.

OK, that's not right either. I don't know that my plan *will* work . . . but I know that it *could* work. That it ought to work.

As I start writing, there's a lightness in my heart. An excitement. I'm doing something. I'm *achieving* something. Derek Smeath is right, positive action *does* boost the soul.

'We need a bunch of balloons,' adds Danny, who is getting more and more enthused. 'And everyone needs to wear shades, even inside the casinos. In fact, I'm styling all of you,' he announces with animation. 'We can't be Becky's Eleven and not rock a great look. What's the plan, anyway, Becky? Drive to Vegas, check into the Bellagio, pull off the con and then watch the fountains while the music plays?'

'Pretty much.' I nod.

'Cool.' Danny looks around. 'Well, I'm in. Are you in or out, Suze?'

'In,' says Suze emphatically.

'In,' agrees Tarquin.

'In,' chimes in Janice.

Everyone else is nodding around the table, although

Dad looks anxious. 'Becky, darling, what *exactly* is your plan?'

'I'll tell you when I've worked it all out properly,' I say, still scribbling. 'We need to make some reservations, get back to Vegas, sort a few things out. But actually, before the plan . . .' I beam at him. 'I think there's one other crucial thing we should do first.'

SEVENTEEN

'Dearly beloved,' intones Elvis. 'Uhuh-huh. We are gathered here. Uhuh-huh.'

Oh God. I'm going to get the giggles. Is he going to say 'Uhuh-huh' after every line?

He's a pretty impressive Elvis. He's in a black spangled suit, with the most massive flares and platforms, and a really good wig (you can't see his real hair at all) and he's already sung 'Can't Help Falling in Love' with lots of reverb and pelvic thrusts.

It's two days since we left Sedona and we're clustered in the Silver Candles Elvis Wedding Chapel in Las Vegas. Everyone's overexcited – especially Minnie, who is dressed up as a 'ring girl' even though there aren't any rings. Suze is in a floaty white dress with a flower garland in her hair, and she's never looked more beautiful. Mum's sitting in the front pew and she's already thrown a handful of confetti over Suze, although we haven't started yet. (I found Mum and Dad at the bar of our hotel this morning, quaffing glasses of champagne. And judging by their bill, they'd each had more than one.)

'To witness the promise of renewed love between this couple. Uhuh-huh.' Elvis surveys Suze. 'I believe you have written your own vows.'

'That's right.' Suze clears her throat, and glances at Tarkie, who's standing nearby, a look of huge pride on his face. 'I, Susan, vow to you, Becky, always to be your friend.' She gazes seriously into my eyes. 'For richer, for poorer, in daytime and at three a.m. And I swear this on my new cowboy boots.'

'Uhuh-huh,' says Elvis with a nod.

'Hurrah!' Mum gives a whoop and throws some more confetti over Suze's head.

'And I, Becky, swear to be your friend for ever, Suze,' I say, my voice trembling slightly. 'For richer, for poorer, in daytime and at three a.m. Let no one put us asunder.'

Especially Alicia Bitch Long-legs, I don't add – but we all know that's who I mean.

'I swear this on my new cowboy boots,' I add for good measure, and do a little twirl. I love my cowboy boots. I'm never wearing anything else, ever. And they're *brilliant* for line dancing, as I discovered last night, because we went to a line-dancing bar. Suze insisted we went, and it was the best fun. Now I just need to get Luke to buy a pair of cowboy boots, and we'll match.

(I already know, this is never going to happen.)

'And I swear never to leave you, Suze.' Tarkie steps forward for his turn. He takes Suze's hands and holds them tight. 'I swear to love and protect you, and keep you for ever, as long as Owl's Tower shall stand. Or longer, if it falls down,' he adds hastily, as he sees Suze open her mouth. 'Much longer. For ever.'

'I vow to be your wife for ever, Tarquin,' says Suze, her voice a whisper. 'And to stay faithful only to you, my beloved husband.'

She looks like an angel in her wispy dress, her face all lit up with hope and love and relief. I feel a bit misty-eyed as I watch them, and I'm wondering if I have a tissue anywhere, when Luke rises to his feet.

'I want to make a vow to you, Becky,' he says, his deep voice filling the chapel, and I jolt in surprise. This wasn't in the plan. We even talked about it, and said, 'Shall we?' and then laughed and decided we didn't need to renew any vows. But here he is on his feet, looking almost startled at his own behaviour.

And as I look into his face, I think I know why he's doing it. It's because of . . . stuff. Our own private stuff. What happened in LA. Seeing Suze and Tarkie stumble, and looking at our own marriage in that light. And, maybe most of all, hearing Suze's news and realizing it's not us, not this time. Last night, in bed, we talked about it. Way into the night. And . . .

Well. I can be honest with Luke the way I can't with anyone else, even Suze. So. He knows.

'I vow . . .' Luke pauses, as though searching for the right words. I can practically see his mind rifling through possibilities and rejecting them. The truth is, I don't think he's going to find them. The truth is, he doesn't need to find them.

'I know,' I say to him, and my throat is suddenly tight. 'I know. I vow too.'

Luke's eyes are locked on mine, and my head feels a

bit swimmy and I wish we had this chapel to ourselves for a good few hours. But we don't. So, somehow, I get my poise back and nod a couple of times, and whisper, 'Amen'. Which doesn't really make sense, but then neither does anything else in Las Vegas.

'All righty!' says Elvis, who's looking a bit confused by Luke's interjection. 'So. Ladies and gentlemen. Let's love each other tender. Let's have no more suspicious minds. Uhuh-huh. By the power vested in me by—'

'Wait. I haven't finished,' Luke interrupts. 'Mother.' He turns to where Elinor is sitting in a back pew, in a black-and-white silk suit so elegant and perfect it makes me want to weep. We reconnected with her in Las Vegas this morning, and she was predictably unfazed by hearing all our plans. Now here she is, sitting upright and composed, with a pillbox hat perched over one eye.

(She always travels with a hat, it turns out. In fact, she was surprised that none of the rest of us had one.)

'I want to make a vow to you, too,' Luke continues. 'Things will be better between us. I promise.' He takes a deep breath. 'We'll spend time together. Holidays. Fun times. We'll be a family. If . . .' He hesitates. 'If you like that idea.'

I don't think I've ever seen Luke and his mother look so similar. They're gazing silently at each other with those unmistakable dark eyes. His expression is taut and kind of yearning. And so is hers.

'I do.' She nods.

'And I do too!' exclaims Mum, who has *definitely* had too much champagne. 'Of course Elinor's part of the family.' She leaps to her feet and brandishes her confetti.

'I, Jane Bloomwood, vow to honour and respect my son-in-law's mother, Elinor. And my wonderful neighbour, Janice.' She turns to Janice with sudden tears in her eyes. 'Janice, where would I be without you? You're always there for me. In sickness and in health . . . when my ankle broke . . . that time the lights fused and you came to our rescue . . .'

'OK, we need to move on, folks.' Elvis is glancing at his watch. 'Uhuh-huh.' He turns to Suze. 'Say after me, "I will not step on your blue suede shoes."'

But Suze doesn't even hear him. She's too riveted by Mum and Janice.

'Oh, love,' says Janice, looking flustered. 'Anyone would have done the same.'

'You gave us your shepherd's pie, Janice! *Your shepherd's pie!*'

'You said we weren't doing vows.' Dad tugs at Mum's dress.

'We're not!' retorts Mum.

'Yes you are! You're making vows all over the bloody place!' he says hotly. 'So I'm going to make one, too.' Dad stands up and turns to face Mum. 'I, Graham, swear never to leave you again, my darling Jane. Never.' He grabs Mum and holds her tight. '*Never.*'

'Enough!' Elvis definitely sounds tetchy now. 'Folks, you can't all be making vows. You didn't pay for this.'

'And I vow always to trust you,' says Mum to Dad, her voice quivering. 'And I don't care where your Big Bonus comes from – I'm proud of you.'

'No more vows!' Elvis practically yells, and at once Danny stands up, a wicked look in his eye.

'I have a vow,' he says brightly. 'Elinor, I vow to make you a mind-blowing new wardrobe, if you'll vow to wear me at the Met Ball.'

'By the power vested in me—' Elvis tries again.

'Sunglasses?' says Minnie, approaching Elvis. She offers him Janice's white sunglasses, while pointing lovingly at his own spangly shades. 'Like *sunglasses*? Pleeeease?'

'Jesus H Christ!' Elvis erupts. 'By the power vested in me by this chapel, I pronounce you committed to one another.' He sweeps a hand around. 'All of you. You deserve each other. Fruitloops. Uhuh-huh.'

EIGHTEEN

Well, if nothing else, our costumes are awesome. Absolutely awesome.

Danny has dressed Luke, Dad and Tarquin in amazing suits with broad silk ties and sheeny shirts that they would never normally have picked out, in shades of mauve and beige. When he was all dressed up, Luke looked at his reflection in horror and said, 'I look like an off-duty gangster,' like that was a *bad* thing. Honestly, has he actually seen *Ocean's Eleven*?

Suze and Elinor are looking super-glam. Elinor, in particular, is wearing thousands of dollars' worth of high-end clothes, just to reinforce the point that she's a Major Player, whereas Suze is in a bouclé dress with pearls, because she's playing Titled Nobility. (She didn't want to be Titled Nobility. She wanted to be The Amazing Yen, squish herself up in a food trolley and do a back-flip. But like I keep telling her, there is no The Amazing Yen in Becky's Eleven.)

Danny himself is in jeans and a ripped T-shirt, but

that's OK, because he's playing himself. Meanwhile, Mum, Janice and I are all in different versions of the domestic staff uniform of the Las Vegas Convention Center, which is where everything's going to take place.

Danny got us the uniforms, I have no idea how, except it was through a 'contact'. I'm in a tailored housekeeper's dress with a badge reading *Marigold Spitz*. Janice is in a black dress and little apron – not sure what she's supposed to be. Part of the catering team, maybe? And Mum has an important-looking jacket-and-skirt combo. She must be some kind of manager or concierge or something.

The most crucial thing is that we've got the meeting rooms exactly as I ordered – interconnecting with double doors. I've nicknamed one 'Ben' and the other 'Jerry's', and the doors are firmly shut between them. For now.

'Right.' For the millionth time I survey the team. 'Does everyone know what they're doing?'

I've got the *Ocean's Eleven* theme music pulsing through my head, because we watched it last night on DVD, to get us in the mood. We also played cards and drank beers and kept saying, 'Are you in or are you out?' to each other.

'You've got the cupcakes ready?' says Suze, and I produce the box from a side cupboard. I place ten cupcakes on a plate and for a silent moment, the two of us survey it.

'You think we need one more cupcake?' I ask.

Suze doesn't move. But I can read that little crinkle in her brow.

'You think we need one more cupcake,' I say.

Still she doesn't move. I know what's going on here. She's being Brad Pitt and I've got to be George Clooney.

'OK,' I say deadpan. 'We'll have one more cupcake.' I place the final cupcake on top of the pile and dust down my hands. 'We're set.'

'Corey's here,' says Luke, looking at his phone, and my stomach gives a sudden heave of nerves. Oh God. He's here. It's starting. And just for a moment I feel engulfed by terror. Are we actually, really doing this?

At least Minnie is safely in our hotel room, being looked after by the lovely Judy. (We brought Judy with us from Sedona as a temporary nanny, which was Luke's idea, and it was a brilliant move.)

'Cyndi's ten minutes away,' reports Danny, consulting his phone. 'It's on. Good luck, everyone.'

My hands are damp and my heart is suddenly pounding. I half-want to run away and forget we ever planned this. But everyone's looking at me for instructions. This is my gig, I tell myself firmly. I need to make it happen. And although I'm terrified, I'm exhilarated, too.

'OK,' I say briskly. 'Party time. Dad, you need to get out of the way. Luke, you head down to the lobby to collect Corey.' Luke nods, and strides out of the room, giving me a brief kiss on the way.

'Attagirl,' he whispers in my ear, and I give his hand an answering squeeze.

'Tarkie and Elinor, into Ben,' I instruct. 'Danny, stay in phone contact with Cyndi. Ulla and Suze, into Jerry's. You all know what to do. Mum and Janice . . .' I look at them both. 'We need to disappear.'

I pick up the plate of cupcakes, give a quick glance around the room and head out to the corridor. The worst thing about this whole plan is, I have to wait now. And I've never been good at waiting. How am I not going to explode with frustration?

'I brought a book of Sudoku to pass the time,' says Janice helpfully, as we all squeeze into the little back room I located earlier. 'And my iPad, with some nice films on it.' She beams at me and Mum. 'Shall we have a little watch of *The Sound of Music*?'

Sometimes, I really love Janice.

Twenty minutes later, even with *The Sound of Music* distracting me, I'm almost popping with tension. What is going on in there? *What?* But at last the agreed time is up, and I sally forth with my bucket of cleaning materials. (We bought them especially at a hardware store.)

I knock on the door of Jerry's, wait till I hear Danny call, 'Come in,' then make my way in, my head bowed right down.

I'm counting on the fact that Cyndi won't recognize me from the children's party, because being in a house-keeper's uniform is such good camouflage. But even so, I keep my gaze down. I just about take in the fact that Cyndi is seated in a low chair by the window, with Suze, Danny and Ulla grouped around her like acolytes. There are glasses of champagne on the coffee table, and a stack of Danny Kovitz boxes on the floor.

Cyndi clearly hasn't recognized Suze either, from their brief previous encounter. Which isn't surprising, as Suze has been transformed from a desperate-looking girl with lank hair and shadowy face into a society lady with a chignon, full make-up and a cream bouclé dress with humongous pearl choker. Ulla, meanwhile, is looking exactly as she did when I first met her in Las Vegas, and is sketching Cyndi in charcoal.

Cyndi is all rosy in the face, and her eyes are bright, so I guess I've missed the bit where Danny told her he'd seen her photo in the society pages of magazines and greatly admired her style.

'Housekeeping?' I mutter, practically in a whisper.

'Oh hi,' says Danny, sounding irritated. 'This really isn't a good time for us.'

'Sorry, sir,' I mumble. 'Shall I come back?'

'Maybe just like, polish that screen?' He points to the widescreen TV on the wall. 'It's filthy.'

It's filthy because we smeared it with oil, earlier on. I hastily head over to it and start spraying on glass cleaner. As I rub away, my ears are almost tingling with desperation to hear the conversation behind me.

'So as I say, Cyndi,' Danny continues. 'I would love to give you this jacket, which I feel encapsulates your style.'

'Oh, my!' Cyndi seems overcome. 'For me? Really?' She pauses, the jacket half on. 'You know, when I got your assistant's email, I couldn't believe it. I mean, Danny Kovitz wants to meet *me*?' She peers over at Ulla's drawing. 'Oh, that's *too* flattering.'

'Not at all,' says Danny. 'Ulla draws all my muses.'

'Muses?' Cyndi looks even more overcome. 'Me, a *muse*?'

'For sure!' Danny nods. 'Now, go ahead, put the jacket on.'

As Cyndi puts on the jacket Suze makes admiring noises.

'Very nice,' says Danny. 'Very nice indeed.'

'So, you're organizing a fashion show for charity?' says Cyndi, as she admires her reflection in the free-standing mirror we ordered from Conference Accessories.

'That's right,' says Danny. 'Fashion by me, Danny Kovitz, and hosted by Lady Cleath-Stuart of the British aristocracy. That's why we got in touch with you.' He beams at Cyndi. 'We felt sure that you, as a top socialite and philanthropist, would want to be involved.'

I can see Cyndi goggling at the name 'Lady Cleath-Stuart', not to mention Danny himself. As well she might! I mean, it's a pretty starry line-up. But it had to be, to lure her here.

As I'm polishing the TV, I keep sneaking glances at Cyndi. And I can see why Corey's smitten. She's so *pretty*. Her skin is like a peach. She has these plump lips which she keeps biting, and these wide innocent eyes. If I were a man, I'd probably fall in love with her, too. I don't blame Corey for being besotted.

And this is how we're going to get him. Not by forcing him or threatening him, but by shaming him, in front of the one person in the world he cares about most.

'My husband knows Lord Cleath-Stuart, you know,' says Cyndi, as she adjusts the sleeves of the jacket.

'Absolutely,' says Danny smoothly. 'That's another reason we thought of you. Does your husband know you're here today?' he adds casually.

'I didn't say *exactly* what I was doing.' Cyndi colours

slightly. 'I said I was meeting friends. But he'll be so excited to hear about it!'

'Good!' Suze beams at her. 'Danny, why not show Cyndi the next outfit?'

I've heard enough. I give a final wipe at the screen, then dump my cloth back in my bucket and retreat into the corridor. I head next door to Ben, knock, and shuffle in.

'Housekeeping,' I murmur, but no one even responds, so I start randomly wiping the TV screen. Luke, Tarquin, Corey and Elinor are all sitting around a conference table and Corey is in the middle of some story involving a rifle and a bear. As he finishes, Luke and Tarquin burst into polite laughter, and Elinor inclines her head.

'But Lord Cleath-Stuart, you must be quite a shot yourself!' says Corey, looking flushed in the face. 'What with your grouse moors and so forth.'

'Absolutely,' says Tarquin. 'Perhaps you'll see for yourself one day.'

'Well!' Corey reddens still further. 'Now that would be an honour, your Lordship.'

'And your wife?' enquires Tarquin mildly. 'Would she like to visit England?'

'She would go *nuts*,' says Corey. 'And Mrs Sherman, I must say . . .' He turns to Elinor. 'Your invitation to the Hamptons is very kind.'

'Perhaps your wife would like an invitation to the Met Ball?' Elinor gives him a chilly smile. 'I'm always happy to introduce my investment partners into society.'

'Now that . . .' Corey seems momentarily speechless. 'That would make Cyndi's *year*.'

I catch Luke's eye and he gives me a tiny wink. OK. So far so good.

I retreat from the room, and pause for a moment, breathing hard. Right. Next stage. I must say, it would be a *lot* easier if we had video cameras, like in the real *Ocean's Eleven*. But we don't.

I hurry back to the little room, knock five times, which is our signal, and let myself in.

'It's all going fine,' I say breathlessly. 'Janice, you're up.'

I pick up the vase of flowers that we ordered earlier, and place it on a room-service trolley. (Luke found it on another corridor and we just turned the tablecloth over.) My job was to establish that the conversation was going in the correct direction in each room. Which it is. Now Janice's job is to give the signal: move to the next level.

As she takes hold of the trolley, I see that her hands are shaking, and I turn to her in surprise.

'Janice, are you OK?'

'Oh Becky,' she says desperately. 'I'm not cut out for this.'

'For what?'

'For this!' Her voice rises in agitation. 'High-level criminal high-jinks!'

My heart sinks. We should *never* have shown the film to Janice. I think in her head she honestly believes she's robbing the casino vault.

'Janice, this isn't high-level criminal high-jinks!' I say.

'It's only a little heist, love,' says Mum soothingly.

'It's not a *heist*.' I knock a fist to my head. Honestly. Does Mum even know what a heist is? 'Janice, you'll be fine.' I try to sound reassuring. 'Just take the flowers into the room, put them down, and leave. OK?' I clasp her hand, but she flinches. 'Look, I'll come with you. It's fine. It's all good.'

I open the door for her, and she pushes the room-service trolley out. We start slowly progressing along the corridor, Janice trembling all the while. I had no *idea* she'd be so nervy. I should never have put her in the Eleven. But I can't change the plan now.

'Look, you see?' I say as we turn the corner. 'Easy-peasy, we're nearly there . . .'

'Where's that going?' A nasal voice hits the back of my head.

What?

I wheel round to see a woman in the same braid-trimmed jacket as Mum. She has badly dyed black hair and is coming out of a room on the other side of the corridor. As she nears us, she eyes the vase narrowly. 'Which flower arrangement is that?' she demands. 'I don't recognize it.'

Oh for God's sake. That's because I arranged it myself, in about five seconds.

'Er . . . not sure,' I say, as Janice seems incapable of speech.

'Who are you?' The woman squints at my badge.

'I'm Marigold,' I say confidently.

'Marigold?' Her eyes narrow further. 'I thought she left.'

Honestly, what's wrong with this woman? Why does she have to be so *suspicious* the whole time? I'm sure it's not good for her health.

337

'Well.' I give a shrug, and the woman whips round to Janice.

'What's your name?'

Oh no. Poor Janice. I turn to give her some moral support – and blink in shock. Janice is transfixed. I've never seen such terror on a face. Before I can even open my mouth, she's collapsed on the floor.

Oh my *God*.

'Janice!' I cry in horror and kneel down beside her. 'What happened? Are you OK?'

She's not even moving. This is bad.

'Janice!' I tug at her clothes and try to listen to her heartbeat.

'Is she breathing?' demands the black-haired woman.

'I don't know!' I say furiously. 'Let me listen!'

I put my ear to her chest, but I can't tell if I'm hearing her heartbeat or my own pulse, so I rest my face against her mouth. I'll be able to *feel* her breath, surely?

And the next moment I hear a watery whisper in my ear:

'I'm acting, love. Like in the film.'

She's . . .

What?

I don't believe it.

This was *not in the plan*. I am so going to tell Janice off. But for now I'll just have to go with it.

'She's unconscious!' I say dramatically, sitting back on my heels. 'I think you should call a doctor. So, um . . . you stay with her and I'll just quickly deliver this.'

I get up and grab the trolley. I need to get into the

room with these wretched flowers. Danny and Suze need the signal. They'll be waiting and wondering and not knowing what to do . . .

'Wait,' says the black-haired woman.

'Call the doctor!' I repeat urgently, and the woman glares back, but gets out her phone and dials. 'Juliana?' she says. 'It's Lori. Can you put me through to the health centre?'

'Hey, Becky!' A cheery male voice hails me. 'Becky, is that you? Over here!'

Argh. What *now*? My head has turned instinctively before I can stop it – and it's Mike, the guy from the roulette table. The one who didn't want me to leave. He's waiting for the lift about twenty yards down the corridor, wearing a blue suit and waving with a huge beam on his face. 'How's the winning streak?' he calls. 'Hey, you really work here?'

I feel prickly all over. *Please shut up*, I think silently. *Please shut up!*

'*Becky?*' Lori gives me an evil look. Thankfully the lift doors close before she can question Mike.

'Isn't that weird?' I give a shrill laugh. 'Who *was* that man? He must have me confused with . . . I have no idea . . . Oh my God! Is she still *breathing*?'

As Lori glances down again at Janice, I practically gallop away with the trolley. I knock on the door of Jerry's and enter without waiting for a reply. By now, Cyndi is wearing a full-length coat, and turning this way and that in front of the mirror.

'He's just naturally generous,' she's saying earnestly. 'You know? *Generous*. Like, he took my whole family on vacation, last year, no expense spared. My mom, dad, my sister Sherilee . . .'

'He sounds amazing,' Suze murmurs.

'Flowers,' I say, unnecessarily, and put them on to a side table. As I do so, I catch Suze's eye and give her a tiny wink. She winks back, then addresses Cyndi.

'You know, Cyndi, I once heard about your husband's generosity from someone else,' she says casually. 'Have you ever heard of a man called . . . Brent Lewis?'

There's silence in the room. I'm completely still, waiting for her answer.

'Brent Lewis?' Cyndi says at last, her brow wrinkling. 'No, I don't believe I have.'

'Oh, it's a great story,' enthuses Suze. 'A wonderful story. And the best thing is, Corey comes so *well* out of it. I can't believe he hasn't told you what happened!'

'Too modest, I'm sure,' puts in Danny.

'He *is* too modest!' Cyndi nods fervently. 'I always tell him that. I say, Corey, hon, shine your light! So what's the story?'

'Well.' Suze beams. 'It starts with the spring. You know the famous balloon spring that launched Corey's business all those years ago?'

'Well, I've *heard* of it . . .' says Cyndi doubtfully.

They're off. It's all under control.

I back out of the room, close the door quietly and draw breath. OK. So far so good. Mum's up next.

But what's happened to Janice? I look in slight bewilderment at the empty floor. She was lying here a moment ago. And what about Lori? Has the doctor been already? Have they taken Janice away? What on earth—

Oh my God, there they are.

Lori is about ten yards down the corridor, walking slowly along with Janice leaning heavily on her arm. As though she can sense me watching her, Lori turns round and scowls.

'Hey, you!' she calls. 'I want to talk to you!'

'Don't stop!' moans Janice at once. 'I need the Ladies! I feel very ill!' She clutches Lori's arm harder. 'Please don't leave me! You're all I have!'

I can feel an almighty giggle rising inside me. Janice is amazing!

'You!' barks Lori again, but I pretend I can't hear and hurry the other way.

'Mum!' I gasp breathlessly as I reach our little back room and fling open the door. (I can't be bothered with signals any more.) 'It's all going to plan except Janice got a bit diverted. You ready?'

'Oh, love.' Mum looks apprehensive. 'I'm not sure about this.'

'Not you too!' I say in exasperation.

I gave Mum and Janice the simplest possible jobs. And they've both lost their nerve!

'Becky, come in with me,' Mum begs. 'I can't do it on my own.'

'But I've already been in once! Corey will notice!'

This was my whole reason for having all of us play different domestic staff – so Corey wouldn't suspect anything.

'No he won't!' says Mum. 'Did he even notice you before?'

341

I consider for a moment. Actually, he probably didn't. Men like Corey don't notice the staff.

'All right.' I roll my eyes. 'I'll come in with you. And I'll text Dad.'

I was so paranoid about Dad being spotted by Corey that I made him wait on a separate floor. But it's safe now. It's his time.

Mum and I take up our positions outside Ben, and a few moments later, Dad comes striding up the corridor.

'All set?' he says to me.

'All going to plan.' I nod at the door. 'He's in there.'

'I can't believe we're doing this.' Dad looks at Mum with a kind of wry, incredulous smile, and gestures at the closed door. 'Can you believe we're doing this? Of all the mad things Becky's talked us into doing, over the years . . .'

'Oh, I've given up even thinking that way,' replies Mum. 'I just go with the flow. Far easier.'

Honestly. What do they mean? I never talk people into doing things.

'But if it works . . .' Dad suddenly takes my hand and squeezes it. 'Becky, you've achieved a lot in your life. But this will be your finest hour. I mean that, love.'

'Oh, well,' I say awkwardly. '*If* the plan works.'

'Of course it'll work!' insists Mum.

Both my parents are looking at me proudly, as if I'm ten years old again, and have raised the most money for the new school netball court. (How I did it, by the way, was: I wrote stories about all of my classmates and illustrated them with little paper dolls and made them cut-out outfits and all the mothers paid *loads*.)

'Don't jinx it!' I say. 'Mum, we need to go.'

As she's smoothing down her jacket, I turn to Dad. 'What are you going to say to Corey?' I ask curiously. 'Where will you even start? I mean, he wouldn't take your call, he wouldn't speak to you . . . I'd want to slap him!'

But Dad shakes his head. 'This isn't about Corey and me. This is about Corey and Brent. Off you go now.' He steps away and I knock at the door, and before I know it, Mum and I are in the room.

Corey, Luke, Tarquin and Elinor are all still sitting around the table; Tarquin is saying something about 'equity' and they look up with what is quite convincing surprise.

'Yes?' says Elinor.

'I'm so sorry, sir,' says Mum, bustling in, looking exactly like a hotel manager. 'I believe you ordered a double conference room.'

Her American accent is absolutely atrocious, but Corey doesn't seem to notice. Or if he does, he doesn't make any comment.

'That's right, we did,' says Luke with a frown. 'I was going to complain about that.'

'My apologies, sir. I'll open the double doors right now.'

I don't know why Mum wanted moral support – she's brilliant! She heads over to the right-hand wall – the wall separating Ben from Jerry's – and my heart begins to thump in excitement. Here we go. *Here we go*.

All these conference rooms have magic doors. It's why I chose this particular business centre. The doors slide right into the walls, so you can have a big opening between rooms, join rooms up, close them off, do what you like.

Unhurriedly, looking for all the world like a bored hotel manager, Mum approaches the doors that open into Jerry's, and pushes them apart. It takes a moment for anyone to realize what's happened, then suddenly—

'Corey?' Cyndi's voice pipes up excitedly from the next room. She jumps up and hurries towards the opening. 'Corey, is that *you*? Oh my God, babe! What a *coincidence*!'

I've been watching Corey all this time, and he jerked with shock when he heard Cyndi's voice. But he at once regained control of himself. Now he gets to his feet, his eyes watchful and suspicious.

'Hi, sweetheart,' he says, his gaze roaming around and fixing on each face in turn, as though to find the answer to this, *now*. 'What are you doing here? Who are these people?'

'This is Danny Kovitz!' gushes Cyndi. 'The famous fashion designer! He's going to put on a fashion show and he wants me to model for it. And this is Lady Cleath-Stuart . . .'

'Your wife.' Corey whips round to Tarquin.

'Ah yes! So she is,' says Tarkie, in tones of surprise that make me want to giggle. 'Hello, dear.'

'Peyton and I are going to open the show!' Cyndi bubbles over. 'We're going to wear matching dresses. Isn't that fun?'

'Great,' says Corey shortly. His eyes are still darting around as though he's trying to work out what's

344

happening. I mean, he's not stupid. He must realize this can't be a coincidence.

And all we need now is for Cyndi to play her part. She doesn't know it, but she's the star of the show. She's like a peach hanging from a tree, I think. A big, ripe peach, all heavy and ready to fall . . . Go on . . . go *on* . . .

'Oh Corey!' Cyndi exclaims. 'I've just been hearing about Brent and all. You are such a sweet, sweet man.'

Thud. The peach has landed. Although, from the atmosphere in the room, it could have been a bomb. I risk a tiny glance at Corey, and my stomach lurches. His expression is absolutely livid.

'What, honey?' he says at last, in almost-pleasant tones. 'What are you talking about?'

'Brent!' she says. 'You know. The settlement.'

'*Settlement?*' Corey sounds like he can't quite pronounce the word properly.

'Ah yes,' says Luke cheerfully. 'We were about to get to that. Another of our valued associates is Brent Lewis, who obviously was very instrumental in helping you in the early days of Firelight Innovations, Inc.'

'I don't know what you're talking about,' says Corey tightly.

'Corey!' Luke gives an easy laugh. 'Don't be so modest!' He turns to Cyndi. 'The wonderful news is, your generous husband is going to provide a settlement for Brent, in recognition of his input to the success of Firelight Innovations. Isn't that kind? The lawyers are waiting downstairs with the documents, so we can get this all wrapped up super-quick.'

'Oh, Corey, you're an angel,' says Cyndi, blinking

earnestly at him. 'Haven't I always said, what goes around comes around?'

'It certainly does,' says Luke.

'Karma,' puts in Danny wisely.

'Of course, Corey doesn't *legally* owe Brent anything,' Luke continues. 'But he would never leave an old friend to starve on the streets.' Luke slaps Corey on the back. 'Would you, Corey, old chap?'

'Of course he wouldn't!' says Cyndi, seeming shocked at the idea. 'Corey's always looking out for others, aren't you, babe?'

'And a settlement of this modest size . . .' Luke gives Corey a significant look. 'You'll barely notice it.'

Luke and the lawyers have pitched the settlement at just the right amount. Enough to make a huge, life-changing difference to Brent . . . but not so much that Corey will feel any hardship. In fact, as Luke says, he'll barely notice it.

(I was all for trying to get squillions out of Corey, but Luke said no, we need to be pragmatic, and I suppose he's right.)

Corey's eyes are sparking with fury. His nostrils are white around the edges. He's opened his mouth and closed it again quite a few times during this conversation – but no words have made it out yet. And I can see his problem. He's kind of in a trap, what with Cyndi gazing lovingly at him.

'Sweetheart, we should have this Brent over for dinner,' says Cyndi earnestly. 'You never even mentioned him before.'

'Dinner?' Corey's voice sounds strangled.

346

'In fact, you guys should *all* come to dinner!' Cyndi looks around, her eyes sparkling. 'Let's do it tonight. We'll set up the grill by the pool, play some music . . .'

'I don't think—' Corey begins.

'*Please*, Corey!' she cuts him off. 'We never have anyone over!' She looks around, counting up people. 'You guys got kids? Bring 'em along! Is there anyone else we should ask?'

But no one answers, because the door behind her has opened, and in walks Dad. He stops, a few paces in, and surveys Corey with a wry expression in his kind eyes. And I want to freeze-frame this moment. Finally, *finally*, after all these years, Dad and Corey are face to face.

As I watch them, all I can think of is that old photo of them. Four young guys on their road trip, not knowing where life would lead them.

Corey may be the richest. But my dad wins in *every way*, I think fiercely. *Every way*.

'Corey,' he says simply. 'Good to see you again.'

'Who are you?' asks Cyndi in bewilderment.

'Oh, I'm with the lawyers,' answers Dad, giving her a charming smile. 'I just wanted to say to Corey: I'm so glad you've decided not to abandon your old friend.'

I'm studying Corey in fascination, to see if any flicker of remorse passes across his face. Or regret? Sorrow? Shame? *Anything?* But his face is impassive. Which could be because of his facelift, I suppose.

'So,' says Dad pleasantly. 'Shall we get this document signed?'

He smiles at Corey and gestures to the door. But Corey doesn't move.

347

'Corey?' prompts Dad again. 'It'll take five minutes of your time. No more.'

Still, Corey is motionless. But I can see his brain working. His eyes are busy. He's thinking ... he's thinking ...

'Lord Cleath-Stuart,' he exclaims and pointedly sits back down at the table next to Tarkie. 'I was interested to hear about your charitable foundation. It supports local entrepreneurs, you say?'

'Ahm ... yes.' Tarquin looks confused. 'Did I mention that?'

'I would love to pledge half a million dollars,' says Corey in loud, clear tones. 'Half a million dollars, today. Give me the details and I'll arrange a bank transfer.'

'Babe!' Cyndi's voice rockets through the room. Her face is glowing and she looks like she might expire from pride. 'You are *amazing*! You are *awesome*!'

'Well, what's the use of having good fortune if you can't share it?' says Corey stiffly, as though he's reciting a memorized line. He glances at Dad and adds casually, 'Shall we leave the other matter to another day?'

Another day?

In consternation, I meet Luke's eyes. No. Nooo.

Corey's so *snaky*. We had him, we totally had him. And now he's wriggling out of our trap.

Cyndi is his Achilles heel. Cyndi would have got him to sign the settlement; that's what the whole plan is based on. But now she's captivated by this new, super-generous donation to Tarkie, she won't care so much about Brent. Corey will be able to put it off and put it off and never do it ...

348

I feel a sudden loathing for Corey, even stronger than before. What kind of twisted man is this? He'd rather spend half a million dollars on some random charity he's only just heard about, than take the chance to right the terrible injustice he caused. All because of some grudge. All because they fought over a woman. It's awful. It's tragic. It's despicable.

But luckily . . .

I don't want to boast, *but* . . .

I saw this coming. Ha.

OK, that's not quite true. I didn't predict *exactly* this happening. But I do have a contingency plan. And it looks like I'm going to have to put it into action, right now.

Trying to look unobtrusive, I start to sidle towards the far partition wall in Jerry's. Because we have a third room booked. (I've nicknamed it 'Häagen-Dazs'.) And we have an eleventh member of the team. And she's waiting patiently in Häagen-Dazs, on standby, just in case she should be needed.

Slowly, almost silently, I push the doors aside and beckon to her.

It took a whole evening of talking to persuade Rebecca to take part in this. She's no big fan of Brent – she doesn't care if he starves. And she's no big fan of Dad either. (My theory is, he broke her heart back in the day. Although I am never, ever sharing this thought with either of my parents.) But she's even *less* of a fan of Corey – and that's what tipped the balance. Sometimes you really need to appeal to people's worst instincts. Which is a bit depressing, but there you go.

As Rebecca approaches the double doors that lead from Häagen-Dazs into Jerry's, I can sense the team behind me swinging into action. Everyone knows about the contingency plan. We've practised it. We've choreographed it. I glance round briefly to see Suze moving into place, while Ulla and Danny stand by her side, looking alert. They all know their briefs. In fact, there is only one brief, for everybody: *Don't let Cyndi turn round. Don't let her see Rebecca.*

'So, Cyndi!' Suze exclaims in animation. 'How many children did you say you have?'

'You should choose some drawings to take home,' adds Ulla, holding up her sketchpad. 'Have a look.'

'Oh yes!' encourages Danny. 'See this one of you in my jacket? Divine.'

'Goodness!' says Cyndi in delight. 'May I really? Oh, I look so *elegant* . . . I just have one child,' she continues to Suze. 'My one precious gift. And you? You have kids?'

Rebecca is standing in the far doorway now. Not moving, not waving, not speaking. Just standing, waiting to be noticed.

My eyes are fixed on Corey. He's listening to Tarquin . . . he's gazing absently up at the ceiling, he's frowning with slight impatience . . . And then, as his gaze drifts past Tarkie, past Cyndi, his whole face jerks with horror.

OK. He's seen her.

If I was hoping for a reaction, I'm not disappointed. His eyes have gone all starey. The colour has drained from his cheeks. He looks like he's in a nightmare. In fact, he looks so ill, I almost feel sorry for him, loathsome as he is. This man has tried *so* hard to airbrush out his past. He's had a facelift. He's lied about his age. He's denied his friends. He doesn't want the past to exist. But here it is, standing in front of him in a floaty purple dress and kohled eyes.

For a moment, Rebecca just surveys him, with that witchy, catlike gaze she has. And then, silently, she prepares to hold up the signs. We made them together, with cardboard and a Sharpie, and checked that they would be legible.

(I didn't get this bit from *Ocean's Eleven*. It's from *Love Actually*. Suze said, why don't we rechristen it *Becky Actually* for the occasion, but that makes no sense. Anyway. Not the point right now.)

The first sign just says:

Hi Corey.

She holds it in place for a few seconds – then replaces it with her second sign:

Long time.

And somehow the contemptuous way she's looking at Corey gives those two words real bite. Her eyes are fixed on him as she produces the next sign:

I'd love to meet your wife.

Her eyes flick to Cyndi, and Corey's eyes follow, and I can see the fury pulsing in his face. Only he doesn't dare

make a sound, in case Cyndi notices. He's trapped.
Again.

Chat with her about old times.
Or maybe that's not such a good idea?

Corey's face is rigid. He looks like he's undergoing
torture. Well, in a way, he is. And Rebecca's *loving* it.

'And what about nurseries? Or do you call them "pre-
schools" over here?' I can hear Suze asking Cyndi
brightly. 'Because it's *so* hard to find places in the UK.'

'Tell me about it!' exclaims Cyndi, completely
oblivious to the drama going on around her. 'And you
know, Peyton is super-talented, so . . .'

What about Brent's settlement, Corey?

Rebecca practically brandishes the sign at him, then
substitutes the next one.

You owe him.
YOU OWE HIM, COREY.

And now she's writing an extra sign we didn't agree
on. She holds it up and her eyes glitter wickedly.

I could make your life a misery.
I would LOVE to make your life a misery.

Crikey. Well, that's honest. I glance at Corey, and the
veins are standing out on his forehead. His fists are
clenched. He looks like he wants to attack her.

Just sign it and I'll be gone out of your life.

Rebecca gives him a long, challenging gaze. Then she starts holding the signs up more and more quickly, almost as if she's dealing cards.

Just sign it.
Just sign the settlement, Corey.
Do it.

Corey is breathing harder and harder. He looks like a man about to explode.

Just fucking DO IT.
DO IT, Corey.
DO IT DO IT DO IT DO IT.

'OK!' Corey suddenly erupts like a bull snorting. '*OK!* Let's get this goddam settlement done. Give me a pen. Let's get it done.'

Oh my God. Did he just say—

I meet Rebecca's eyes for a breathless moment. Have we *done* it? Have we won?

I think we've won.

Slowly, silently, Rebecca closes the double doors . . . and it's as if she was never there.

'Marvellous!' says Luke smoothly. 'Very kind of you, Corey. Shall we sort that out straight away?'

'You OK, babe?' says Cyndi, looking away in surprise from Suze, Danny and Ulla and surveying Corey.

'Sweetheart, is something wrong? You look like you're burning up!'

'Nothing's wrong.' Corey gives her a fixed smile. 'Just want to get this all wrapped up.'

'Good man,' says Dad, in cheerful tones. 'Let's go and find my legal colleagues.'

Without any further delay, Dad ushers Corey towards the door. I catch his eye as he walks past, and feel a weird bubble rising up inside me. But I'm not sure . . . is it a bubble of relief? Hysteria? Disbelief?

As Cyndi babbles on about Peyton's amazing ballet potential, I meet Suze's eyes . . . then Mum's . . . all around the room. Tarquin's . . . Danny's . . . Ulla's . . . Elinor's. And last of all, Luke's. He gives me a little grin and lifts his coffee cup to me as though in a toast. And I can't stop a smile spreading across my face. After all that. We've done it.

We've actually done it.

NINETEEN

The Bellagio fountains are magical. And OK, I *know* they're touristy and I *know* they're a cliché, and I *know* there's a load of other sightseers crowding around. But right now, I feel as if they're gushing up, over and over, just for us. For us ten. They're our reward.

We're leaning against the balustrade, all in a line, just like at the end of the *Ocean's Eleven* film. That ripply piano music is playing in my head, and nobody's saying anything. We're just looking at each other and smiling, and I haven't felt so good for ages. For *ever*. We did it. We got justice. And the ridiculous thing is, Brent doesn't even have any idea yet . . . but somehow that's not the point.

I don't think I've ever felt so content. I don't think life has ever fallen so perfectly into place.

The plan worked so brilliantly. Everyone played their parts immaculately, from Tarquin to Janice . . . Especially Janice. (Apparently she locked herself in a cubicle in the Ladies, moaning, until Lori went for help, whereupon

Janice scurried away.) Over our celebratory drinks I regaled everyone with how fantastic she'd been, and she got all flustered and had to have more champagne, and then everyone had to rehash all their various moments, and Dad wanted to hear it all about ten times, because he'd been stuck waiting for so long, and Mum said, 'Don't you wish we had it all on video?' and Luke said, 'Well, maybe, if we wanted to end up in prison for coercion.'

I'm still not totally sure if he was joking or not. But I don't care. The documents are signed. Brent's going to get the money. He'll be able to buy a house. And that's all that matters.

Rebecca isn't with us. She didn't even stay to say goodbye. Which – you know. Fair enough. That's her choice. To be honest, I'm glad. I'll be happy if I never see her again. I'm over poking around in the past. I want to move forward. Move on. It's time for Luke and me and Minnie to head home. Not home LA, *home*, home.

Suze and Tarkie are heading home, too. I think they'll probably scoop up the children and get on a plane as soon as they can. Back to England, back to Letherby Hall, back to real life. Tarkie can't wait to get stuck in to all his development plans. Suze can't wait to go and find Owl's Tower. She told me she's going to feed it Growmore every week, just to make sure. (Actually, she'd better not do that, she'll probably kill it.)

Luke and I need to pack up the house in LA, give notice at Minnie's pre-school, do all those final things you do when something's over. And it'll be sad in a way . . . but it'll be right. I smile up at Luke, whose face is all shining from the fountain lights, and he puts his arm around my shoulders.

What's supposed to happen now is we all silently drift off without saying goodbye, into our separate lives, with our millions. Except that's where real life and *Ocean's Eleven* really *are* different, because we can't drift off silently, we've got a table reserved for all of us at this really nice steak restaurant that was recommended to Luke. (Plus, obviously, we don't have any millions.)

So I glance at Mum and she nods, and nudges Dad, and Janice looks up from her phone and says, 'Martin's just boarding at Heathrow! Won't be long now!'

Janice's husband, Martin, is coming out for a few days and they're going to visit some vineyards in California with Mum and Dad. I think they'll have a wonderful time, and it's a really nice way for my parents to thank Janice. She deserves it.

'Shall we go?' says Mum.

'Let me get a piccie first!' says Janice. 'All line up in front of the fountains!'

OK, we have *majorly* digressed from *Ocean's Eleven* at this point. I can't imagine Brad Pitt accosting a random tourist and asking him to take a quick 'snap of the gang'.

Then Mum wants a photo of her and Dad, and then they want one with Janice, and I'm just wondering whether I should ask Suze to take one of me and Luke, when I notice a stocky man nearby, watching us. I wouldn't even have noticed him, except he's staring quite fixedly at my dad, and as the stranger turns his head, the light catches his face and—

I gasp so loud, Luke whips round in alarm.

'Look!' I flail my arms. 'Is that him? Is it *Brent*?'

The man takes a step backwards and from his caught-out expression I just know it's him. He looks like the photo, only craggier and sadder. He also looks as though he's having second thoughts about being here.

'Don't go,' I add hastily. 'Please.' I hurry over to Dad and tug his sleeve. 'Dad, look who's here!'

He turns, and I can see the light of surprise in his eyes.

'Brent! You made it! I didn't think you'd . . .'

'I got a voicemail from Rebecca,' says Brent. 'She told me . . .' He rubs his brow. 'Told me you'd be here. Told me some other stuff. Not sure what to believe.'

Slowly Suze, Tarkie and the others are gathering around, peering at Brent, almost in disbelief. We've been chasing, discussing, focusing on this guy for all this time. And finally, here he is.

He's not a well-looking man. He's still got the square brow of his youth, but his grey hair is going, and the rest of his face is jowly, with sunken, defeated eyes. He looks like he's had a hard life. He's wearing an old, cheap-looking jacket, and a backpack is slung over his shoulder.

Now his eyes are moving suspiciously over all of us, as though expecting a trick.

'Did Rebecca tell you—' Dad breaks off. 'Did she mention a settlement at all?' he says carefully. 'Did she mention the money?'

Brent's expression immediately becomes more defensive. His glower deepens and his shoulders tense.

Which I can understand. If I were him I wouldn't want to believe it either. I wouldn't want the hope till I had the proof.

'Makes no sense,' he says. 'Why would Corey suddenly cave in? I tried in 2002.'

'I know,' says Dad quickly. 'Brent, like I tried to tell you before, I had no idea you were approaching Corey then. None. I would *never*— You have to know . . .' As he gazes at Brent he seems a bit overcome. 'Here. Read this.' He takes out of his pocket a copy of the settlement agreement. 'It's what you're morally owed. No more.'

Tourists are pressing backwards and forwards, trying to get a view of the fountains, but the ten of us are totally engrossed in Brent's face as he reads the words of the document.

I'm pretty sure he reads the whole thing three times before he reacts. Then he looks up, gives a brief nod and says, 'I see. Yes. Can I keep this?'

And you might think he was totally callous and ungrateful, if you couldn't see his hands, shaking and shaking. And a sudden tear plops on to the paper, which we all pretend we didn't notice.

'Of course.' Dad nods. 'We have copies.'

Brent carefully folds the paper up small and puts it in his backpack, then surveys the group of us again.

'I guess I need to thank . . . you, Graham?'

'All of us,' says Dad quickly. 'We all pulled together.'

'But who *are* you?' Brent looks around the faces, as though totally confused.

'Friends of Graham's,' says Janice.

'And Becky's,' says Danny, as Ulla nods.

359

'I am Rebecca's mother-in-law,' says Elinor.

'It was Bex who made the plan to get Corey,' puts in Suze.

'We called it Becky's Eleven,' explains Mum brightly. 'Have you seen the film?'

'Which one's Becky?' demands Brent, and nervously, I step towards him.

'Hi. I'm Becky. I met your daughter, Becca. I came to the trailer, I don't know if she mentioned it . . . and I told my dad you'd been evicted . . . That's how it all began, really.'

'We wanted to get justice for you,' chimes in Janice. 'That Corey is a low-down snake, pardon my French!'

'You're from Britain.' Brent looks more and more bewildered.

'Oxshott. But I flew over to help,' continues Janice cheerily. 'Well, anything for Jane and Graham.'

'And anything for Becky,' adds Suze. 'She got us all going.'

'It was a group effort,' I say quickly. 'Everyone was brilliant.'

'But . . .' Brent rubs his face again. 'Why? Why help me? You're strangers, most of you. You don't know me.'

'We were helping Becky's dad,' says Danny simply.

'You need to thank my daughter,' puts in Dad. 'She's the powerhouse behind all this.'

'Oh and by the way, Brent, thanks for the CB and MMM tip!' I exclaim, suddenly remembering. 'That's like, my motto for life!'

But Brent doesn't respond. He's looking around at the

ten of us, a sort of wonder in his face. Then, at last he turns to me.

'Young lady, you must be very lucky in your friends,' he says. 'Or maybe they're lucky in you.'

'I'm very lucky in my friends,' I say at once. 'That's what it is. Definitely. They're amazing.'

'It goes both ways,' says Ulla, and we all peer at her in surprise. (She's not the most talkative, Ulla, although she was brilliant at distracting Cyndi.)

'Hear hear,' confirms Suze.

'Well, anyway,' I say, a bit awkwardly. 'The main thing is, we did it. And now you're here! You *must* come for supper . . .' I swing back round to take up the conversation with Brent. But I can't see him any more. What happened? Where is he?

We all scan the crowd in confusion, and Luke searches around the area a bit – but it's soon obvious he's not coming back.

Brent's gone.

The steak-house that was recommended to Luke *is* amazing. We all order steaks and fries and pretty much every side dish on the menu. The waiter pours out a delicious red wine, and as we toast each other I can sense everyone breathing out. Properly. Finally. We made it.

As I look around the table, I feel a little wash of happiness. We're all in such a better place than we were. Mum and Dad are sitting side by side across the table from me with Janice. They're all looking at photos on Dad's phone of the red-rocks canyons, and making plans for their vineyard trips. All of Mum's hysteria has evaporated; all of her tension has gone. She keeps stroking Dad's arm, and he squeezes her back as though he's never going to leave her again.

Elinor is looking pretty relaxed, too. She and Luke are chatting away about the holiday we might all take in the Hamptons, with Danny chipping in every now and again with local gossip that makes even Elinor snort with laughter.

If you were brutally honest you might say that Danny has *mostly* become best friends with Elinor because she's planning to spend a small fortune on his clothes and help him launch a whole new older women's market which will do great things for his profits . . . But there's more to it than that. There's a genuine bond between them. I really do believe that. Like, they've already discussed how they'll give Cyndi a wonderful time at the Met Ball because none of this was her fault. (I'm going to try and go, too.)

As for Suze and Tarkie, they're completely different people. Suze has relaxed. She's the old Suze. She laughs at silly things. Her frown has eased. And Tarkie is a revelation! I keep watching him, trying to work out what's different – but I don't think it's one thing. It's lots of little things. Apparently one of the pieces of advice Dad gave him on the road was: 'Fake it till you make it.' Well, I don't know what's fake and what's real, or whether he even knows himself – but it's working. He's going to make a kick-ass Lord of the Manor when he gets back to England.

'We're going to plant over a thousand trees next year,'

he's telling Dad. 'Of course, Suze won't notice any of them.'

At once, Suze flushes red and says hastily, 'I will! I'll help plant them and look after them and everything. I *love* trees!'

Tarkie flicks a tiny, teasing smile at her, and she flushes even deeper, and it's quite obvious she's confessed all about Owl's Tower. Well, that's good. It was stressing *me* out, never mind them.

As if she's reading my mind, Suze gently nudges my foot with hers under the table. We're both wearing our cowboy boots. They feel so right, I can't believe I'll ever wear anything else again. The Wild West has really got under my skin. Into my soul. The clothes, the sunshine, the desert, the music . . .

Ooh, which reminds me of something.

'Hey, Luke!' I say brightly. 'I forgot to tell you. When I was out with Suze this afternoon, I tried out a banjo and I think we should get it.'

'*What?*' Luke looks up from his conversation with Elinor, aghast.

'I told her you wouldn't go for it,' puts in Suze, spearing a piece of steak.

'Don't look like that, Luke!' I say, affronted. 'It'll be good for Minnie to learn an instrument, so why not the banjo? And we can all have lessons together, and become a family folk group, and it'll *totally* be a good investment . . .'

BUCKINGHAM PALACE

Mrs Luke Brandon
c/o The Pines
43 Elton Road
Oxshott
Surrey

Dear Mrs Brandon

The Queen wishes me to write and thank you for the good wishes which you have sent to Her Majesty.

I am glad to hear that Mr Derek Smeath of East Horsley (formerly of Fulham) has proved such an invaluable friend, not just to you but to 'the causes of love and justice'. I can well believe that he has made the world a better place.

However, I'm sorry to say, there is no 'instant fast track' to a knighthood; nor does the Queen have any 'spare OBEs' that she could 'just put in an envelope for him'.

On behalf of Her Majesty, I thank you again for writing.

Yours sincerely

Lavinia Coutts-Hoares-Berkeley
Lady-in-Waiting

LONDON BOROUGH
OF HAMMERSMITH & FULHAM
TOWN HALL
KING STREET
LONDON W6 9JU

Mrs Rebecca Brandon
c/o The Pines
43 Elton Road
Oxshott
Surrey

Dear Mrs Brandon

Thank you for your letter. It is always pleasing to hear from former residents of Fulham.

I was glad to hear about your friend Derek Smeath, who managed the Fulham branch of Endwich Bank for so many years. He sounds a most helpful man, and I'm sure you are right that many residents of Fulham have benefited from his wisdom.

However, it is unfortunately not within my powers as a councillor to 'award him a medal' or 'the freedom of the city'.

I thank you for your interest in the council and enclose a leaflet on our latest progress in green waste-management.

Yours sincerely

Councillor Elaine Padgett-Grant
Hammersmith & Fulham Council

East Horsley Horticultural Society
'Little Whisperings'
55 Old Oak Lane
East Horsley
Surrey

Dear Mrs Brandon

Thank you very much for your letter. What a story you have to tell!!!

As one of Derek's gardening 'chums' I could not agree more with your sentiments that he is an all-round good egg. I was delighted to learn that Lord and Lady Cleath-Stuart are naming a new avenue of trees on their estate, 'Smeath Walk', after him. He deserves no less!!!

It will be my absolute pleasure to organize a society 'day out' to Letherby Hall for the 'opening ceremony', and your cheque should amply cover our expenses. I assure you, Derek will be none the wiser, until you land the 'surprise' on him. I should think he won't believe his eyes!! Meanwhile, 'mum's the word'.

I look forward to meeting you on 'the day'. Meanwhile, stay well and no more adventures!!!

Yours very kindly

Trevor M. Flanagan
President, EHHS

PS: Are you the 'Rebecca' who gets into such trouble in Derek's book? Don't worry, your secret's 'safe' with me!!!

Acknowledgements

Writing a book is much like going on a road trip, what with the snacks, the constant looking out of the window and the panics that you have no idea whatsoever where you're heading . . . I'm endlessly grateful to all who have been in my metaphorical RV. I couldn't have done it without you. Thank you. xxx

The British RV

Araminta Whitley, Peta Nightingale, Jennifer Hunt, Sophie Hughes, Nicki Kennedy, Sam Edenborough and all the team at ILA, Harriet Bourton, Linda Evans, Bill Scott-Kerr, Larry Finlay, Sally Wray, Claire Evans, Alice Murphy-Pyle, Tom Chicken and his team, Claire Ward, Anna Derkacz and her team, Stephen Mulcahey, Rebecca Glibbery, Sophie Murray, Kate Samano, Elisabeth Merriman, Alison Martin, Katrina Whone, Judith Welsh, Jo Williamson, Bradley Rose.

The American RV

Kim Witherspoon, David Forrer, Susan Kamil, Deborah Aroff, Kesley Tiffey, Avideh Bashirrad, Theresa Zoro, Sally Marvin, Sharon Propson, Loren Noveck, Benjamin Dreyer, Paolo Pepe, Scott Shannon, Matt Schwartz, Henley Cox.

Read on for the first, hilarious chapter!

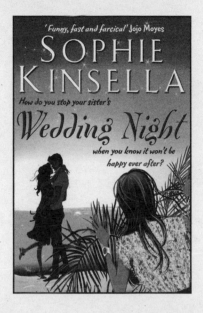

What do you do when you think your sister's about to marry the wrong man?

It's all gone wrong with the man Lottie thought was Mr Right. Then out of the blue she gets a call from her first love. She decides it must be Fate, and rushes off to marry him and rekindle their sizzling Greek island romance.

Lottie's older sister can't believe she's doing something so crazy. No more Ms Nice Sister, she's stopping this marriage. Right away! And she'll go to any lengths to do so . . .

'Funny, fast and farcical. I loved it'

Jojo Moyes

Out now in paperback, ebook and audio

PROLOGUE

Arthur

Young people! With their hurrying and their worrying and their wanting all the answers, *now*. They wear me out, the poor, harried things.

Don't come back, I always tell them. *Don't come back.*

Youth is still where you left it and that's where it should stay. Anything that was worth taking on life's journey, you'll already have taken with you.

Twenty years I've been saying this, but do they listen? Do they hell. Here comes another of them now. Panting and puffing as he reaches the top of the cliff. Late thirties, I'd guess. Attractive enough, against the blue sky. Looks a bit like a politician. Do I mean that? Maybe a movie star.

I don't remember his face from the old days. Not that that means anything. These days I barely even recall my own face when I glimpse it in the mirror. I can see this chap's gaze raking the surroundings, taking in me, sitting in my chair under my favourite olive tree.

'Are you Arthur?' he says abruptly.

'Guilty.'

I scan him adroitly. Looks well-off. Wearing one of those

expensive-logo polo shirts. Probably good for a few double Scotches.

'You must want a drink,' I say pleasantly. Always useful to steer the conversation in the direction of the bar early on.

'I don't want a drink,' he says. 'I want to know what happened.'

I can't help stifling a yawn. So predictable. He wants to know what happened. Another merchant banker having a midlife crisis, returning to the scene of his youth. The scene of the crime. Leave it where it *was*, I want to answer. Turn round. Return to your adult, problematic life, because you won't solve it here.

But he wouldn't believe me. They never do.

'Dear boy,' I say gently. 'You grew up. That's what happened.'

'No,' he says impatiently, and rubs his sweaty brow. 'You don't understand. I'm here for a reason. Listen to me.' He comes forward a few paces, an impressive height and figure against the sun, intentness of purpose on his hand-some face. 'I'm here for a reason,' he repeats. 'I wasn't going to get involved – but I can't help it. I have to do this. I want to know *what exactly happened* . . .'

1

Lottie

Twenty days earlier

I've bought him an engagement ring. Was that a mistake?

I mean, it's not a *girly* ring. It's a plain band with a tiny diamond in it, which the guy in the shop talked me into. If Richard doesn't like the diamond, he can always turn it round.

Or not wear it at all. Keep it on his nightstand or in a box or whatever.

Or I could take it back and never mention it. Actually, I'm losing confidence in this ring by the minute, but I just felt bad that he wouldn't have anything. Men don't get the greatest deal out of a proposal. They have to set up the occasion, they have to get down on one knee, they have to ask the question *and* they have to buy a ring. And what do we have to do? Say 'yes'.

Or 'no', obviously.

I wonder what proportion of marriage proposals end in a 'yes' and what proportion end in a 'no'? I open my mouth automatically to share this thought with Richard – then hastily close it again. *Idiot.*

'Sorry?' Richard glances up.

'Nothing!' I beam. 'Just . . . great menu!'

I wonder if he's bought a ring already. I don't mind either way. On the one hand, it's fabulously romantic if he has. On the other hand, it's fabulously romantic to choose one together.

It's a win-win.

I sip my water and smile lovingly at Richard. We're sitting at a corner table overlooking the river. It's a new restaurant on the Strand, just up from the Savoy. All black and white marble and vintage chandeliers and button-back chairs in pale grey. It's elegant but not showy. The perfect place for a lunchtime proposal. I'm wearing an understated, bride-to-be white shirt, a print skirt, and have splashed out on stay-up stockings, just in case we decide to cement the engagement later on. I've never worn stay-up stockings before. But then I've never been proposed to before.

Ooh, maybe he's booked a room at the Savoy.

No. Richard's not flash like that. He'd never make a ridiculous, out-of-proportion gesture. Nice lunch, yes; overpriced hotel room, no. Which I respect.

He's looking nervous. He's fiddling with his cuffs and checking his phone and swirling the water round in his glass. As he sees me watching him, he smiles too.

'So.'

'So.'

It's as though we're speaking in code, skirting around the real issue. I fiddle with my napkin and adjust my chair. This waiting is unbearable. Why doesn't he get it over with?

No, I don't mean 'get it over with'. Of course I don't. It's not a vaccination. It's . . . Well, what is it? It's a beginning. A first step. The pair of us embarking on a great adventure together. Because we want to take on life as a team. Because we can't think of anyone else we'd rather share that journey with. Because I love him and he loves me.

I'm getting misty-eyed already. This is hopeless. I've been like this for days, ever since I realized what he was driving at.

He's quite heavy-handed, Richard. I mean, in a good, lovable way. He's direct and to the point and doesn't play games. (Thank *God*.) Nor does he land massive surprises on you out of the blue. On my last birthday, he hinted for ages that his present was going to be a surprise trip, which was ideal because I knew to get down my overnight bag and pack a few things.

Although, in the end, he *did* catch me out, because it wasn't a weekend away, as I'd predicted. It was a train ticket to Stroud, which he had biked to my desk with no warning, on my midweek birthday. It turned out he'd secretly arranged with my boss for me to have two days off, and when I finally arrived at Stroud, a car whisked me to the most adorable Cotswold cottage, where he was waiting with a fire burning and a sheepskin rug laid out in front of the flames. (Mmm. Let's just say that sex in front of a roaring fire is *the best thing ever*. Except when that stupid spark flew out and burned my thigh. But never mind. Tiny detail.)

So this time, when he started dropping hints, again they weren't exactly subtle indications. They were more like massive signposts, plonked in the road: *I will be proposing to you soon*. First he set up this date and called it a 'special lunch'. Then he referred to a 'big question' he had to ask me and half winked (to which I feigned ignorance, of course). Then he started teasing me by asking if I like his surname, Finch. (As it happens, I do like it. I don't mean I won't miss being Lottie Graveney, but I'll be very happy to be Mrs Lottie Finch.)

I almost wish he'd been more roundabout and this was going to be more of a surprise. But there again, at least I knew to get a manicure.

'So, Lottie, have you decided yet?' Richard looks up at me with that warm smile of his, and my stomach swoops. Just for an instant I thought he was being super-clever and that *was* his proposal.

'Um . . .' I look down to hide my confusion.

Of course the answer will be 'yes'. A big, joyful 'yes'. I can still hardly believe we've arrived at this place. Marriage. I mean, marriage! In the three years Richard and I have been together, I've deliberately avoided the question of marriage, commitment and all associated subjects (children, houses, sofas, herbs in pots). We sort of live together at his place, but I still have my own flat. We're a couple, but at Christmas we go home to our own families. We're in *that* place.

After about a year I knew we were good together. I knew I loved him. I'd seen him at his best (the surprise birthday trip, tied with the time I drove over his foot by mistake and he didn't shout at me) and his worst (obstinately refusing to ask for directions, all the way to Norfolk, with broken sat nav. It took six hours). And I still wanted to be with him. I *got* him. He's not the show-offy kind, Richard. He's measured and deliberate. Sometimes you think he's not even listening – but then he'll come to life so suddenly, you realize he was alert the whole time. Like a lion, half asleep under the tree, but ready for the kill. Whereas I'm a bit more of a gazelle, leaping around. We complement each other. It's Nature.

(Not in a food-chain sense, obviously. In a *metaphorical* sense.)

So I knew, after a year, he was The One. But I also knew what would happen if I put a foot wrong. In my experience, the word 'marriage' is like an enzyme. It causes all kinds of reactions in a relationship, mostly of the breaking-down kind.

Look at what happened with Jamie, my first long-term boyfriend. We'd been happily together for four years and I just happened to mention that my parents got married at the same age we were (twenty-six and twenty-three). That was it. One mention. Whereupon he freaked out and said we had to take 'a break'. A break from what? Until that moment we'd been fine. So clearly what he needed a break from was *the risk of hearing the word 'marriage' again*. Clearly this was such a major worry that he couldn't even face seeing me, for fear that my mouth might start to form the word again.

Before the 'break' was over, he was with that red-haired girl. I didn't mind, because by then I'd met Seamus. Seamus, with his sexy Irish lilting voice. And I don't even *know* what went wrong with him. We were besotted for about a year – crazy, all-night-sex, nothing-else-in-life-matters besotted – until all of a sudden we were arguing every night instead. We went from exhilarating to exhausting in about twenty-four hours. It was toxic. Too many state-of-the-nation summits about 'Where are we heading?' and 'What do we want from this relationship?' and it wore us both out. We limped on for another year, and when I look back, it's as though that second year is a big, black, miserable blot in my life.

Then there was Julian. That lasted two years too, but it never really *took*. It was like a skeleton of a relationship. I suppose both of us were working far too hard. I'd recently moved to Blay Pharmaceuticals and was travelling all over the country. He was trying to get partnership at his accountancy firm. I'm not sure we ever even broke up properly – we just drifted apart. We meet up occasionally, as friends, and it's the same for both of us – we're not quite sure where it all went wrong. He even asked me out on a date, a year or so ago, but I had to tell him I was with someone now, and really happy. And that was Richard. The guy I really do love. The guy sitting opposite me with a ring in his pocket (maybe).

Richard is definitely better-looking than any of my other boyfriends. (Maybe I'm biased, but I think he's gorgeous.) He works hard as a media analyst, but he's not obsessed. He's not as rich as Julian, but who cares? He's energetic and funny and has an uproarious laugh which makes my spirits lift, whatever mood I'm in. He calls me 'Daisy' ever since we went on a picnic where I made him a daisy chain. He can lose his temper with people – but that's OK. No one's perfect. When I look back over our relationship, I don't see a black blot, like with Seamus, or a blank space, like with Julian; I see a cheesy music video. A montage, with blue skies and smiles. Happy times. Closeness. Laughter.

And now we're getting to the climax of the montage. The bit where he kneels down, takes a deep breath . . .

I'm feeling so nervous for him. I want this to go beautifully. I want to be able to tell our children that I fell in love with their father all over again, the day he proposed.

Our children. Our home. Our life.

As I let my mind roll around the images, I feel a release inside me. I'm ready for this. I'm thirty-three years old and I'm ready. All my grown-up life, I've steered away from the subject of marriage. My friends are the same. It's as though there's been a crime-scene cordon around the whole area: NO ENTRY. You just don't go there, because if you do, you've jinxed it and your boyfriend chucks you.

But now there's nothing to jinx. I can *feel* the love flowing between us, over the table. I want to grab Richard's hands. I want to envelop him in my arms. He is such a wonderful, wonderful man. I'm so lucky. In forty years when we're both wrinkled and grey, perhaps we'll walk up the Strand hand in hand and remember today and thank God we found each other. I mean, what were the chances, in this teeming world of strangers? Love is so random. *So random.* It's a miracle, really . . .

Oh God, I'm blinking . . .

'Lottie?' Richard has noticed my damp eyes. 'Hey, Daisy-doo. Are you OK? What's up?'

Even though I've been more honest with Richard than I have with any other boyfriend, it's probably not a good idea to reveal my *entire* thought process to him. Fliss, my big sister, says I think in Hollywood Technicolor and I have to remember that other people can't hear the swooping violins.

'Sorry!' I dab at my eyes. 'Nothing. I just wish you didn't have to go.'

Richard is flying off tomorrow to a secondment in San Francisco. It's three months – could be worse – but I'll miss him terribly. In fact, it's only the thought that I'll have a wedding to plan which is distracting me.

'Sweetheart, don't cry. I can't bear it.' He reaches out to take my hands. 'We'll Skype every day.'

'I know.' I squeeze his hands back. 'I'll be ready.'

'Although you *might* want to remember that if I'm in my office, everyone can hear what you're saying. Including my boss.'

Only a tiny flicker of his eyes gives away the fact that he's teasing me. The last time he was away and we Skyped, I started giving him advice on how to manage his nightmare boss, forgetting that Richard was in an open-plan office and the nightmare boss was liable to walk past at any minute. (Luckily, he didn't.)

'Thanks for that tip.' I shrug, equally deadpan.

'Also, they can see you. So you might not want to be *totally* naked.'

'Not *totally*,' I agree. 'Maybe just a transparent bra and pants. Keep it simple.'

Richard grins and grasps my hands more tightly. 'I love you.' His voice is low and warm and melting. I will never, ever get sick of him saying that.

'Me too.'

'In fact, Lottie . . .' He clears his throat. 'I have something to ask you.'

My insides feel as if they're going to explode. My face is a rictus of anticipation while my thoughts are spinning wildly. *Oh God, he's doing it . . . My whole life changes here . . . Concentrate, Lottie, savour the moment . . . Shit! What's wrong with my leg?*

I stare down at it in horror.

Whoever made these 'stay-up stockings' is a liar and will go to hell, because one of them *hasn't* bloody well stayed up. It's collapsed around my knee and there's a really gross plastic 'adhesive' strip flapping around my calf. This is hideous.

I can't be proposed to like this. I can't spend the rest of my life looking back and thinking, *It was such a romantic moment, shame about the stocking.*

'Sorry, Richard.' I cut him off. 'Just wait a sec.'

Surreptitiously I reach down and yank the stocking up – but the flimsy fabric tears in my hand. Great. Now I have flapping plastic *and* shreds of nylon decorating my leg. I cannot believe my marriage proposal is being wrecked by hosiery. I should have gone for bare legs.

'Everything OK?' Richard looks a little baffled as I emerge from under the table.

'I have to go to the Ladies,' I mutter. 'I'm sorry. Sorry. Can we put things on pause? Just for a nanosecond?'

'Are you OK?'

'I'm fine.' I'm red with embarrassment. 'I've had a . . . a garment mishap. I don't want you to see. Will you look away?'

Obediently, Richard averts his head. I push my chair back and walk swiftly across the room, ignoring the looks of other lunchtime diners. There's no point trying to mask it. It's a flappy stocking.

I bang through the door of the Ladies, wrench off my shoe and the stupid stocking, then stare at myself in the mirror, my heart pounding. I can't believe I've just put my proposal on pause.

I feel as though time is on hold. As though we're in a sci-fi movie and Richard is in suspended animation and I've got all the time in the world to think about whether I want to marry him.

Which, obviously, I don't need, because the answer is: I do.

A blonde girl with a beaded headband turns to peer at me, lipliner in hand. I guess I do look a bit odd, standing motionless and holding a shoe and stocking.

'There's a bin over there.' She nods. 'Do you feel OK?'

'Fine. Thanks.' I suddenly have the urge to share the momentousness of this occasion. 'My boyfriend's in the middle of proposing to me!'

'No *way*.' All the women at the mirrors turn to stare at me.

'What do you mean, "in the middle of"?' demands a thin redhead in pink, her eyebrows narrowed. 'What's he said, "Will you . . ."?'

'He started, but I had a stocking catastrophe.' I wave the hold-up. 'So he's on pause.'

'On *pause*?' says someone incredulously.

'Well, I'd get back out there quick,' says the redhead. 'You don't want to give him a chance to change his mind.'

'How exciting!' says the blonde girl. 'Can we watch? Can I film you?'

'We could put it on YouTube!' says her friend. 'Has he hired a flashmob or anything?'

'I don't *think* so . . .'

'How does this work?' An old woman with metal-grey hair cuts across our discussion imperiously. She's waving her hands angrily underneath the automatic handwash dispenser. 'Why do they invent these machines? What's wrong with a bar of soap?'

'Look, like this, Aunt Dee,' says the redhead soothingly. 'Your hands are too high.'

I pull off my other shoe and stocking, and, since I'm

here, reach for the hand lotion to slather on my bare legs. I don't want to look back and think, *It was such a romantic moment, shame about the scaly shins*. Then I get out my phone. I *have* to text Fliss. I quickly type:

He's doing it!!!

A moment later her reply appears on my screen:

Don't tell me u r texting me in the middle of a proposal!!!

In Ladies. Taking a moment.

V exciting!!! You make a great couple. Give him a kiss from me. xxx

Will do! Talk later xxx

'Which one is he?' says the blonde girl as I put away my phone. 'I'm going to have a look!' She darts out of the Ladies, then returns a few seconds later. 'Ooh, I saw him. The dark guy in the corner? He's fab. Hey, your mascara's smudged.' She passes me a make-up eraser pen. 'Want to do a quick fix?'

'Thanks.' I smile companionably at her and start to erase the tiny black marks below my eyes. My wavy chestnut hair is swept up in a chignon, and I suddenly wonder whether to let it down so it tumbles over my shoulders for the big moment.

No. Too cheesy. Instead, I pull some tendrils out and twist them around my face while I assess everything else. Lipstick: nice coral colour. Eyeshadow: shimmery grey to bring out my blue eyes. Blusher: hopefully will not need touch-up as will be flushed with excitement.

'I wish *my* boyfriend would propose,' says a long-haired girl in black, watching me wistfully. 'What's the trick?'

'Dunno,' I reply, wishing I could be more helpful. 'I suppose we've been together a while, we know we're compatible, we love each other.'

'But so do my boyfriend and I! We've been living together, the sex is great, it's all great.'

'Don't pressure him,' says the blonde girl wisely.

'I mention it, like, once a *year*.' The long-haired girl looks thoroughly miserable. 'And he gets twitchy and we drop it. What am I supposed to do? Move out? It's been six years now.'

'*Six years?*' The old woman looks up from drying her hands. 'What's wrong with you?' The girl with the long hair flushes.

'Nothing's *wrong* with me,' she says. 'I was having a private conversation.'

'Private, pfft.' The old woman gestures briskly around the Ladies' room. 'Everyone's listening.'

'Aunt Dee!' The redhead looks embarrassed. '*Shush!*'

'Don't you shush me, Amy!' The old woman regards the long-haired girl beadily. 'Men are like jungle creatures. The minute they've found their kill, they eat it and fall asleep. Well, you've handed him his kill on a plate, haven't you?'

'It's not as simple as that,' says the long-haired girl resentfully.

'In my day, the men got married because they wanted sex. That was motivation all right!' The old woman gives a brisk laugh. 'All you girls with your sleeping together and living together and *then* you want an engagement ring. It's all back to front.' She picks up her bag. 'Come along, Amy! What are you waiting for?'

Amy shoots us all desperate looks of apology, then disappears out of the Ladies with her aunt. We all exchange raised eyebrows. What a nutter.

'Don't worry,' I say reassuringly, and squeeze the girl's arm. 'I'm sure things will work out for you.' I want to spread the joy. I want *everyone* to have the good luck that Richard and I have had: finding the perfect person and knowing it.

'Yes.' She makes an obvious effort to gather herself. 'Let's hope. Well, I wish you a very happy life together.'

'Thanks!' I hand the eraser pen back to the blonde girl. 'Here I go! Wish me luck!'

I push my way out of the Ladies and survey the bustling restaurant, feeling as though I've just pressed 'play'. There's Richard, sitting in exactly the same position as when I left him. He's not even checking his phone. He must be as focused on this moment as I am. The most special moment of our lives.

'Sorry about that.' I slide into my chair and give him my most loving, receptive smile. 'Shall we pick up where we left off?'

Richard smiles back, but I can tell he's lost a bit of momentum. We might need to work back into things gradually.

'It's such a special day,' I say encouragingly. 'Don't you feel that?'

'Absolutely.' He nods.

'This place is so lovely.' I gesture around. 'The perfect place for a . . . a big talk.'

I've left my hands casually on the table, and, as I

intended, Richard takes them between his. He takes a deep breath and frowns.

'Speaking of that, Lottie, there's something I wanted to ask.' As our eyes meet, his crinkle a little. 'I don't think this will come as a *massive* surprise . . .'

Oh God, oh God, here it comes.

'Yes?' My voice is a nervous squawk.

'Bread for the table?'

Richard starts in shock and my head jerks up. A waiter has approached so quietly, neither of us noticed him. Almost before I know it, Richard has dropped my hand and is talking about brown soda bread. I want to whack the whole basket away in frustration. Couldn't the waiter *tell*? Don't they train them in imminent-proposal spotting?

I can tell Richard's been thrown off track, too. Stupid, *stupid* waiter. How dare he spoil my boyfriend's big moment?

'So,' I say encouragingly, as soon as the waiter's gone. 'You had a question?'

'Well. Yes.' He focuses on me and takes a deep breath – then his face changes shape again. I turn round in surprise, to see that *another* bloody waiter has loomed up. Well, to be fair, I suppose it's what you expect in a restaurant.

We both order some food – I'm barely aware of what I'm choosing – and the waiter melts away. But another one will be back, any minute. I feel more sorry for Richard than ever. How's he supposed to propose in these circumstances? How do men *do* it?

I can't help grinning at him wryly.

'Not your day.'

'Not really.'

'The wine waiter will be along in a minute,' I point out.

'It's like Piccadilly Circus here.' He rolls his eyes ruefully, and I feel a warm sense of collusion. We're in this together. Who cares when he proposes? Who cares if it's not some perfect, staged moment? 'Shall we get some champagne?' he adds.

I can't help giving him a knowing smile. 'Would that be a little . . . *premature*, do you think?'

'Well, that depends.' He raises his eyebrows. 'You tell me.'

The subtext is so obvious, I don't know whether I want to laugh or hug him.

'Well in that case . . .' I pause a delicious length of time, eking it out for both of us. 'Yes. My answer would be yes.'

His brow relaxes and I can see the tension flood out of him. Did he really think I might say no? He's so unassuming. He's such a darling man. Oh God. We're getting married!

'With all my heart, Richard, yes,' I add for emphasis, my voice suddenly wobbling. 'You have to know how much this means to me. It's . . . I don't know what to say.'

His fingers squeeze mine and it's as though we have our own private code. I almost feel sorry for other couples who have to spell things out. They don't have the connection we do.

For a moment we're just silent. I can feel a cloud of happiness surrounding us. I want that cloud to stay there for ever. I can see us now in the future, painting a house, wheeling a pram, decorating a Christmas tree with our little toddlers . . . His parents might want to come and stay for Christmas and that's fine, because I *love* his parents. In fact, the first thing I'll do when this is all announced is go and see his mother in Sussex. She'll adore helping with the wedding, and it's not as though I've got a mother of my own to do it.

So many possibilities. So many plans. So much glorious life to live together.

'So,' I say at last, gently rubbing his fingers. 'Pleased? Happy?'

'Couldn't be more happy.' He caresses my hand.

'I've thought about this for ages.' I sigh contentedly. 'But I never thought . . . You just don't, do you? It's like . . . what will it *be* like? What will it *feel* like?'

'I know what you mean.' He nods.

'I'll always remember this room. I'll always remember the way you're looking right now.' I squeeze his hand even harder.

'Me too,' he says simply.

What I love about Richard is, he can convey so much simply with a sidelong look or a tilt of his head. He doesn't need to say much, because I can read him so easily.

I can see the long-haired girl watching us from across the room, and I can't help smiling at her. (Not a triumphant smile, because that would be insensitive. A humble, grateful smile.)

'Some wine for the table, sir? Mademoiselle?' The sommelier approaches and I beam up at him.

'I think we need some champagne.'

'*Absolument.*' He smiles back at me. 'The house champagne? Or we have a very nice Ruinart for a special occasion.'

'I think the Ruinart.' I can't resist sharing our joy. 'It's a very special day! We've just got engaged!'

'Mademoiselle!' The sommelier's face creases into a smile. '*Félicitations!* Sir, many congratulations!' We both turn to Richard – but to my surprise he's not entering into the spirit of the moment. He's staring at me as though I'm some sort of spectre. Why does he look so spooked? What's wrong?

'What—' His voice is strangled. 'What do you mean?'

I suddenly realize why he's upset. Of course. Trust me to spoil everything by jumping in.

'Richard, I'm so sorry. Did you want to tell your parents first?' I squeeze his hand. 'I completely understand. We won't tell anyone else, promise.'

'Tell them what?' He's wide-eyed and starey. 'Lottie, we're not engaged.'

'But . . .' I look at him uncertainly. 'You just proposed to me. And I said yes.'

'No I didn't!' He yanks his hand out of mine.

OK, one of us is going mad here. The sommelier has retreated tactfully, and I can see him shooing away the waiter with the bread basket, who was approaching again.

'Lottie, I'm sorry but I have no idea what you're talking about.' Richard thrusts his hands through his hair. 'I haven't mentioned marriage or engagement, or anything.'

'But . . . but that's what you meant! When you ordered the champagne, and you said, "You tell me," and I said, "With all my heart, yes." It was subtle! It was beautiful!'

I'm gazing at him, longing for him to agree; longing for him to feel what I feel. But he just looks baffled and I feel a sudden pang of dread.

'That's . . . *not* what you meant?' My throat is so tight I can barely speak. I can't believe this is happening. 'You didn't mean to propose?'

'Lottie, I *didn't* propose!' he says forcefully. 'Full stop!'

Does he have to exclaim so loudly? Heads are popping up with interest everywhere.

'OK! I get it!' I rub my nose with my napkin. 'You don't need to tell the whole restaurant.'

Waves of humiliation are washing over me. I'm rigid with misery. How can I have got this so wrong?

And if he wasn't proposing, then *why* wasn't he proposing?

'I don't understand.' Richard is talking almost to himself. 'I've never said anything, we've never discussed it—'

'You've said plenty!' Hurt and indignation are erupting out of me. 'You said you were organizing a "special lunch"!'

'It is special!' he says defensively. 'I'm going to San Francisco tomorrow.'

'And you asked me if I liked your surname! Your *surname*, Richard!'

'We were doing a jokey straw poll at the office!' Richard looks bewildered. 'It was just chit-chat.'

'And you said you had to ask me a "big question"!'

'Not a big question.' He shakes his head. 'A question.'

'I heard "big question"!'

There's a wretched silence between us. The cloud of happiness has gone. The Hollywood Technicolor and swooping violins have gone. The sommelier tactfully slides a wine list on to the corner of the table and retreats quickly.

'What is it, then?' I say at last. 'This really important, medium-sized question?'

Richard looks trapped. 'It's not important. Forget it.'

'Come on, tell me!'

'Well, OK,' he says finally. 'I was going to ask you what I should do with my airmiles. I thought maybe we could plan a trip.'

'Airmiles?' I can't help lashing out. 'You booked a special table and ordered champagne to talk about *airmiles*?'

'No! I mean . . .' Richard winces. 'Lottie, I feel terrible about all this. I had absolutely zero idea . . .'

'But we just had a whole bloody conversation about being engaged!' I can feel tears rising again. 'I was stroking your hand and saying how happy I was and how I'd thought about this moment for ages. And you were agreeing with me! What did you *think* I was talking about?'

Richard's eyes are swivelling as though searching for an escape. 'I thought you were . . . you know. Going on about stuff.'

'"Going on about stuff"?' I stare at him. 'What do you mean, "Going on about stuff"?'

Richard looks even more desperate.

'The truth is, I don't always know what you're on about,' he says in a sudden confessional rush. 'So sometimes I just . . . nod along.'

Nod along?

I stare back at him, stricken. I thought we had a special, unique silent bond of understanding. I thought we had a private code. And all the time he was just nodding along.

Two waiters put our salads in front of us, and quickly move away as though sensing we're not in any mood to talk. I pick up my fork and put it down again. Richard doesn't seem even to have noticed his plate.

'I bought you an engagement ring,' I say, breaking the silence.

'Oh God.' He buries his head in his hands.

'It's fine. I'll take it back.'

'Lottie.' He looks tortured. 'Do we have to . . . I'm going

away tomorrow. Couldn't we just move away from the whole subject?'

'So, do you *ever* want to get married?' As I ask the question I feel a deep anguish inside. A minute ago I thought I was engaged. I'd run the marathon. I was bursting through the finishing tape, arms up in elation . . . Now I'm back at the starting line, lacing up my shoes, wondering if the race is even on.

'I . . . God, Lottie. I dunno.' He sounds beleaguered. 'I mean, yes. I suppose so.' His eyes are swivelling more and more wildly. 'Maybe. You know. Eventually.'

Well. You couldn't get a much clearer signal. Maybe he wants to get married to someone else, one day. But not to me.

And suddenly a bleak despair comes over me. I believed with all my heart that he was The One. How could I have got it so wrong? I feel as though I can't trust myself on anything any more.

'Right.' I stare down at my salad for a few moments, running my eyes over leaves and slices of avocado and pomegranate seeds, trying to get my thoughts together. 'The thing is, Richard, I *do* want to get married. I want marriage, kids, a house . . . the whole bit. And I wanted them with you. But marriage is kind of a two-way thing.' I pause, breathing hard but determined to keep my composure. 'So I guess it's good that I know the truth sooner rather than later. Thanks for that, anyway.'

'Lottie!' says Richard in alarm. 'Wait! This doesn't change anything—'

'It changes everything. I'm too old to be on a waiting list. If it's not going to happen with us, then I'd rather know now and move on. You know?' I try to smile, but my happy muscles have stopped working. 'Have fun in San Francisco. I think I'd better go.' Tears are edging past my lashes. I need to leave, quickly. I'll go back to work and check on my presentation for tomorrow. I'd taken the afternoon off, but what's the point? I won't be phoning all my friends with the joyful news after all.

As I'm making my way out, I feel a hand grabbing my arm. I turn in shock to see the blonde girl with the beaded headband looking up at me.

'What happened?' she demands excitedly. 'Did he give you a ring?'

Her question is like a knife stabbing at my heart. He didn't give me a ring and he isn't even my boyfriend any more. But I'd rather die than admit it.

'Actually . . .' I lift my chin proudly. 'Actually, he proposed but I said "no".'

'Oh.' Her hand shoots to her mouth.

'That's right.' I catch the eye of the long-haired girl, who's eavesdropping blatantly at the next table. 'I said "no".'

'You said "*no*"?' She looks so incredulous I feel a pang of indignation.

'Yes!' I glare at her defiantly. 'I said "no". We weren't right for each other after all, so I took the decision to end it. Even though he really wanted to marry me and have kids and a dog and everything.'

I can feel curious eyes on my back, and swivel round to confront yet more people, listening agog. Is the whole bloody *restaurant* in on this now?

'I said "no"!' My voice is rising in distress. 'I said "no". *No!*' I call over loudly to Richard, who is still sitting at the table, looking dumbfounded. 'I'm sorry, Richard. I know you're in love with me and I know I'm breaking your heart right now. But the answer's "no"!'

And, feeling a tiny bit better, I stride out of the restaurant.

I get back to work to find my desk littered with new Post-its. The phone must have been busy while I was out. I slump down at my desk and heave a long, shuddering sigh. Then I hear a cough. Kayla, my intern, is hovering at the door of my tiny office. Kayla hovers a lot round my door. She's the keenest intern I've ever met. She wrote me a two-side Christmas card about how inspiring I was as a role model, and how she would never have come to intern at Blay Pharmaceuticals if it weren't for the talk I gave at Bristol University. (It *was* a pretty good talk, I must admit. As recruitment speeches for pharmaceutical companies go.)

'How was lunch?' Her eyes are sparkling.

My heart plummets. *Why* did I tell her Richard was going to propose? I was just so confident. It gave me a kick, seeing her excitement. I felt like an all-round superwoman.

'It was fine. Fine. Nice restaurant.' I start to riffle through the papers on my desk, as though searching for some vital piece of information.

'So, are you engaged?'

Her words are like lemon juice sprinkled on sore skin. Has she no finesse? You don't ask your boss straight out, 'Are you engaged?' Especially if she's not wearing a huge, brand-new ring, which clearly I'm not. I might refer to this in my appraisal of her. *Kayla has some trouble working within appropriate boundaries.*

'Well.' I brush down my jacket, playing for time, and

swallowing the lump in my throat. 'Actually, no. Actually, I decided against it.'

'Really?' She sounds confused.

'Yes.' I nod several times. 'Absolutely. I concluded that for me at my time of life, at my career point, this wasn't a smart move.'

Kayla seems poleaxed. 'But . . . you guys were so great together.'

'Well, these things aren't as simple as they appear, Kayla.' I riffle the papers more quickly.

'He must have been devastated.'

'Pretty much,' I say after a pause. 'Yup. Pretty crushed. In fact . . . he cried.'

I can say what I like. She'll never see Richard again. *I'll* probably never see him again. And like a bludgeon to the stomach, the enormity of the truth hits me again. It's all over. Gone. All of it. I'll never have sex with him again. I'll never wake up with him again. I'll never hug him again. Somehow that fact, above all others, makes me want to bawl.

'God, Lottie, you're so inspiring.' Kayla's eyes are shining. 'To know that something is wrong for your career, and to have the courage to make that stand, to say, "No! I *won't* do what everyone expects."'

'Exactly.' I nod desperately. 'I was making a stand for women everywhere.'

My jaw is trembling. I have to conclude this conversation right now, before things go horribly wrong in the bursting-into-tears-in-front-of-your-intern department.

'So, any vital messages?' I scan the Post-its without seeing them.

'One from Steve about the presentation tomorrow, and some guy named Ben called.'

'Ben who?'

'Just Ben. He said you'd know.'

No one calls himself 'Just Ben'. It'll be some cheeky student I met at a milk-round talk, trying to get a foot in the door. I'm really not in the mood for it.

'OK. Well. I'm going to go over my presentation. So.' I click busily and randomly at my mouse till she leaves. Deep breath. Firm jaw. Move on. Move on, move on, move on.

The phone rings and I pick it up with a sweeping, authoritative gesture.

'Charlotte Graveney.'

'Lottie! It's me!'

I fight an instinct to put the receiver straight back down again.

'Oh, hi, Fliss.' I swallow. 'Hi.'

'So, how *are* you?'

I can hear the teasing note in her voice and curse myself bitterly. I should never have texted her from the restaurant.

It's pressure. All hideous pressure. Why did I ever share my love life with my sister? Why did I ever even tell her I was dating Richard? Let alone introduce them. Let alone start talking about proposals.

Next time I meet a man, I'm saying *nothing to anybody*. Nada. Zip. Not until we've been blissfully married for a decade and have three kids and have just renewed our wedding vows. Then, and only then, will I send a text to Fliss saying: 'Guess what? I met someone! He seems nice!'

'Oh, I'm fine.' I muster a breezy, matter-of-fact tone. 'How about you?'

'All good this end. So . . . ?'

She leaves the question dangling. I know exactly what

she means. She means, *So, are you wearing a massive diamond ring and toasting yourself with Bollinger as Richard sucks your toes in some amazing hotel suite?*

I feel a fresh, raw pang. I can't bear to talk about it. I can't bear her sympathy gushing over me. Find another topic. Any topic. Quick.

'So. Anyway.' I try to sound bright and nonchalant. 'Anyway. Um. I was just thinking, actually. I really should get round to doing that Masters on business theory. You know I've always meant to do it. I mean, what am I waiting for? I could apply to Birkbeck, do it in my spare time. What do you think?'

Before **Sophie Kinsella** wrote the *Shopaholic* series,
she wrote seven acclaimed novels under her real name

MADELEINE WICKHAM

Her collection of bestselling books examine universal ideas
of love and hate, sex and romance, family and single life
with emotional understanding and an incisive wit:

The Tennis Party
Mixed doubles, anyone?

A Desirable Residence
What goes on behind closed doors . . .

Swimming Pool Sunday
An idyllic day . . . and then everything changes

The Gatecrasher
A shoulder to cry on, a hand on your wallet . . .

The Wedding Girl
When 'I do' gives you déjà vu it could be a problem . . .

Cocktails for Three
Secrets, strangers, and a splash of scandal . . .

Sleeping Arrangements
Two families, one villa – who's sleeping with whom?

Visit

www.sophiekinsella.co.uk

The official website of

SOPHIE KINSELLA

for more on all the Sophie Kinsella novels.

Be the first to find out when there's a new book coming. Plus find updates from Sophie, news, videos, audio clips, downloads and some great prizes up for grabs.

Keep up to date with all the latest news on Sophie's books, events and more with Sophie's official e-mail newsletter.

You can also join Sophie on her official Facebook fan page

f facebook.com/SophieKinsellaOfficial

or follow her on Twitter 🐦 **@KinsellaSophie** and Instagram 📷 **@sophiekinsellawriter**